The RESURRECTION *of* Hucklebuck Jones

PAUL E. WOOTTEN

Grebey Creek Publishing

To the men in my family -
Cody, Bryce, and Geoff.

This one's for you.

***

Dedicated also to the memory of Nathaniel Parker.

And of course, to Robin, with love!

PART ONE

SOUTH FLORIDA
1955

ONE

"Pete?"

Lost in concentration, laboring over the ancient Royal typewriter, Pete almost fell from his chair when she barged in.

"Let me do that for you, hon."

"Thanks, Doris, but I'm nearly finished."

She made that tsk-ing sound, the one that drove him nuts. It was almost as annoying as when she called him hon.

"I hate seeing you have to try so hard, hon. Typing on that old thing is bad enough with two arms." She stopped to take a wheezing breath. "Besides, your grandpa sent me down here to do that kind of work for you."

Bullshit. Dad and Papú had exiled Doris to the warehouse because she'd grown too old and cantankerous to work in any of the stores.

Pete took a deep breath, but didn't look up from his work. Doris would see that as an invitation to sit down, light up a Parliament, and stay a half-hour.

"Really, Doris, it's okay."

"Tsk, tsk..." She tried to look over his shoulder. "What is it you're working on, anyways?"

Pete leaned in to shield his work from her prying eyes. "Just some stuff for the weekly meeting."

She nodded, but didn't ask any more questions. "Well, I don't have anything else to do, so…"

There it was. She wanted to go home early. Again. He'd pushed for firing her, but Papú had angrily put his big Greek foot down. She'd been with Demo-Fresh in one capacity or another for twenty-five years, and it was easier to saddle Pete with her than let her go. Lately, he'd insisted she stay for her entire four-hour shift, but today he needed the solitude to finish the most important proposal he'd ever put together.

"Sure, Doris, go on home. I'll see you tomorrow."

***

Twenty minutes later, Pete pulled the final sheet from the typewriter, glanced over it, and laid it on the stack with the rest. Dad and Papú would be impressed that he'd typed it himself. If they were as impressed with the suggestions in the proposal, Demo-Fresh Markets might even become one of the big boys. Just the thought of it made his heart race.

Winn-Dixie… Publix… Demo-Fresh.

The telephone jarred him from his thoughts.

"Demo-Fresh Warehouse, Pete Demopoulos."

"He's at it again! You need to go up there, Peter. *Now.*"

He'd heard it all before: the grating pitch of her voice, the demand that he act immediately, the assumption that he was at her beck and call. Reflexively, he held the phone a few inches from his ear.

"Elena, what are you talking about? Who's at it again?"

"That ugly slob of a Headmaster. He's saying Gwendolyn called the science teacher a fat pervert. Peter, I told you we need a better school."

Pete glanced at his desk calendar. Two appointments with suppliers and his monthly visit to Dove's Barber Shop. Dad would be unhappy if the supplier meetings were cancelled, but his wrath was nothing compared to what Pete would face from Elena.

"I'm on my way."

***

The drive to Gwendolyn's private school provided him with forty-five minutes of solitude; perfect for rehearsing his presentation. It would take place first thing in the morning. Dad, Papú, and his brother Chris would be the only attendees. Dad oversaw the day-to-day operations, but had avoided all but the most necessary improvements for years. Part of the reason was Papú. The Demo-Fresh founder was irritable and unwilling to accept change, so Dad avoided issues that would trigger the old man's wrath.

But Dad could also be his own worst enemy, often becoming so involved in little things that he failed to see how times were changing. Air conditioning was one example. All the big stores in Florida were installing it, and people were even starting to get it at home. Pete figured it was a matter of time before customers bypassed Demo-Fresh for their air-conditioned competitors.

His proposal was ambitious, for sure. Expansion of six stores, extensive renovation of all eleven, automation, express lanes for small purchases, home delivery for a nominal fee. The associated costs were high, but it wasn't as if they didn't have the money. The stores close to the resorts made money hand over fist, and Dad and Papú had socked away plenty. It was the others, those where Demo-Fresh entered the market late, where sales were flat. It was time to move forward.

The key would be Papú. Even though he'd turned over leadership of Demo-Fresh to Dad five years before, he still came to work every day, overcrowding the small office in the back of the Dickerson Springs store so much that Chris often found reasons to be out. Papú made it clear that he still had a vote on all matters. Sadly, he often rode roughshod over Dad, and his single vote usually became two that trumped the two votes of Pete and Chris.

Thankfully, Pete could count on Chris if things started going off the rails. They'd always been tight, and despite their five-year age difference, Chris had looked out for his older brother. Pete was puny, always had been. Losing his arm in a playground accident had left him bedridden for a year. While Chris had excelled in Little League and on the gridiron at Dickerson Springs High School, Pete spent his time in the stores, yearning for the day when he would take his place in the company. He'd hoped to go to college and major in business management, but Dad preferred that he learn on the job. Chris had flunked out of junior college before operating a fishing charter that went belly-up after seven months. The next several years were filled with stints as a truck driver, bricklayer, and encyclopedia salesman. No one was happier for Chris's return to the family business than Pete. They often talked about running the company together.

And tomorrow might be the beginning of that dream becoming reality. But first, Pete had to contend with Gwendolyn.

***

Having personally experienced Elena Demopoulos' fury, Headmaster Ricketts visibly relaxed when he spotted Pete waiting outside his office. He waved him in and closed the door.

"Mr. Demopoulos, I'm sorry to make you drive all the way up here. I considered waiting until school was out, but Gwendolyn's outburst was…" The Headmaster's eyes held a sadness that Pete understood. He was a good man stuck at a middling private school in nowhere, Florida. At the back end of middle age, his prospects for career advancement to one of the elite private schools in Tampa were behind him. Having to deal with Gwendolyn Abbott only added to his despair.

Pete considered speaking up for Gwendolyn. Elena expected it, and would have herself had she not been banned from campus after an altercation with the school receptionist earlier in the year. Try as he might, he couldn't summon the will.

"You know she's not really my daughter... I mean, I married her mother, but..." That was the best he could do. Headmaster Ricketts nodded in commiseration.

"This time she really crossed the line, Mr. Demopoulos. I'm forced to suspend her for a week. It's only the second time in..." he looked toward the ceiling as he counted to himself "...twenty-four years that I've had to suspend a student."

They were silent for a moment; each aware of the common obstacle they faced. Of course, only one of them had to go home to her.

***

Gwendolyn alternated between bawling and tantrums of red-hot anger. During the crying jags, tears and snot tracked down her face to the blouse of her school uniform. She beat the dashboard of Pete's Chevy with her fists. The histrionics worked on Elena, but Pete wanted to reach across and slap her spoiled ass to Tallahassee. Instead, he concentrated on the road. It was better that way.

He could envisage the scene that would play out at home. Elena would hug dear Gwendolyn and whisper into her ear, occasionally turning to Pete, saying things like, "She shouldn't have to endure this. She's only a child." Pete would be expected to stay in the room and witness the farce, nodding sympathetically and agreeing with whatever plan Elena cooked up to get Gwen back in school. Gwendolyn wasn't a child. She was fifteen, but dressed like twenty-one; quite beautiful, with long blonde hair and, when she wasn't throwing a tantrum, an angelic face. When boys had started calling the house in eighth grade, Pete put his foot down, or tried to. Elena found it adorable and overrode his objections. That was the last time he'd tried. Two years later he was beyond caring.

The house was one of the nicest in Gullford, but not good enough.

Too far from the beaches.

No culture.

No civic organizations for the 'right' people.

A country club run by local lawyers and physicians, ham-and-eggers all of them. Nothing, Elena was quick to point out, like the community leaders in Sarasota.

Ahhh, Sarasota. A hundred miles away. The weekends when Elena and Gwendolyn went to visit Elena's mother were the best. He was never invited, of course. "You'd be bored," Elena would coo in that placating tone, but he knew the truth. She was ashamed to be seen with him in her hometown. She didn't want some long-ago high school beau to find out she was married to a scrawny Greek merchant ten years younger, two inches shorter, and missing an arm.

The car had barely stopped before Gwendolyn threw open the door and stomped toward the house. Pete watched her for a moment before engaging the transmission and heading for the street. This time the spectacle would commence without him. In the rearview mirror, he saw Gwendolyn had paused on the front step and was watching him.

"Where are you going?" she yelled.

He slowed and stuck his head out the window. "Back to the warehouse. I have work to finish."

"Mother will want you here. We have to do something about…"

The rest of her screed faded into the distance as he accelerated away.

TWO

"Conveyor belts? *Conveyor belts?*"

The way Hal Demopoulos spun around in his chair, one would think Pete was proposing burlesque dancers in the candy aisle.

"What happens when they break down?"

Pete's mouth was dry. He considered excusing himself from the hot cramped office for a quick run to the watercooler, but didn't want to give the others an opportunity to escape before hearing him out. Instead, he reached to turn on the ancient box fan sitting on a table in the corner.

"Don't," his grandfather said sharply.

"Papú," Pete protested, "it's hotter than blazes in here."

"You know I can't hear when it runs. Leave it off."

"Why don't we move these meetings to the warehouse?" Pete asked, using a handkerchief to wipe sweat from his neck and forehead. "This little office is so cramped with you and Dad. You add Chris and me and it's intolerable."

"We can't leave the store unattended, son," Dad said, always the peacemaker. "Now, back to my question. What happens when these conveyor belts break down?"

"If they break down, we do like we do now: take the groceries from the cart and place them by the cash register."

"If we have to do that anyway, why bother with conveyor belts?"

"We won't *have to*, Dad. The only reason they would stop working is if the electricity goes off."

Pete eyed his brother, slumped in his usual seat in the corner, doodling on a notepad.

"Chris, anything to say?"

Chris glanced up, meeting Pete's expectant gaze. He could usually count on Chris to take his side in these weekly meetings or, as they joked behind their father's and grandfather's backs, the *weekly beatings*. This time though, Chris shrugged and returned his attention to his notepad.

"And another thing: they're so noisy," Dad continued his argument. "All that humming... and what if they knock over the milk? Oh, my gosh, son, you know what happens when the milk bottles get knocked over."

Dad shuddered as he spoke; Papú did, too; as if a gallon of spilled milk would be the death of the Demo-Fresh Supermarket chain.

"Dad, the milk will be fine. We need to start thinking about—"

"Pelope! Enough!"

It was never good when his grandfather called him by his given name. The old man swore Greek epithets as he leaned heavily against stacked cases of Pepsi-Cola bottles to pull himself up from his chair. The bottles swayed and jangled against one another, concerning Pete that spilled milk might be the least of their worries.

"You no right. No belts in my stores."

His stores. It irked Pete to no end when Papú referred to Demo-Fresh like that. They were his stores, too. Nobody worked harder and, sadly, no one got less credit. Chris was treated that way, too. Pete wondered when that would change. Papú was eighty-two. He couldn't last forever.

Usually by that point, it was time to surrender, but Pete had an ace up his sleeve; a bit of information not known to the others.

"Winn-Dixie's opening a store in Beardon."

Papú froze. Dad inhaled sharply. Chris looked up from his doodling, mouth agape.

"And Orchard City."

Papú clutched his chest. Dad's cheeks turned red. Chris appeared confused.

"When?" Dad was the first to recover.

"How you know?" Papú was next, his English more heavily accented than usual.

"Next fall in Beardon," Pete said. "Orchard City's store is scheduled for the summer of '56. I got it from the editor of the *Beardon Banner*."

The room was quiet as three generations of the Demopoulos family came to grips with the news. Orchard City and Beardon ranked fifth and sixth in sales among eleven Demo-Fresh Markets. Winn-Dixie could potentially put those stores out of business. Pete wanted to hammer away at that fear to get what he thought was needed.

"They'll be air-conditioned," he said, "and have four checkout lines... with conveyor belts."

Papú spewed more Greek expletives. "Our customers... they do not want 'dez belts and they sure as hell don't want air conditioning."

This was absurd, but Pete wasn't going to point it out. He pushed ahead, ignoring as best he could the sweat trickling down his back into his underwear.

"It's just the beginning, Papú. Winn-Dixie and Publix are looking at Florida's smaller towns. We need to start planning for—"

"We can beat 'dem," Papú scoffed. "We ran Piggly Wiggly outta Lakeville."

"Papú," Dad said, "the Lakeville Piggly Wiggly was demolished by Hurricane Easy."

"But 'dey never came back!"

Pete turned to his father. "We have eight months before the Beardon Winn-Dixie opens and a year before Orchard City. I've put a plan together that will help us meet the challenge head-on." He reached into his satchel and pulled out a wire-bound binder.

"I typed this myself, and I'd like you to take it home and read it." Pete could see that, despite their opposition, Dad and Papú were impressed. Dad flipped through it for a few moments, then looked up.

"Let's get back together next week. Papú and I will have to think on this. But seriously, Pete, *conveyor belts?*"

THREE

Satisfied he'd gotten his point across, Pete left the stuffy office in the rear of the Dickerson Springs store; Demo-Fresh #1, as he and Chris liked to call it. Dickerson Springs had been a wide spot in the road when Papú opened the store in 1922. Though small, compared to the larger supermarket chains that arrived after the Second World War, Demo-Fresh #1 had the advantage of being the last stop before crossing the bridge to the barrier island beaches. Thirty-three years later, fishermen and beachgoers flocked in daily, making the cash registers sing, despite a lack of conveyor belts.

Papú had quickly parlayed the success in Dickerson Springs into two more Demo-Fresh Markets. Pete's father, who was in his mid-twenties at the time, liked to recall his skepticism at Papú's site selections. "Dirt roads and sand dunes" were how he'd described the towns.

Then, the tourist boom hit. Dirt roads were widened, paved, and widened again. Sand dunes were leveled, making way for motels and bungalows. Right in the middle of everything, Demo-Fresh Markets.

The eight stores added since then were in less-desirable locations, but were profitable nonetheless. These were the stores that Pete was fighting to improve.

The narrow hallway between office and store was crammed with merchandise, leaving barely enough room to pass. Pete bristled at the stacked pallets of Merita Bread. He'd admonished Byron, the Merita truck driver, for trying to cut his workload by delivering two days a week instead of three. He could forgive Papú for not noticing, but Dad and Chris should know better. He pulled out the tiny spiral notebook he always carried, balanced it against the stub that used to be his left arm, and jotted a note.

Past the bread, where the dark hallway opened to the store, Pete heard a mewling squeal that made him smile.

"Blahhhhhh!"

Hucklebuck, waving like an old friend returning from war.

Pete moved into the bright fluorescent light of the store, preparing for one of Hucklebuck's enthusiastic handshakes.

"Where have you been?"

Hucklebuck looked at him, confused. Pete spoke slower, using hand gestures.

"Where... have... you... been?"

His face lit up with understanding. His hands flew as he mimed, waved, and emitted a variety of wails and guttural sounds. People who didn't know Hucklebuck, mainly tourists and children, were sometimes frightened by his mannerisms. Locals knew better. Huck was harmless. Deaf and colored, but harmless.

"Sick?" Pete feigned a cough. Hucklebuck nodded, pitching forward as if he was vomiting.

"But you've been gone two weeks." Pete pointed at a wall calendar and counted the days. No one knew if he could read or count, but Hucklebuck seemed to understand the passage of time. He held out his left hand, palm up, and used the fingers of his right hand to imitate walking.

"Where?"

Hucklebuck waved into the distance.

"Why so far?"

He didn't understand.

Pete grinned. "Do you have a girlfriend someplace? Some pretty girl at Clearwater Beach?"

"Gul?"

"Girlfriend. Sweetheart." When Pete puckered his lips and mimed a kiss, Hucklebuck's loud cackle echoed across the store.

"Naaaaaaa. Naaaaa gul, Blahhhh."

Then, abruptly he stopped laughing. Regarding the stump that ended where Pete's elbow would have been, his face grew sad. He reached out and patted it like one might an injured kitten. He did this every time.

"Awwwwwww, Blahhhh."

"I'm okay. Really, it doesn't hurt." Pete shook his head and gave that thumbs-up symbol that fighter pilots had popularized during the War. "I lost it when I was five. You don't have to worry."

Pete waved good-bye and moved toward the front of the store. In Aisle Four a stout woman in her forties was kneeling as she removed cans of green beans from a box and placed them on the shelf. Her Demo-Fresh smock rode up over a roll of fat around her midsection.

"Linda, you shouldn't be stacking those heavy cans. Leave that for Orman or David."

She looked up, startled.

"It's okay, Mister Pete. They're unloading a truck."

He patted her shoulder. "Well, thanks for seeing what needed to be done. You're off to a good start."

"I'm trying," she said, pushing aside the box and struggling to her feet. "I gotta tell you, Mister Pete, that one scares me." She motioned to the end of the aisle where Hucklebuck smiled maniacally.

"Don't worry about Huck. Dad has been giving him odd jobs for years. A few cents here and there tides him over."

Linda tugged at her smock, her eyes darting from Pete to Hucklebuck. "Some of the boys at the brickyard say he's been in jail for…" she lowered her voice, "…stuff we don't talk about."

"It's all gossip, Linda. My father's known Huck since he was a boy. He disappears at times, but always comes back."

"Where does he live?"

Pete shrugged. "I'm not sure exactly. Out in the woods near the swamp. He and his father lived together until Ready Bill – that's what they called his father – passed away." Pete glanced back as he spoke. Hucklebuck was still there, still grinning.

"Blahhh!"

"Huck took it pretty hard when his father passed. We didn't see him for a couple months."

Linda's expression transformed from fear to sympathy. She smiled at Hucklebuck and he waved in return.

"Why does he keep saying, 'blahhhh?'"

Pete felt his cheeks redden. "He's saying 'black.' Since I'm dark-complected, he thinks I'm colored like him."

It was Linda's turn to be embarrassed. "That's not very nice."

"He doesn't mean anything," Pete smiled. "My Grandmother was from an area of Greece whose people were dark-skinned. Everyone who knew her says I look just like her. Besides, I'm the only person who Huck calls by name."

"How old do you think he is? Would he like it if I brought him some food? Leftovers from supper?"

"He'd probably love it, but we never know when he's coming in. As far as how old he is, there's no telling. I'm thirty-three, and I remember him when I was a kid. I think he's younger than me, but how much I couldn't—"

Something on the shelves caught Pete's eye.

"Linda, last week I had Orman rearrange the canned goods so the Delaney brands were on the top shelf. They're on bottom again."

Linda turned and examined the shelves.

"We did that yesterday. Mister Hal and Mister Chris made us put them back."

"But..." Pete scanned the length of the shelf. Sales for the Delaney brand had been lagging behind the nationals, and he'd read in one of the trade magazines that moving them to eye level could spur sales. He'd shared the article with his father and Chris and assumed they agreed. But now, things were back as before, and they hadn't even consulted him first.

Oh, well, that was an issue best saved for another day.

"Continue on, Linda. Have a nice day." He turned to Hucklebuck and waved.

"Buh, Blahhhh!"

FOUR

Horace Atteberry grabbed a dip net and used it to manhandle the fish past Pete to the floor of the boat.

"You'll be eating well tonight, buddy. That one's huge."

Pete set aside his rod and went about removing the hook and wrestling the fish toward the cleaning area of Horace's thirty-foot Hatteras Sport Fish. It had been a good day so far, and the sun still hadn't reached its apex. Snook, drum, and red snapper were jumping for their bait.

As expected, Elena and Gwendolyn had embarked for Sarasota the morning following the school suspension. That was three days ago. They'd taken the car, but Pete had use of a Demo-Fresh panel truck, which worked just fine. Elena had ripped him a new one when he'd returned home that night, but since she'd prefaced it by saying they were leaving the next morning, he took it without complaint. A chewing-out was fair recompense for six days of silence and relaxation. Horace Atteberry's offer of a day of Gulf fishing made it even sweeter.

"Pete, if you don't mind me saying," Horace nodded at Pete's stump, "I've known you awhile and I'm yet to see anything you can't do. You fought that snapper like a pro."

"It's all what you're used to, I guess." Pete held the fish against his chest and propelled it onto the cleaning table, nimbly dodging its razor-sharp dorsal fin, then stepped out of the way to allow Horace to begin cleaning it. Watching him wield the knife, his face weathered and bronzed from the sun, gray hair blowing in the breeze, a stranger would never guess he was the owner of a chain of department stores that were a staple in several small Florida towns. Atteberry's Dry Goods shared a parking lot with the Demo-Fresh Market in Groveside, a fact that had caused much gnashing of teeth in the Demopoulos family a decade before. It boiled down to an issue of parking lot maintenance, a cost Papú felt should be shared fifty-fifty. When Horace presented a three-week study that showed that seventy percent of the cars in the lot were going to Demo-Fresh, the elder Demopoulos refused to budge, despite Pete's protestations.

It took two years and a parking lot full of moon-sized craters before Pete stepped in and amiably settled the matter with a sixty-forty split. A friendship was born in the process, and while they didn't see each other on a regular basis, they remained close. The bond had grown over the past eighteen months since the untimely death of Horace's wife, Betty.

Pete baited and cast his line into the blue-green Gulf. The day was warm, high-eighties, with a breeze from the southwest. There were no other boats visible on the horizon, and other than the gulls diving for the fish entrails Horace tossed over the side, they were alone. Just the way Pete liked it.

No Elena. No Gwendolyn.

No Dad. No Papú.

They would reconvene on Monday to discuss Pete's plan. Chris had called twice, mainly questions about easements and the difficulty of stores remaining open during the renovation process. Good questions, Pete thought. Questions that showed that at least one Demopoulos was interested.

Unfortunately, he was the wrong Demopoulos.

"So, Elena's in Sarasota?"

Pete glanced over his shoulder. Horace had the fish cleaned and was stowing it in a cooler with the others.

"Yeah, through Tuesday."

Horace retrieved his reel and joined him at the stern.

"A good woman, Pete. You did an admirable thing."

Everyone said that. Good old Pete; rescuing the war widow. They'd never found Walter Abbott, a fighter pilot. After three years, it was assumed he was dead. Ha! Pete figured old Walt was out there someplace, sipping a cold beer and laughing at the poor schmuck who was saddled with Elena and their spoiled, overprotected daughter.

Pete had often wondered about the many fine men Elena glowingly spoke of back in Sarasota. Wouldn't one of them have been interested in saving the poor damsel, Elena? Apparently, they knew better. She was a bitch on wheels, but Pete's family had been so quick to push him to the altar, there hadn't been time to find out.

Changing the subject, Pete filled Horace in on his plans for Demo-Fresh. He listened closely, clearly interested.

"Does the company have the funds?"

"Yep," Pete grinned. "We don't blow our money on fancy fishing boats."

Horace laughed at the running gag. "I like to enjoy the fruits of my labor," he said. "Something your cranky-ass grandfather should've done, too."

Horace was one of few people who dared speak so frankly about the Demopoulos patriarch. They did, after all, have a history.

"I've never understood why he's such an SOB," Horace said, casting his line on the boat's port side. "He's been successful in business, great family. And your grandmother, rest her soul, she was one of the most remarkable women I ever knew."

Pete turned to face his friend. "I had no idea you knew my grandmother, Horace."

Horace nodded. "I was still a pup, maybe thirty, when she and your grandfather opened the Dickerson Springs store. I stopped in there a couple times a week. Angela, your grandmother, ran the cash register. She was in her forties, but just beautiful. She had the same dark skin that you have. I was there a couple times when people stopped in and thought they'd come into a colored store.

"I get that occasionally, too," Pete said quietly.

"But your grandmother..." Horace searched for the words. "...she had a way about her that captivated people. They would go out of their way to see Angela. I always said that if Angela Demopoulos hadn't died so young, Demo-Fresh might've—" Horace stopped suddenly and looked at Pete.

"I'm sorry," he said. "I shouldn't have... it's just... your grandmother was very special and I never understood why she'd married an old grouch like Eli."

Pete smiled. "It's okay. I didn't know her, and Dad and Papú don't say much."

"There's no doubt that Eli Demopoulos knew how to build a business," Horace said, seemingly grateful for the chance to move on to another subject. "It's just unfortunate that he can't see the need to look ahead. The sixties and seventies are going to be very different, and companies like yours and mine need to be ready."

"So, you like my proposal?"

"I do," Horace said. "We're facing competition from the larger stores in a couple towns. If I was younger, like you, I'd move in the same direction. I've made my money, so I'll probably hang on until I can't anymore, then get on my boat and head for Key West; maybe buy a house next door to Ernie Hemingway and breed dogs that eat six-toed cats."

"Sounds good, but Hemingway left Key West twenty years ago."

"Yeah," Horace winked, "but the damn cats are still there."

They fished in silence for a few minutes, then Pete had a thought.

"Am I missing anything, Horace?"

The older man turned his way, squinting into the sun's glare off the water.

"No, they've just stopped biting. You might check your bait, though."

"I mean about the plan I presented to Dad and Papú."

Horace considered the question.

"Business-wise, it makes sense. In ten years, Winn-Dixie and Publix will be in your market. Florida isn't going backward. The tourism's getting bigger every year. Clearwater and St. Pete Beach can only grow so much. Towns like Beardon and Groveside are next. You're smart to get ahead of the growth. So yeah, you're on the right track..."

"But?"

Horace shook his head.

"Horace? Don't hold back. I asked."

More silence, before Horace finally spoke.

"I've seen Chris in the Groveside store several times lately. He's been telling your manager there, Frank, that big things are ahead for Demo-Fresh. What do you know about that?"

Pete scratched his head and squinted at the sun.

"Chris is with me on this. He wants the company to grow as much as I do."

Horace nodded, a skeptical look on his face.

"I know you guys are close. It's just... you run circles around your brother, Pete. Everybody knows that; suppliers, vendors, everybody. They all say the same thing: if you want something done right at Demo-Fresh, go to Pete."

"Thanks, Horace." Pete waved his hand for him to continue. "Now stop beating around the bush."

Horace rubbed his neck. "I'd already heard about your plans through Frank. Chris told him everything... but he said the ideas were his."

FIVE

Monday came and went, still no meeting. Dad had called the warehouse first thing. Something had come up. Pete pushed, but Dad remained vague. Something couldn't wait. They'd shoot for Tuesday afternoon.

Usually Pete stayed at the warehouse until six, an hour after the drivers clocked out. But with Elena and Gwendolyn still in Sarasota, he went home early, made himself a sandwich, and fell into his Barcalounger for an evening of mindless television. Kukla, Fran, and Ollie, George and Gracie, and Lucy and Desi were interspersed with short catnaps and trips to the bathroom. The bachelor life was pretty satisfying. If only...

They would be home tomorrow. Elena had called twice. Gwendolyn would return to school to finish out the last few weeks of the year, but that would be it.

"I've talked to some people who are connected to the Montfried School in Tampa," she'd told him over the phone. "They assured me there would be a spot for Gwendolyn in the fall."

What she left out was the cost. He considered recommending to Elena that she get out of the house and find a job to make it affordable, but decided to delay that discussion until she returned home. Why spoil the last days of an otherwise blissful week?

Just before eleven the telephone rang. Pete considered not answering, before recalling that at Elena's mother's house, everyone was in bed by nine-thirty.

"Hello."

"Pete."

Hearing his brother's voice brought to mind the conversation on Horace Atteberry's boat two days earlier. Horace was astute, but in this case, he was mistaken. Chris might have mentioned Pete's plans, but he wasn't the kind to take credit. The more he'd thought about it, the more convinced Pete was that his brother's discussion with outsiders was a good thing. It meant he was enthused.

"Hiya, Chris."

"Dad got a call from Stu Sacks at Merita Bread. He said you jumped all over them about their delivery schedule."

No pleasantries, no brotherly insults. Just plow ahead. This was unlike Chris.

"I don't know about 'jumping all over them,' but I warned them about cutting back on our deliveries."

"Yeah, that's what I figured." Chris grew quiet for a moment. "We decided to let them continue coming by twice a week."

"What?" Pete gripped the phone tightly, his voice growing louder. "That's not acceptable. It means we'll be selling day-old bread on Saturdays and Sundays."

Chris took a breath. "Stu said their delivery guys are stretched thin, and since we're not on the main route—"

"That's stupid. We're a mile and a half from the main highway. Their trucks are up and down that road all week."

Chris was silent.

"I guarantee they stop at the Piggly Wiggly three times a week. And besides, why is Dad getting into this? Distribution is my area. And why did our meeting get cancelled today? I know you were in the stores on the west side, but did you hear anything?"

23

Chris mumbled something about meetings and paperwork before quickly bringing the conversation back to bread.

"Like I said, Dad and Papú decided to let Merita continue with two deliveries."

"Did you speak up?"

Again, a mumbled response, but this time Pete wouldn't let it slide.

"What's been up with you lately, brother. You hardly said a thing at the meeting last week. Are you in trouble with Dad? Did you say something Papú didn't like? I can help you out if you let me."

"It's nothing," Chris said. "Just tired, I guess."

"But you'll be there tomorrow, right? I need you in my corner when I make my pitch."

"I'll be there."

SIX

Cancelled again. Pete couldn't blame his father this time, though.

Demo-Fresh #8 in Tocoboga had a busted water main.

Pete got the call from the store manager at six-fifteen that morning. By seven he was there and had made the decision to shut the store down and call in all available employees to help with cleanup. The plumber had the problem fixed by noon, and the store was ready to reopen at two. Chris had called twice, but Pete was tied up and couldn't break away. Dad had made a last-minute decision to take the day off, saying something about Mom and an appointment in Tampa. Papú showed up long enough to curse out the store manager and plumber before heading back to Dickerson Springs.

Worn out and soaked to the skin, Pete took a few minutes to sit with the store manager and catch his breath. That's when the phone call came.

A storm had hit Gullford.

Not an actual storm, though that might have been preferable. This storm had a name: Elena. She'd tracked him down, insisting they needed to talk immediately. At home. Pete rolled his eyes, aware the store manager could hear her braying over the phone. The manager smiled, then excused himself to check on something. After hanging up, Pete called the office, hopeful of another water main break, but finding that all was quiet in the Demo-Fresh Kingdom.

He would have to go home.

***

Elena spread the colorful brochure out on the dining room table and dared him to object. The pictures were of happy young coeds reading, studying, and socializing in gowns that cost more than Pete made in a month.

"They pride themselves on turning out well-heeled young ladies," she gushed, pointing to the photographs of young maidens in formal attire, escorted by boys sporting uniforms and fake sabers. "Over half of their graduates attend college; some even go to the Seven Sisters."

"Is that a Catholic School?"

Elena stared at him like one might a chinchilla in a wedding dress. Deciding to ignore what was a serious question, she continued.

"The girls attend sporting events and social functions at Burkemper Military School." She clutched her hand to her chest as if she might get the vapors. "Now *there* are some outstanding young men. Can you imagine if Gwendolyn caught the eye of a *General's son*? Or *an Admiral*?

Pete didn't bother to mention that the offspring of an Admiral would be unlikely to attend a military school with ties to the Army; or that Gwendolyn would likely be more interested in the twenty-something roustabout son of some scullery worker.

"Oh, Peter, I'm just *so excited*." And breathless, like she'd run home from Sarasota. "I've filled out the application. Mother's friend, Eudora, is a Montfried alumni. She said she would speak on Gwendolyn's behalf."

Dear cultured Elena didn't know the difference between alumni and alumna. Even stupid one-armed Pete knew that much.

"What does Gwendolyn think of boarding school?"

Elena took a breath. "She's still warming up to the idea. The rules are rather restricting."

Pete knew better. Gwendolyn was playing Elena like a violin. The girl would fight an alligator for the chance to be away from home, rules be damned. Pete wondered for a moment if there were boarding schools for grown men. Then he remembered there were. They were called jails. And sometimes jail didn't sound so bad...

He knew he shouldn't bring it up, but common sense got the best of him. "We need to look at the cost. The way things stand right now boarding school would be a stretch."

Stretch? Pete was bringing home $435 a month after taxes. The Montfried brochure listed room, board, and tuition at $2,600 a year. Half his annual salary.

"I've thought about that," Elena replied, her tone more conciliatory than Pete expected. Perhaps she was thinking of returning to the job market. But then, he remembered, she'd never been *in* the job market.

"You need a raise."

Pete felt his muscles tense. They'd been down this road before, and it never ended well. In the past, he had rushed to his own defense, but this time he bit his lip and waited, knowing Elena would frame her argument with a story of one of her mother's friends.

"Fran Hearthway was telling me about her son, Ronald. You remember Fran, don't you? From Mother's church?"

No. Those old cacklebirds never left an impression on him one way or another, especially since he was only in Sarasota every two or three years.

"Oh, yes, from church."

"I knew you would," Elena nodded. "Anyway, Ronald took over the family paving business last year. Howard, Fran's husband, decided to retire so they could travel. They went to Cuba on a pleasure cruise last fall, and Fran says they're thinking about a *driving trip* to the

Grand Canyon. Can you imagine? Driving all the way to the Grand Canyon?"

Pete flashed a fake smile and glanced at the telephone, willing it to ring and bring an end to his misery.

"Fran said Cuba is just beautiful, though Howard got seasick on the trip and... I guess *that* wasn't a pretty sight."

If the phone wasn't going to ring, how about someone at the door? Salesman, lost traveler, Girl Scout. Anyone.

"They're hoping to leave for the Grand Canyon just before the tourists start showing up here in October. Four weeks. They'll stop and see her cousin Lil in Biloxi, then..."

The rest of what Elena said sounded like a distant foghorn through the cracking pain developing in Pete's head. He nodded at the appropriate moments, or so he hoped. Then, something happened that hadn't occurred in at least two years.

Elena grabbed his hand. Squeezed it, even. Startled by the suddenness of the gesture, Pete almost pulled it away.

"Peter, you'll never guess how much Ronald is making."

"Who's Ronald?"

Elena's eyes darkened. "Fran's son. Weren't you listening?"

Pete felt himself starting to perspire. "Well... of course I was listening. I guess I got carried away thinking about Fran's trip to the Grand Canyon."

"It is exciting, isn't it?" Elena beamed. She was still holding his hand. Please, God, let her stop. "We'll make a trip like that someday; maybe while Gwendolyn is away at boarding school next fall. Anyway, back to Ronald." She lowered her voice, like the IRS might be lurking outside, waiting for information they could use against Fran's son Ronald. "He's making *nine-thousand dollars a year.*"

And there it was. Ronald, son of Fran the world traveler, nine-grand. A total that was—"

"Three times what Hal and Elias are paying you."

No, it wasn't. It wasn't even double. And why did Elena insist of calling Dad and Papú by their given names? Even Papú's friends, when they were alive, shortened his name to Eli. Chris's wife, Becky, called them Dad and Papú. It was no wonder Dad didn't trust Elena and Papú openly detested her.

Ahhh, one of the few things Pete and Papú agreed on.

"Actually, before taxes nine thousand is only—"

"They should be paying you more, Peter. It's as simple as that. You need to march in there tomorrow and demand a raise to nine thousand. Then, we'll have no problem with the tuition at Montfried and we can take that trip to the Grand Canyon."

She was still holding his hand.

He needed a way out. Something that would end the conversation. Perhaps he should tell her about his plan... No, not that. The last thing he wanted was for her to know about that.

"Well, if things go like I think they'll go, I might be getting that raise."

Crap. Why had he gone and told her that?

A wide grin spread across her plain face. "Peter? Are you keeping a secret from me? Is something good about to happen?"

He looked at the table, embarrassed. "I've put together a plan..." He spent the next few minutes describing the changes he would be proposing, and how he anticipated a raise in return for overseeing the renovations.

Elena listened intently, even asking questions. She moved from hand-holding to hand-caressing, occasionally running her palm up his arm. Nothing got Elena's motor revving faster than money. Pete had to admit, it felt good. She was forty-two, nearly ten years his senior. She wasn't as attractive as she'd been when they'd married six years ago. She wasn't attractive back then, come to think of it.

But she was a woman. And, bursting with excitement over the possibility of Pete's advancing position in the family business, she led him upstairs and reminded him for the first time in more than two years why having a woman around could be a good thing.

SEVEN

Not cancelled again. Postponed.

Seven o'clock. Over dinner. The Alpine Inn in Neptune Beach.

Mom would be attending. Chris's wife Becky, too.

And the clincher: Elena.

Dad was vague about the evening's agenda, but was definite about spouses being included. Pete was uneasy about it, but Elena was ecstatic. The Alpine Inn wasn't a five-star restaurant like the places she claimed to have frequented with her beaus back in Sarasota, but it was good. She'd called him after lunch to tell him she was already getting dressed, calling him Snuggles in the process.

Snuggles. Wow. He hadn't heard that one in a while. Maybe there was hope. After all, she'd taken him to bed last night and burst the dam that had been building inside him for months. He'd even caught himself whistling a couple times as he supervised the loading of delivery trucks.

When he arrived at home after work, Elena was standing at the door, resplendent in a white sleeveless dress that was probably a bit over the top for The Alpine Inn, but appeared to make her happy.

"Peter, hellooooooo," she called out, waving her fingers at him from the step. As he got out of the car, the door behind her was flung open. Gwendolyn appeared in pajamas, bawling like a two-year old.

"She's upset that she can't go," Elena said to Pete. Then, turning around, she yelled at Gwendolyn, "It's not going to work, so stop trying. Tonight is adults only. Peter is going to be discussing his exciting new position with the company."

Gwendolyn's shoulders heaved as she turned and went back inside, slamming the door behind her.

"Give me fifteen minutes to get ready," Pete said, climbing the steps. Elena met him with a big wet kiss on the lips.

"I waited to put my lipstick on so I could do that," she cooed, patting him on the backside as he passed.

***

Demopoulos family dinners could play out any one of four ways. Only one of them was good. The common denominator was Elena.

Silent Elena was the least problematic. When she refused to talk to the others because of some previous slight remembered only by her, they ignored her, but it would be hell at home for Pete.

Snippy Elena could make a night drag on interminably. Chris and Becky were usually the targets, as their two children, Jamie and Colleen, seemed incapable of doing any wrong, a fact that led Snippy Elena to point out even the smallest things in an effort to make up for Gwendolyn's misbehaviors.

Devious Elena was directed at Papú. The old man couldn't hear well. Everyone knew it and compensated by facing him and speaking up. Devious Elena would not only do the opposite; she would arrange things so Papú also missed out on the conversations of others, often without their realizing it was happening. Too proud to let on, Papú would sit in silence, but it would be hell at work for Pete the next day.

Flattering Elena showed up after she'd angered the others and was trying to make amends. She was certain that she was smarter than the rest of the Demopoulos family, and she would use those perceived smarts to lay on the false praise. This one drove everyone up the wall, and it would be hell for Pete at work the next day.

Pete could usually tell in advance which Elena was accompanying him. If necessary, he would give Mom and Dad a heads-up. They, in turn, could enlighten Chris and Becky. No one bothered to let Papú in on the mood of the evening. He'd just have to find out for himself.

As they entered the private dining alcove of The Alpine Inn, however, Pete was at a loss. The lady holding onto his arm wasn't silent, snippy, devious, or flattering. She was just... nice. How would that go over?

"You look lovely, Corrine. Have you lost weight?"

Mom appeared momentarily flummoxed by Elena's kind words and warm hug. This was real. It was obvious she wasn't being Flattering Elena. Dad, Chris, and Becky gaped at her like one might a traffic accident. Papú appeared to be scoping out the exits.

"Thank you, dear." Mom smiled as she deftly removed herself from Elena's embrace. "Twenty pounds."

"Well, you've got to tell me how you did it." From there, Elena made the rounds, hugging and air-kissing as she went. Anticipating her approach, Papú brushed past Chris to a spot at the far side of the round dining table, making it impossible to get stuck in Elena's clutches.

Once everyone was seated, a server took food and drink orders. During the polite conversation that followed, Pete checked and rechecked his satchel, ensuring it was close by and the notes he'd brought were readily available. He had no idea what questions they might ask, but he was ready for anything.

Almost anything.

Dad gulped his martini, stood, and cleared his throat. This was his way, standing even when there were only the seven of them. Mom sat to his right, Papú to his left.

"I'm always happiest when my family gathers together," he said, smiling broadly. "Before I begin, I'll offer a toast."

Dad looked around the table as glasses were raised.

"To the future."

"The future!" they echoed.

Pete watched his family slug their drinks. They weren't a cultured group, but they liked the occasional nip.

"Now, I know you're wondering why I brought you here," Dad said. Elena squeezed Pete's hand under the table. "We usually do business at the store, but tonight is special."

Dad looked at Pete as he continued. "Last week, Pete… Pelope brought me a proposal that got me thinking about the future of Demo-Fresh. I went home that evening and told Corrine, and she agreed… it was a sign from God."

Uncomfortable smiles flashed around the table. Since Mom and Dad had started going to the holy roller church in Dickerson Springs two years ago, they'd been tossing God and Jesus into their conversations. They'd been members of the local Greek Orthodox Church for years, attending sporadically but donating regularly. The change didn't make sense, but it was their life.

"I've always considered myself pretty indispensable to Demo-Fresh," Dad continued, "but recently it's become evident that our family has several leaders."

Out of the corner of his eye, Pete saw Elena beaming at him.

"Papú gives us a link to our past," Dad said, "while Pete and Chris represent our future."

"You're important too, Dad," Chris said.

"Indeed," Becky echoed.

Dad's face reddened. "Thank you both, but I must say that when Pete submitted his proposal, I found myself digging in my heels, wanting to keep things the same. That's when I realized, the company can do fine without me."

Pete's breath caught. He looked at the others. Mom was watching Dad, her pride evident. Chris was studying his drink, his left arm intertwined with Becky's right. Papú stared blankly into the distance.

"Mom and I made the decision this weekend to follow our hearts. We're leaving in three weeks for New Guinea. We'll be there for two years, maybe longer, doing mission work for our church. We'll be working with natives, helping them learn better ways to live. We can't wait—"

"Dad are you nuts?" Pete was on his feet, his tone loud enough to attract a waitress. He shooed her away. "Do you know what you're getting yourself into? And Mom?"

Dad stared at him, his expression a mix of irritation and confusion. "Pelope, don't you think we've considered this thoroughly? Have you ever known your mother and me to go off half-cocked?"

"New Guinea has cannibals, Dad. *Cannibals!*"

Elena gasped. Instinctively, Pete touched her shoulder, before noticing that the reactions of the others were unchanged by this revelation. Chris continued to study his drink. Becky sat impassively. Mom seemed unperturbed. Papú stared at the wall.

That's when it became obvious.

"You've already told them of your plans," Pete said. "Why did you leave me – us out?"

Dad sat down slowly, buying time. Pete remained on his feet.

"Papú knew. Chris knew. Even Becky knew, and she's not even a blood relative," Pete said angrily. "Why am I finding out tonight?"

"Easy, Pete." Chris finally looked up, his voice soothing.

"Stay out of this, Chris. Dad, I think you're making a big mistake. I've read about New Guinea. It's dangerous. It's also your life, and if you and Mom want to preach to headhunters, that's your business. What I don't understand is why I'm learning of this for the first time tonight, after everyone else has obviously been told before."

"*Pelope*, enough." Papú had finally torn his gaze away from the wallpaper. His tone invited no rebuttal, but Pete wasn't in the mood for the old man's churlishness.

"Am I the only one here who cares? Do any of you read *National Geographic*? Do you have any idea of what it's like there? Do you even know where New Guinea *is*?"

Silence. Uncomfortable silence.

Shaking his head, Pete took a deep breath and sat down. Seeing his opening, Dad spoke. "I appreciate your concern, Pete. We've considered several options, but feel New Guinea is where we can do the most good. We won't be spending our time in the areas with the cannibals, but there is the chance of occasionally meeting them."

"We're finally doing something together, Pete," Mom said as she took Dad's hand. The simple gesture gave Pete pause. He'd never seen such obvious affection between his parents.

As Mom spent the next few minutes describing the work they'd be doing on the other side of the world, Pete's feelings changed. Her excitement was evident, as was the amount of study and consideration she and Dad had put into the decision. At one point, Elena leaned close and whispered in his ear, "Have they gone batty?" But by then, Pete was sure they'd made the right decision. He'd not seen them this animated in years. Certainly, the daily rigors of running a chain of grocery stores didn't compare. By the time Mom finished he was envious.

Then the other shoe fell.

"Effective the beginning of the month, I'll no longer be on the Demo-Fresh payroll," Dad said. Then, turning his attention to Pete, he continued, "Papú and I have looked at how to best organize the company for the future. Pete, you've done an outstanding job getting the warehouse in order. We never have to worry about whether our stores have what they need when they need it."

Elena grabbed his hand again.

"The renovations you've proposed are needed. We've decided to start with Beardon and Orchard City. More square-footage, air-conditioning..." Dad stopped and grinned. "...and check-out stands with conveyor belts. Winn-Dixie won't have a chance."

This brought soft laughter from the others.

"Take a bow, Pete. Your proposal will lead the way to Demo-Fresh's next generation."

Pete was speechless, embarrassed by his father's glowing words and the applause that followed.

"I'm so proud of you," Elena effused.

"By the time the work is done," Dad continued, "I expect our sales to rise by half or more. In some ways, I'm sorry I won't be here for it, but the excitement of Mom's and my future more than makes up for it."

Dad reached into his back pocket and pulled out an envelope.

"Papú and I agree you've earned something extra for the work you put into your proposal. Please accept this with our love and appreciation." Pete opened the envelope and found a Demo-Fresh payroll check for five-hundred dollars, more than a month's salary.

"Tuition for Gwendolyn's new school," Elena squealed. Pete noticed the looks of dismay around him. They didn't like Gwendolyn, either. Even Mom, who everyone loved, couldn't warm up to her step-granddaughter.

"Thank you, Dad... Papú," Pete said.

"With the increased sales, the warehouse will be more important than ever," Dad said. "Pete, as Warehouse Manager, we would like you to oversee a fifteen-thousand-foot expansion over the next twenty-four months. Papú and I also feel a ten-percent salary increase is in order."

Pete nodded appreciatively, but still had one question.

"Dad, what about your—"

Dad waved for him to stop.

"I know what you're about to ask. We've decided that Chris will take my position as General Manager. He'll work closely with Papú in Dickerson Springs... and you, of course." Dad paused to pat Chris on the shoulder.

"Demo-Fresh will continue to be one big happy family."

EIGHT

"It's a damned travesty, Peter! You *cannot* let them treat you like this!"

The force of Elena's purse thrown against the kitchen cabinet knocked over the flour and sugar canisters and sent the cat scurrying for safer ground. She'd delayed her explosion until they were home, quietly steaming in the car for the thirty-minute ride from The Alpine Inn.

Then, the sound of approaching footfalls from someplace deeper in the house. Gwendolyn appeared in the kitchen.

"What's going on? Mother, are you—"

"Gwendolyn! Back upstairs! Now!"

Unused to being the subject of one of her mother's full-frontal attacks, Gwendolyn retreated meekly.

"What has *Chris* done to deserve anything?" she ranted. "The only reason he's back is because he screwed up everything he tried."

"Leave him out of this, Elena. The problem's not Chris; it's Dad and—"

"*Chris knew*, Peter. He knew all along. Your father and grandfather told him and that dimwit Becky. You and I were the only ones who didn't know." Elena leaned against the counter, catching her breath and preparing for the next salvo. "You can't let them get away with it. I'm telling you, you must do something. Those bastards *need* you."

She was right. Pete knew it. He also knew how difficult it would be to say anything after the scene they'd left at the restaurant.

"Elena, you shouldn't have called Papú an asshole."

"Somebody had to stand up for you." She'd turned to face him, her eyes sizzling with disdain. "Because you certainly weren't doing a very good job of it. And he *is* an asshole. I've known that since I met him. He's as mean as a snake. You're used to it, because you've dealt with it your whole life, but that man hates everything and everybody."

Right again.

"And your father... he's so intimidated by the old man that he's going to live with headhunters. *Headhunters!*"

She had a point.

"If you're so all-important to Demo-Fresh like Hal said, why are they leaving you in the warehouse? A *monkey* could run the warehouse."

"A monkey? Now that's enough." It was Pete's turn to be angry.

"You said as much yourself," Elena retorted. "Earlier tonight, before we left. You said you'd gotten the warehouse to where it could run itself. You said that!"

She had a good memory. But a monkey?

Peter stood straighter, preparing to unleash a few shots of his own. "I might have been able to talk to Dad tonight, if you hadn't dumped a salad on Becky's head."

"That bitch was smirking!"

"Elena, you shoved my mother!"

That one hit home. She nodded, guilt spreading across her face.

"I shouldn't have done that," she admitted. "Corrine was trying to make peace, but the others..."

"I'll talk to Dad tomorrow. I'll let him know he's made the wrong decision. I'll demand to be made General

Manager. I'll even…" Shaking his head, Pete turned to leave the kitchen, Elena in hot pursuit.

"You'll what? What else were you going to say?"

Pete reached the stairs before turning.

"I'll quit."

Elena looked as if she'd just been given a death sentence.

"No, Peter. Whatever you do, don't quit."

Pete looked at her uncertainly.

"Just a minute ago you were telling me to fight for my career. Now… what changed?"

"You need this job. Even if it's still in the warehouse. We need income to support Gwendolyn. She's starting at Montfried next year. We need to make sure—"

A smile slowly came to Pete's face. He looked at Elena, at the bottom of the stairs, a pleading look on her usually smug face.

"That's all it's about for you, isn't it, Elena? Money."

"Don't you say something like that to me—"

"Money, money, money," he taunted. "It's all about the money."

"Peter, how can you say that? You need to be reasonable. How many companies are going to hire a one-armed little man who's spent his entire adult life catering to his Papú's and Daddy's every command?"

The way she dragged out the name, 'Papooooooo,' and the mocking way she said 'Daddy,' like Pete was a child, were cold and unsettling. The same for the look in her eyes – her eyes said it all.

Elena hated him.

But not as much as he hated her.

NINE

Dad showed up at the warehouse at eleven-thirty with sandwiches. Ham, bacon, and cheese.

"We had to use up the ham and bacon today," he said, handing Pete one of the two sandwiches and situating himself in the folding chair next to Pete's tidy desk. "They were starting to smell up the meat case."

This declaration might turn the stomach of many people, but the Demopoulos family was accustomed to eating smelly, outdated meat from the butcher case. Pete shrugged, unwrapped the wax paper, and took a bite. Not as bad as some they'd eaten. Pete had seen Papú slice away the mold from a chunk of turkey breast until there was almost nothing left, then shove it in his mouth. It's what they did.

They sat for a few minutes, chewing quietly, each waiting for the other to go first. Both knew why they were there, so there was little sense in waiting. Pete set aside his sandwich, wiped his hand on a paper towel, and charged ahead.

"Dad, I resent that everybody knew your plans except me. And why is Chris taking your place? I'm older, I've worked longer, and you said yourself, I've done a good job with the warehouse. You have no right to pass me over!"

Pete hadn't expected the anger that accompanied his words, and judging by the way his father recoiled, he hadn't either.

"Watch your tone, Pelope! This is still my company, and if I want to do something, *I will do it!*"

It was Pete's turn to flinch. Seldom did Papú's legacy of anger rear up in his father. Pete hung his head, then remembered how things had played out the night before. This wasn't the time to back down, despite the fluttery feeling in his gut.

Remember why you asked him to come here. Get what's owed to you.

"Dad, I demand to be made General Manager. It's what I've worked for since high school. You know that."

Dad met his steely gaze with one of his own, causing Pete to realize he had started the conversation all wrong. Rather than calmly discussing what had happened, he had set them up for an argument. If anything good was going to come out of this, he had to change the tone.

"Look, I'm sorry for the way that came out. It's just that last night was a huge shock. Put yourself in my shoes. Decisions were made about Demo-Fresh that I knew nothing about. You've said yourself, Dad, that we're a team. Right now, I don't feel like I'm part of it."

Dad looked away for a moment, his posture growing less tense.

"Son, I understand… and I'm sorry." His father's eyes grew misty. Demopoulos men didn't show emotion, other than anger, so this was rare. "You *have* done a good job with the warehouse, it's just…" he coughed and scratched his head, "…Chris is better cut out for being General Manager. I mean, he went to college, and—"

Pete's voice started to rise again. "He got drunk every weekend and skipped his classes until they threw him out. And where was I?" Pete stopped for a breath. "I was right here. Working my ass off for Demo-Fresh."

Dad bit his lip. "But he did go to college. Papú and I feel that will help Chris—"

"He flunked out!" Pete banged his fist on the desk, startling his father. "He flunked out of junior college! Dad, nobody flunks out of junior college."

Dad rose quickly, sending sandwich crumbs flying from his shirt. "Pete... Pelope, the fact is, Chris has done well for us despite his earlier setbacks. He married well, he has two beautiful children. He's made a good life for himself."

Dad's face grew deeper red as he continued.

"Your family life is a mess. Look at Elena. She's a dreadful woman, Pelope. Did you see the way she pushed your mother? It was all I could do not to kick her ass out of that restaurant. You should have done something, but you didn't. You just let her walk all over you, Pelope. And Gwendolyn? That one is a tramp, I'm telling you—"

"What the hell do you want me to do, Dad?" Pete was on his feet, he and his father were eye-to-eye across the table. "Want me to divorce Elena? Given the way you and Mom pushed me to marry her, that should be the last thing you want."

That one stung. Pete could see it. Dad remembered. His eyes fluttered rapidly as he took several breaths.

"We just thought... I mean with your..." Dad didn't say anything, but Pete didn't miss the glance in the direction of his missing arm.

"You didn't think I'd find a wife on my own, did you? You and Mom thought nobody would marry poor, one-armed Pete, so when you saw the chance, you pushed Elena on me. Am I right?"

Dad didn't respond. He didn't have to.

"Well, there you go, Dad. Before you get too haughty, remember you had something to do with her being part of this family."

He shook his head. "She wasn't like that then."

They grew quiet; the truth hanging in the air like the Florida heat. Dad slumped back into his chair, seeming ten years older than when the conversation had begun. Pete's gut told him he wasn't going to win, no matter what he said.

"Who knows, son, maybe in a few years, when Papú retires, or… and Chris takes his spot, you'll be our General Manager." He paused and looked up at Pete. "To be honest, we might have done you a favor. Dealing with Papú everyday takes so much out of a man." Tears rimmed his eyes, but he smiled nonetheless. "I mean, I'm going all the way to New Guinea to get away from him. Being eaten by cannibals actually sounds better than being beaten down every day by Papú."

Dad stood. Pete followed him to the door. As he turned to leave, he put his hand on Pete's shoulder.

"I've told no one this, Pete, but I've prayed for him to die in his sleep. Not a painful death, but just going to sleep and not waking up. That's terrible, isn't it?"

Dad didn't expect an answer, so he didn't wait for one. As the door closed, Pete thought of his own situation. Yeah, praying for someone to die in his sleep was terrible, but hadn't he uttered the same prayers? About Papú? About Elena?

TEN

The fish weren't biting, so Pete and Horace Atteberry had plenty of time to talk.

"I still have a spot for you, Pete. I just lost my manager in Sebring." Horace relaxed in a deck chair, fishing rod in one hand, cold beer in the other. "It would be a pretty long drive from Gullford, but it's yours if you want it."

Standing to one side, Pete reeled in his line and cast out again, watching as the sinker pulled the baited line into the azure Gulf waters. It was the third time in the six months since Dad's decision to leave that Horace had offered him a position with Atteberry's Dry Goods.

"I can't leave Chris in the middle of the building project," he said. "Beardon is two-thirds done. We took bids on the work at Orchard City last week…"

And I'm hating every minute of it.

For several minutes the only sounds were the groans of the vessel as it gently rocked. Horace stood up and moved to the side of the boat to relieve himself, grabbed another beer, and returned to his seat.

"Hear anything from Hal?"

"I got a postcard last Wednesday. It took a month to get here. He and Mom are doing well. They're living in a small village, no cannibals yet. Mom is teaching the women how to preserve food. Dad's working with the men on some farming ideas."

Horace laughed. "I didn't realize Hal knew anything about farming."

"He doesn't, but they don't know that... yet. He took some seeds and farming books with him, so I guess that helps."

Horace nodded. "I suppose anything that keeps the natives from eating each other is good."

More silence. Both men preferred it that way. Occasional talk interspersed between long periods of quiet. Pete reeled in a pretty good-sized gray snapper.

"I've been thinking about getting a boat of my own," Pete said, dropping the snapper into the cooler. "Nothing as big as this, but something I can use to get away."

"Excellent investment," Horace effused. "I can put you in touch with a guy at the marina where I bought *Misty*. He'll treat you right. Of course, you'll have to promise to still come out with me every now and then."

"Of course, Horace." Pete cast his line and stared at the horizon. "Do you know if they set up payment plans?"

"I've seen signs about it," Horace said, eyeing his friend. "But the discounts come from paying cash. Use some of that Demo-Fresh money, son. I see the business you guys do. You're swimming in cash."

Pete shrugged. "Yeah, on paper I guess. We've always plowed it back into the business, though. That's the way Papú and Dad prefer to do it."

Horace shook his head, a frown overriding his usually pleasant face.

"It's not my business, Pete, but it's those kinds of decisions that drive guys like Hal off to places where cannibals live."

Pete said nothing, memories of his father's comments about wishing Papú would die in his sleep replaying through his mind.

"How is Chris doing working with the old bastard?" Horace asked.

"He doesn't say much. I guess okay." Truth was, Chris and Papú had formed a bizarre bond that left Pete on the outside looking in. Papú seemed happy to be free of Dad's daily involvement, going so far as criticizing him for the way he'd led Demo-Fresh as General Manager. Chris was able to move past that and get closer to Papú in the process. He was still the same, crusty, grouchy Papú, but somehow, he now viewed Chris as the golden one. And almost as an equal.

And Pete as the outcast.

"Well, if you change your mind about coming to work for me…"

"I appreciate it, Horace. I really do."

But the truth is, I'm sick of warehouses and retail stores.

And brothers and grandfathers.

And bitchy wives and trampy daughters.

And private schools that we're mortgaging our house to pay for.

"Hucklebuck was in my place last week, looking for work."

Pete looked at his friend. This was news.

"I called Chris. He said they didn't want him around the store anymore. Something about being bad for business."

Papú had gotten to Chris. He detested Hucklebuck, like he detested colored people in general. But the poor man needed a little spending money. They'd always taken care of him. Dad had seen to it.

"He's coming back this week," Horace said. "I guess I can find some things for him to do."

"If you don't mind, Horace, send him to me."

Horace, reeling in his empty line, glanced at Pete. "At the warehouse? Pretty far from Dickerson Springs to Gullford. Do you think he can walk that far?"

Pete nodded. "Huck lives a few miles out of Dickerson Springs, in the swamp out on Route 31. He can do it."

"Well then," Horace smiled, "It sounds like you have yourself a new warehouse assistant."

***

The house was quieter with Gwendolyn away at boarding school. Other than Christmas, she'd only come home twice since last September. An added benefit was that Elena had started visiting her mother in Sarasota every other weekend. Unfortunately, Pete thought as he entered the kitchen through the back door, this wasn't one of those weekends.

He laid the four snappers he'd caught on the kitchen countertop and was getting ready to clean them when he heard her come downstairs.

Clean those outside! That's what she would say when she entered the kitchen. Always the same. Elena loved eating his catches, but found the spectacle of cleaning them repulsive. He started to gather the fish back into the container, when she entered the kitchen.

"Hello, Peter."

What?

"Those look delicious!" she said, coming up behind him, towering over him as she peered over his shoulder. "Are you grilling them or would you like me to bake them?"

"Well... I was going to grill them..."

What in the heck was going on?

Pete took a quick inventory of reasons Elena might be pleasant. She hadn't wrecked the car; he'd seen it parked outside. It had to be money. Maybe she'd been shopping.

"So, what did you do today?"

"I've been deliciously engrossed in *Marjorie Morningstar*," she said, sighing deeply. "You really should read it, Peter. I'm finding so much of... of *myself* in Marjorie."

She hadn't been shopping. That was good. It had to be something else.

"Did you know that as a young girl I planned to be an actress, Peter?"

He hadn't. And speaking of acting, what was making her act so nice?

"People in Sarasota still talk about my performance in the Class of 1931's production of *Apron Strings*. Why, just last weekend, Mother's friend Fran – you remember Fran, don't you, Peter?"

Pete eyed the filet knife in his hand, considering it's many possible uses.

"Uh, yes. Fran. Of course. The world traveler. Went to Cuba."

Elena smiled. "You *do* remember."

"Didn't she go to the Grand Canyon this winter?"

"Oh, they were supposed to, but Howard has gout. Anyway, I played the role of Tommy in *Apron Strings*. It was a most difficult role, Peter. The entire play centered on—"

She hadn't wrecked the car. She hadn't been shopping...

"Wait a minute. Tommy? A girl named Tommy?"

Elena blushed. "Actually, Tommy was the male lead. You have to remember, Peter, it was during the Great Depression. The boys had dropped out of school to find work, except for Robbie Placek who was almost blind and a couple boys who were gimps and... oh I'm sorry Peter, I didn't mean..."

That meant there was just one thing left. One reason why she was being so kind.

"... anyway, I was the most statuesque of the girls in our class, so I played Tommy. It was amazing, Peter. I wish you could have—"

"Did Gwendolyn's tuition bill from Montfried come today?"

Elena's babbling came to an immediate stop. She looked at him anxiously. Pete saw it in her eyes – that moment of indecision where Elena had to choose how to respond. Would she continue to be bubbly, happy Elena?

Or would she go on the offensive.

Pete was betting on the latter.

He won that bet.

50

"It's on your desk. It needs to be paid by the end of the month. Peter, Montfried has been so good for Gwendolyn. She's meeting important people. Going to social functions—"

"Smoking in her dormitory room."

Elena's nostrils flared, and her cheeks grew red. Her hands clenched into fists. This was going to be one for the ages, but it had to be. His anticipation – his hope – that Gwendolyn would flunk out by Christmas hadn't come to fruition. He already knew what the figure on the tuition bill would be: thirteen-hundred dollars. Their bank account, after his next paycheck, would have three hundred less than that.

"It was one time, Peter. *One time!*" On this, she was right, though there had to be more. Gwendolyn certainly hadn't gone off to boarding school and become *more* disciplined. Pete suspected that the Montfried administration, to protect the school's bottom-line, turned a blind eye to some things. Of course, like any school, they had limits. Gwendolyn's decision to light up in her room probably would have gone unchecked had she not ignited her roommate's comforter, then expelled the contents of two fire extinguishers to put it out. Pete had hoped that the extinguishers wouldn't be the only thing expelled, but Montfried was a forgiving institution, so here they were.

"Elena, we just don't have the kind of money it takes to send Gwendolyn to Montfried." Pete resisted the urge to duck as he said this. Elena hadn't slugged him. Yet.

"Peter," her voice grew quiet, which scared him even more, "you knew the costs when we enrolled Gwendolyn last September. Your exact words were, *we will figure it out.*"

Turning to leave, she spoke softly over her shoulder.

"Get figuring."

ELEVEN

There was a chill in the air as Pete drove toward the warehouse in the predawn light. A cold front had arrived the day before, and high temperatures were expected to only reach fifty-five.

The temperature at home had been considerably chillier.

There were no words between him and Elena the day following the argument. She'd remained holed up in their bedroom, dreaming of what could've been as she plowed through *Marjorie Morningstar*. Pete commandeered the den, where he mindlessly watched television and considered how he would come up with the tuition money. He'd decided to approach Chris and Papú about a company loan, to be repaid by pulling weekend shifts in the Beardon store. It was demeaning and unnecessary, and the thought of asking caused him to break out in hives. Chris would be particularly difficult. In the months since he'd assumed their father's role with the company, his regard for Pete's ideas and opinions had lessened. What's more, Chris's wife Becky had started coming to work part-time, taking over a corner of the already-cramped Dickerson Springs office. "Typing and filing," Chris had offered in way of an explanation, but it seemed lately that Becky's role had expanded, mostly at Pete's expense. The extra money Becky brought in was certainly coming in handy, as Chris had hired the construction crew that was building out the Orchard City store to add a den and swimming pool at his home.

Pete considered lobbying for a position within the company for Elena, but knew better. Since the scene at The Alpine Inn, she'd refused to be in the same room with any Demopoulos other than Pete. Besides, what could she do, other than get in the way? His taking a shift in Beardon was the only solution.

It was just after six when he pulled into the deserted warehouse parking lot. The only light emanated from a single security light near the front of the building. It would be two hours before the drivers arrived. He parked in his usual spot, off to one side of the building and made his way to the back door.

"Blahhh!"

The sudden noise caused him to jump, then duck. He considered fleeing, before realizing who it was. He turned around, pushed aside his initial fear, and smiled.

"Hucklebuck."

"Blahhhh!" Grinning from ear to ear, Hucklebuck waved as if they'd just spotted each other across a crowded train terminal. Then, as something occurred to him, he pulled a crumpled slip of paper from his pocket and thrust it at Pete. Pete unlocked a padlock, pulled open the door, and motioned for Hucklebuck to follow him inside. After turning on the lights, he looked at the slip of paper.

Pete, Huck showed up at my store Saturday evening. I told him to come see you. It was good fishing with you Saturday. Regards, Horace.

Hucklebuck looked at him expectantly.

"Yeah, Huck," he nodded. "I can use some help." Pete pantomimed sweeping the floor. Hucklebuck smiled joyfully, then as he'd done many times, grew instantly somber as he reached out and touched Pete's stump.

"Awwwwwww, Blahhhh."

"Thanks for your concern, Huck," Pete said, patting him on the arm. "It hasn't grown back yet, but if it does you'll be the first to know. Now let's get you started."

Pete located a push broom, and handed it to him. The man nodded appreciatively and started sweeping. Pete tapped him on the shoulder.

"Not here," he said, using gestures to make his point. "Out front."

He signaled for Hucklebuck to follow him. Outside, the light was still dim. "I'll go inside and open the bay doors. That should give you plenty of light to sweep by," Pete said.

Pete was pointing to the areas he wanted swept when a car pulled into the far end of the lot; it's headlights illuminating them as it came to a stop at the opposite end of the warehouse, fifty yards away. Pete gave Hucklebuck some final instructions while keeping an eye on the car. By the dim glow of the security light he could make out two people, probably Demo-Fresh employees from one of the stores that didn't get Monday deliveries. It wasn't uncommon that a store might need something and would arrange for someone to stop by on their way to work. He watched as they opened the doors and got out. Men, his age, maybe a little older. Not Demo-Fresh people, for sure. Workingmen, it appeared. Not big, but not little. They said something to each other that Pete didn't catch, then approached. Hucklebuck stopped sweeping to smile and wave.

"Good morning, Gentlemen," Pete said casually. "Can I help you?"

They stopped side-by-side, a few feet away. Their eyes moved from Pete to Hucklebuck and back. Hucklebuck was still waving, hoping for a response that didn't come.

The smaller of the two spoke first.

"You niggers know the man that runs this place?"

Pete's breath caught. He sputtered something unintelligible as he tried to get his wits about him.

"C'mon, boy. It ain't a hard question. The smaller one took a step forward. I need to see the man in charge. Is he inside?"

Dumbfounded by the turn of events, Pete shook his head.

"This one's stupid," the smaller man said dismissively, then turning to Hucklebuck. "How about you, boy; tell me who runs this place."

"Blahhhh," Hucklebuck said loudly, pointing at Pete, the grin never leaving his face.

The men laughed, then the larger one spoke for the first time. "What we got here is a couple of nigger retards, Jerry."

The one named Jerry moved closer. His eyes were menacing and a little crazy.

"Who's inside?"

Pete took a deep breath, trying to push away the creeping fear that something wasn't right. Most likely there wasn't anyone within three miles of the warehouse. If this confrontation, whatever it was about, was going to be settled, it would be up to him.

"I'm in charge."

More laughter.

"You must think we're stupid as posts, boy. Them Demo-Fresh people sure as hell ain't leaving a nigger in charge." He nodded at Pete's stump and grinned. "Especially no one-armed nigger."

"I'm Pete Demopoulos. I own Demo-Fresh." He hoped they couldn't see his knees shaking. Something was definitely off about these two.

Jerry looked over his shoulder at his partner, his gaze less certain.

"Marvin?"

The other one came closer, looking down his nose at Pete, inspecting him.

"Might be white. Hard to say. Them Greeks come in all colors."

55

"Maybe you is white," Jerry said, grinning menacingly, "but it don't really matter. What does matter is how much money you got inside the building. That's the only color me and Marvin's interested in."

Pete scoffed. "It's a warehouse, asshole. We don't have money."

Jerry's fist to the side of Pete's head sent him scrabbling to the concrete.

"Blahhh!" Hucklebuck's response was instant and feral. Tossing aside the broom, he lunged at the attacker, awkwardly and off-balance. Jerry side-stepped the advance and laughed as Huck tumbled to the ground next to his friend. Any further resistance was dampened when Jerry pulled a hunting knife from a sheath on his hip.

"Watch 'em, Marvin. I'm going inside." Jerry handed his partner the knife and disappeared into the warehouse. Marvin scowled at them.

"While we're waiting, you boys give me your wallets."

Pete searched the surroundings as he pulled his wallet from his back pocket, hopeful of finding something nearby that he might use against Marvin, but coming up empty. Wordlessly he handed over the wallet. Marvin opened it and removed the bills, two tens and a single.

"How about you, nigger, he said, brandishing the knife in Hucklebuck's direction. Huck's eyes followed his every move. If he was scared, it wasn't showing. Perhaps he didn't understand.

"He's deaf," Pete said quietly.

Marvin moved closer, waving Pete's wallet in his face.

"Yourrrr mo-neee!" he said loudly, drawing out his words as if it would make a difference. Hucklebuck stared at him for a moment, then pulled a tattered change pouch from his front pocket and held it out. Closing the remaining two feet between them, Marvin grabbed for the pouch, not seeing Hucklebuck's left leg swing out like a pendulum, striking him just below the knee and sweeping his legs out from under him.

Hucklebuck was on him in a flash, landing blows while he tried to avoid Marvin's awkward stabs with the knife. Pete jumped up and moved in to help, but with Hucklebuck on top and seeming to have the advantage, there was little he could do. The blade of the knife glinted in the dim morning light as it weaved back and forth, jabbing and zigzagging as the men struggled for control. Then, Pete saw it plunge through Hucklebuck's left hand. He screamed in agony as he fell away. Emboldened by the damage he'd done, Marvin pounced, thrusting and slashing with the knife. It pierced Huck's hand again, then his upper arm.

Then his throat.

Despite the blood gushing from his wounds, Huck continued to fight. He tossed Marvin aside like a ragdoll and staggered to his feet. The guttural roar that emanated from him came from someplace deep and otherworldly. Pete instinctively rushed toward their assailant, but Marvin spun and waved the knife menacingly, backing him up before returning his attention to Huck. Stumbling back, Pete tripped and fell against the side of the warehouse. A searing pain tore through his lower back. He'd fallen upon a red brick used to conceal a spare key to the warehouse. He shakily picked it up and crept toward the fray. Marvin's attention was zeroed in on finishing off Hucklebuck, who was still fighting, but now had a vacant look in his eyes. Blood from his wounds gushed down his shirt and onto the concrete.

Marvin didn't see the blow coming that knocked him down instantly and heavily. Hucklebuck collapsed to the ground at the same time. Pete stepped past the attacker to see if Huck was still breathing. He wasn't. The spot on his neck where one would check for a pulse was a large open gash.

His adrenaline raging, Pete moved to the side of the warehouse. He was uncertain if the one inside, Jerry, had heard what was happening, but he doubted it. The warehouse was large, and the exhaust fans tended to drown out noise from outside. He considered jumping in his car and making a run for it, but the thought of Hucklebuck lying out front kept him from fleeing. He had to do what he could for the man who had saved his life by giving his own.

But first, he had to flush out Jerry.

Moving to the rear of the warehouse, he replaced the padlock he had removed ten minutes earlier. That left one way out. Then he stopped at the outside breaker box. With his hand shaking, he unlocked it, reached inside, and pulled the main breaker. With the bay doors still closed, there would be no light in the warehouse. Whatever Jerry was doing inside, he was doing in the dark.

Scrambling back to the front, he jumped into the late-forties Dodge coupe in which the men had arrived and fired up the engine. It would be a matter of time before Jerry came out. A minute passed, then another. Through the smeared and dirty windshield, he could see them lying on the ground, Hucklebuck and his attacker. Neither was moving. Daylight was approaching, and he could see the swaths of blood covering the area where the men had fought.

The door was flung open and Jerry emerged, carrying a box of shotgun shells and some moon pies.

"The damn lights went—" He froze at the sight of the carnage, dropping his spoils. Hesitantly he moved toward his partner, then, seeing there was nothing he could do, turned and started running toward the car at the same time Pete pumped the gas and surged toward him.

It became a game of cat-and-mouse, and Pete planned to win. Running no more than a few feet ahead, Jerry juked left and right across the parking lot, but Pete kept coming. Jerry began screaming at the top of his lungs as he took off on a dead run toward the main road. That was his mistake. It was a straight path, with no place to hide. The road was two hundred yards away. By seventy-five yards, Pete had closed to with twenty feet. At a hundred yards, he could see the sweat flying from Jerry's face and body as he ran for his life. At a hundred and fifty yards Jerry was under the Chevy's front axle. It was such a satisfying thump that Pete slowed, shifted into reverse, and did it again. And again.

He shut down the car and sat back, exhaustion setting in. It was six-thirty. The entire ordeal had lasted less than twenty minutes. It took several moments for the shaking to subside; the sight of Jerry illuminated in the headlights, crumpled on the asphalt in front of the car didn't help. His left leg was bent at an obscenely impossible angle and his head was caved in.

Pete shook off the cobwebs and checked his watch again. Six-fifty. Somehow, he had lost twenty minutes. The sky was brighter, but still murky with the threat of rain. He froze as a car passed by, but it kept going, too far away to see what had taken place.

Then, clarity. He had to do something. He got out of the car and trudged back toward the warehouse. His head was pounding from Jerry's fist, and his knees and legs struggled to move him forward. His mind, however, remained clear. He would call the county sheriff. He would know what to do. But had he gone too far? Should he have let Jerry run away rather than giving chase? Running him down had definitely brought the drama to an end, but running over him the second time? A third? How would that be viewed?

At the warehouse door, he gazed down at their lifeless bodies. The other one, Marvin, looked as if he were sleeping peacefully. The only sign of trauma was blood trickling from his ear. Somehow, Pete thought with no small amount of satisfaction, he had delivered the blow with the perfection of someone schooled in hand-to-hand combat. It was luck. And anger. Hucklebuck didn't deserve the hand he was dealt. There was no truth to the rumors that made the rounds at the brickyard and other places. Huck had been a peaceful person who never hurt anyone. Yet there he lay.

As he reached out to open the warehouse door, Pete spotted something on the ground. Huck's change pouch. He picked it up and looked inside. Forty cents and a tattered plastic card, an expired Florida driver's license, issued six years earlier. Unbelievably, his name really was Hucklebuck. His middle names, Theodore Roosevelt. The picture, a largely unchanged Hucklebuck, beaming at the camera. The address, General Delivery, Dickerson Springs. Birthdate, June 1929. Huck had been twenty-six, six years Pete's junior.

At the bottom of the license the words *Deaf Mute* had been stamped. Pete was familiar with this type of addendum, having the word, *Invalid,* etched into his. He'd hated it from the moment he saw it, but the driver's license office said it was the closest description they had of a one-armed man. He examined the license closely, then stuck it in his pocket. He cinched up the purse and placed into in his friend's cooling hand.

"Hucklebuck, you deserved better," he said quietly. "But then again, so did I."

PART TWO

KIRKMONT, IOWA
1959

TWELVE

"Jonesy, I can't tell you how much we're going to miss you." When Dr. Laidlaw grasped his hand, Jonesy detected that currency of some denomination was coming his way. Knowing the good doctor, it was probably a single, but that was all right. Jonesy had already shaken hands that morning to the tune of forty-seven dollars. The dinner shift the night before netted sixty-one. More than enough for a bus ticket out of Kirkmont.

It was just before ten when the last of the breakfast diners cleared out of the Cheshire Room. In the adjoining lobby, hotel guests were moving to and fro, most in town for Kirkmont College's graduation, where, in a few hours, seventy-three students would be receiving their diplomas. Jonesy would be one of them.

The three boys who worked the midday shift swept in to replace tablecloths and prepare place settings for lunch. Jonesy looked around one last time before heading to the rear of the restaurant to turn in his jacket and tie. Morris, the manager, was waiting for him.

"Well, I guess this is it, huh?" Morris said, snuffing out a cigarette and struggling to pull his ample girth from a saggy office chair. Jonesy smiled as he removed his tie and placed it and the jacket on a coat rack in the corner.

"Father was just saying last night, Jonesy, how you've done better than anybody expected. Why, if you wanted to, you might be able to move up to shift manager or assistant manager at a diner someplace. You ever think of doing that? Maybe in a bigger town with more colored trade?"

Shift Manager. Assistant Manager. It was all Jonesy could do to keep from laughing in his face. Morris was stupid and lazy and, above all else, clueless about how to run a restaurant, hanging on to his job only because his father was one of four owners of the Dancy Hotel, where the Cheshire Room was located. Neither Morris nor his father was aware that the other three owners had approached Jonesy several times over the last few months, imploring him to stay and replace Morris as manager.

"It's certainly a thought, Morris," Jonesy said, making a point to use the man's first name. Morris blanched, but recovered quickly. It was an expectation at the Cheshire Room that employees referred to the manager as Mr. Dixon. Comfortable in his standing, Jonesy had seen fit to scrap that formality six months earlier. Morris had mentioned it a couple times in his passive-aggressive manner, then given up.

Taking his leave, Jonesy strolled out the front door of the hotel and in the direction of the cramped walk-up he'd called home for the past four years. Kirkmont had recommended it in lieu of a room in the tiny men's dormitory, thinking Jonesy and Spencer Shay, the other colored male student, would be more comfortable there. Spencer left after freshman year, having had enough of being a token negro in small-town Iowa.

It was Saturday, and many Kirkmont and Kirk County residents were shopping on the square. Several men, women, and especially teenagers said hello as Jonesy passed. After much hesitation, and more than a little arm-twisting by some of the community's more prominent citizens, the Kirk County Board of Education had relented and permitted Jonesy to student-teach at Kirk County High School during the previous fall semester. In the opinion of most everyone, he had excelled at the endeavor, but a full-time position wasn't in the offing. It was one thing for those progressives out at the college to admit coloreds, but Kirk County Schools couldn't have a colored teacher responsible for white boys and girls. Jonesy had no plans on staying anyway. He'd done his part to enlighten the people of Kirk County and had to admit he'd enjoyed it greatly. But it was time to move on. Staying anyplace for too long wasn't advisable.

He said a quick hello to Mr. Bishop in the filling station as he headed around back and up the stairs to his place. Bishop looked and acted the part of a Midwestern redneck, but Jonesy saw through the facade early on. Bishop was a good Presbyterian who, though he would never consider letting his sweet daughter, Joanne, date a colored man, had no problem with one living over his filling station, particularly if he paid his rent on time. Fortunately, he'd never learned of the nights Joanne, a closet liberal-communist-sympathizing wild-child sociology major, had also spent above the filling station, exploring racial taboos illegal in twenty states. Jonesy would miss her.

Everything Jonesy was taking with him was crammed into a weathered footlocker and two cardboard suitcases, setting in the middle of his living room. It was a lot for a cross-country bus trip. He stepped around them and into the closet-sized bedroom, where he put on his one suit, grabbed his gown, and headed back out. Though it was outside the city limits, Kirkmont College was less than a half-mile away. As he walked toward campus, several cars passed, the drivers blowing their horns in recognition. A couple stopped and offered rides, but it was a beautiful late spring day, his last in Kirkmont, and Jonesy wanted to experience the walk to campus one final time.

It was far different from four years earlier, when he, Spencer Shay, Vonda Barnett, and Deborah Grimes, had arrived to begin their freshman year. They'd represented the first colored co-eds in the small liberal arts school's fifty-year history. The girls were given a dormitory room on campus, so they missed out on some of the more interesting events of that first semester. Not so for Jonesy and Spencer. It wasn't uncommon for their walk to campus to be accompanied by racial taunts and slurs. Spencer had taken the bait a few times, including one epic scuffle in front of the Seventh-Day Adventist Church that ended with the high school basketball team's star forward in the emergency room. Jonesy stayed clear of confrontation; it was obvious to even the narrowest-minded bigot that Jonesy wasn't going to put up much of a fight. White or black, picking on someone who couldn't take care of himself wasn't acceptable in Kirk County.

***

Backstage at the Kirkmont College Assembly Hall, Jonesy walked into a sea of mint-green and white.

Mint-green was the color of the gowns worn by the graduates and the official color of the Kirkmont College Knights. It was a running joke among students that if the lack of size and talent didn't allow the opposition to rest easy, the sissy-looking mint-green uniforms would.

White was the color of their faces, except for Jonesy's. He moved about the gathering, saying a few good-byes before taking his place in the spot reserved for class valedictorian.

"I still can't believe I let a coon beat me out," the voice came from behind him. Taunting, familiar, friendly. Jonesy didn't bother to turn around.

"Don't start crying in front of your family, Suggs. You can console yourself with the knowledge that you're the smartest white boy."

Willard Suggs brayed loudly, then gave Jonesy a playful shove.

"Just remember, if it weren't for Chancellor Mathers, you'd be standing *behind* me."

"Yes, and every sophomore would still be putting up with Adeline Akers for English."

"That is true," Willard conceded. "I sure don't miss that old cow."

The old cow, Dr. Akers, had flunked the first three papers Jonesy submitted in her class. Exasperated, he had gone to Chancellor Mathers, himself a former English professor, who actually wrote Jonesy's next paper for him. When Dr. Akers flunked it, her tenure was cut short. It was only after her departure that her family's ties to the Missouri and Iowa Ku Klux Klans were discovered. When Dr. Akers had died suddenly the year before, Jonesy overheard someone at the hotel say her funeral was so sparsely attended it could've been held in a telephone booth. Despite their history, that comment made him feel something for the old cow.

At one on the dot, the graduates marched into the assembly hall to the strains of "Pomp and Circumstance" performed with great enthusiasm and middling results by a combined ensemble of Kirkmont College and Kirk County High School musicians. The packed hall held four-hundred, and each graduate was given five tickets for graduation. Jonesy had given his to Willard Suggs, the oldest of eight children, and the first in his family to make it past high school. Willard's mom, Delphine, had promised that the entire Suggs clan would cheer for him as if he were their own.

After faculty introductions, Chancellor Mathers ascended to the podium, unfolded a sheet of paper, and gazed upon the gathering.

"Five years ago, a landmark decision was made by the Kirkmont College Board of Governors to actively seek out and enroll Negro students." He paused to wipe a trace of perspiration from his forehead. "Nine-months later, four colored students arrived on campus. Three of the four chose to leave for various reasons along the way."

True, Jonesy thought, as he sat and waited. Spencer grew tired of the honky attitudes, Vonda got pregnant over Christmas break of their sophomore year, and

Deborah had transferred to the University of Michigan to get a jumpstart on their pre-med program. That left him.

Chancellor Mathers continued, "The fourth student is sitting amongst our graduates today. He has made his mark both academically and as a resident of our community. Like all graduates, he will be moving on after today, assuming a teaching position back East. I speak for myself, but also for our faculty and the people of Kirkmont when I say he will be missed. So, without further ado, I introduce our commencement speaker..."

The room grew quiet as Chancellor Mathers checked his notes.

"and Valedictorian of the Class of 1959..."

The Chancellor beamed at Jonesy.

"Hucklebuck Theodore Roosevelt Jones."

PART THREE

TWINTON COUNTY, MARYLAND 1959-61

THIRTEEN

As the Greyhound bus rolled into Sheffield on Maryland's Eastern Shore, Jonesy was taken by the community's beauty. Stately Victorians enveloped in shady canopies of mature trees lined both sides of the street. The downtown business area was easily three times the size of Kirkmont's. This was going to be okay.

The bus dropped him and two other passengers off in front of Werner's Drug and Soda Bar. The latest Paul Anka hit sprang from a jukebox inside. It had been a long four-hour trip from the transfer station in Baltimore, and Jonesy considered going inside to wet his whistle.

"Mr. Jones? Hucklebuck Jones?"

The man was older, late-fifties. Colored, wearing work clothes and a straw hat.

"Yes?"

Jonesy's confirmation brought a wide grin to the man's face. "I be Lucius Tapper. Doctor Mister up to the school board sent me to get'cha."

Lucius was a throwback to another time. A step-and-fetchit, as some called them. His way of speaking, his stooped posture, and conciliatory demeanor signaled a life spent bowing to and serving white people who would never view him as anything close to their equal. He genuflected and looked away when Jonesy offered his hand.

70

"If you'll come with me I'll take you to Doctor Mister's office."

The bus driver had placed his luggage on the sidewalk. Jonesy reached for his trunk, but Lucius stepped in, took it by the handle and lifted it.

"I got it, suh. You just stand in the shade over there while I get it loaded up."

"Nonsense, Lucius. Besides, I have two more over here." Jonesy moved closer to the bus, retrieving one of his bags. Lucius froze, wide-eyed.

"How you gonna get them two bags with…" Lucius didn't finish what he was about to say, but it wasn't necessary. Jonesy had caught him glancing at the empty jacket sleeve a couple times already.

"Been like this since I was a little boy," Jonesy said, holding one suitcase against his chest while he wrestled the other into his grasp.

Though delivered in a kindly manner, Lucius was flustered by the response. "Uh, uh, I din't mean nothin', suh. I was just—"

Jonesy laughed, an attempt to put Lucius at ease. "Don't give it a second thought, Lucius. And stop calling me sir."

Lucius looked at him like he might be from another planet.

"You workin' for Doctor Mister up to the school. What you want me to call you, suh?"

The simple question brought Jonesy up short. He'd hated being called Jonesy from the moment it had been stuck on him at Kirkmont, but it was certainly preferable to Hucklebuck. That one made people laugh. Still, he hadn't considered a name for this new chapter in his life. He had plenty to choose from, with a name like Hucklebuck Theodore Roosevelt Jones.

Huck? Nah too Mark Twainish.

Teddy? Fine for a bear, but worse than Jonesy for a man.

Rosey? A woman's name.

"How about..." Jonesy paused for a second. It was going to be Jonesy by default. Then, an idea.

"Call me Buck," he said. "Buck Jones."

"Okay, Mr. Buck. This be my car here. You get on in and I'll load your stuff. Doctor Mister be waitin' for you up to the school."

Jonesy looked longingly at the drug store. "Have I got time to run inside and get a cold drink?"

Lucius gasped, causing him to drop the end of Buck's trunk.

"Mr. Buck? You can't go in there. That be the *white* drug store."

White drug store?

"Don't worry, suh. We stop at Mister Billy's filling station up a piece. He sell to everybody."

Jonesy took a lingering look at Werner's Drug Store. *The white drug store.* Kirkmont had been segregated to a point, but had mostly welcomed the handful of colored students who found their way to the college. Heck, Jonesy had become a bit of a celebrity, greeted warmly by Kirkmont's most influential residents.

Greeted, but invited into their homes?

Nope. Not once. But then, he'd been too busy to notice.

Could it have been that they liked him for the same reason people in Sheffield liked old Lucius? Because he was harmless and served their needs?

No. Not the same... was it?

He could just make out the printed bus schedule posted on the drug store window. The next bus to Baltimore left in three hours. It was Tuesday. He could be back in Kirkmont by Friday. They'd welcome him back at the Cheshire Room. Probably make him manager, like the owners had mentioned.

It was good to be welcome someplace.

Then, another thought. He was welcome at the Cheshire Room as Jonesy, the trusted employee and potential manager. But how about Jonesy the man?

Could Jonesy the man be accepted into the inner sanctum of the Cheshire Room? Could he reserve a table and be served on the fine china and tablecloths?

Jonesy wracked his brain trying to remember. Had he ever seen a colored person in the Cheshire Room?

Nope.

Suddenly aware of his naiveté, he swore under his breath.

"You say something, Mr. Buck?"

Jonesy looked at Lucius blankly. "What?"

"You said something, suh, but I din't hear."

One final look at the bench in front of Werner's, a totem for buses leaving Sheffield for points North, South, and West.

North? Who did he know there? Colored people were fleeing to the North in droves. He'd be arriving with no prospect of work and no support.

South? Definitely not. Maryland was as close to Florida as he dared go. What if someone...? The thought made him shudder.

West? Lingering thoughts of Kirkmont played at the fringes of his mind, but no. It was apparent now that his lot in life there would be little more than a cleaned-up version of Lucius' life in Twinton County.

But what if... he could always... *be white again.* That would make it easier. A white man with a college degree could find his way no matter where he went.

His mind flashed to the early dawn hours of a day four years ago. A man fighting to save his life. To save both their lives.

The sight of that knife piercing the man's neck still woke him up from the soundest of slumbers. For all intents and purposes, the man was dead, yet he rose and continued fighting. Until there was no fight left.

Jonesy couldn't desert that man's memory, though it would be easy enough. Jump the next bus North, be white again, use the Kirkmont degree to get a job.

Except the degree wasn't his. Neither was this life, really. Had it not been for Hucklebuck Theodore Roosevelt Jones, he might have died that morning. Really died. Not a staged disappearance that had confounded Florida police.

It wasn't going to be easy, but Jonesy would continue down the road he'd ventured upon years ago. He'd remain Hucklebuck Theodore Roosevelt Jones. A black man.

Pete Demopoulos was dead.

Hucklebuck was alive. Buck, as he would be known now.

"Let's go see Doctor Mister."

***

That really was his name. Kenneth J. Mister, Ph.D. Doctor Mister to everybody in Twinton County. When Buck was escorted into his office, the superintendent openly gaped at his missing arm. Buck was used to it, but had expected a man as learned as Doctor Mister to rein it in a little.

"Sit down, Mr. Jones." He motioned to a maroon leather chair across from a desk large enough for a family of six to enjoy dinner. The entire office was a testament to Doctor Mister's position in life. Superintendent of Twinton County Schools. It smelled faintly of leather, Old Spice cologne, and furniture polish. The lighting was sedate.

Doctor Mister made a show of flipping through a folder with Buck's name on the label. There were several pages, including a letter Buck recognized as being from Chancellor Mathers, another from the head of Kirkmont's English Department, and a third from a Kirkmont banker. When the superintendent looked up, his eyes showed suspicion.

"Nobody said you were missing an arm, Mr. Jones. You never mentioned it in our telephone interview, either."

"It's not important, sir. As my references write, and as you'll learn, I can handle any responsibility thrown my way."

Doctor Mister nodded, his face pensive. "War injury? I noticed you're…" he referred to the application Buck had filled out several months earlier. "thirty-two. That would have put you at the right age…"

"It's hard to talk about, sir," Buck said, lowering his head somberly. Let the judgmental bastard think what he wanted to think.

Superintendent Mister grew contrite. "I understand completely, Mr. Jones. I'll not say another word. Our local boys saw a lot of difficult things over there, too. Your scholastic and employment records from Iowa speak for themselves. In fact," he paused for a second, pulling a scrap of paper from under a paperweight replica of a negro lawn jockey. "I have something that might interest you, provided you want to make a little extra money."

***

Lucius was waiting when Buck stepped out of the office and into the bright afternoon sunshine.

"Thanks for waiting, Lucius. I guess I need to find a place to stay."

"Of course, suh. What you looking for?"

"Do you know of any rooming houses here in Sheffield?" Buck said, as they got into Lucius's car. "Maybe something that includes meals?"

"Colored people don't be living in Sheffield, suh. You gots to look in Pine Hammock. The colored town. That where I live. Fact is, I know a lady be looking to rent a room in her house. Nice older woman. Already gots one person living with her, but looking for another."

Shaking his head, Buck said, "More surprises every minute around here, Lucius. White drug stores, colored towns."

"That be the way it always been here, suh. We just go along and get—"

Buck turned sharply in his seat. "Lucius, cut the bullshit."

Brought up short, Lucius grew silent.

"Seriously, is this how you talk at home? 'Yes, suh' and 'this be my car, suh.' If we're going to be neighbors… and friends, you need to be straight with me."

Lucius remained quiet, but his jaw moved slightly, like he was considering his next response. Then, a sudden jerk of the wheel and they peeled off onto a dirt road. For a moment, Buck considered the possibility of Lucius taking him someplace to dump and leave him. It was ten minutes before they came to a small structure backed up against a thick woods. A shack really. No sign. Nothing more than a door and some darkened windows. There were a half-dozen battered vehicles parked around the periphery. Lucius pulled in amongst them, shut off the motor, and motioned for Buck to follow him.

Inside the place was dark and reeked of sweat, cigarettes, stale beer, and something stronger.

"He makes his own, just beyond the tree line," Lucius said, motioning to a slender dark-skinned man behind the bar.

"Who the one-armed boy?" a bald-headed man seated at the end of a ten-stool bar asked Lucius.

"Buck Jones. New teacher up at the school. Buck, this is Remy Robertson." Buck approached and offered his hand, but Remy only stared at it."

"Where the other one?" he asked gruffly. Buck stared at him, waiting for him to say something else, but Remy grinned and stuck out a chubby hand.

"Just jakin' you, brother. Welcome to Moonie's." For the next few minutes, Lucius took him from person to person, making introductions along the way. The entire place would have easily fit inside Superintendent Mister's office. The bar, four scratched and wobbly lacquered tables with mismatched chairs, and a cigar store Indian filled the cramped space. Moonie was the owner, second generation. Moon Junior, actually. Moon Senior had, according to the stories the men openly told in front of Moon Junior, run off three years earlier.

"With a white woman," they said reverently. "A *married* white woman," one added. Moon said nothing; just listened and dispensed drinks.

"Two choices," Lucius explained as they took seats at the bar. "National Boh or moon juice." While not much of a drinker since his days in Florida, Buck knew his selection would say a lot.

"Give me the juice."

A small cloudy glass of clear liquid was placed in front of him. He tipped it at Lucius and knocked it back. Fire burned from tongue to ass, but he did his best not to let it show. He ordered a second, then a third. Talking and answering questions along the way, but mostly listening to the tales spun by those around him. Three days earlier, he was overseeing breakfast at the Cheshire Room. This was about as far from there as one could get. Moonie's was hot, smelly, and cramped.

Damn near perfect, actually.

I could get comfortable here, Buck thought, waving at Moonie for another hit of juice.

FOURTEEN

"That's a new one from The Platters, *Smoke Gets in Your Eyes*, going out to Harold who is on his way home from the second shift at Ocean Star Tuna. Harold, Althea says get home quick and get yourself ready for *the third shift*. She said you'd know what she meant." Buck paused for a moment, before continuing in his slow easy cadence, "Harold, I think we *all* know what Althea means."

He allowed the moment to linger before leaning closer to the microphone. "This is *Night Side* on WSCM. It's eleven-thirty, my friends; time for your good-night calls from across the countryside." He pushed a button on the telephone. "Who's got Hucklebuck's ear tonight?"

"It's me, Hucklebuck... Marguerite." Her voice was breathy, sexy. "I'd like to say goodnight to Ricky and his love and Karvin and his love and Natalie and her love... and to my special love, Malcolm. And goodnight to you and your love, Hucklebuck."

"Always a pleasure to hear from you, Marguerite. Now you go and keep Malcolm warm on this cool summer night. Who's next?"

"Hucklebuck, it's Frank, man. I gotta tell ya, my girl Donna said we is done..." The line grew quiet. Buck had been through this before. He allowed Frank time to compose himself.

"Anyway, man, I want to tell Donna good night, and I'm sorry. I..." Another pause. "... really want to..." Frank's sobs came through the line.

"Be strong, Frank. All those people out there who are the praying types need to be saying one right now for Frank. He's going through some bad times, for sure. Frank, you call back in a few days and let Hucklebuck know you're doing okay. All right, brother?"

Most likely, Frank was in his late teens or early twenties. This was the audience Buck's show had been attracting since kicking off the month before. Getting the job had been a stroke of luck. Mr. Adams, the station owner, had contacted Superintendent Mister, looking for a colored person who sounded white and wanted a part-time job. Fortunately for Buck, the superintendent offered him first crack. After a twenty-minute training session with Buster Key, the afternoon announcer, an openly hostile redneck who wanted nothing to do with Buck, he was declared ready to fly solo.

WSCM had been battling low nighttime ratings since losing the Baltimore Orioles games to a competitor the year before. "All people want to do anymore is watch television," Mr. Adams had said during the interview. He'd tried everything – country western, big bands, rock and roll. Nothing worked.

"Finally, it came to me," he'd said. "Nobody was playing music for the coloreds." Buck suspected it wasn't an original idea, as much as one born after reading of the success of radio stations in Baltimore and Philly that were raking in big money catering to black listeners. Whatever. It provided him with a job in addition to the teaching gig that would start in a couple months. He worked Monday through Friday for twenty-five bucks a week, doing the seven to midnight shift and cleaning the station restrooms before leaving. It figured out to less than minimum wage, but there would be time to correct that. Besides, he'd already figured out how to put on longer album versions of songs that gave him time to get the restrooms cleaned during the show.

The evening hours allowed Buck to experiment. The good-night calls were a tremendous success, with callers patiently waiting their turn on the station's four telephone lines. The innuendo that slipped through would probably have gotten Buck fired if Mr. Adams didn't have to go to bed early each night so he could be at the station for his 5 am farm reports. As long as Buck kept it clean until eight, he was home free. No white person would ever admit to listening to *Night Side,* though he suspected some did, and his colored audience ate it up, as evidenced by the amount of fan mail he received.

The good-night calls continued until just before midnight, with Buck doling out advice on lost and unrequited love and offering congratulations on newfound love. His tone was soft and easy, like the night itself. None of that loud, harsh deejay stuff the daytime guys relied on.

"The clock is about to strike midnight," he purred into the mic. "Another day is done. Hucklebuck thanks you for tuning in and hopes you find the love you're looking for." He paused, allowing the moment to draw out. "Everyone should be going off to bed. Some alone, some with a special person. Whatever your story, Hucklebuck hopes all your love is good love... Good night."

***

The time of day or night didn't seem to matter. There were always thirsty customers hanging around Moonie's. In just a few short weeks, Buck had become a regular. The late-night crowd was different from the after-work crowd; most were younger, tougher men coming off the four-to-midnight shift at the tuna and shrimp packing plants. Fish and body odor created a sickening funk that required Moonie to open the back door, allowing some cross-ventilation.

Buck still wasn't much of a drinker, mostly out of necessity. After paying room and board at Mrs. Mitchell's place and the monthly payment for the 1950 Dodge Coronet that Lucius found for him, there wasn't a lot left. It would be a couple months before the school paychecks started, so he had to be prudent. Still, hanging at Moonie's for an hour or so after shutting down the radio station had become a pleasurable pastime.

They greeted him as an old friend when he breezed in. Clarence, Johnny, and Poop had saved him a seat at a corner table, close to an oscillating fan that mitigated some of the smell. Buck waved at Moonie and received a nod in return. He'd still not heard Moonie speak.

"The one-armed wonder has arrived!" Johnny was on his feet, palm outstretched, waiting for some skin. The men who frequented Moonie's earlier in the day were traditional hand-shakers, if the moment called for it. The night guys had taken up the habit of saying, "give me some skin."

Buck signaled for some moon juice and took his seat at the table. The others had a several-drink lead on him, and he had no intention of catching up. Poop's head was already starting to list, his eyes were growing heavy.

"You ain't gonna believe this, man," Clarence said, leaning in, bringing his wicked breath too close for Buck's liking, "but Moonie's started playing your show."

"Yep," Johnny said. "Never heard nothing but man-talk in here before last week. Kinda makes the place seem like a real bar, if you know what I mean. Next thing you know, old Moonie be adding a jukebox."

As if on cue, Moonie appeared and set a glass down. Buck flashed his biggest, fakest smile at him. "I hear I'm providing the evening's entertainment these days, Moonie. That should at least be worth a drink or two a night, don't you think?" Moonie stared at him, but said nothing before returning to the bar. Buck watched him walk away before turning back to the others.

"Think that worked?"

Even Poop cackled at that one.

"Moonie would charge to throw water on you if you was on fire," Johnny said, laughing.

The conversation was light and easy for the next half-hour, as one-by-one, other customers walked or staggered out the front door into the night. By one o'clock, Poop was completely out, his head resting on the sticky table. Clarence flashed a conspiratorial look at the others before downing the last of Poop's beer.

"You ain't gonna be hanging with us much longer, right Buck?" Johnny asked. "Soon be time to get on with being *Mister Jones*."

"I have a few more weeks, but I'll try to stop in now and again when school starts."

"A man's gotta sleep sometime," Clarence said. Then motioning to Poop, he added, "I guess you can just sleep here." Their laughter didn't stir Poop; nor did Johnny's placement of several beer labels on the back of the dozing man's head. Poop had recently started pulling double-shifts at the fish plant, and was expected back there in just five hours. Buck had encouraged him to give up the couple hours at Moonie's, but old habits were hard to break.

"I'm betting you have my boy, Terrence, in your class," Clarence said. "He be going into tenth grade."

"I haven't been told where I'm teaching yet." Buck's reply brought head-shaking and looks of confusion from the others.

"Nobody got to tell you where you're teaching. You're teaching at Pine Hammock with the rest of the coloreds."

"I'm not sure about that, Johnny. My student-teaching was in advanced classes. Doctor Mister said that would come in handy, so I'm assuming I'll be at one of the larger schools."

They laughed at this.

"Look, Buck," Johnny said. "Ain't gonna be no colored students or teachers at Sheffield High School.

Ever. That cracker superintendent ain't changing because some smart high-yella boy come in here from out west."

Buck looked at him quizzically. "High yellow?"

Johnny and Clarence exchanged looks.

"What?" Buck pressed.

Clarence spoke first. "You never heard high yella before? Where you from, boy?"

"I've told you before. Florida. Iowa."

"Ain't nobody never called you, 'high yella' in them places?" Johnny asked. "How long you been black, brother?" The question brought another round of ribald laughter from both men, unaware of how close Johnny's question hit home.

Buck proceeded cautiously. "Nobody used it in Florida, and in Iowa people didn't really talk about color much."

Clarence got his laughter under control, then said, "High yella is a colored person who has light skin, like you."

"Some high yella people who grew up around here went off to other places where they could pass." Lowering his voice, Johnny nodded at a man sitting at the far end of the bar. "Albert's wife, Mary, she always had the boys chasing after her because she was high yella. Albert was the one who caught her, but he couldn't hold on. Word is, Mary's someplace up in New York, *passing*."

"Passing?" The conversation was getting further and further away from anything Buck thought he knew about life as a colored person.

"*Passing*, man... as a *white person*."

Buck glanced over at Albert, hoping the man didn't notice.

"That's a thing? Passing?"

More laughter.

"You mean to tell me you never... *never* tried to pass? Even once?" Another question from Johnny that needed to be addressed carefully.

Why, yes, Johnny. I passed for thirty-two years.

"I guess not. Never saw the need, really." Buck's response seemed to please both men.

"That's the way to be, Buck," Johnny said. "Be proud of your blackness. That's what that Dr. What's-his-name King preaches."

"He that Methodist preacher from Salisbury?" Even Buck laughed this time.

"Albert, man, don't you listen to the radio or nothing?" Johnny teased. "Dr. King's the one who helped our people get to ride in the front of the bus down in Alabama. He about the only colored man you ever see on the news."

Albert nodded thoughtfully. "That Methodist preacher from Salisbury is pretty good too."

FIFTEEN

Other than four cars parked close to the main entrance, the lot was empty when Buck arrived. It was his second trip. His first, three days before, had been for naught. Summer hours for the library at Maryland State College were eight to noon. He'd arrived at ten past noon the first time. He hadn't made that mistake again.

Inside, he found his way to a deserted reference desk where he waited. A few minutes later an elderly woman with patchy gray hair passed by and took note of him.

"Can I help you," she asked, not unkindly.

Buck introduced himself, then got into why he'd come. "I'm doing a bit of research and need to find some old newspapers."

"From?"

"1955. Dickerson Springs, Florida. The paper is the *Dickerson Springs Examiner*."

The woman shook her head. "Never heard of it. How about a newspaper from a larger community?"

Buck thought for a moment. It had been a few years.

"The *Beardon Banner*?"

"Sorry, Mr. Jones. We have limited space and resources and must be discriminating about what periodicals and newspapers we take. The only Florida paper we receive regularly is the *Miami Herald*."

Buck sighed. "Thanks, but that's the wrong part of Florida." He was headed for the exit when she called out.

"Mr. Jones?" He turned.

"You did say 1955?"

Buck nodded.

"We took the *Tampa Tribune* through last December. Would that be helpful?"

"It would," Buck smiled. "That's close to the area... uh... that I'm researching."

"Follow me." She led the way through a maze of bookshelves to an area in the library's nether reaches where she pulled open a squeaky wooden door and flipped on a light switch, revealing a massive storage area. The smell of must, mold, and newsprint assaulted Buck's senses.

"I haven't seen you here before," the lady said, motioning for Buck to follow her through a series of narrow aisles with books and newspapers shelved from floor to ceiling.

"I'm not a student, ma'am. I moved here recently from Iowa. I'm going to be teaching in Twinton County."

She stopped and offered her hand. "I'm Mrs. Budd, the head librarian, Mr. Jones. I'll be glad to issue your first library card and hope you'll consider enrolling here and get started on your master's degree. I believe you'll find Maryland State College does a good job for our people."

Mrs. Budd showed Buck the general location of the *Tampa Tribune* and left him to his own devices. The air was thick and old, and Buck had several coughing jags as he searched for what he was looking for.

He didn't have to look long.

SIXTEEN

TAMPA TRIBUNE
February 3, 1955

SEARCH CONTINUES FOR GULLFORD MAN

Police in several south Florida counties continue their search for a Gullford man missing since January 23.

Authorities were summoned to the Demo-Fresh Market warehouse at eight-twenty on the morning of the twenty-third by an employee who had just arrived for work. At the scene, police immediately cordoned off an area in front of the warehouse where a struggle had evidently taken place. Bloodstains covering a swath of concrete indicated multiple individuals were likely involved. The only car at the scene belonged to Pelope "Pete" Demopoulos, 32, the warehouse manager. According to Demopoulos' wife, he had left for work at his usual time that morning.

After hearing of the incident, a Gullford resident reported to police that he saw what might have been a late 1940's to early 1950's coupe in the warehouse parking lot at approximately six-fifteen on the morning in question. Additionally, a box of shotgun shells and some snack cakes had been dropped near the warehouse entrance, but attempts to retrieve fingerprints proved unsuccessful. A brick, also near the scene, had blood smears on one side, but again no fingerprints were found. Residents with additional information are encouraged to notify the Gullford Police Department.

SEVENTEEN

TAMPA TRIBUNE
February 21, 1955

REMAINS NOT THOSE OF MISSING
GULLFORD MAN

Speculation that the remains found in a Central Florida swamp might be those of missing Demo-Fresh Warehouse Manager Pelope "Pete" Demopoulos was dashed yesterday after further investigation.

The remains, found washed ashore in a remote area of Gull County were determined to be those of two males. The bodies, badly decayed and partially eaten by alligators were identified after divers retrieved additional evidence from the swamp. The bodies were those of Jerry Mark Lester, thirty-one, and Marvin Roger Conrad, thirty-five. The most recent address for both men was the Florida State Penitentiary in Chattahoochie, from where they were released on successive days in mid-January after serving three and six-year terms for a number of crimes. A man matching Lester's description was seen stealing a 1948 Dodge coup from the home of a St. Petersburg woman on January 19.

According to an official with the Florida State Police, a knife found at the swamp's edge still had small amounts of blood on the blade. It is not known if Lester and Conrad were involved with the disappearance of Demopoulos, but police are continuing to pursue all leads.

***

"Mr. Jones?"

Buck was startled by the sound of Mrs. Budd's voice. He wheeled around quickly, hopeful she hadn't been there long enough to see him clipping the articles.

"The library is closing in five minutes. I almost forgot you were back here." She smiled. "It would've been a shame for you to be locked in overnight."

Buck got to his feet, dusting off his pants and straightening the stack of newspapers. "I didn't get as far as I had hoped. Perhaps I'll come back after school gets started in a couple weeks."

Mrs. Budd handed him an envelope. "Here's your library card and some information about our graduate programs." Then, leveling her gaze at him, she added, "We prefer that our patrons take notes for their research, but since you're the only person I can ever remember asking for the Tampa newspaper, I can make an exception."

Buck winced. She had seen him.

"In fact..." She pushed past and pulled a stack of Tribunes from the shelf, "why don't you take the rest of 1955 with you. Just remember to bring them back."

EIGHTEEN

Buck rushed in at one minute before eight, thankful to arrive on time after forgetting to set his alarm. Seventy-five teachers were clustered at one end of the Sheffield High School library. Glancing around, he became aware that he knew no one.

"Come in, Mr. Jones." Doctor Mister was at a podium in the front, watching Buck's sudden entrance. "And remember, sir, in the Twinton County Public Schools..." the superintendent nodded at the staff, who replied in unison, *"on time is late."*

Buck's face grew hot as he searched for a seat. Spying an open spot at a table off to one side, he moved down a side aisle, keeping his head down, careful not to draw more attention. It didn't work.

"Mr. Jones, I think you'll be more comfortable over here." Doctor Mister pointed to a table on the opposite side of the room. Though it would have been closer to cut across the front, Buck wanted to stay as far from the superintendent as he could. He reversed course and moved around the periphery of the library, feeling all eyes upon him, until he reached an open seat. A gangly colored man in his early forties pulled out a chair for him. "Welcome to Twinton County... Hucklebuck," he whispered. Buck looked at him sharply.

91

"I'm Biggerstaff, we're neighbors at Geraldine Mitchell's place. Has she put the moves on you yet?"

"Mr. Biggerstaff, will you please share the forecast for Pine Hammock School?" Superintendent Mister had spotted his whispering. Biggerstaff quickly rose to his feet.

"Sunny with a chance of Negroes," he said loudly, drawing tittering laughter from those at his table and scathing looks from the others. Doctor Mister looked upon him as one might a miscreant child.

"*Enrollment* forecast, Mr. Biggerstaff."

The meeting continued at a slow, boring pace, Doctor Mister doing all the talking other than a few pointed questions to others seated about the library. As he took copious notes, Buck stole glances around the room. It occurred to him that the colored teachers were seated together, fifteen of them, at three round tables. The remaining dozen or so tables were occupied by white teachers. Buck was struck by how casually they were attired compared to the colored staff, most of whom wore dresses or shirts and ties. In his blue short-sleeved shirt and corduroy trousers, Buck felt underdressed.

At ten, Doctor Mister announced a fifteen-minute restroom and cookie break. Buck scrambled to his feet and headed toward the front of the room.

"Don't go up there," Biggerstaff said.

"But I want to apologize for—"

"Don't go being an Uncle Tom to him," Biggerstaff replied. "Don't give him the satisfaction. Stay here and meet your new colleagues."

Buck looked from Biggerstaff to Doctor Mister and back again. Biggerstaff said nothing else, just motioned for him to come closer.

"Gather around, Pine Hammock Professionals," he said loudly, again drawing disapproving looks from white faculty still in the room. "This is Buck Jones, our newest addition. Buck, these well-dressed and well-coiffed individuals are your colleagues. They will do everything within their power to make sure you find success at Pine Hammock School."

All around him, colored faces nodded and smiled.

"I'm not sure yet," Buck said, nodding in return. "Doctor Mister hasn't indicated yet where I'll be teaching." Like the guys in the bar, the teachers laughed.

"Mr. Jones," Biggerstaff said, shaking his head, "your lot has been cast with these fine folks. That's the way it is in Twinton County. Now you can go up and speak to the good doctor, but you'll be wasting your breath. No colored man is going to be teaching his precious white boys and girls."

One-by-one they approached and introduced themselves. Though he was still uncertain if Biggerstaff knew of what he spoke, Buck made a show of shaking hands and learning names. Most of the fifteen were considerably older. Only two were close to his age. One was a portly guy with a deep southern accent, named Muskett.

The other, a shapely woman in a dress that looked like something you'd see in the movies, approached and looked Buck in the eyes. When Buck offered his hand, she shook her head disapprovingly.

"Mr. Jones, a man does not offer his hand to a lady. Were you raised in a barn?"

Buck, taken aback by her brashness, was speechless.

"Dottie teaches citizenship and Home Economics," Biggerstaff said, grinning at the obvious discomfort she'd caused.

After the break, Doctor Mister continued to drone on about rules, policies, and other things not at all related to teaching. Twice, Buck actually caught himself about to doze off, then noticed he wasn't the only one. White and black teachers in Twinton County had one thing in common: their superintendent's monotone sent many to the edge of slumber. Biggerstaff went a step further, and for several moments was snoring softly in his seat. Buck was about to touch his arm when the teacher on his other side shook her head.

"Sometimes he snores louder than that," she whispered. "Leave him be."

***

At noon, Doctor Mister dismissed the staff with an announcement that a tasty lunch would be served at Willoughby's Blue Rose Diner, after which teachers would reconvene at their respective schools. Buck stood with the others and glanced around. Biggerstaff, who had awakened just in time to hear the superintendent's final words, spoke to the colored teachers who, other than Buck, had remained seated.

"Billy Goat's, half-hour." Like good soldiers, the colored staff gathered their things and headed for the door. Biggerstaff, noting Buck's hesitation, wrapped his arm around him and pulled him along.

"Willoughby's don't serve us," he said. "And for that, you can be glad. You been to Billy Goat's?"

Buck hadn't, though he'd passed it regularly. Like a lot of establishments in Pine Hammock, it didn't look like much from the outside.

***

If the disembodied head of a goat impaled over the door made Buck think twice about going inside, the smells wafting out pulled him in like a magnet. The place was immaculately clean, and while not on a scale with the Cheshire Room, was well-appointed. An old woman met him at the door.

"Name's Ruby," she said, sticking out her hand. "Your people is in back."

Buck walked in the direction she pointed, passing working men, farmers, and a couple gentlemen in suits and ties. All enjoying heaping plates of food, all nodding friendly hellos as he passed, all colored.

Most of the staff were already seated at a round table, large enough for everyone. There was small talk for a few minutes as the others drifted in. They made a point to pull Buck into their conversations. Asking questions about his background and family. A few were aware of his night gig at the radio station.

"I heard my boy Yancy listening to you a couple weeks ago," said a matronly woman with a broad beam. "Mr. Jones, you need to be watching yourself. That show of yours damn near burned off the dial of my radio." The others laughed good naturedly.

"C'mon, Hester," another teacher said. "You have to admit, it beats that hillbilly shit they were playing before."

Conversations ceased when Biggerstaff came barreling in.

"Sorry I'm late, people," he said. "The Man caught me on my way out." Then, changing his voice to a nasally whine, he continued. "Landon, I want you to remember the responsibilities that accompany your position." It was a spot-on impression of Doctor Mister that had the others howling. Buck wasn't sure how to respond. What position? Who exactly was Biggerstaff?

The questions would have to wait, as Ruby and two young men entered bearing pots brimming with chicken and dumplings, green beans, rolls, and butter. The smell was intoxicating, making Buck realize how poorly he'd been eating since arriving in Twinton County two months ago. Mrs. Mitchell's boarding house fare was filling, but bland. As he'd been the only boarder that summer, she'd tended to get lazy and serve the same few things in a constant rotation of mediocrity. He already knew from the smells around him that Billy Goat's was going to join Moonie's as one of his homes away from home.

The conversation remained light and unguarded as everyone dug in. The attire and decorum this group had displayed at the meeting with the superintendent were cast aside as they filled themselves with Ruby's grub. At one point, Buck looked up from his plate and saw Biggerstaff grinning at him.

"The hoi-polloi are probably nibbling on watercress sandwiches at Willoughby's Blue Rose Diner," he cracked.

"I hope they never find out what they're missing," a teacher said, dumpling sticking from his mouth. Buck wondered if this was true. Were they really okay with being excluded? He wasn't sure how he felt about it, but the chicken and dumplings were out of this world.

"How much they give you, Biggs?" a female teacher asked.

"Enough for all this," Biggerstaff said. "... and a little bit more." As if on cue, Ruby returned with pitchers of beer and frosty mugs. The teachers applauded, then started pouring. This was moving far from what Buck had imagined a teachers' meeting would be like. Not that he cared, he thought, holding out his mug.

After a half-hour of drinking, talking, and laughter, Biggerstaff tapped his water glass with a spoon to get their attention.

"We need to go over some things before the show starts day after tomorrow." He stopped and turned to Buck. "First, let's again welcome our newest faculty member, all the way from Florida by way of Iowa." Biggerstaff flipped through the pages of a notepad he held in front of him. "Mr. Jones graduated valedictorian from Kirkmont College with dual majors in History and English." The others applauded. "He arrived in Twinton County in June and has been burning up the nighttime airwaves at WSCM as," his voice grew deeper, "Hucklebuck, the Godfather of Love." More laughter. Buck wanted to crawl under the table.

"When's your last day?" Biggerstaff asked. Buck looked at him, confused.

"I... guess I don't have a last day." The others expressed surprise at his response, but Biggerstaff shushed them.

"You plan to teach *and* work at the radio station?"

Buck nodded. "If it gets to be too much, I'll give it up, but I'm used to working long hours."

Biggerstaff eyed him curiously, before breaking out in a big smile. "Okay, then, I guess you can do it. Just remember, teaching school is what you came here for. *As your principal*, I will expect your very best every day." Biggerstaff raised his hand for attention.

"Now, let's head over to school and get ready."

***

When Buck saw the inside of Pine Hammock School, he almost turned and ran out. It was a hell-hole. The schools in Kirkmont where he'd done his student teaching, and Sheffield were palatial when compared to the dilapidated conditions at Pine Hammock.

Biggerstaff had assigned Buck to teach high school English and History. Three sections of each, with forty students per section. The desks, what few there were, were ancient, scarred, and wobbly. Still, the twenty-five students who lucked into getting them would be the fortunate ones. Ten other students would make do with hard wooden chairs along the back wall. Five students would sit on the floor.

"We may get more chairs," Biggerstaff explained noncommittally on a stop by Buck's classroom. "I have a request in. Actually, you have a couple more than the guy before you." The principal sensed Buck's dissatisfaction with the environment and worked to assuage his concerns.

"Look, man, things are tough here, but not much harder than a lot of other places. What was the school like that you went to?"

Though it had been a few years, Buck had fond memories of Dickerson Springs High School. Hallways waxed to a shine, new books and desks.

"Pretty good, I guess," he said.

"Florida must be doing better by its colored kids than Twinton County," Biggerstaff said, staring out the window. Then, returning to the moment, he continued. "I joke a lot and talk too much. Some people in the white man's office think I'm a smart-ass nigger. Maybe I am." He paused, his eyes boring into Buck. "But if you remember one thing, *Mr. Jones*, remember that this raggedy-ass school is the only hope the colored kids around here have. If I ever... *ever* find out you're not giving them all you've got, I'll come down on you the likes of which you've never seen."

***

Biggerstaff's words echoed in Buck's mind as he worked his shift at the radio station, causing several moments of dead silence as records ended without him noticing. He even found himself cutting some of his good-night callers short as he watched the clock creep toward midnight.

Could he do this? Teach school by day and be Hucklebuck at night?

His drive to the boarding house was consumed by doubt. Did he even want to teach at Pine Hammock? He could've kicked himself for not checking out the school earlier. Heck, he'd been in town for two months.

Did he even want to teach? He had to admit, the radio gig was pretty easy. There had to be a market for colored disc jockeys particularly in the city. He wouldn't have to worry about desks and lessons and being responsible for the future success of every little colored son of a fisherman's mate in Twinton County.

And that Doctor Mister! What an ass. Those white teachers in Sheffield were getting ready to teach in their shiny nice school with its library full of books. The library at Pine Hammock consisted of two old sets of World Book Encyclopedia and a bunch of beat-up old books cast off by the white school. And the textbooks? One English text for every three students. No History books at all.

The boarding house was dark when he parked in his usual spot out front. Biggerstaff parked his Oldsmobile in the dusty driveway, close to the back door. He'd lived there longer and that was his spot, Mrs. Mitchell had warned. Where the heck had Biggerstaff been all summer, anyway?

Buck silently ascended the front steps, avoiding the squeakiest boards on the front porch, as he thought about the few precious hours of sleep he'd get before heading back to Pine Hammock for the one full day of preparation teachers were provided prior to school opening on Wednesday.

"Decided to skip Moonie's tonight?" Biggerstaff's voice caused Buck to jump. There were no street lights in Pine Hammock, and he hadn't seen him seated on the far end of the screened porch.

"Probably be skipping Moonie's a lot," Buck replied, turning the knob on the front door, hopeful of avoiding further conversation. Unfortunately for him, Biggerstaff wasn't having any of it.

"Sit your black ass down," he said, quietly but firmly. Buck did. They didn't speak for a few minutes, just listened to the night sounds. Pine Hammock had a population of 725, according to the signs on each end of town. It seemed smaller.

Buck was starting to nod off when he heard Biggerstaff shift in his seat.

"You're going to be fine."

His eyes now accustomed to the darkness, Buck could see Biggerstaff looking at him. He didn't know what to say. It was like the man was reading his mind.

"I knew it the minute you walked into the library, before you said a word." Biggerstaff stifled a yawn. "For a few moments, you owned that room. You weren't intimidated by all those white faces." He laughed. "Did you see the way those old white teachers looked when they thought you were going to sit at their table?" Buck hadn't.

"Most of our teachers at Pine Hammock, they were born and brought up around here. They still have a lot of the old ways about them. Please the white man, kiss his ass, yassah, that kind of thing. You're different, though. You've run in whitey's circles, Buck. You know how to fit in and make a difference."

"Like Dottie?" Buck's reference to the Home Economics teacher who'd given him a lesson on hand-shaking brought a snort of laughter from Biggerstaff.

"Now *that one* is a handful," he said. "Grew up in D.C. Went to Howard University. Taught in the city for a couple years before divorcing her husband and deciding to get away from it all. You watch her, Buck. She's a pretty one, but... whew. She's also the best teacher I've got."

Buck nodded, but didn't speak.

"You getting along okay with Mrs. Mitchell?"

Buck nodded. "I'm not here much. Where were you all summer?"

"Down in Virginia, picking cotton. Didn't Mrs. Mitchell say anything?"

"No. How long have you been—" Buck didn't finish his question, as Biggerstaff was laughing so hard.

"Are you *sure* you're colored?" he asked, doubled over in laughter. He held out his hands. "Do these look like the hands of a cotton picker?"

Buck shrugged, uncertain how to respond. The man could certainly keep a person off-balance.

"Nah, man. I've been in Cambridge, Massachusetts. Harvard Grad School."

Biggerstaff saw the surprise in Buck's face, which made him laugh harder. The porch light came on. Mrs. Mitchell's wide frame filled the door.

"Landon Biggerstaff you need to keep it down out here, or I'm—"

"Get yourself back to my bed, Geraldine," Biggerstaff shouted. "I'll be in to pleasure you in a bit."

Mrs. Mitchell stepped out onto the porch, waving her fist. "I'd kill myself before I got in bed with you!"

"That's not what you said last night, sweetheart."

Mrs. Mitchell let loose with a string of expletives Buck wouldn't have expected from the elderly woman. She slammed the door and turned the light off. Biggerstaff shook his head.

"Geraldine and Mama were best friends before she died seven years ago."

The surprises never ended.

"You grew up here?"

Biggerstaff nodded. "Graduated from Pine Hammock School. Went to Maryland State to get my teaching degree, then high-tailed it right back."

"I was at Maryland State a couple weeks ago."

"I know," Biggerstaff replied. "Mrs. Budd called me. Who do you think told her it was okay to let you take those newspapers you've got strewn all over your room."

They heard the tinny chime of Mrs. Mitchell's hallway clock as it struck one.

"Morning coming quick," Biggerstaff said, yawning again.

"Mr. Biggerstaff, if you don't mind me asking—"

"Call me Biggs, or Landon. At least when we're not at school. And you can ask me damn near anything."

"Why do you live here?"

Biggerstaff glanced around like he was seeing his surroundings for the first time. A trace of discomfort showed in his eyes. "Haven't you figured it out by now? Geraldine and me got *a thing*."

"Seriously, sir. Why?"

"Well," Biggerstaff cracked his knuckles, "I had a house, up until four years ago. Wife, too, for that matter. Her name was Hazel." He shifted uncomfortably in his chair. "First colored people to live in Sheffield, though we weren't actually in the city limits. We bought a place about a half-mile out."

Buck listened intently, not liking the direction in which this story was going.

"Some people didn't like us living there. Must've burned a half-dozen crosses in our yard. Trash dumped all over the place. Mailbox blown up. It got to be too much for Hazel; we'd met in college. She wasn't from here."

Biggerstaff took a deep breath. "Anyway, one night I heard something outside, so I grabbed my shotgun and went out to check. A couple redneck crackers were about ten seconds from burning down the place. I held them at gunpoint while Hazel called the Sheriff."

He grew silent. Buck didn't want to push, but he had to know the rest of the story.

"Don't tell me they got away with it."

"Hell, no." Biggerstaff answered. "Four years each in the state penitentiary. My family had known or worked for every juror in that box." He paused again, rubbing his palms together. "That was enough for Hazel. She said I had to make a choice."

He looked up at Buck. "I guess I did. Only God knows if it was the right one."

***

The clock raced past two, then three, but sleep was elusive. The conversation with Biggerstaff had left him more apprehensive than before. Did he really want to make his living as a teacher? In Twinton County? Did he want to wind up like Biggerstaff? Alone. Involved in battles he probably wasn't going to win.

Choosing to stop fighting the insomnia, he turned his attention to the stacks of *Tampa Tribunes*. He'd finished looking through February and March, but there were no more follow-up stories about the incident at the warehouse.

Then, barely into April, he found what he was looking for.

NINETEEN

TAMPA TRIBUNE
April 6, 1955

REMAINS IDENTIFIED AS MISSING
GULLFORD MAN

After an investigation, state authorities have identified the remains found in a barn fire in Hacker County on January 22 as those of Pelope "Pete" Demopoulos, 33. Demopoulos has been missing since January following an early-morning altercation at the Demo-Fresh Warehouse in Gullford.

Among the items recovered from the rubble of the blaze was the monogrammed back of a silver wristwatch. Authorities were able to trace the watch to a store in Neptune Beach. The store owner stated it was sold three years ago to Corrine Demopoulos, 57, mother of the victim.

The fire, authorities say was purposefully set to hide the location of Demopoulos' body. Evidence suggests that the victim had been stabbed, beaten, then placed in the trunk and driven to the location. It is not known if he was alive at the time the fire started, as the only evidence authorities were able to recover from the burned out remains of the car were teeth fragments and the aforementioned watch.

Speaking to the *Tribune*, Highway Patrol spokesman Carter Mulch stated, "Based upon what we've been able to put together, we are now certain that on January 23, two men, Jerry Mark Lester and Marvin Roger Conrad, appeared at the Demo-Fresh warehouse in the early morning hours. After what appears to have been a bloody altercation, they placed Mr. Demopoulos in the trunk of a stolen 1948 Dodge, and drove him seventy-eight miles to a remote area of Hacker County. There, they parked the car in an abandoned barn and used gasoline to set fire to the barn and its contents. Lester and Conrad then left the area on foot, and were traversing a rural area of Gull County late at night when they stumbled or fell into what is known locally as Killday Swamp, where it is speculated that they drowned or were killed by alligators that are common in the area.

Reached for comment, Helio "Hal" Demopoulos, father of the victim, stated the family was heartbroken by the news. "We're in a state of shock," Demopoulos said. "We've been praying for answers to our son's disappearance, but had hoped it wouldn't be like this." Demopoulos said his wife and he had planned to return to New Guinea last month on a church mission, but the trip had been delayed.

"We needed to know," he said. Adding that they would likely still go later in the year.

TWENTY

TAMPA TRIBUNE
April 8, 1955

Obituary
Pelope Helio "Pete" Demopoulos
June 28, 1923 – January 23, 1955

A Memorial Service for Pelope "Pete" Demopoulos will be held Monday, April 11, at the Gullford Community Center, with interment to follow at the Dickerson Springs City Cemetery.

Pete was born June 28, 1923, in Dickerson Springs to Helio "Hal" and Corrine Demopoulos. Despite a childhood accident that cost him his left arm, Pete lived a full and happy life. He graduated third in his class from Dickerson Springs High School in 1939, where he was active in Debate and Commercial Club.

Following graduation, Pete entered the family business. For the past ten years, he was responsible for Demo-Fresh Market's warehouse operation, considered by many to be a model for other retailers.

In 1948, Pete and Elena Dodd Abbott, a war widow, were united in marriage. At that time, Pete also assumed the role of stepfather for Elena's daughter, Gwendolyn Abbott.

Pete was involved with several local organizations and activities in Gullford.

Surviving are wife Elena and stepdaughter Gwendolyn of the home, grandfather Elias Demopoulos; parents Helio "Hal" and Corrine, a brother Chris and wife Rebecca, and two nephews, all of Dickerson Springs.

***

Buck carefully folded the newspapers into a pile for return to the college that weekend. It was after four. He would have to be up by seven to get to school at eight. It would be a hard, long day, followed by his night shift at WSCM.

He smiled wistfully. Getting through a day on little sleep shouldn't be that difficult.

After all, he'd already beat death.

TWENTY-ONE

Buck was three minutes into his first day as a teacher before all hell broke loose. It could have been sooner, but Jerome Gilliam was tardy.

"I'm supposed to be in here," he proclaimed loudly, barging into Buck's classroom as if he owned the place. For a few moments, he did.

Jerome Gilliam looked like two different people; his lower torso resembled a ten-year-old, with spindly bowed legs and toes that pointed in. Above the belt, he was a man; squat and muscular, with immense shoulders and no neck. Class records indicated he was fifteen.

Jerome took his time surveying the classroom, nodding at friends and winking at girls. Then his eyes settled on Buck, dressed in his best white shirt and insistent on keeping his sport coat on despite temperatures already soaring into the eighties. Jerome did a double take.

"Where the hell's your arm?"

The class laughed uproariously.

"You must be Mr. Gilliam," Buck said, ignoring the outburst. "You'll have to sit on the floor."

"First tell me where's your arm at." The laughter was more subdued this time, as thirty-seven teenagers waited to see how the new teacher would react. At first Buck didn't, choosing to lock into a stare-down with Jerome

Gilliam. His Education professor at Kirkmont had said this was an effective tactic for getting students to stop misbehaving. Sadly, no one had taken time to let Jerome Gilliam know this. He remained unblinkingly focused on Buck's eyes until the teacher finally broke.

"Find a seat, Mr. Gilliam," he sighed, turning his attention to the cracked slate blackboard mounted on the front wall. He printed *Mr. Jones* in large letters, followed by *Tenth Grade English*. When he faced the class again, Jerome Gilliam hadn't moved. Buck wracked his brain to come up with some further pearl of college wisdom, but when nothing came to mind, he forged ahead.

"You will be sharing textbooks with two classmates. When there is homework, I'll give you time in class to copy the pertinent information from—"

"Where's. Your. Arm. At?" Jerome said it slowly, as if he were talking to an imbecile. Buck continued to ignore him.

"There will be a test every Friday. It will cover proper grammar and usage. Reading assignments will also be part of—"

"Where's. Your. Arm. At?"

"—this class. We will read some of the classics, but you'll also get to choose—"

Jerome raised the stakes, asking the same question, but throwing in an obscene reference to proclivity between a woman and her son. The students gasped.

"Mr. Gilliam, that is enough. You will find a seat—"

"Jerome Gilliam!"

Everyone, Buck included, shuddered at Biggerstaff's thundering voice. Standing in the doorway, glowering into the classroom, he didn't wait for an invitation to come in.

"Clear the middle of this room," he thundered. "Move these desks!" When students didn't move fast enough, he restated his demand, louder, with no room for confusion. The two-foot long wooden paddle he carried spurred the students' hasty retreat. A six-by-six area in the center of the room was quickly emptied of students and furniture, like a boxing ring in the middle of a crowded arena.

"Jerome Gilliam, put your hands on your knees and bend your ass over."

There was no stare-down this time. Jerome stepped forward, meekly, his lips quivering. "Mr. Biggerstaff, all I done was ask about that man's arm." His confidence and bravado were gone. From his spot on the outside of the gathering, Buck could see the boy was fighting tears.

"I heard everything, boy. So, you're going to get even more for lying to me. Bend over."

Jerome approached Biggerstaff as one might an electric chair. Tears dripped from his cheeks as he bent over. Biggerstaff ran his hand up and down the length of the paddle, warming it up.

"Time for your first lesson of the year, Jerome, and I'm sad I had to be the one to give it to you."

Whack.

There was a collective inhalation of air as thirty-six students and one teacher recoiled from the center of the room, trying to move as far away as they could.

"First, your teacher's name is Mr. Jones. Say it."

Whack.

"Mmmmm. Mmmmm."

Whack.

"Say it!"

"Mmmmmm. Mmmmmm-Mister Jo-Jo-Jones."

Whack.

"Second, it's impolite to ask personal questions of people you don't know."

Whack.

"Ye-ye-ye-yesssir."

"So, what should you say to Mr. Jones?"

Whack.

"Suh-suh-suh-Sorry."

"Sorry, who?"

Whack.

"Mmmmm-Mmmm-Mister Jones."

Satisfied that his point was made, Biggerstaff stepped back. Jerome remained bent over, not daring to look up. Aghast at what he'd just witnessed, Buck looked on helplessly.

"Students," Biggerstaff said calmly, "please straighten up Mr. Jones' classroom." Wordlessly the desks were returned and students reclaimed their seats. Jerome, his face covered with tears and snot, limped to an area under a window and lowered himself, wincing audibly when floor and backside met. When Biggerstaff exited the scene of the carnage, Buck numbly returned to the lesson. He was certain by the end of the period that no one had gained anything from it. Later in the day, he had Jerome in his Mathematics class. The boy arrived on time and took a seat as far from Buck as he could. They never spoke nor made eye contact.

Only a hundred and fifty days to go until summer vacation.

TWENTY-TWO

Buck rolled over and checked the clock on his bedside table.

Three-fifteen.

In the afternoon.

Well past time to get up, but he didn't have it in him. Two days of school had left him exhausted. Thank goodness the first day had come on Thursday, but next week would be five days. Five long days.

What had he been expecting, and how could it be so different from student-teaching in Kirkmont? He'd excelled at the public high school there. Kids were kids, weren't they? He mulled it over until he fell back asleep. When he awoke, it was after four, and his stomach demanded to be fed. Mrs. Mitchell didn't put out supper until seven-thirty on Saturday nights, so if he wanted something he would have to go find it.

Pulling himself from the bed, Buck headed into the hallway. Biggerstaff's door was open, and the room was empty. He went to the bathroom they shared, splashed cool water on his face, returned to his room, and pulled on a pair of casual pants and a light sweater. No one was downstairs as he headed out the front door.

First stop – Billy Goat's. As it was between meals, the place was empty. Standing at an old wood cookstove,

Ruby was stirring a pot of something that smelled delicious.

"Whatchu need, Hucklebuck?" she asked, throwing him a flirty wink that would have been laughable if he weren't mired in a post-sleep fugue.

"Chicken and rice," Buck said, taking a seat at a table against a wall and resting his head against a gently-humming drink cooler. There was much to do. He'd quickly come to the realization that he needed to spend more time preparing his lessons if he was going to have a chance. Classes were twice the size they had been in Kirkmont, and there were more than a few unruly students willing to take advantage of every unplanned moment, even after Jerome's first-day whipping.

And that still bothered him. He'd spent a lot of time thinking back to how he could have handled the situation better. One thing was certain: Biggerstaff seemed like a good guy, but most kids at Pine Hammock lived in fear of him. Perhaps it needed to be that way, but Buck hoped he could get to the point where students minded in his class as they did in Dottie Hanford's. He'd walked past her Home Economics classroom a couple times. Students appeared to hang on her every word. He'd considered asking how she did it, but given how haughty she'd been when they'd first met, he couldn't bring himself to make the overture.

Ruby appeared with a heaping plate of steaming chicken and rice. "Whatchu wanna drink?" she asked, setting it in front of him. Buck glanced into the cooler, but already knew that Billy Goat's didn't have what he needed.

"Ruby, would you mind making this order to go?"

***

Buck was awakened by a gentle nudge. When he lifted his head, Moonie was staring at him. A mostly-eaten plate of cold chicken and rice was beside him. The once-enticing smell made him nauseous. He pushed it away.

"What time is it?"

Moonie pointed to a large Schlitz Beer clock over the bar, then returned his attention to a sink full of dirty glasses.

One-fifty. In the morning.

He'd been there for almost seven hours.

Buck tried to straighten himself, but a stiff back made it hard. The crack of bones or vertebrae or whatever was in there echoed through the deserted bar, but was nothing compared to the cracking in his head. How much Moon Juice had he drunk?

He turned slowly on the barstool and attempted to get up, but even that movement caused his stomach to lurch. He didn't so much get off the stool as fall off, staggering in the general direction of the door and missing it twice before getting outside and hurling a vile concoction of baked chicken, rice, and hooch into the dirt. Despite the warmth of the September night, he shivered.

Reaching his car, he crawled inside and sat back to regather his senses. The next time he awoke, a sliver of daylight was visible. He got out and urinated against the front tire, then drove home.

Home.

Was that what he was calling Mrs. Mitchell's place now? Home?

***

Buck made it upstairs undetected. It was six-forty, but Biggerstaff's room was empty. Where did that man go all the time?

He filled the bathtub with hot water. If Mrs. Mitchell knew how full and how hot his bath was, she'd raise the roof. Fortunately, Sunday was the landlady's day to sleep in. He could enjoy the bath in peace. The hot water started to eat away at the fringes of his headache, and after a half-hour, he started to feel close to normal as his brain emerged from its pickled state.

Certain things became clear as the morning sunlight entered the room through the bathroom's single window. First, he had to stop drinking. In the months he'd been in Twinton County, Moonie's had progressed from social outlet to necessity. Moon Juice was consuming his mind and wallet. He decided to give Moonie's one night a week, tops. And no more than two glasses of juice.

Second, he had to cut back his hours at the radio station. It was a fun gig, but a five-hour shift after a full day at school would kill him. He'd been wrong. He couldn't do both.

And finally, he would be damned if those kids were going to get the best of him. Biggerstaff would never again come into his classroom and light into one of his students. Buck would show up prepared to teach, and woe be to the student who tried to slow him down. They'd owned the first two days, but from there on out, Buck would be in charge.

TWENTY-THREE

It had seemed like such a simple gesture. Three weeks earlier, Buck had written on the board that he would stay after school two hours each Tuesday and Thursday for students who needed extra help. Tuesday would be for Math, Thursday for English. He hadn't expected many kids to stay; most had to get home to take care of younger siblings while parents went to night jobs. Others had jobs of their own.

He was wrong.

Somehow, they found the time. A dozen for Math; almost as many for English. In the process, Buck had learned something important: Pine Hammock parents desperately wanted a future for their children that was better than what they'd had.

Most eeked out livings on the margins of society as fishermen's helpers, farm hands, and factory workers. In almost every case, they took jobs left over after the white people of Twinton and surrounding counties had their picks. The fish-packing plants were a good example. Buck had learned that eighty-percent of the employees were Negro, but none were supervisors. Even among the rank-and-file, white people had the more desirable jobs.

"We clean up the guts," Darrell, one of his students, told him. "The white people check to make sure we cleaned 'em up." Darrell was one of several students

115

working the three-to-eleven shift at Talley-Ho, a fish-packing plant that employed many Pine Hammock residents.

Despite their difficult lots in life, most parents went out of their way to make sure their children attended school and did their best. That was why the number of students staying after school was so high.

"Luther's really been doing better with them fractions," a parent effused to Buck one Saturday evening as he was exiting Billy Goat's. He'd been hearing that a lot, and it made him happy. After seven weeks, he was finally achieving some recognition as Mr. Jones, the schoolteacher, and not just as Hucklebuck on WSCM's *Nightside*.

Not that the radio show wasn't doing well. Mr. Adams had been able to sign on a bevy of new advertisers interested in spots on *Nightside*, many from Salisbury, the largest community on Maryland's Eastern Shore, forty-five miles away.

"Your program is coming in loud and clear up there," Mr. Adams said happily. "I didn't even know Salisbury had colored businesses, but they do and they want to be part of your show."

Buck had smiled appreciatively, but said nothing. Neither Mr. Adams nor any other white person in Sheffield had a clue as to how much colored money left Twinton County for businesses in other communities where Negro trade was accepted. Still, despite the station owner's shortcomings, Buck was grateful that he'd allowed him to shorten *Nightside* from five hours to three.

"There's nobody awake in Twinton County after ten anyways," Adams had said. He hadn't even cut Buck's salary, a fact that wasn't lost on him.

Buck, fresher after a couple extra hours of nightly sleep, and sharper-minded after cutting out his nightly treks to Moonie's, was plowing his extra time and energy into Pine Hammock. The results were encouraging. Even Biggerstaff had noticed. They'd talked about it several times over dinner at Mrs. Mitchell's before Buck rushed off to the radio station. Biggerstaff asked lots of questions about what he was doing in class; questions that led to more questions, then more. It took Buck a while to realize that Biggerstaff's questions ultimately led him to come up with answers of his own, some of them for problems he didn't realize he was having.

Like discipline. There were still a few boys who drove Buck nuts by cutting up in class. Fearful of another visit by Biggerstaff and his paddle, Buck never mentioned it, but somehow Biggerstaff had intuited there were still problems. Through his series of questions, Biggerstaff had helped him see that most of the boys were acting the fool to get attention. Possibly Buck's attention, but more likely the attention of the girls in the classroom. The principal then guided him as he developed ways to handle the problems.

It was late-November, however, when Buck proposed a problem that even stupefied Landon Biggerstaff.

TWENTY-FOUR

"We need more books."

Biggerstaff wiped his face with a napkin and sat back in his chair. Respectful of their conversations, Mrs. Mitchell silently cleared the table.

"I'm always pushing for more from the people up in Sheffield, Buck. You know that. Are you running short of Math books?"

"Not textbooks. Library books. By tenth grade my kids have run through everything we have."

Biggerstaff rubbed his chin and shifted in his chair.

"We haven't gotten new library books in a couple years. Let me go see Doctor Mister. Maybe it's time."

"Buck, you need to get going." Mrs. Mitchell called from the kitchen.

"I'm good," he replied. "They're carrying the President's speech from seven to eight." Then, reconsidering, he stood up suddenly.

"But I do have a stop to make," he said, heading for the door.

***

The Twinton County Library was a stately edifice, built in the previous century and tucked neatly between the Presbyterian Church and the Rialto Theater on

118

Sheffield's tree-lined Second Street. As he'd remembered from passing by on his way to work, the sign in front said the library was open until eight on Tuesday night. The clock over the front door indicated it was seven-fifteen.

The street was deserted. *Some Like It Hot*, the seven-o'clock show at the Rialto had already started. The entrance to the library was awash in light from the theater billboard, giving it a show-bizzy feel at odds with what one expected from a library. He pushed open the large glass entrance door and immediately encountered the pleasing smell of books. A few people were scattered about, none taking note of him as he made his way to the circulation desk. A fiftyish woman who was sorting through a stack of magazines looked up and smiled.

"Help you?"

"Yes, ma'am. My name is Buck Jones. I moved here last summer and—"

"You want a library card," she said, pulling a small form from a stack and passing it across the desk. "Fill this out and I'll have your card ready in ten minutes."

Buck filled out the form, signed, and placed it in front of the librarian. Automatically, she reached into a drawer, removed a blank library card, and started filling in the spaces. Buck watched closely. She was almost done when she stopped, pen poised in mid-air. She squinted at the form for a moment, then raised her head and carefully considered Buck. Her eyes told him what he suspected.

"You're colored."

"Why would you say that?"

Buck's response startled her. Considering that perhaps she'd made a mistake, she looked again at his application.

"You live in Pine Hammock."

Buck nodded.

"Then you're... aren't you...? I mean, you don't necessarily *look*... But you are? Aren't you?"

Buck stood a little taller, which still left him a couple inches shorter than the librarian.

"Is there a law against colored people using the public library?"

For a fleeting moment, he saw her fear. Fear of what? He was smaller than she was and was missing an arm. How much damage could he do? She glanced around, looking for support that Buck guessed wouldn't be coming. After all, it was Tuesday night. Most people were home, and the rest were next door getting an eyeful of Marilyn Monroe. The only people likely to be in the library were the die-hard reading set.

Finally, she returned her gaze to him. Her eyes weren't scared anymore. She looked indignant.

"The library is only for Sheffield residents." She started to step away, but Buck moved slightly to remain in her line of sight.

"This is the *Twinton County Public* Library," he said. "Since June, I've been a resident of Twinton County. I would like a library card, please."

"It *says* Twinton County Public Library," she snipped, "but it *belongs* to the people of Sheffield. Since you don't live in Sheffield, I'll have to ask you to leave."

Her raised voice had attracted the attention of patrons seated nearby. Buck played through a variety of possible responses, before deciding it was a battle best saved for another day. When he reached across the desk, the woman instinctively stepped back.

"Thank you for your time," he said, picking up his completed application. "I'll be on my way."

***

"That was Jackie Wilson with, "Lonely Teardrops." You're tuned to *Nightside*. This is Hucklebuck."

Buck stopped for a moment to gather his wits. Since leaving the library, he'd considered what he was about to say. He hoped he had considered it enough. There was a real possibility that a few of Twinton County's white population hadn't yet turned the dial after President

Eisenhower's regular radio address. If so, they were about to get an earful.

Taking a deep breath, Buck pulled the microphone closer.

"I'm going to be changing things up a little bit tonight, so forgive me if you turned in expecting Wilbert Harrison or Lloyd Price. I had an experience earlier this evening that I want to share with you. To some, it won't be anything new. To others, it will come as a surprise. I'll tell you about it, then open the phone lines to get your thoughts."

As Buck related his encounter at the library, his plan to remain detached quickly started to fall apart as he recalled the librarian backing away when he'd reached over to retrieve his completed application. That would have never happened to Pete Demopoulos.

He considered bringing up the sorry state of the Pine Hammock School Library, but decided it might be too much too quick. Besides, when he glanced at the studio telephone, he noticed that all lines had callers waiting.

"Now that I've shared what I had to say, let's hear from you. Thanks for calling *Nightside*. Who is this?

"Hucklebuck, this is Larry. Man, can I tell you about what I went through last week?"

And for the next two hours, Buck got an earful. After the fifth call, he started making tick marks on a notepad. Twenty-seven calls by the time his shift ended, ranging from small slights to outright humiliations. All because of skin color. Larry, the first caller, had spent six weeks training a white person he thought was going to be working beside him at a commercial bakery, only to discover that the new hire was replacing him. The stories were heartfelt, sometimes accompanied by tears. Good radio, indeed, but for all the wrong reasons.

The most indicative of the state of things was a woman working as a maid in a Sheffield hotel who was fired because she became too large for the uniform. It was easier to replace her, she was told, than to get a new uniform.

Not all the calls were from Twinton County. Some came from surrounding communities. A couple came from as far away as the District of Columbia, over a hundred miles away. "We listen every night," one DC caller said before launching into an emotional account of being turned away from a suburban restaurant.

By sign-off Buck was physically spent. He concluded with some remarks that he knew didn't touch the gravity of what his listeners had shared. His senses on overload, he exited the building into the station's small parking lot. It was dark and empty, and for the first time, a sense of fear and foreboding struck him as he crossed the lot to his car. What if someone was listening and didn't like what they were hearing? Everyone within fifty miles knew the exact location of the WSCM studio. He made a mental note to park closer to the door next time.

The combination of the cold autumn air and the emptiness of the parking lot put Buck's senses on full alert. Exiting the parking lot, he drove south toward Pine Hammock. At a crossroads a couple miles out of Sheffield, he made a last-minute decision to turn left instead of going straight. Fifteen minutes later, he was in the dirt parking lot at Moonie's.

***

The signs of first frost were appearing when Buck parked on the street in front of Mrs. Mitchell's. His steps were mincing, as the cracked sidewalk was slippery in spots. The wooden porch was even worse, and he caught himself on a railing, saving himself from going down.

"Careful there."

Biggerstaff was seated in his usual spot, wearing a coat.

"Cold to be sitting outside," Buck said. "Late, too."

When Biggerstaff didn't respond, Buck assumed he was dismissed. "Well, good night."

"I heard it. Everything."

Buck couldn't make out Biggerstaff's expression, and his tone gave nothing away, so he waited.

"What happens next?"

Buck shrugged. "I haven't thought that far ahead."

"You need to," Biggerstaff said sharply. "You got a lot of people stirred up tonight."

"Twenty-seven. That's how many called."

Buck could see him shift in his chair. "You think that's it? How about the people who have stories to tell but didn't call in? Maybe they don't have telephones, or they're afraid *the man* will recognize their voices and fire them from jobs they need to support their families."

Biggerstaff's voice was rising as he continued. "Buck, you could go to any house on this street - hell, any house in Pine Hammock and hear stories like those on your show; some a lot worse."

"Then it's time to speak out."

Biggerstaff became quiet, and Buck could hear him breathing deeply. He reached over and removed a stack of books from a wooden rocking chair.

"Sit down."

Buck shivered and wasn't certain if it was because of the frigid air or what he might hear. "It's pretty cold, Mr. Biggerstaff, and I really need to get some sleep."

"Wasn't too cold to stop off at Moonie's, boy. You probably have enough juice in you to handle ten minutes on this cold porch. I won't need any more than that."

"I only had one, sir... Moon Juice, I mean. First time in weeks."

Biggerstaff grinned, the first time since Buck had shown up. "We've all gotten a bit too friendly with Moonie at one time or another," he said. "Were Clarence and Poop out there tonight?"

"Almost every night, sir. Johnny, too."

Shaking his head, Biggerstaff said, "Poop Chester was Twinton County's first attempt at school desegregation."

This was news. The few times Poop could stay awake, he'd never mentioned anything about that. Biggerstaff could see Buck's disbelief.

"You might find this hard to believe, but Poop played pro baseball. Negro Leagues in the '30's and '40's. After Jackie broke in with the Dodgers, Poop signed with the Detroit Tigers, but never made it to the big leagues. Money was tight, so he decided to get into teaching. That's how he wound up in Twinton County."

When Biggerstaff paused, Buck leaned in closer, willing him to continue.

"The Sheffield principal at the time was a progressive man who'd been brought in from up North. He remembered seeing Poop play against the Pittsburgh Pirates in an exhibition game. Well, Jackie had opened up baseball a couple years before, and this principal thought it would be a good idea if Poop coached the Sheffield varsity."

Buck tried to imagine Poop in the dugout, leading a team... a white team. He couldn't get past the sight of him lolled over in his usual spot at Moonie's, though.

"Poop spent his days teaching at Pine Hammock, then he'd hightail it over to Sheffield for practices. The white boys took to him pretty quick, especially after they saw him hit. Then, the season started. I can't even remember against who, but the coach refused to let his players take the field against a team with a colored coach."

Biggerstaff shook his head sadly. "Next game, same thing. After it happened a third time, the parents got angry at the principal. Superintendent Mister – he was here back then – he reassigned Poop," Biggerstaff made quotation marks with his fingers, "*practice* coach. Poop said screw that and quit on the spot. He went to work at the tuna plant and started hanging out at Moonie's."

Buck pulled his jacket around him and checked his watch. It was half-past midnight. Time for bed.

"You're probably wondering why I brought it up," Biggerstaff said. "You need to know about Twinton

County. It's not like some of those places you read about down South. Whites and coloreds generally get along pretty well here, provided everybody stays in their place."

"Like when you and your wife bought that house in Sheffield?"

Biggerstaff waved his hand dismissively. "A white jury put those boys away—"

"And you gave up and left." Buck could see his words had wounded him. When Biggerstaff spoke again, his tone was sharp.

"Tell me about where you grew up. Down in Florida, right? Did you and Whitey get along? Did you date his daughters?"

"It was different," Buck said cautiously. "It's hard to compare."

"Well, why don't you try," Biggerstaff challenged. "You've been here for five months and nobody knows anything about you, except that you went to college in some cow pasture in Kansas—"

"Iowa... it was a cow pasture in Iowa."

Buck's attempt to deflect the conversation with humor didn't work.

"What about Florida? Were you in trouble there or something, Buck? I saw those old Tampa newspapers. You were looking for something or other." Biggerstaff paused. "You rob a bank down there? Get a white girl pregnant? What is your story?"

Buck took a minute to gather his thoughts. He'd concocted a story several years ago, but had never had to use it. The kids back in college were too self-centered to care about someone else's life story. Sitting with Biggerstaff, he wondered if that story would hold up to scrutiny.

"Lived with my father, little place in the woods. Went to school, worked in a grocery store—"

"Doing what?"

"This and that. Stocking shelves, putting—"

"What was the name of the store?" Biggerstaff was zeroing in like a prosecutor.

"It was... um..." He couldn't say Demo-Fresh. That would be too easy to trace. "...Atteberry's Dry Goods. I worked there for—"

"Dry goods? I thought you said it was a grocery store."

This was getting harder by the moment, and who the hell did Biggerstaff think he was, anyway? And what was he doing looking around Buck's room?

"Who the hell do you think you are, Biggerstaff? What right do you have to be digging into my past?"

"I have a right to know who's working in my school, and ever since I met you I've thought there was something... *off* about you, boy."

Buck stood quickly. "I don't have to take this from you—"

"Sit back down, Buck. If I was worried, we'd have had this conversation by now."

Obediently, Buck returned to his seat.

"You started something tonight when you called out the people at the library. Nobody has ever questioned the way things are in Twinton County, publicly at least. I could hear it in the voices of the people who called your show. They're tired of how things are. They're hearing the stories on the radio about Negroes having sit-ins and protest marches, and they're thinking, why are things like they are here in Twinton County?"

Biggerstaff leaned forward and took a breath.

"Now what will you do if one of those listeners goes off half-cocked and gets into a scuffle with a white man, or worse yet a white woman? That'll be on you, Buck."

"What are you saying?" Buck asked incredulously. "You telling me to just leave it alone?"

"Nah, man. Not at all. Just know that what works other places won't work here. Integration will come in its own time. You don't need to be pushing it. People get along here, and when they get along, change comes along right when it's supposed to."

Biggerstaff got to his feet and patted Buck on the shoulder.

"Cool it on the integration shit, you hear?"

TWENTY-FIVE

Whether they entered the classroom individually or in small groups, students stopped and considered him carefully. Many had listened to the previous night's show. Those who were working or out doing who-knows-what had heard about it.

There were only a handful of televisions in Pine Hammock, and most families still turned to the radio for their evening entertainment. Since last summer, most of those radios had been tuned to WSCM's *Nightside*.

He noticed their silent gazes. They were seeing him different than before. Though he was doing a credible job teaching English and Math, he'd remained aloof; reticent to talk about things other than academics. As a result, students hadn't warmed up to him and vice-versa.

He called first period to order with instructions to copy thirty math problems from the board and begin solving them. Students eyed him curiously, none moving to begin work. This had been an issue early in the school year, but Buck assumed it had been solved by now. Perhaps it was time for a reminder of who was in charge.

"I'm not seeing any work getting done," he said, looking about the room.

There were no replies, nor did anyone make a move to get started.

"Need I remind you that Mr. Biggerstaff is just up the hallway."

"What are you gonna do?" Jerome Gilliam, the subject of Biggerstaff's whipping the first day of school, spoke from his seat on the floor. Buck moved past the front row of students, his eyes locked on the boy.

"Mr. Gilliam, I thought you'd learned your lesson back in September."

Jerome raised his hands in front of him. "No. Not like that, Mr. Jones. What are you gonna do about…"

"About what, Mr. Gilliam?"

A short silence was broken by a female student seated in front.

"Jerome's talking about the library. In Sheffield."

Several students nodded in agreement. Buck noticed their attention was riveted on him; not like most classes where they alternated between staring into space or dreamily gazing out the windows.

Moving back to the front, he leaned against the edge of his desk and wiped chalk dust from his hand as he considered how to proceed. It wasn't uncommon for them to try to get him off topic, hopeful the math could wait another day. This didn't seem like one of those times.

"I don't know," he said quietly. "What do you think I should do?" The simple question opened a floodgate of responses.

"Keep going back until they let you in."

"Get yourself arrested, like Dr. King."

"Write a letter to President Eisenhower."

"The Atlanta library got integrated last year. They need to do that here."

Michelle, a petite dark-skinned girl who hadn't spoken ten words all year, said, "I think we should do a sit-in."

Michelle's suggestion met with enthused echoes of support loud enough to draw the history teacher across the hall from her classroom to shush them. Buck closed the door and returned to his perch.

"Guys," he said, drawing a deep breath. "Last night I was angry. Really angry. I'd just experienced something I didn't expect, and then I went on the radio and ranted about it." He stopped, Biggerstaff's admonition from the night before jabbing at his brain like a stick. "Maybe I shouldn't have said anything. Perhaps that wasn't the best way to handle it..."

A cacophony of negative responses rained down, along with a few quietly-uttered expletives.

"Mr. Jones, my Daddy is the janitor at Sheffield School," one boy said, getting to his feet. "Have you been there?"

Buck nodded.

"Think about how that place looks, then look at the shit they give us. Mr. Jones, it ain't right."

"The Supreme Court said separate but equal ain't okay," a girl said.

"This sure as hell ain't equal." Jerome Gilliam's declaration met with the full support of his classmates. Buck considered reprimanding him and the others for their language, but the spark in their eyes was real.

***

When the school day had ended, he found them clustered outside his classroom door, waiting. The entire Pine Hammock staff, save Biggerstaff and Dottie Hanford. Their question was the same one asked by the students.

"What are you going to do?"

His answer remained as it had for each class period; he didn't know. His colleagues offered their ideas; many the same as he'd heard from students. Buck remained non-committal, uttering something like, *I guess you'll have to wait and see,* when in truth he didn't know himself.

It wasn't until he was heading to his car that he ran into Dottie Hanford. His relationship with the Home Economics teacher had remained distant.

"We talked about you in my Citizenship class today," she said, tossing her purse and a book bag into the back seat of her car.

Buck smiled as he got into his car, closed the door, and rolled down the window. "Did you come up with any ideas?"

"Lots," she replied. "The students are big on letters to the President."

"Yeah, they gave me that suggestion, too." Buck looked through the windshield for a few seconds. When he turned again, Dottie was standing next to his car.

"Biggerstaff told me you wanted more library books," she said softly. "Frankly, I didn't think you gave a damn."

What?

"I've watched you this year, Mr. Jones," she said, crossing her arms. "At first, I thought you only cared about yourself, but I've seen how you stay after school to help our students."

Buck didn't reply, surprised at the slight crease in the armor of the Queen of the Cold Shoulder.

"I think you're right," she said. "Our kids do deserve more books... more everything. What we can't do is have them heading into Sheffield with a chip on their shoulder and no plan in their brain."

"You make a good point, but what should we do?"

"I've been thinking about that," Dottie said. "Have you got a few minutes?"

TWENTY-SIX

Buck parked his car a block away. They got out and started walking along the busy sidewalk. He would never admit that he was nervous, but suspected Dottie could tell. She appeared to be as cool as a cucumber, despite the sidelong glances they received from passers-by.

"*Sleeping Beauty*," Buck said, as they approached the Rialto. "Last time it was *Some Like It Hot*."

"Have you been?" Dottie asked. "Inside the Rialto?"

He shook his head. "Too busy I guess."

"Coloreds still sit in the balcony," she bristled. "That needs to change."

"One thing at a time, Miss Hanford."

Her giggle was girlish, light, pleasing.

"Don't worry… Mr. Jones. I won't throw too much at you at once. I see how your hand is shaking."

Buck jammed it into his pants pocket. He felt his face grow warm and hoped it didn't show.

"A blushing negro," she said teasingly. Then as they passed under the theater marquee, she grew serious. "We've talked this through, Buck. Remember the plan and everything will be okay."

Buck glanced around as they reached the bottom step of the Twinton County Public Library. While the streets and sidewalks were busy, the number of people coming and going from the library on the cool but sunny Saturday morning was small.

"I wish there were more of us," he said.

Dottie reached over and squeezed his arm. "It's better that there isn't."

Buck was opening the large glass door when he heard a shout.

"Miss Hanford!"

They turned and spotted a young colored man sprinting their way. He wore a gray suit and matching hat. A large camera tucked under one arm nearly fell to the ground when he stumbled over a crack in the sidewalk. He slowed as he approached.

"Desmond Henry," he said, gasping for air. "Reporter for the *Baltimore Black Advocate*." He offered his hand, first to Buck, then to Dottie. She gripped it warmly despite the same lack of protocol that had led her to upbraid Buck back in August.

"I got lost," he puffed, placing his left hand on his knee while making sure to protect the camera. "Then, I parked on the other side of downtown. By the time I realized I was in the wrong area it was too late to get back to my car, so I ran."

He pulled a peculiar-looking device from his pocket, placed it in his mouth, and breathed in sharply. The action slowed his breathing.

"Asthma," he said, replacing the device.

Buck, having watched the interaction with great interest, finally spoke. "Did you know he was coming?" he asked Dottie.

"I hoped someone might," she said. "I wrote a letter to his newspaper last week.

"Our publisher, Mr. Conklin, sent me. He sends his regards and wishes you Godspeed today. I'll remain in the background, documenting what happens."

Buck checked his watch. Ten-o'clock on the nose. "Let's go."

Inside, daylight from large windows bathed the library in a warmness that contradicted the forty-degree temperatures outside. In one corner, a woman read from a picture book to a dozen young children. A smattering of mothers sat at the periphery, listening or whispering among themselves. Chairs were placed around a half-dozen tables in the center of the building, some occupied, most not. As they approached the circulation desk, Buck looked closely at the two women seated there. Neither was the woman from last time.

"We would like to register for library cards," Buck said, pulling out his driver's license. Dottie did the same. "We've been Twinton County residents for eight months and two years, respectively."

While one woman, a younger blonde, scrutinized them closely, the other, an emaciated-looking gray-haired woman in her sixties, quickly stood and retreated to a side room.

The blonde picked up their licenses and inspected them closely. Buck noticed she did not reach for the stack of applications as the librarian had two weeks earlier. After a few moments, she replaced their licenses on the counter.

"I'm sorry," She smiled apologetically. "You don't live in Sheffield. The library is for Sheffield residents only."

Dottie reached into her purse, pulled out a pink slip of paper, and placed it next to her license.

"This is the 1958 tax bill for my home in Pine Hammock," she said. Then pointing to a small box in the lower left corner, continued, "I paid three dollars and eighty-one cents for a County Library Use Tax." Dottie looked up. "If I'm being *taxed* for library use, it would make sense that I be able to *use* the library."

As Dottie spoke, Desmond Henry snapped photographs. The flash of his camera brought curious looks from all corners of the library. Even the lady reading to the children stopped.

"Sir, please don't take my picture," the librarian said, backing away as she ran her hand through her hair.

"I'm press, ma'am." Henry's declaration turned the librarian's white face even whiter.

"Look... Mr. Jones and Miss Hanford," she stammered. "All I can tell you is that the rules say that only people from Sheffield can use the Twinton County Library."

"Do you know how *ridiculous* that sounds?" Buck asked, his voice rising. "It's the Twinton County Library, but only—"

"We would like to take this before your Library Board," Dottie said, cutting him off.

The librarian's eyes grew large. "Oh, I don't think that can happen, I mean they're—"

"They're meeting at this moment, aren't they?" Dottie asserted. "The sign outside says they meet the first Saturday of the month at ten in the library basement."

The librarian glanced around anxiously, looking for support but not finding any. "I don't think they... I mean... they aren't meeting today... I don't think."

For a moment, Buck felt for the young girl. She was having to say something that wasn't true when she obviously wasn't up to it. Several times, he saw her glance at the stairs as she looked for the words she needed, while Desmond Henry continued to snap pictures.

"Let's go," Dottie said quietly, picking up her driver's license and tax bill from the counter. Buck followed closely, with Desmond Henry right behind. They walked toward the exit, but at the last minute veered toward the stairs. The young librarian opened her mouth in protest, but nothing came out.

At the bottom of the stairs was a short hallway with just three doors. The first was an exit, another said *Storage*. That left one. Buck pushed ahead of Dottie and opened it, allowing her to step in first.

Five people, three men and two women, were seated behind a long table. In front of them were a dozen chairs arranged for attendees who weren't on the board. Two of them were occupied. One by the skinny woman who had left the young librarian to fend for herself, the other by the librarian who had denied Buck's request on his first visit. All eyes were on the new arrivals. Buck took the lead this time, as planned.

"We would like to address the Library Board."

"Obviously apprised of their arrival in advance, a man seated at the center of the table smiled. "I'm sorry, but our agenda is set three days prior to the meeting." He flipped through several sheets of paper. "And I don't see any request from you folks."

"You don't even know who we are," Buck said moving closer.

"We've been told why you're here," the man replied. "Unfortunately, since you aren't on our agenda, we won't be able to accommodate you."

The response left Buck stumped. Dottie, not so much. She touched his arm and motioned to the empty seats. They moved away from the table and sat on the front row, next to the skinny lady, who moved to leave a space between herself and them. The man at the center of the table watched them for a moment, then spoke.

"Folks, since you aren't on the agenda, I'll have to ask you to leave."

"This is an open meeting," Dottie said, pulling out a copy of the notice she'd clipped from the newspaper. "It says so right here."

The room grew quiet. Desmond Henry, taking advantage of the moment, snapped a picture of the library board. Like the girl upstairs, this caught them by surprise. A man seated to one side of the table, rose from his seat, angrily jabbing his finger at Desmond.

"Boy, you can't take pictures of—"

"I'm not boy, sir," Desmond said, snapping another shot, "I'm a man. *Mister* Desmond Henry. Reporter for the *Baltimore Black Advocate*. I'm here on assignment."

"Well, no pictures!"

Desmond's response was to snap two more pictures. Buck thought the man who was questioning Desmond might come across the table, but another board member, a rotund woman in a dark-blue dress, spoke up.

"Let them stay. We can't exclude people from public meetings. The press either. Ralph, you know that. We let Kendall from the *Sheffield Times* take our picture every year."

The man looked less certain, but that didn't stop him from speaking. "Yeah, Dora, but Kendall doesn't come here to cause trouble like these…" He nodded at Buck, Dottie, and Desmond, the slur he'd been about to utter was left unsaid, but still hung over the room.

"Fine enough," the chairman said. "Let's continue."

Uncertainty remained in the air as the board moved through its agenda. Buck felt it emanating from board members as they sneaked occasional glimpses at the interlopers. The skinny lady from upstairs glowered at them for the entire meeting.

After forty-five minutes of mundane business, the Board President arrived at the final item on the agenda.

"We've been given a list of seventeen new books that Mrs. Cogdon has recommended purchasing. Would you like to speak about these books, Carol?" The librarian who had denied Buck's initial request for a library card stood and went through a short description of books in a monotone that would have put Buck to sleep if his nerves weren't on edge. The drooping eyelids of two board members confirmed their mutual disinterest.

"Do we have a motion to purchase these books?" the chairman asked, perusing the faces of his board mates.

"I would like to make the motion with an amendment." It was the first time the second female board member had spoken. Dottie whispered to Buck, "she teaches at Sheffield."

"I would like to amend the motion to say that we buy these seventeen books and… an additional seventeen books for the Pine Hammock School Library." She paused and smiled at Buck and Dottie. "Miss Hanford has an outstanding reputation as a teacher at Pine Hammock. She can help select the books."

The faces of the other board members ranged from confused to defiant.

"I second the motion and amendment," the other woman on the board said.

"We have a motion to buy seventeen books for the library and another seventeen for the Pine Hammock School Library." The board president remained poker-faced as he spoke. "Is there any discussion?"

"I want to say something," Mrs. Cogdon, the librarian, rose to her feet. "We have a budget and, quite frankly, books for the colored school aren't part of it. Now if you are going to start doing this—"

"Carol," the board president said sharply. "You aren't part of the board. Discussion is among board members only."

Flustered, the librarian took a seat. The skinny lady continued to scowl at Buck and Dottie.

The Board President waited a few beats, then said, "If there's no more discussion, we'll vote. All in favor of buying seventeen books for the public library and seventeen books for the Pine Hammock School Library raise your hand."

The board president, the two female board members, and one of the men raised their hands.

"All opposed, like sign." Ralph, the man who had challenged Buck and Dottie's attendance, raised his hand but said nothing."

"The motion carries, four to one." The board president rapped a small gavel on the table, then turned his attention to Dottie. "Miss Hanford, will you please work with Mrs. Cogdon to make sure we get the correct books for the colored school?"

"Yes, sir, I will," Dottie said pleasantly.

The board, except Ralph, was all smiles; happy they had averted trouble.

"Is there anything else to be brought before the Library Board before we adjourn?" the chairman asked pleasantly, as the other board members started packing away their papers. The simple question was a gaping hole in protocol large enough to drive a truck through, and Buck wasn't going to let it pass.

"I'd like to speak," Buck said, getting to his feet and approaching the board.

Smiling, still unaware he'd opened a door best left closed, the chairman nodded at Buck.

"Yessir. State your name, please."

"Buck Jones, teacher at Pine Hammock School. I'd like to thank the board for the kind purchase of books for our library."

The board members beamed.

"You've probably not seen our library..." *Fat chance of that, as Buck had never seen a white face in Pine Hammock School, including Superintendent Mister.* "... but we are in desperate need of books. Our students have access to only a few dozen volumes, most of which are castoffs from Sheffield School."

While Buck was speaking, the skinny lady who'd glared at him for the last hour, abruptly got up and exited the room, making a show of moving past Buck, Dottie, and Desmond as if they might have a contagious disease. Buck and Dottie ignored her. Desmond took her picture. When she was gone Buck continued.

"While these new books will certainly be treasured, they are only a drop in the bucket. It's imperative that our students have access to the public library that their parents' taxes are supporting."

The smiles were still there, frozen in place. The board members knew they'd been had.

"With that in mind, Miss Hanford and I are here to sign up for library cards. Once that is completed, we will start bringing students from Pine Hammock to get their own cards and start using the vast resources of this fine library."

Silence.

Buck peeked back at Dottie, seated behind him. Her head was high. Desmond snapped another photograph. It seemed almost surreal as he waited for the board to respond. Several moments passed, but nothing.

Then, the door from the hallway opened and two police officers entered, followed closely by the glaring old lady.

TWENTY-SEVEN

BALTIMORE BLACK ADVOCATE
February 24, 1960

TWINTON COUNTY LIBRARY DESEGREGATES

By: Desmond K. Henry

A milestone was achieved in Twinton County on Maryland's Eastern Shore this week, when two residents applied for and received the first library cards issued to Negroes.

Hucklebuck Theodore Roosevelt "Buck" Jones, 31, and Dorothy Elizabeth "Dottie" Hanford, 25, both of Pine Hammock, made an impassioned plea at the monthly meeting of the Twinton County Library Board of Directors on Saturday, February 20. This followed an unsuccessful attempt by Jones to secure a library card two weeks earlier.

At one point in the proceedings, two officers from the Sheffield City Police Department entered the meeting room and moved to arrest Jones and Hanford for disturbing the peace. The officers were directed by two Library Board members to stand down while a vote was taken regarding the issuance of library cards to Negroes. By a vote of three to two, the motion passed, and Jones and Hanford were issued their library cards.

Immediately after the vote, another motion was made to open library facilities to all Twinton County residents regardless of race. This motion passed by the same three to two margin.

Jones, a first-year teacher at Pine Hammock School, the county's colored school, was pleased with the results.

"Miss Hanford and I had the best interests of our students in mind when we made our appeal," Jones said. "We look forward to their having access to the wonderful selection of books the public library has to offer."

While the *Baltimore Black Advocate* applauds the willingness of the Twinton County Library Board to open its doors to Negroes, it must be pointed out that there is still much to be done. Twinton County lags behind most Maryland counties in regard to desegregation of its schools and businesses. With leaders in the colored community, such as Mr. Jones and Miss Hanford, there is hope that much more can be achieved.

TWENTY-EIGHT

"Forty-six," Dottie whispered to Buck as they passed on their way to their last period classes. "Seven more yesterday."

It was a far cry from the entire population, but residents of Pine Hammock were making their way into the Twinton County Public Library and getting their library cards. Two days earlier, Miss Sophie Ann Dickers had been wheeled to the library's front door by her grandson. There, the ninety-seven-year-old pulled herself from her wheelchair, climbed the steps, secured a library card, and checked out her first book.

"*Onion John*," she'd proclaimed, holding up a children's book for all to see. "I always loved me some onions."

As a special guest on *Nightside* the evening before, Miss Sophie had proudly declared that things were "gettin' good in Twinton County." Judging by the calls Buck received, Miss Sophie was a hit with listeners.

The article the week before in the *Baltimore Black Advocate* opened a floodgate of sorts; letters started arriving at Mrs. Mitchell's, first one or two at a time, now at least a dozen a day. Dottie was receiving the same volume at her home. Most were postmarked from locations far from Pine Hammock: Baltimore, of course, but also Washington, Richmond, and a myriad of small towns they'd never heard of. Many congratulated them on their efforts at integrating the library. A few challenged them to go further.

A couple included threats.

Dottie had received the first, a barely legible scrawl with a Winchester, Virginia postmark. *Niggers can't reed and shudnt be in the liberry. Niggers who go to the liberry get shot.* It frightened Buck more than Dottie. Then, when they got out an atlas and found that Winchester was a couple hundred miles away, he'd relaxed. A little.

The next one came from Snow Hill, Maryland. That was much closer. It was addressed to *Buck Nigger Jones* and the sentiment made Dottie's letter seem genteel in comparison.

"Expect it," Desmond Henry had cautioned. "Dr. King gets them all the time. Anybody involved in the civil rights movement has to deal with it."

Civil rights movement?

Buck had laughed when Desmond used the term. He wasn't involved in the civil rights movement. That was people like Rosa Parks down in Montgomery and Dr. King. All Buck wanted was for his students to have library books.

***

At the end of the day Buck was exiting the school with Dottie when Biggerstaff intercepted them.

"I need you both in my office in ten minutes."

They nodded their assent and Biggerstaff headed off toward the back of the school.

"What's this about?" Buck asked.

Dottie shrugged. "He hasn't said a word to me since our meeting at the library. You?"

"Nothing."

They went to the sparsely-furnished principal's office and waited until Biggerstaff returned. Uncharacteristically, he closed the office door before

144

taking his seat. He sat back and held his hands in front of his face, almost like he was praying. His eyes said otherwise.

"Why didn't you tell me what you were up to?"

His voice was flat. Emotionless.

Dottie spoke first. "If you're referring to the library, we—"

"You know *damn well* I'm referring to the library, Dottie!"

Buck shrank back in his seat. Dottie went in the other direction.

"Do *not* swear at me, Mr. Biggerstaff."

The man's eyes grew large. Buck thought his probably did, too.

Biggerstaff retorted, "If you think you're going to involve this school in your race battles, you have another thing coming. You two have got everybody in Pine Hammock stirred up. Parents are upset. Kids are coming to school upset—"

"Upset?" Dottie interjected, now on the edge of her seat. "If you call finally being allowed to go to the public library that their taxes pay for being upset, then yes, Mr. Biggerstaff, they're upset."

"We don't teach agitation, here," Biggerstaff snapped. "We teach math, reading, and writing. This outside stuff you're bringing in gets in the way. We need to lift these children up so they can find their way in the world."

"You mean find their way in the white man's world?" Dottie asked, her voice growing more animated. "Because if that's what you mean, I'll give you my resignation right now."

Dottie looked at Buck, expecting a show of agreement, but he was too shell-shocked to offer anything.

"Wait a minute," Biggerstaff said, raising his hands, his voice turning conciliatory. "Dottie, you're not resigning. We just need to make sure we're working together."

"What is this really about, Mr. Biggerstaff?"

Biggerstaff looked past them, focusing at a spot on the wall. His eyes were troubled, not confident like Buck and Dottie were used to seeing from the man who controlled Pine Hammock School with an iron fist. Buck instinctively picked up on the problem.

"Doctor Mister's giving you trouble?" he asked gently.

Biggerstaff's nod was so slight they almost missed it.

"He thinks you're going to try to integrate the schools," Biggerstaff said quietly. "He said I need to control you or the school board will find a principal who can."

***

The meeting with Biggerstaff had left Buck numb, and after a quick nap and bite to eat, he headed to the radio station. The days were getting longer, but it was still dark when he pulled into the station parking lot at six-thirty. Buster Key's car was there, as always. Buck's stomach seized when he saw a second car: Mr. Adams' gleaming Chevy Impala.

Buck entered silently, but Mr. Adams must've heard him. He stepped out of his office and greeted Buck with a handshake.

"You're here late, sir," Buck said.

"We need to talk, Buck." Mr. Adams waved him into his office and closed the door; Buck's second closed-door meeting of the day.

"I wanted you to hear this from me before you heard it from Buster or somebody else," Mr. Adams said.

Fat chance of hearing anything from Buster, as the afternoon DJ still wasn't giving him the time of day.

Mr. Jones picked up a sheaf of paper that Buck recognized as advertising invoices. He held them for Buck to see.

"Seven advertisers are threatening to take their business elsewhere," Mr. Adams said. "You know Ralph

Crosswaith? He's on the Library Board." This jogged Buck's memory of the man who had voted against integrating the library.

"Yes, sir. We've met."

Mr. Adams nodded. "Ralph owns that little hardware store behind the bowling alley. He does some business with me. Not a lot, but every little bit helps."

Buck remained quiet.

"He's pulling his business unless we take you off the air."

Ouch.

"And he says he's got these six businesses joining him."

Ouch.

Buck picked a piece of lint from his sleeve as he stared at the floor, buying time before being fired. He could get by without this gig, but would've preferred to exit on his own terms.

"So… you're letting me go, Mr. Adams?"

The station owner blinked several times, then grabbed another handful of invoices.

"Buck, these are new accounts that have come in over the last few months. Almost all of them choose to advertise exclusively on your program."

Buck gazed at the invoices, but could glean nothing from them, so he waited.

"Even if all seven of these…," he pointed to the stack containing Ralph Crosswaith's invoices, "… decide to leave, and I don't think when it comes down to it they will; anyway, if they leave, I'll still be bringing in twenty-percent more revenue than I was before your show started."

"I'm glad to hear that, sir."

"Me too, Buck." Mr. Adams laid aside the invoices and rested his arms on the desk. "You probably think I'm focused on nothing but making a profit," he didn't stop to see if Buck would acknowledge this, "but I've listened to your show, Buck. Now, I don't much care for the music, but I think you're moving Twinton County in the direction it needs to go."

Buck had to force himself to take a breath. Was he really hearing his boss correctly?

"If my radio station can play a small part in that, then I'm all for it. In fact," Mr. Adams handed across an envelope, "I'm giving you a twenty-percent raise, effective this week."

Buck knew his smile probably looked silly, but didn't care.

"If you ever decide you don't want to teach anymore, Buck, I'd like to expand your shift. Maybe cut Buster back and have you on from five to ten."

"Mr. Adams, I'm not sure my show would play well to your white audience driving home from work."

The station manager shrugged. "I think we'd be surprised how many white listeners you've picked up over the last couple months, Buck... real surprised."

White listeners? Really? Buck hadn't considered the possibility. When he looked up, Mr. Adams was watching him, a kindly smile playing across his face.

"I'm proud of you, Buck. Keep up the good work."

TWENTY-NINE

The weeks following the library integration were uneventful, as Dottie and Buck were uncertain how to proceed. They wanted to build on the progress already made, and *Nightside* listeners were pushing for more, but they were confounded about how to handle the issue Biggerstaff was facing with the superintendent and school board. Nothing else had been said, but they'd sensed a change in him. He was less certain, and more prone to overlook things that would never have escaped his attention before. He seemed to be a man struggling to hold onto his job.

Winter's frosty grasp had given way to spring, and farmers and watermen were returning to fields and rivers. School attendance started to drop, as many students were needed to plant crops or man fishing boats. Most asked for and received their schoolwork with the promise of getting it done at night. A few, sixteen-year-old boys mostly, simply disappeared. For them, school was over permanently.

"Pine Hammock will never get ahead until parents see what they're doing to their kids," Dottie lamented over supper. She and Buck had started dining together occasionally, usually lunch or supper on Saturdays. Their first dinner together had been at Billy Goat's, and tongues had immediately started wagging. Since then, they'd become smarter and headed to Salisbury or Princess Anne.

In many ways, Buck wanted their dinners to become something more than two colleagues discussing work and social issues. The only woman he'd ever been romantic with was Elena, and she'd been foisted upon him by his well-meaning family and friends; a mistake he'd never make again.

Dottie was pretty and smart, once you got past the cool exterior. Her Washington upbringing gave her a perspective that no Pine Hammock woman could match. Compared to them, she was an exotic bird. Buck loved when she'd open up about her past: hard-working, dedicated parents who demanded excellence from their daughter, college at Howard University, involvement in student groups that had integrated Washington restaurants. Dottie had done much in her short life, and she was willing to talk about everything. Almost.

One topic she refused to discuss was her former marriage. Buck had broached it once, tentatively, but she'd quickly changed the subject. He certainly couldn't blame her; after all, he'd omitted discussion about everything in his life prior to college. When Dottie would ask about racism and segregation in his hometown, Buck would offer generalities. Yes, he'd say, there was some racism, but not bad. Yes, he'd gone to segregated schools, not mentioning he'd attended the white ones. No, he'd never been married. Lying to someone he cared about was hard, but necessary. Besides, he rationalized, Hucklebuck Theodore Roosevelt Jones had never been married.

And Pete Demopoulos was dead. He had the *Tampa Tribune* article carefully tucked away in a tattered college textbook in his room at Mrs. Mitchell's to prove it.

"You know, we can't just ignore the obvious," she said, taking a bite of salad. Johnny and Sammy's in Salisbury had become one of their favorite places to dine. Prices were compatible with a teacher's salary, and the restaurant had been integrated for several years.

"About what?" Buck was busy tearing into a steak he'd asked to have sliced before it was served, one of the few accommodations he ever requested because of his missing arm.

"Our next step in Sheffield. People are waiting."

"Does there have to be a next step?"

Dottie waved away cigar smoke wafting from a neighboring table, leveling the culprit with the same no-nonsense stare she used on wayward students. "Don't you listen to your own show? People want more, Buck. The movie theater is still segregated. All the restaurants. And we haven't even mentioned the schools."

Buck shrugged. "I would feel terrible if we messed up things for Biggerstaff. He's done a lot for me, and—"

"Tell me one thing Landon Biggerstaff's done for you." Dottie bristled as she took a sip of water.

Buck didn't know what to say. Sure, Biggerstaff had engaged him in several chats on Mrs. Mitchell's front porch, and he'd beaten Jerome Gilliam into submission, but what *had* he done?

"Did you know that he used to live in Sheffield?" Buck asked.

Dottie smirked. "Everybody knows that. I'm betting he gave you the cleaned-up version."

Buck watched her across the table, waiting and noticing again how pretty she was.

"He lived on the road to Pine Hammock, a mile or so from Sheffield."

That much Buck had heard.

"And he told you how some white men tried to burn his house?" Dottie asked.

"Yes."

"All true, but what he probably didn't mention was that Hazel, his ex-wife, had been running around with one of them behind his back."

Whoa.

"No, that didn't come up."

Dottie nodded. "Earlier that night, Biggerstaff and some colored boys he used to run with from college paid a visit to the white boy Hazel had been seeing. They whipped him bad. The boy went to the Emergency Room to get stitched up, then came back after midnight to get his revenge." She paused for another sip of water. "Biggerstaff suspected something might happen, so he was ready. There were whispers around Pine Hammock that the gas cans the cops found when they arrived were planted by Landon Biggerstaff himself."

Buck's breath caught at this revelation.

"Crazy, isn't it?" Dottie said.

"Do you believe it?" Buck asked.

Dottie's face twisted as she considered the question. A waitress came by and refilled their glasses, then stepped away.

"Yes, I do. Biggerstaff likes being the big fish in a small pond. I wonder sometimes if Superintendent Mister really threatened him or if he just said that."

"But... why?"

"To keep his precious job. If the schools integrate, Landon Biggerstaff won't be in charge anymore. They'll close Pine Hammock as sure as I'm sitting here. He'll either be out of a job or have to go back to teaching, because there's no way they'll have a black principal right off the bat. It just doesn't happen."

Buck took another deep breath. "That's a lot to think about, Dottie. I guess everybody has their secrets."

Dottie put her fork down and leaned closer. "Yes, they do, *Mr. Jones*. And what, may I ask are yours?"

Buck chewed his steak slowly, buying time.

"No secrets. I just don't like talking about my—"

Dottie waved him off. "Don't try to pull the wool over my eyes, Buck. There's a whole lot in your past you aren't telling. Like why you dug through five years of *Tampa Tribunes*."

His surprise must have been evident.

"Biggerstaff told me. I think he was worried I'd be attracted to you. He's been carrying a torch for me since I arrived. He thinks you had some kind of secret life down there that you're not telling anyone about."

Things were starting to hit too close to home. Buck hoped he wasn't giving away the fear he felt building in his gut. He also hoped that Biggerstaff hadn't been digging through his room when he was out. It wasn't likely that he'd find the articles he'd clipped, but if he did...

"Like you said, Dottie," Buck said, trying to remain nonchalant, "everybody has secrets. Mine aren't substantial, but I suppose I have them."

She smiled, relaxing into her chair. "Well, anyway, back to the point where we got off topic, I think it's time to take on the school system."

"What do we tell Biggerstaff?"

"We don't tell him anything," Dottie said. "Our next steps will be made as residents of Twinton County, not as teachers. We'll make a point never to mention our activities in school, so Biggerstaff or anyone else can't say we were out of line."

Buck started to look down, but Dottie wouldn't let him, bending low to catch his gaze.

"Are you in?"

***

The porch was deserted when he returned to Mrs. Mitchell's. Biggerstaff's car was parked out front, but the door to his room was closed. Buck walked quickly down the hall to his own room, closed the door, and picked up the textbook where he'd hidden the articles about his past.

They were still there.

Aware of the threat they could pose, and familiar now with Biggerstaff's background, Buck went downstairs to the dark kitchen. Mrs. Mitchell still did most of her cooking on an old wood stove, and the remnants of that day's fire still burned faintly. Lifting one of the burner covers, he fed the articles in and watched as they were reduced to ash. Satisfied, he replaced the burner cover and turned to go back to his room.

From the stairs, Biggerstaff was watching.

"Burning memories doesn't make them go away," he said, his eyes flickering like the fire in the stove.

THIRTY

The next assault on the segregation practices of Twinton County would come on a Saturday evening in June, and it would be double-barreled.

School had dismissed for the summer on the tenth of June, with Buck and Dottie both receiving contracts to return in the fall. They had worried about that, as Biggerstaff had said little to nothing regarding the coming school year. They were given until the fifteenth of July to sign. Both chose to wait.

Nor had anything else been said about the late-night encounter in Mrs. Mitchell's kitchen, though Biggerstaff had grown more aloof with Buck than before. Dottie noticed the change, and even asked Buck about it, but when it came to his past, the less said the better.

Buck met the group of seven at a table in a far corner of the Twinton County Public Library, the meaningfulness of the location not lost on anyone. Desmond Henry and his camera were waiting up the street.

"Walk alone or in groups of two," Buck explained, speaking softly so other library patrons wouldn't overhear. "It's just three blocks, and we shouldn't run into any trouble." The eyes of the people meeting his gaze were tired, old, and wise. For a couple the walk wouldn't be easy. Two women and five men, all over sixty, revered in the colored community and respected by many whites. Dr.

155

Elijah Watson, the local black doctor, had been the first to volunteer. Buck had been surprised to learn he was a faithful *Nightside* listener. "I love me some Ike and Tina," he'd said the first time they'd met. Two preachers, a preacher's wife, a carpenter, a waterman, and Buck's landlady, Mrs. Mitchell, rounded out the group.

"If you run into any trouble and want to quit, just—"

"Ain't nobody quitting," the preacher's wife said. Nods of affirmation came from all sides of the table.

Buck checked his watch. "It's six-twenty. If we start walking now, we'll get there by six-thirty, do our business, and move on to the second part of our evening." Wordlessly they struggled to their feet and exited the library, their presence barely raising the interest of the dozen or so white residents in the building.

Outside, the early summer air was warm, but a breeze drifting from the west kept things comfortable. The group immediately split up into twos, with Dr. Watson joining Buck. They watched the others depart.

"I've actually sat at the Miggett's lunch counter once before," Dr. Watson said, steadying himself with a walking stick as they took off. "Back in thirty-nine. A white doctor in town, Dr. Grayber, was eating lunch and had a heart attack right at the counter. The man who ran the lunch counter back then, I can't remember his name, came out on the street and started yelling for somebody to help. I was coming out of the post office and heard him, so I ran over and did what I could." Dr. Watson pulled a neatly folded handkerchief from the inside pocket of his jacket and wiped perspiration from his forehead. "I wasn't able to save the poor man; it turned out he'd had another attack a few months before. Anyway, I worked on him until the boys from the funeral home showed up. It was hot as blazes, late July or thereabouts, and Miggett's didn't have air conditioning like they do now. As they were loading his body onto a gurney, I backed up against the counter and sat down, without thinking. One of the girls who worked there was looking at me, so I asked for a sip of water."

Buck kept an eye open for cracks in the sidewalk that might trip up the doctor, but wasn't missing a thing he said.

"The girl said they didn't serve coloreds... actually she didn't say coloreds." The doctor glanced at Buck. "And that was that."

It was when he heard accounts of past injustices like Dr. Watson's that Buck felt most inadequate for the role he had reluctantly assumed. Pete Demopoulos was more than five years in his past, but that life was far removed from anything the people walking ahead of him toward Miggett's Department Store had experienced. More than once, he'd concluded that he should step back from the movement, but then Dottie would say something or he'd get a letter from Desmond and the fire to continue would reignite.

Still, the thought of a white man as the unofficial leader of the integration of Twinton County seemed wrong. And the fact that nobody had questioned his blackness somehow made it more difficult. Still, he reminded himself, if not him, who?

When Buck and Dr. Watson turned the corner onto Main Street, they saw the others were assembled in front of the post office across the street from Miggett's. Desmond was standing at a distance, discretely snapping photographs. Dottie was chatting with two of the participants, but Buck saw her eyes scanning the sidewalk for signs of trouble. When she spotted him she nodded, checked for traffic, and crossed the street, the others following behind.

Traffic on Main Street was scarce on weekend evenings, as most people parked in the large public lots tucked behind the storefronts. This gave Main Street a feel more like a pedestrian walkway, an image aided by careful landscaping and colorful awnings. Pedestrian traffic, however, was thick, and the sight of a group of

Negroes congregating in front of the post office had garnered attention. Of the nine businesses on the north side of Main Street, only one, Vesper Hardware, welcomed colored trade. Vesper's decision to open its doors to all customers had come just a week after the integration of the library and was viewed as a victory by many in Pine Hammock. It also had signaled the beginning of the end for Irving's, a small white-owned hardware store in Pine Hammock with exorbitant prices and back-breaking credit plans. Nobody shed a tear when Irving's had closed its doors six weeks earlier.

"Dr. Watson, you go on ahead, sir," Buck said, gently patting the old man on the shoulder. "I'll stay here and make sure everything's okay outside." Silently, Dr. Watson made his slow trek across Main Street, joining up with the others. At the entrance, Dottie glanced back at Buck, whose slight nod meant all was good. She opened the door and held it for the others. Passers-by gawked at what was happening, unsure how or if they should respond.

"Having the old folks do this was genius," Desmond said as he hurried past. "I'll make sure to get some good pictures."

When the last of the group had entered the store, Buck started across the street.

"What the hell's going on?" The man was mid-forties, dressed in khakis and a blue and white plaid shirt. "Niggers at it again?"

He obviously assumed Buck was white. It had happened before, and Buck had chosen to let it slide, then felt badly. He was to some degree, as Johnny, Clarence, and Poop back at Moonie's had described, *passing* as white to avoid conflict.

But not this time. Not after hearing Dr. Watson's story of being refused a glass of water at this same lunch counter.

"You're not fit to hold the hats of any of those fine people," Buck said, shouldering past. "And for your information, I'm one of them."

Buck fully expected to be shoved from behind or have an epithet yelled at him, but nothing came. Not daring to glance back, he walked briskly toward Miggett's, pushed open the door, and went inside. The lunch counter was straight ahead and slightly to the left. Walking toward it, he watched seven elderly black people find seats at the counter. Like outside, they sat in groups of two. Dr. Watson sat at the far end of the counter, alone, with at least six seats between him and anyone else. Buck instinctively knew why he'd chosen that seat and hoped the old hero finally got his sip of water.

After everyone was seated, Dottie found a spot for herself a few seats away from Dr. Watson. Buck joined her. Behind the counter, confusion reigned. Three waitresses gaped at their new customers, then quickly clustered to one side, whispering among themselves before one excused herself and headed toward a staircase.

The lunch counter was laid out shotgun-style, with two dozen green leather and polished chrome swivel seats. Buck counted six white customers already seated when the Pine Hammock contingent arrived. Some were eating; a couple were waiting for food. Their responses ran the gamut from disbelief to acting as if the new arrivals weren't there. One little girl, no older than four, eating a dish of ice cream, turned to her mother and said loudly, "Mama, they're *brown*." It sounded to Buck as if she'd never seen Negroes before, a real possibility for a child in Sheffield. The mama shushed her, encouraging her to finish her ice cream.

"We're not going to have to wait long to find out what happens next," Dottie said motioning to the returning waitress followed by a middle-aged man with a mottled face, dressed in a white short-sleeved shirt and tie.

"Folks," he said, moving behind the counter and positioning himself at the midpoint. "Miggett's has a policy of not serving coloreds at the lunch counter. I'm sorry for the inconvenience, but you'll have to move on."

Nobody moved, except the mother and her daughter, the little girl starting to cry because she wasn't allowed to finish her ice cream. The waitresses had backed up against the wall as if they were about to face a firing squad. Behind the stools, a group of eight or ten white customers had congregated. Things grew quiet, as everyone waited for someone else to take the next step. Buck felt his heart racing, as he could see the gathering crowd behind him in the mirror over the lunch counter. All it would take was one person to make this situation go bad really quick. Then, from several seats down the counter, Mrs. Mitchell picked up a menu, scanned it, then turned to the man who'd just arrived.

"I'll have a dish of chocolate ice cream, please. Just like the little white girl's."

"Same here," said another.

"Me, too," said one of the preachers.

"Ice cream and a sip of water," Dr. Watson said from the end of the counter.

Buck saw the blood rising to the white man's face as orders came at him. The crowd behind them continued to grow, but they seemed more curious than angry. Then, he saw someone slip through the gathering, sliding onto the stool next to him.

"Good evening, Buck." Mr. Adams, the radio station owner said with a smile. Then, directing his attention to the man behind the counter, said, "Buzz, ice cream for everybody at the counter." He turned and looked at the gathering behind him, now approaching twenty-five. "And for these fine people, too. Put it on my bill."

Buzz, the white man behind the counter, stared at Mr. Adams for a moment. Buck could see how ill-prepared he was for a situation like this.

"Mr. Adams, you know we can't... I mean if Grandpa Miggett was here, he'd—"

"Otis Miggett's been dead for fifteen years, Buzz. It's 1960, son. Time to move ahead."

All eyes were glued on Buzz. He looked from one end of the counter to another, desperately hoping for a last-minute reprieve. Then, turning slightly, he nodded to the waitresses.

"Serve the ice cream," he said.

"And a glass of water for me, please," Dr. Watson interjected.

Buzz nodded, then looked at Mr. Adams. "Make sure you put it on his bill... and no discounts." With that, Buzz stepped away, headed back to wherever he'd come from. The waitresses began filling bowls with chocolate ice cream. As planned, the seven Negroes who were about to enjoy their first serving at the Miggett's lunch counter remained quiet and pleasant. Even Desmond and his camera were unobtrusive. Some in the crowd behind them turned to walk away, but most crowded closer for free ice cream, filling in the vacant seats between white and black.

"That's one down," Dottie whispered.

***

The line for tickets at the Rialto was fifty deep, typical whenever a new Western came out. John Wayne's *The Alamo* had been garnering a lot of attention in recent weeks, and Buck felt it was the perfect film to integrate the theater.

The seven people who had enjoyed ice cream at the Miggett's lunch counter an hour earlier took their place in the ticket line, again in groups of two. Initially, Buck had considered expanding the group to include younger Negroes, but Dottie had been rightfully concerned that the size of the audience for *The Alamo* might make it hard to find enough seats.

Black faces in the ticket line were nothing new and caused nary a wayward glance, despite word quickly spreading about what had happened at Miggett's. There were a few Negroes in line who weren't part of the planned integration, but like everyone around Pine Hammock, they were aware of what was about to happen. Still, no one said or did anything that would tip off the Rialto management.

Desmond Henry worked his way back down the line to Buck and Dottie, his camera concealed in a carrying case.

"I have to give Twinton County credit," he said, speaking quietly so others wouldn't hear. "Locals seem to have heard about the integration problems elsewhere and want to avoid the violence."

After purchasing their tickets, Buck placed his hand on Dottie's elbow and led her through the lobby and into the cool dimly-lit theater. Stairs leading to the balcony were on each side of the auditorium, but in twos or threes, seven elderly heroes bypassed the stairs in favor of seats on the lower level. The air was filled with laughter and friendly conversation, as neighbors visited with neighbors. No one seemed to notice the arrival of the seven.

Except one man.

***

It was after midnight when Mrs. Mitchell slowly awakened. The doctor had given her painkillers and a mild sedative, so her consciousness was fleeting. The gaze from her rheumy eyes floated about the tiny hospital room, ultimately settling on Buck and Dottie. She smiled, then winced at the pain. Reaching up groggily, she touched the bandages that swathed the back of her head.

"What was it?" she asked, her voice a shadow of its usual level.

"A mason jar," Buck said, rubbing her hand. "Half-full of bootleg."

Mrs. Mitchell nodded faintly. Her head was starting to totter to one side.

"You're going to be fine," Buck said reassuringly. "The doctor said—"

The force with which Biggerstaff pushed open the door caused them to jump. Despite the lateness of the hour there was no effort to remain quiet. He made a beeline for Buck, pulling him away from Mrs. Mitchell's bed and shoving him hard against the wall.

"You stupid son-of-a—"

Dottie's scream drowned out what Biggerstaff said next, but did nothing to take away from his fury. Considerably stronger and more physically able than Buck, he repeatedly shoved him against the wall, then lifted him until they were eye level, causing a picture of two colored angels to fall to the floor and break.

"You just don't know any better, do you?" he snarled. "Getting your own landlady hurt - an old woman - because you're too chickenshit to put your own ass on the line."

Dottie pulled at Biggerstaff, but couldn't budge him. Buck was certain he was about to get decked, but with little he could do to stop the onslaught, he took a page from Dr. King's playbook, growing limp and meeting the eyes of his assailant.

"Landon Biggerstaff! You stop that right now!" Amazingly, Mrs. Mitchell was sitting up, and just the sight of her trying to crawl from bed was enough to get Biggerstaff to back off.

"Lay back down, Geraldine!" Biggerstaff ordered. "You're hurt too bad to be trying to get up." He returned his attention to Buck, who he still held at eye-level. "This asshole knew better. I told him to leave it alone. Now look what's happened."

"You better know something, Landon." Mrs. Mitchell had gotten to her feet and was doddering toward them. "The minute the doctor lets me out of this hospital, I'll be back at that movie theater trying again!"

Biggerstaff, watching her over his shoulder, finally relented and lowered Buck to the floor. After regaining his balance, Buck scooted out of his reach. Mrs. Mitchell continued, unconcerned that the hospital gown she was wearing provided minimal coverage.

"I'll go back because it's the right thing! You know it is, Landon. The question is, why wasn't *you* out there with us?"

Mrs. Mitchell glared up into his face, fists clenched, daring Biggerstaff to argue. He appeared to deflate under her steely gaze, glancing around as if just becoming aware of the commotion he'd caused.

"Now you go on back to the house," she said angrily, "and you'd better not lay a hand on Buck. Him and Miss Dottie are heroes. They're trying to fix a lot of what's wrong in Twinton County. I would 'spect you would be in the middle of this instead of fighting against your own."

"Look, Geraldine," Biggerstaff said, holding his hands out as if surrendering, "you and I have been here a lot longer than they have. We know that things around here aren't perfect, but this isn't Mississippi or Alabama, either. Whites and blacks respect each other here. If we take our time, things will change without good people like you getting hurt. We just have to respect each other."

"I respect white people just fine, Landon. It's that white boy that struck me in the head with a mason jar who don't have no respect. What did I do to deserve that?"

Doubt clouded Biggerstaff's eyes. He didn't answer.

"Landon, I'm sixty-four years old. I got ten, maybe twenty years left. If I can help make things better for our people, I'll die a much happier woman." Mrs. Mitchell looked at Dottie and Buck as she gently lowered herself to the bed. "I got these two to thank for allowing me to be part of what happened tonight. I'll take a jar of hooch to the head anytime if I know I'm making a difference. Now... leave an old woman to get some sleep, all of you."

***

"Would you like a drink?"

It was after one in the morning, and Buck's body ached all over, but adrenaline was a tricky thing. His senses were still on overload, and maybe Dottie's offer would calm him enough to go home and get some sleep.

He followed her up the steps and inside her tiny Pine Hammock bungalow. Though they had taught together for almost a year, and lived just three streets apart, it was his first time in her house. Dottie was big on maintaining appearances.

"Nobody's up this late anyway," she said, drawing the shades then heading into the kitchen. Buck took a seat on a worn sofa and looked around. Nice, but not fancy. A large desk dominated one wall. There was a radio but no television. A couple family pictures. Dottie's college diploma.

In a few moments, she reemerged with two glasses, taking a seat on the other end of the sofa.

"Brandy," she said, handing him one. "It'll help us sleep."

"Are you as wired as I am?" he asked, accepting the glass, knocking it back, then grinning at her wide-eyed stare.

"Boy, you'd better slow down," she said, taking a sip. "But then, I've heard how you like your Moon Juice, so I shouldn't be surprised."

Buck laughed. "I haven't been to Moonie's since winter," he said. "I'll have to go back again sometime and take you with me."

Dottie raised her hands, as if fending off evil spirits. "I've seen how sketchy that place looks in the daylight," she said, shaking her head. "There is no possibility of my going at night."

For a few moments, they sat quietly. Buck rested his head against the back of the sofa and watched Dottie take several more sips. The conversation was in a lull, but both knew what the other was thinking. It had been a good night, despite Mrs. Mitchell's injuries. There was, however, more to be done. That could wait for another time. For tonight, they could relax.

"Would you like another?"

Buck considered his empty glass. The weariness was starting to spread, and he certainly wouldn't need another to fall asleep. Still, the thought of encountering Biggerstaff back at the boarding house gave him pause. He held out the glass.

When Dottie returned this time, she kicked off her shoes and stretched her legs demurely across the couch in his direction. They sipped silently as Buck's head started to nod. Without thinking he reached out and started massaging her feet. Through a blissful haze of brandy and fatigue, he heard her groan appreciatively.

Awakening quietly, Buck checked his watch and saw that forty-five minutes had passed. He also saw that Dottie had changed position, and that her head was resting on his shoulder. Thinking she was asleep, he leaned closer and smelled a floral fragrance that must have been shampoo. It felt good, as intoxicating as the brandy. Then, she stirred, turned her face to his and pulled him close. She kissed him gently on the cheek, then the lips. He kissed her back, noticing that she was even more beautiful up close and wondering how he could have been so wrong about her when they first met. Dottie Hanford was no snow queen. She was more of a… Juliet.

But Pete Demopoulos is no Romeo.

Disconcerted by his thought, he pulled away, startling Dottie.

"What?" Her eyes showed confusion. And hurt, maybe?

"Sorry," he said, pulling her toward him. She settled back into the same spot, facing him. Still close. Then, closing her eyes, she moved even closer. Their lips touched and stayed that way. Searching. Finding.

Pete Demopoulos.

Damn.

Pete's gone.

I'm Buck.

No, you're not.

And then, Buck was gone too.

***

The packed dirt lot was empty, but light emanated from inside. Did the place ever close?

Buck was worn to a nub, but had little desire to return to the boarding house; at least not without more liquid courage.

The place was empty, the air still reeked of cigarette smoke, spilled booze, and piss. Buck considered a back table before choosing a stool. The bar was sticky, but that was nothing new. It was always that way.

Moonie appeared from the back room. It had been months since Buck had stopped in, but Moonie didn't raise an eyebrow.

"Juice," Buck said in way of a greeting. Moonie nodded, then looked past Buck toward the open door.

"Were you getting ready to close?" Moonie shook his head as he reached for a glass and moved down the counter to fill Buck's order. Buck looked around, suddenly missing the place and wondering if life could be as simple as it had been the year before.

The flies were thick, and Buck was waving them away when Moonie brought his drink. Buck smiled appreciatively and knocked it back, eager for the burn that would remind his insides that he was alive and well.

Nothing.

No burn. No taste.

Water.

"Moon, what the hell?" Buck eyed him over the top of the glass. "If you've started cutting drinks to make money, I don't like it."

Wordlessly, Moonie took the glass, moved back down the counter, and placed it in a small sink behind the bar. Buck watched his every move, uncertain what had gotten into a man who, though he'd never heard him speak, still considered a friend. Moonie carefully washed and dried the glass, then disappeared into the back.

Buck waited. It was five minutes before Moonie returned. Still no juice. Instead, he held a yellow scrap of newspaper, which he laid on the bar in front of Buck. Buck glanced at it, then at Moonie. He waved his hand as an invitation for Buck to read, so he did.

"Did you know these guys?" Buck asked, pushing the clipping away. Moonie nodded.

"Friends?"

Moonie looked at him like he was nuts.

"Well, I don't understand..." Buck glanced at the article again. Seven years ago. Two men shot to death outside a Baltimore bar. No suspects. "Moon, were you there."

Moonie nodded. "I did it."

They weren't the first words he'd hoped to hear Moonie say, but at least Buck now knew he could talk. His voice was quiet and unassuming. He expressed neither pride nor remorse. Buck didn't know what to say in return, so he waited.

And waited. Moonie seemed content to leave it hanging there. He turned his attention to the glasses in the sink, washing, wiping, and placing them on the shelf for the next day. Buck let it go for about three minutes before he couldn't stand it anymore.

"Did you get caught?"

Moonie barely looked up as he shook his head.

"So, what the hell happened? Moon, you can't throw something like this out there and not expect me to want to know more."

Moon kept his head down, his attention on the glasses.

"Couple of Army boys, home on leave. I was tending bar at Papscott's on Monument. These boys wanted money, so they waited out back until I got off. They jumped me. One of them had a gun, then he didn't."

Holy cow. This was the last thing Buck would have thought he'd hear from Moonie, even if he'd known he could talk.

"So, it was self-defense?"

Moonie shrugged. "They white."

Now it became clearer. White army boys killed in an alley. Even acting in self-defense, Moonie never would've stood a chance in court. A year ago, maybe even six months, Buck would have asked why he didn't turn himself in. Now, after a few stares of incredulity and questions about whether he was really black, he'd learned. There were situations where the Negro was always guilty.

But why was Moonie telling him this now?

Moonie wiped the last glass, then came closer, leaning in as if to share a confidence.

"You ain't who you say you is," he said, his voice remaining calm. Buck started to protest, but Moonie cut him off.

"It don't matter, man. Most people ain't who they say they is. There's people in Sheffield, important people, come to see me for things they don't want nobody to know about. Juice, weed... women."

Buck nodded, suddenly thirsting for some of the moon juice those important people craved.

"Like I says, you ain't who you say you is, but you are who you is now. Just like me."

This took a minute for Buck to decipher. When he did, he felt as if Moonie was looking into his soul.

"That teacher woman likes who you is, man. Now, I know you're running scared." Moonie stopped for a moment, taking a look around the bar. "But she don't give a rat's ass who you *was*. You need to get past that and make a life for yourself *now*."

Buck could do little more than shake his head, astonished at the depth of understanding coming from a man who never said anything.

"But... is it fair to her if I don't tell her?"

"Will she still be there if you *do* tell her?"

Buck read Moonie's expression perfectly.

"I'm just afraid my past might catch up to me." Buck laughed harshly. "There aren't a lot of one-armed light-skinned black guys out there."

"You gotta make sure that don't happen," Moonie said. "But don't let whatever happened back then stop you from living now." Moonie became quiet. There was hurt in his eyes that Buck suspected came from missed opportunities or, more likely, from loves lost. He took another look around the bar, his eyes registering everything.

"Last thing you want is to be stuck someplace like this."

Buck got up to leave. Unsure what, if anything, he could offer in the way of thanks. He nodded at Moonie and made his way to the door. Like everything he'd shared that night, Moonie's final words stayed with him.

"Grow a beard, man. And let that afro grow out, too. A yella one-armed Negro sticks out like a hog in a chicken coop."

THIRTY-ONE

BALTIMORE BLACK ADVOCATE
June 27, 1960

ONE INJURED IN TWINTON COUNTY DEMONSTRATION

By: Desmond K. Henry

What started as a peaceful night of segregation protests in Sheffield ended with a Pine Hammock woman in the hospital.

Mirroring the sit-ins conducted earlier this year in Greensboro, North Carolina, a group of seven Negroes made their way to the lunch counter of Miggett's Department Store Saturday evening. Once inside, the seven seated themselves and, after some initial reluctance from Miggett's management, were served without incident.

Later that evening, the same seven, all elderly residents of neighboring Pine Hammock, attempted to integrate Sheffield's Rialto Theater, which had previously allowed Negro seating only in the balcony.

Again, the protesters made it to their seats without incident, despite a near-capacity audience. Minutes later, however, a disturbance arose from an aisle when a theater employee approached two of the protesters and asked them to relocate to the balcony. When the protesters stood up, one of them, Geraldine Mitchell, 64, was struck from behind by a glass jar. Mitchell collapsed to the floor and had to be carried out by others in her group.

Police were called to the scene and used information gathered from witnesses to arrest George M. Stern, 31, of Sheffield, on charges of assault and battery. Having fled the scene, Stern was found at his house several blocks away.

Following the disturbance, a theater manager informed the audience that the evening screening of *The Alamo* would be cancelled and tickets would be refunded.

Reached for comment prior to this story going to press, Rialto Theater Manager Joseph Huxtable stated that the theater was evaluating its seating practices, but had not arrived at a conclusion.

Speaking on behalf of the protesters, local educator and radio host Buck "Hucklebuck" Jones expressed regret that injuries resulted from the evening's activities, but remained optimistic.

"Sheffield has come far in the past few months in terms of opening facilities to Negroes," Jones said. "We will continue our efforts until all barriers are removed."

THIRTY-TWO

Pine Hammock School was deserted. Windows were closed and shades were drawn. Biggerstaff's car was the only one there when Buck and Dottie arrived.

"He wouldn't tell you anything?" Dottie asked, as Buck opened her car door.

"He's not said anything since last week at the hospital. When we pass in the hallway at Mrs. Mitchell's he acts like I'm invisible. By the way, did you bring your contract?"

"I have it right here," she replied, patting her purse.

"Mrs. Mitchell said he's leaving for Harvard tomorrow," Buck said, climbing the front steps and pulling open the door. "I'm betting he wants our contracts before he goes."

The air inside was oppressively still. The hallway was dark, except for the first door on the left. Biggerstaff's office.

"Maybe we can come to an understanding," Dottie said, walking slightly ahead of Buck, her hard-sole shoes echoing on the hallway's wood floors. "I like it better when we're not at odds with Landon."

Through the frosted door, they could see him seated at his desk. Dottie knocked softly, then went in. When Biggerstaff looked up from his desk, Buck knew this meeting wasn't going to go well. The principal's eyes were hard, his posture stiff and formal.

"Mr. Jones, Miss Hanley," he said curtly. Picking up on his mood, Dottie instinctively stayed back. Buck moved to take a seat in one of the two wooden chairs across from Biggerstaff's desk.

"Don't sit," he snapped. "You won't be here long."

Caught off guard, Buck stood behind one of the chairs. Dottie moved forward and stood beside him. Whatever was going to happen, they would take it together.

"I'll get to why we're here." Biggerstaff's gaze settled on Buck. "You first, Mr. Jones. As I told you on Mrs. Mitchell's porch last fall, I've had an uneasy feeling about you since the day I met you."

Buck heard Dottie catch her breath at the abruptness of the attack. Figuring he had nothing to gain from speaking, Buck remained quiet, hopeful Biggerstaff would eventually run out of steam.

"You showed me very little early on. You couldn't control your classes. You were the last teacher to arrive and the first out the door. Then, as the year went along, being *Hucklebuck* became more important than your job here."

The way he said it – *Hucklebuck* – came out as a derisive hiss.

"Now I tried to defend you to the superintendent. 'Give him more time,' I pleaded. And I got you more time, but did you appreciate it? Hell no! You get a big head about you and start thinking of yourself as the Martin Luther King of Twinton County."

"Hold on right there, Landon." Dottie's voice remained as quiet as Biggerstaff's was loud.

"I'll get to you in a minute," Biggerstaff roared. "At least there's still hope for you, Dottie, unless you decide to keep spouting off."

Still hope? That could only mean... While the intent of this meeting hadn't been apparent to Buck before, that statement made it clear.

Chastened, Dottie scowled at the floor. Buck knew she wasn't done, but had wisely chosen to follow his lead. Biggerstaff continued.

"Then, when Geraldine got hurt at the movie theater, that was it. I couldn't do anymore for you."

"I didn't hurt Mrs. Mitchell."

"You put her in the position to get hurt. That woman's never harmed a soul, and because of you, she's sitting at home with a big-ass bandage wrapped around her head."

"Proudly," Buck said quietly. "Proudly sitting at home."

This brought a momentary pause to Biggerstaff's harangue. Somewhere, buried deep inside, he had to have a heart for what had transpired in Sheffield.

When he continued, his voice was toned down.

"Your contract is revoked. Since you've not signed and returned it, the school board can do that."

"But I've got it right here, signed." Buck pulled the contract from his pocket, smoothing it out and laying it on the desk.

"Too late," Biggerstaff replied tersely, tearing the contract in half. "I can't do anything else for you. You chewed up your credibility with Doctor Mister when you started agitating."

Buck stood mutely, shocked by the revelation that he no longer was a teacher. He considered pleading for his job, but he'd done nothing that warranted that.

"Dottie, I need to visit with you alone."

For a moment, Buck had forgotten that Dottie was a witness to what had just happened. He stared numbly at Biggerstaff before bringing his head close to hers.

"Will you be okay?" he said quietly. "I can stay if you want."

"I'll be fine," she said, her eyes never moving from Biggerstaff.

***

Fifteen minutes passed before Dottie came out. Her tan cotton blouse was bathed in sweat, but her eyes were resolute.

"What...?" Dottie cut off his question with a quick wave of her hand. She pointed to the door. Once in the car, she spoke.

"They want me to stay," she said simply. "They offered me a three-hundred dollar raise and a promotion. I'm going to be the first colored teacher at Sheffield High School."

Buck felt his heartbeat quicken. "They're integrating? Really?"

Shaking her head, Dottie replied, "they thought it would be good to start with one teacher. Maybe a second in another year, then figure out after that how to proceed from there."

"Is a white teacher coming to Pine Hammock, then?"

Dottie snorted. "What do you think?"

Buck started the car and backed out of the lot, headed for Dottie's place.

"They're going to start a voluntary integration plan in three years," Dottie continued. "Fall of 1963. Families will be able to choose which school they want their kids to go to. Colored kids will be able to go to Sheffield, white kids can come to Pine Hammock."

"Ridiculous," Buck exclaimed. "Want to guess how many white kids transfer?"

"Or colored kids," Dottie said. "From what Landon said, any child going to a school out of the area where they live will have to find their own transportation. No buses from Pine Hammock to Sheffield, or vice-versa."

They rode in silence, considering the paper-thin credibility of the plan Biggerstaff had shared with Dottie.

"There will be a few families, maybe eight or ten, who can afford to drive their children to Sheffield every day," Dottie said. "The rest are stuck."

They turned onto the block where Dottie lived. Children were playing tag under trees on one side of the road, while across from them a makeshift game of baseball was taking shape. Several stopped and waved at their teachers.

"Well," Buck said, nodding at two boys standing on the roadside, "maybe you can help change that. At least you still have a job."

When Dottie looked across the seat at him Buck noticed that softness had replaced the determined look she'd displayed earlier. She reached across and gently touched his shoulder. The feeling was electric.

"No," she said. "I don't need a job where I'm somebody's token colored girl. I turned it down."

Almost running off the road, Buck pulled the car to the side and turned off the engine.

"Dottie, you can't do that. I mean, I still have the radio gig, but what do you have?"

She cupped his hand in hers and pulled it to her face, kissing it softly.

"I guess that all I have... is you."

THIRTY-THREE

Everything inside him told Buck to make a big deal out of being fired. Get a hold of Desmond at the *Baltimore Black Advocate*, tell him about the outrageous actions of the Twinton County Superintendent, maybe get some protests going.

Dottie said no.

Then she said yes, but not to that.

She said no to reacting too quickly to Buck's firing and her resignation. Biggerstaff had left for grad school two days after their meeting, and in the two weeks since, nothing had leaked out. "Let's figure out our next move, then decide if going public is best," she'd said.

Buck's next move was a no-brainer. Mr. Adams had immediately offered him a full-time position with the station. Still nights, but five to ten now. The station owner's appearance at Miggett's had cemented their friendship, and from what Buck had heard, Mr. Adams was doing what he could to convince other downtown Sheffield businesses to integrate.

Still, he felt bittersweet about the opportunity. It was late in the summer, and Dottie was unlikely to find a teaching job in the area. A move closer to her parents' home in Washington was looking more and more likely when she received a call from the friend of a friend at Maryland State College.

"A graduate teaching position," she'd gushed to Buck. "The person who accepted the position backed out. I can get my masters while I teach college classes."

And just like that, it was settled.

Except there was one more thing.

Buck had been feeling it, despite his best efforts to bury it. The time he'd been spending with Dottie over the past few months had blossomed into something special. Buck had never experienced love before, certainly not in this life and even before, as Pete, he'd married for reasons that still confused and angered him.

And, as important, Dottie felt it too. They'd become inseparable over the summer, only parting ways at night for Buck to return to Mrs. Mitchell's. Decorum was everything in Pine Hammock, and the sight of Buck sneaking around Dottie's place at night would get the rumor mill started. As the summer progressed, he spent more time with her, enjoying occasional dinners in Salisbury but mostly sharing the cooking responsibilities at her place.

"You hang on to that one, Buck," Mrs. Mitchell had said several times. With Biggerstaff's departure, Buck and the landlady spent more time visiting one-on-one. Between her encouragement and the advice from Moonie, he'd become comfortable that he could have a future with Dottie.

In many ways, Pine Hammock was becoming home. Despite the decrepit nature of many of the homes, the unpaved streets, the workaday culture, Buck liked it. His role as a teacher and now, as someone concerned with achieving equal rights, made him a leader.

But he even surprised himself when, over a dinner of roast pork, carrots, lima beans, and strawberry pie, he'd abruptly asked Dottie Hanford to marry him. He knew he would eventually, but so quickly? His astonishment only grew when she said yes.

Provided he did two things.

179

THIRTY-FOUR

The heat as Buck and Dottie drove into the District of Columbia was oppressive, with waves undulating from the concrete. Buck's decade-old Dodge had overheated as they came off the Chesapeake Bay Bridge, and he could've kicked himself for not agreeing to take Dottie's two-year-old Studebaker for the ten-day trip they'd planned.

They would be spending the next two days at the home of Leon and Gloria Hendricks, Dottie's parents. It was one of Dottie's two requirements before they got married. It was the easiest of the two to fulfill. The second one scared Buck to death.

Buck's beard was starting to fill in, but was still thin in spots. Dottie hadn't decided if she preferred it, but liked that he was letting his hair grow out.

"It's wavy," she'd said, running her fingers through it. "Not nappy like mine." Buck loved her hair, which she meticulously styled to emulate one of Hollywood's newest stars, Diahann Carroll.

After missing two turns and getting lost within a half-mile of the house, Dottie was finally able to direct Buck to her parent's street. The neighborhood was working-class, Negro. The houses were neatly kept, with manicured lawns and rope swings suspended from oak trees older than the city itself. The Hendricks' home was a tidy gray two-story with a small front porch. It looked exactly as Buck would have expected.

Gloria Hendricks was an older version of her daughter. Early-fifties, perfect posture, elegant. They even spoke the same, with that soft but self-assured voice that Buck had grown to love.

It was a few minutes before Dottie's father joined them in the living room. A brawny and cheerful man who made his living as a pipe fitter. Leon Hendricks wore a plaid shirt, khaki pants, and socks but no shoes. He appeared surprised when he first saw Buck, a not uncommon response when people spotted his missing arm, but he recovered quickly.

Meeting the parents was a new experience, and Buck was uneasy. When Pete had met Elena's mother, it was three days before their city hall wedding. There had been no moment where he had wondered if he was acceptable or not. They were getting married and that was that.

With Dottie's parents, it was different. She'd been married before, but had said little about it. Buck had asked a few questions, but chose to wait until she was ready to talk. After all, he reasoned, he was holding back on his past, too. Mr. and Mrs. Hendricks, though, were full of questions. Buck gave them what he could, but didn't overdo it. "My early life wasn't easy," he'd said, leaving it at that. "Fortunately, I could get away and go to college, and that made all the difference." His parents were dead, he lied. No brothers or sisters; again a lie. He didn't elaborate, hopeful his perfunctory responses would be enough. They must have been, because the conversation quickly moved to other things.

On the second day of their stay, Buck rose early, took a bath, and joined Dottie's mother in the kitchen. Gloria was preparing scrapple, a Maryland delicacy that Buck had grown to love at Mrs. Mitchell's place. Leon entered just as she was putting it on the table.

"I've got eggs, too," she said.

"I'm going to fix that drippy faucet soon as I finish breakfast," Leon said. "Buck, you want to go to the hardware store with me?"

Buck assumed this to be a question with only one answer.

"Yes, sir. And I can help you fix that faucet."

Fifteen minutes later, they were walking in the direction of a neighborhood hardware store. It was already in the low eighties, and the humidity hung over them like a heavy coat.

"Western Auto's just a few blocks up," Leon said, motioning with his head. It was a few more minutes before he spoke again.

"She's happy, Dottie I mean. I can see it."

Buck smiled. "I have to tell you, sir. I never saw it coming." His story about their first encounter at the teacher's meeting, and about how Dottie had chastised him brought a snort of laughter from her father.

"She was always prim and proper," Leon said. "But she also had strong feelings about right and wrong. We read the stories in the paper about the things the two of you did in that little town; the lunch counter and the library. I'm sure Dottie was in her glory, getting to be in the middle of that."

"She had more courage than I did," Buck replied, ducking to avoid a low hanging branch. "She wanted to be out front."

Leon laughed again, then quickly turned somber. "How's the lady who got hit in the head?"

"Mrs. Mitchell spent a couple days in the hospital, then was home and eager to try again. The theater decided to integrate, by the way."

"Sounds like you're making a difference."

"People in Sheffield have been more accepting than some expected," Buck said. "It's going to take some work to integrate the schools, though. I'm sad I won't be working there when the day comes."

Leon patted him on the shoulder. "You'll still have something to do with it, I have no doubt." Then lowering his voice, he said, "You don't say much about your past. Is there something I should know about, just between us men?"

Buck's stomach lurched. Answering Leon's question would require more lies, and he wasn't sure he had them in him.

"Have you known men who had such dismal childhoods that they didn't want to talk about them?" he asked cautiously.

Leon seemed to think on this for a moment, then nodded. "I expect so. More from down South it seems. White man treat you bad?"

Pete shrugged. "I can't really claim that. Just a miserable existence in general. I needed to get away and find what I was capable of. The chance came and I took it."

More silence. When Leon spoke again, his tone was different. More paternal, like Pete's dad had spoken to him when Pete was a boy.

"Whatever your situation was, Buck, you've done good getting past it. Dottie's written to us about how you organize people and work day and night."

"I thought you might wonder when you heard I was fired from the school."

Leon waved his hand like swatting a flea. "Colored people have been taking it for too long, son. You were able to do something about it, and you did. I'm just glad you had the radio job to fall back on, especially when you're marrying my daughter. Speaking of which, when are you tying the knot."

"As soon as we get back to Twinton County," Buck said. Then with a quiet laugh, he added, "She's putting me through the wringer, you know? She demands that I take her to the area where I grew up."

Leon nodded thoughtfully. "What are you going to do in Florida, seeing how you don't have any good memories down there?"

Buck shrugged. "I don't know yet. Maybe take her to the area where I grew up. She seems determined to see it."

Slowing his pace, Leon turned to him. "Determined she is. This isn't like before, with Tyrus. You're a man, Buck. You don't need my blessing on marrying Dottie. Just remember all she went through the first time around and take care of her."

Buck considered asking what Dottie had experienced with her first husband, but in the end left it for later.

"I promise to take care of her, sir."

And that was good enough for Leon Hendricks.

***

They pulled away from Dottie's parents' house with plans to make it to the Georgia line by night. Leon had slipped a copy of *The Negro Motorist Green Book* in Buck's hand as he was getting in the car. The Green Book provided lists of motels and restaurants that were open to Negroes, as well as towns to avoid.

"Things can get strange down that way," he'd offered in the way of explanation. "Of course," Leon added, "you know all about that, being from Florida and all."

Not really, Buck thought. He'd played it white as he made his way from Florida to Iowa five years before. It was only after arriving at Kirkmont that he crossed the racial line for the first time. Nobody questioned the lack of a photo on Hucklebuck's expired driver's license, which he explained had been sliced off by a piece of farm equipment. The Iowa Department of Transportation had been more than happy to issue a new license, with photograph, for Hucklebuck Theodore Roosevelt Jones, a twenty-seven-year-old Negro, just as the remnants of the Florida license stated.

It had been that easy.

"You passed the test," Dottie said, rolling down the window and putting her hand out to draw in some of the slightly cooler morning breeze. She eyed him playfully. "Now let's see how I do in Florida."

It had finally come to this. He had to tell her something, but what? He'd considered taking her to an area of the state as far from Dickerson Springs as he could get. That would pretty much eliminate any chance of encountering people who knew him before.

But it would also be hard to hide his lack of familiarity with the new terrain. He knew the counties where Demo-Fresh markets were located, but beyond there he was less certain.

"I was talking to Daddy," Dottie said. "He really enjoyed your conversation on the way to the hardware store."

"Me too. He's a good man."

"I agree," Dottie said, reaching over and stroking the back of his neck, sending a tingle through his entire body. "He also said I shouldn't make you go home."

What?

"Yeah, he said he'd met men like you before. Who came from bad circumstances. He recommended we change our plans, and I agree. In fact..." she pulled a slip of paper from her purse. "He gave me the name of an Army buddy who lives at a place called Butler Beach. Have you heard of it?"

He hadn't

"It's the only colored beach in North Florida. Mr. Gossetter, Daddy's friend, knows some people there, and he got us a room at the Markwell Motel. Five nights, Daddy and Mother's treat."

It felt like the weight of the world had just been removed from Buck's shoulders.

"There's only one requirement."

Maybe not all the weight of the world.

"We can't stay together until we're married."

"But, we'd talked about having Reverend Tasley back in Pine Hammock marry us."

"Who cares, Buck. I want to marry you and the sooner the better." Dottie's face was animated, happy. "Let's find a justice of the peace as soon as we get there and get it done." She waved a finger at him. "Because, you know, Daddy will be checking."

Buck couldn't imagine being any happier than he was at that moment. He cast a long sideways look at his soon-to-be wife. She was beautiful and smart and she wanted to marry him as much as he wanted her. There was only one small problem.

"We can't make it to Florida by night," he said glumly. "Especially if the car overheats like it did before."

Dottie shook her head, a wry smile on her face. "Sounds like we'll be spending tonight in separate rooms, or you'll be sleeping back there." She motioned to the back seat.

Damn.

Then, a thought.

Buck reached under the seat, pulled out *The Negro Motorist Green Book*, and handed it to Dottie.

"Look and see if there are any Justices of the Peace in Virginia or North Carolina who marry Negroes."

And she did.

THIRTY-FIVE

What started as the happiest moment of Buck's life had become the happiest week. Their wedding ceremony, conducted by a preacher in Mercertown, North Carolina just after sundown was only the beginning. After a honeymoon night in a neat-as-a-pin colored motel on the South Carolina border, they'd continued to Florida.

Everything about Butler Beach was perfect. It was colored only, and the fact that white people were nowhere to be seen allowed everyone to loosen up. There were parties every night, and Buck and Dottie Jones quickly found themselves being pulled into the center of a welcoming and happy culture. A few of their new friends made their permanent homes there. Others were, like Buck and Dottie, visiting tourists from up North.

It was on their next-to-last day that Buck met Vincent Payne. Payne, a long-time Butler Beach homeowner, had made a small fortune in a variety of Florida business ventures. They met over afternoon drinks at the Tic Toc Lounge. Dottie had decided to go to the beach with some of the women she'd met, while Buck joined their husbands at the Tic Toc. The discussion had turned to civil rights, and Buck let slip that he'd been involved with some integration efforts in Maryland.

"I read about that," Payne said. "The *Florida Star* picked up the story. You integrated a lunch counter and a movie theater, right?"

Buck nodded, suddenly uneasy that the story had found its way to Florida. What if someone from Dickerson Springs read it?

"*Florida Star*?"

"The black paper out of Jacksonville," Payne replied. "It's very popular here."

The longer they visited, the more Buck discovered they had in common, particularly on the topic of integration. For Buck, it was a matter of right and wrong. That weighed heavily on Payne as well, but for him integration also made good business sense.

"I know how to make money," he said in a tone that Buck didn't view as bragging, but as a matter of fact. "If integration gives me the chance to make money off white people, I win."

Buck couldn't argue with the logic. He'd taken an immediate liking to Vincent Payne. Fifty-something, svelte, stylish in every way except a conk hairstyle that had been preferred in the forties and fifties by stars like Cab Callaway and Eddie South, Payne had piercing eyes that seemed to bore into Buck when they talked. Though he could have bought and sold most of the men in the Tic Toc, Payne came across as an everyday sort. When he found out about Buck's radio work, Payne's interest increased.

"I'm starting a radio station down the road here a piece," Payne said excitedly. "All black all the time. The signal will reach Daytona and Jacksonville, so we'll have listeners at Bethune-Cookman College down South and Edward Waters College up North."

"That's good coverage," Buck replied, waving at the bartender for another beer.

"Highest radio tower in North Florida," Payne said. "Daytime signal might reach all the way to Orlando. I'd like to do for our people down here what you've been doing in Maryland; help the effort to integrate and everything. Florida has really dragged its feet."

"Programming to Negroes all day will help," Buck said. "I'm only on from five to ten at night. The signal's not that strong, but it does reach parts of Baltimore and DC."

Payne nodded, his eyes continuing to bore in. "You ever thought of a change? I plan to be up and running by the first of January. I could use a station manager who knows how to program to our people."

Buck took a draw from his beer, buying time. He and Dottie had certainly enjoyed their time at Butler Beach. He'd forgotten how nice the beach could be in summer; comfortable despite the pressing temperatures. It was Dottie's first experience on the coast, and, while excited about beginning school at Maryland State, she dreaded having to leave.

But there was also the geography to consider. Butler Beach was less than two-hundred miles from the closest Demo-Fresh store. Was that far enough? The chances of running into someone he knew were certainly more likely than on Maryland's Eastern Shore.

"Is it money?" Payne's question pulled Buck away from his thoughts. His silence had been interpreted by the older man as a negotiating ploy. Might as well play it that way.

"Maybe... and my wife's situation."

"One thing at a time. How much are you making at your station?"

Buck remembered enough from his days at Demo-Fresh not to divulge everything. He named a number that represented his combined salaries at the station and what he'd been making as a teacher. Payne's eyes grew large, like the number was beyond anything he would consider. Buck let him have his moment.

"No," Payne said, turning his stool slightly away. Buck's only response was a shrug of indifference. Payne finally bit.

"Seriously?"

Buck nodded.

"And your wife..."

"Dottie."

"Yes. What does she do?"

"She's starting grad school in two weeks."

Vincent Payne's eyebrows arched slightly. "My brother, Charles is on the Board of Trustees at Bethune-Cookman. I'm sure something could be worked out."

Buck stroked his spotty beard as he considered Payne's comments. He seemed sincere, but it was a lot to digest when he and Dottie were leaving the next day.

"You're heading home tomorrow?"

Was the man a mind-reader?

"Yes, sir."

"Can you stay a couple more days? I can make some introductions for your wife, take you to see where we're building the station." He paused, a smile crossing his face. "Maybe get you to reconsider your salary requirements."

"Let me talk to Dottie, Mr. Payne. I'll let you know."

"Well, if you decide to stay, you'll be guests at my home."

***

Payne picked them up from the Markwell Motel at ten the next morning, stowing their luggage in the trunk of his gleaming white Eldorado convertible. The sun was blazing, and Payne had the top up, but when Buck crawled into the front seat, he knew why. Ice-cold conditioned air blew from air vents on the dashboard, the first time he'd experienced that in an automobile.

Dottie sat in back for the hour-long drive to Daytona Beach. Her excitement the night before at being told of Buck's meeting hadn't waned, and she tossed dozens of questions at Payne as he drove. They had agreed to drop her off for a prearranged meeting with the Head of Bethune-Cookman's Education Department. While they met, Payne would show Buck the site of the new radio station, a remote area near the town of Palm Coast.

"Would there be any possibility of living at Butler Beach?" Dottie asked.

"It would leave you with a bit of a drive to Daytona," Payne said, "but there are people who do it. You could drop Buck off on the way, or leave a spare car at the radio station."

By noon, Buck and Payne were standing in front of a partially completed block building. Behind it, an installation crew was busy putting up what would be the station's broadcast tower.

"It's off the beaten path," Payne said, "but the real estate was inexpensive and, as you know, not many people go to a radio station anyway." He unrolled a set of blueprints and spread them out on the Cadillac's scalding hood.

"The studios are here," he pointed at a sizable area of the design. "These are recording rooms. Offices over here." The studio would dwarf the outdated WSCM facility in Sheffield.

"This area will be the station manager's office." Payne placed a manicured nail on one corner. "Somebody's going to have some pretty sweet digs."

It sounded perfect, as had everything they'd heard thus far. Could it be?

***

They arrived at Payne's elegant home at four. He introduced them to his elderly housekeeper.

"Zella will take care of you this evening," he said apologetically. "I have meetings in Jacksonville that will keep me there until very late. I know you have a lot to discuss, so this will provide you the opportunity. We can visit more tomorrow."

And with that he was gone.

Vincent Payne's was the first house either of them had seen with an indoor-outdoor swimming pool. Given the fact that it and the ocean were less than fifty yards apart, it seemed an unnecessary extravagance, but they sure enjoyed splashing around like little kids while Zella drifted in and out of the house, filling glasses and taking the occasional telephone call.

Zella called them to dinner at six. Payne was a lifelong bachelor who knocked around in a house large enough for a family of ten. Zella, it turned out, had her own quarters in one corner of the home. Dinner was served in a formal dining room, at a table large enough to seat twelve. They'd had so much fun in the pool, they'd barely talked about the day. After serving the food and instructing Buck to ring a small tableside bell when they were ready for dessert, Zella exited, closing the door behind her.

"Bethune Cookman was wonderful," Dottie exclaimed between bites of red snapper, asparagus, roasted potatoes, and a fruit medley. "I was afraid I was being pushed upon them, but Professor Chivas said that wasn't the case. He was excited that I might be coming."

"It all seems so quick, though, don't you think?" The proximity to the Demopoulos family continued to concern Buck. "Besides, I'm not sure Mr. Payne can meet my salary demands."

"Then lower them," Dottie said, waving her fork at him. "Can you imagine living someplace where you can walk to the beach every day?"

"Yeah, but... I'm just not sure. We've really grown to like Pine Hammock and..."

Dottie looked at him skeptically. "What's really bothering you, Buck?"

Buck sat straighter in his chair. "Like I said, Pine Hammock has become our home, and I'd hate to leave."

Dottie stood and moved to a large picture window overlooking the pool and, beyond that, the Atlantic Ocean.

"What is there in Pine Hammock that can compare to *that*?" she asked, waving at the beach.

Her point was well-taken, and she seemed so happy. Her face was glowing, her eyes bright with anticipation. Despite Buck's misgivings, Dottie had, in her mind, already moved to Butler Beach.

And that was good enough for him.

THIRTY-SIX

"And finally, with just days to go until the Presidential election, many voters in Twinton County are still on the fence. A straw poll conducted this week by WSCM Station Owner Paul Adams showed forty-nine percent of residents saying they would vote for Senator John Kennedy, while forty-six percent were leaning toward Vice-President Nixon. Five percent indicated they are still undecided. Time will tell how Twinton County and the nation vote on November eighth. For WSCM News, I'm Buck Jones filling in for Arley Ferguson."

As the midday announcer introduced a Perry Como selection, Buck shucked off the headset and headed for the break room.

"You've got a good voice for news," Mr. Adams said, chewing on a ham and cheese sandwich, "and the beard has come in nicely."

Buck expressed his thanks as he reached into the refrigerator and pulled out a leftover plate of fried chicken. Since informing Mr. Adams of his imminent departure for Butler Beach, the station owner had encouraged him to assume a variety of roles in addition to his regular evening air shift. That week alone he'd been delivering the news while regular newscaster Arley Ferguson visited his daughter in New Jersey. He'd also put together several station announcements, reviewed new music received from various record companies, and even sold airtime. It was proving to be invigorating, further exciting Buck about his new position.

"So, the guy you're working for..." Mr. Adams searched for the name.

"Mr. Payne. Vincent Payne."

Mr. Adams snapped his fingers. "Yeah. He has no experience in radio?"

"None. He's sort of a generalist. Real estate, a bank, even an orange grove."

"Then you need to be ready to hit the ground running," Mr. Adams said, wiping mustard from his face with a soiled napkin. "It sounds like you're going to have a lot to do."

"Hiring the on-air talent will be first," Buck said, chomping into a cold chicken thigh. "The ads are placed, and I'm hoping to get some good applicants."

"If he pays them as well as he's paying you, it won't be a problem." When Buck had first approached Mr. Adams with the news he was leaving, the owner tried to convince him to stay. That included a couple of generous salary increases, but nothing that came close to what Buck's salary would be in Florida. While Buck never told him the exact amount he would be making, Mr. Adams had been able to deduce that it was significant."

Following lunch and a few minutes of conversation, Buck returned to the small room where the hourly newscasts were assembled and delivered. This part of the job wasn't demanding. Most news stories were culled from the various news services to which the station subscribed. Others came from local newspapers. Buck couldn't remember the last time Arley Ferguson had actually investigated and written an original story. It was a matter of minutes before he was ready with the one o'clock report, allowing him time to relax.

He considered calling home, before remembering that Dottie was substitute teaching in Somerset County. After deciding to make the move to Florida, she'd demurred at starting grad school at Maryland State, choosing to spend the time earning extra money as a substitute teacher. She'd recently concluded a six-week gig filling in for an elementary teacher on maternity leave and was now subbing at a Negro high school.

And married life? Buck smiled at the thought. Soon after they'd returned, dozens of students they'd taught at Pine Hammock formed a human chain, moving Buck's meager belongings the three blocks from Mrs. Mitchell's place to Dottie's house. Many of them still stopped by to visit, lamenting how different the school was.

"Nobody tells us to stand up for our rights," Jerome Gilliam confided to Buck. Jerome had come a long way since having the paddle taken to him fourteen months earlier. Now a junior, with arms and upper body testifying to the work he'd put in learning to throw the shot, Jerome was aiming for a track and field scholarship at Maryland State.

But nobody was sorrier to see Buck leave than Mrs. Mitchell. Not wanting to encounter Biggerstaff any more than necessary, Buck only visited his former landlady in the daytime when school was in session.

"Who gonna keep up the fight?" she'd asked several times. It was a question that Buck couldn't answer. Progress had been steady and ongoing since the incident at the movie theater last summer. All but one Sheffield restaurant were integrated, along with every store and even one church. The lone holdout? The school.

"You ask me, Landon Biggerstaff is feathering his own nest," Mrs. Mitchell had said. "They close Pine Hammock, that boy might be without a job." Sadly, she was probably right. It had happened in other counties, where desegregation was heralded until it cost Negro teachers and principals their jobs.

And that had been when Buck had his idea. He'd asked Mr. Adams to set it up, given how respected he was in town. He could easily get an audience with the superintendent, Dr. Leonard Mister. He'd readily agreed, not even asking the nature of the interview. It would take place tomorrow evening. Live.

***

After his last news report at three, Buck raced home to rest up in preparation for his return to the airwaves at five. Dottie was usually home by four, which meant they had thirty minutes to catch up before Buck left again. He sat in the living room and eyed the street as four o'clock came and went. At four-fifteen, he went to the bedroom and changed shirts. When he returned, there was still no sign of her. Resigned that he would have to get by without a few minutes with the person who'd changed his life, he left for work.

Nightside progressed without a hitch, though Buck would be the first to admit that he was mailing it in these days. He picked music he liked by his favorite performers, meaning there was a lot of Jackie Wilson, The Drifters, and Dinah Washington and not so much Chubby Checker or Sam Cooke.

"It's time for your goodnight calls on *Nightside*," Buck intoned into the microphone, stopping for a moment for a quick drink of water to curb the dry throat that came from too much time on the air. The phone lines were already lighting up, and Buck progressed through them one by one, speaking with many voices he'd heard before. Larry, Martinique, Daisy. They were regulars who always made sure to say a special good night to Hucklebuck and his love.

"And who do we have on this line?" Buck asked.

"This is Mrs. Hucklebuck," she replied. And it was. Buck grinned at her playful voice. It was the first time Dottie had called in, and with no idea what to expect he rolled with it.

"And what may I do for you, Mrs. Hucklebuck, you lovely thing?"

Dottie giggled. "I didn't get to say good-bye to my husband before he went off to work the night shift."

"And why was that, Mrs. Hucklebuck? Were you delayed at work?"

"Noooooo," she drew out the word, teasing him. "I had an appointment."

"Um-hmm," Buck said, his voice light. "That's what women say who are stepping out on their men. You're not stepping out on your man, are you, Mrs. Hucklebuck?"

"I'm afraid I am. I stepped out this afternoon... with Dr. Drewson down in Princess Anne."

Buck hadn't known she had a doctor's appointment.

"And did you and Dr. Drewson have a lot to talk about?"

When she spoke again, her voice was emotional. Not sing-songy like before.

"Yes, we did. It seems there's a new development he wanted to tell me about. Something involving you, Mr. Hucklebuck."

Buck flashed through memories of meetings he'd had with Daniel Drewson, an honorable man who cared for many Pine Hammock residents. He recalled a discussion regarding possible protests about segregated wards at two area hospitals. That had to be it.

"Is there a new development at Hickson Memorial Hospital?"

"I don't know anything about that, Mr. Hucklebuck, but there is a new development *in me*. We're having a baby!"

Oh, my goodness. Could it really be? Unable to adequately process this bit of information, Buck started giggling. He knew he sounded like a little girl, but didn't care.

"Dottie? Are you sure?"

"Um-hmm."

The giggling became joyful tears as Buck forgot for a moment where he was.

"I'm on my way home right now, honey. I love you!"

"Buck, you still have another hour—"

"Folks, as you heard, there's going to be an addition to our family. If you don't mind, I'm going to call it a night and go be with my wife. So... I guess that's it... Good Night!"

***

He had no recollection of how he'd gotten home, other than it had taken half the usual time. Dottie looked up from the sofa, surprised at his arrival. He ran to her, tripping and almost falling on a loose floor board before righting himself and plopping down next to her. He started to giggle again.

"You're a real sight, do you know that?" Dottie said playfully, pinching his cheek. "A person would think you just received some good news."

Buck giggled some more.

"Dr. Drewson says it will probably happen next July. He's going to talk to some friends and find us a good doctor in Florida. He said we're okay to head South when we get done here, but we shouldn't plan any long trips after that."

Buck continued to giggle. He didn't realize how silly he looked until Dottie started laughing too.

"I had no idea how you'd respond, but I didn't expect it to be like this," she teased. "Did you even bother to turn off the transmitter or is the station still on the air?"

Buck stopped giggling, his eyes growing large.

"Come on, Mr. Hucklebuck," Dottie said, pulling him from the couch. "Let's go to Sheffield and shut the place down, then we'll come back here and have our own little celebration."

She started toward the door, but he pulled her back and wrapped her in an embrace.

"Dottie Jones, I love you with everything I got in me," he said, looking deeply into her eyes. "You've just made me the happiest man in Twinton County."

He kissed her lightly several times, then harder. She returned his kisses then took his hand and led him from the living room. The transmitter would have to wait.

THIRTY-SEVEN

"It's Friday night and you're listening to *Nightside*. I'm pleased to have in the studio with me the superintendent of Twinton County Schools, Dr. Leonard Mister. Dr. Mister, welcome.

"Thank you, Buck."

Buck looked across the small table where the superintendent was seated. He'd done a monthly segment with Mr. Adams for years, and it was obvious that Dr. Mister was comfortable behind the microphone. As always, he was attired in a conservative suit, white shirt, and maroon tie.

Buck had spent hours mulling over how best to proceed with the interview, knowing from what Biggerstaff had mentioned last summer that the superintendent had a desegregation plan that was pitifully inadequate. Dr. Mister was used to being kowtowed to in Twinton County, and Buck imagined he was expected to follow suit. That wouldn't happen. After learning that he and Dottie had a child on the way, Buck's fervor for equality was reaching new heights. He would remain professional, but there would still be some hard questions.

"Dr. Mister, you've been a regular on this station in the past, but many of our *Nightside* listeners may not be

201

familiar with you. Will you tell our audience a little bit about your background?"

Buck reviewed his list of questions while the superintendent rolled out his credentials. He'd considered referring to him as Leonard, but thought that might come off as disrespectful. He wanted Dr. Mister to convict himself for the slowness of integration in Twinton County and that would best be achieved slowly and respectfully.

"Most of our listeners, you might know, sir, are Negroes. Many have been involved with the efforts to integrate local businesses and institutions, and they're wondering why it's taking so long to integrate our schools. What can you say to them?"

Fully expecting the question, Superintendent Mister leaned into the microphone, never taking his eyes from Buck.

"We have been slow, Buck. I won't deny that. By nature, I'm a cautious man, and the last thing I want to do is disrupt the learning taking place in our schools, white and colored." He took a sip of water and continued.

"With the help of our local school board, we now have a plan that will allow for integration of our schools. Beginning in a couple years, we will offer an innovative program called school choice."

The superintendent went on to describe the same ideas Dottie had gleaned last summer from Biggerstaff. Parents would be able to choose which Twinton County school their children attend, regardless of their race. His pride was evident as he ticked off the benefits of the voluntary program. Buck let him have his moment in the sun.

"In fact, Buck, as you know, your beautiful bride was offered a position at Sheffield High School this past year. We were disappointed that she turned it down, but will begin anew the process of integrating our teaching staff for the upcoming school year."

Buck nodded thoughtfully, as though considering the gravity of Dr. Mister's comments, when he was actually giving his audience time to chew on what the superintendent had just proposed.

"So, Dr. Mister, in two years, colored children will have the opportunity to enroll at the elementary and high schools in Sheffield?"

"That's right," Dr. Mister was smiling, proud that he was paving the way for the next generation of Twinton County Negro children. "We're excited about that, Buck. It's the right thing to do."

"If it's the right thing to do, Dr. Mister, then why isn't it happening this fall?" Buck's question brought a flash of concern to Dr. Mister's face, but he recovered quickly.

"Our school board and I have watched how integration has played out in places like Little Rock. We want to avoid the… hostilities they've experienced."

"And those hostilities will not be a problem in 1965?"

The superintendent licked his lips.

"We feel we can use the time between now and then to… *prepare* people for integration."

"Doctor, are you aware of the successes Twinton County has had over the past year in terms of integration? The library, stores and lunch counters, the movie theater?"

"Well, Buck, I don't live in a cocoon." Mister's laugh was harsh, forced. His eyes were boring in on Buck with a message that warned it was best to tread lightly.

"Then you are aware that, in almost every incidence, integration happened without violence or injury and that—"

"What about that colored lady? The one who got hit in the head? That's the kind of thing we're trying to avoid, Buck."

Buck noticed the phone lines were full, despite having not yet solicited listener calls. This could get interesting.

"Do you anticipate white children transferring to the school in Pine Hammock, Doctor?"

"They'll certainly have the opportunity." Sweat was forming on the superintendent's forehead. Buck plucked a tissue from a box and handed it over.

"But do you think any will transfer?"

Mister dabbed at his forehead. When he finished, a small piece of tissue remained just above his eyebrow.

"I just can't say. I would anticipate that some of the families that live out in the country closer to Pine Hammock might consider it."

"Would you send your children to Pine Hammock, Dr. Mister?"

The superintendent laughed uncertainly. His eyes darting around as if looking for an exit.

"My children are grown... gone off to live other places, so I can't—"

"If they were school age, would you allow them to go to Pine Hammock?"

Mister shook his head, but said nothing. His usual confident demeanor was gone, but Buck expected he might still mount an argument.

"Listen, Buck, as I said earlier, integration is way past due. We have a plan that will remedy that situation. I thought you would find that to be a positive step."

"Dr. Mister, when was the last time you were in Pine Hammock School?"

"I visit all my schools regularly. I can't say exactly when, but... regularly."

"What do you know about the textbooks they use there?"

"They're the same ones we use at Sheffield."

"Aren't they actually the books that Sheffield is no longer using, Doctor? And how about quantities? Can you tell me if students at Sheffield have to share textbooks?"

Mister's fists were balled up in his lap. His face was crimson and growing darker.

"Because they do share books at Pine Hammock. Three books to a student in some classes—"

"That's a lie!"

"Is it? I was there, Doctor. I experienced it every day. And desks – did you know that there aren't enough desks? When the white kids start coming to Pine Hammock, will they get desks, or will they sit on the floor like some Negro children have to do? Are there any white children sitting on the floor at Sheffield School, Dr. Mister?"

Silence.

"This is radio, sir. You must respond. Is there anything I've asserted that you would like to dispute?"

Silence.

"Dr. Mister?"

The superintendent rose from his chair and left the studio. Buck turned his microphone so that listeners could hear the sound of his footsteps and the door closing behind him. Then nothing. Buck let the emptiness hang in the air for fifteen seconds.

"That was Dr. Leonard Mister, Twinton County Superintendent of Schools. He has chosen to leave rather than continue our interview, so I'll open his time to you, our listeners. What are your thoughts about what you've just heard?

For the next hour, the airwaves were filled with anger and impatience.

"It ain't right that we don't have books."

"Why is it taking so long?"

"Why aren't there any Negroes on the school board?"

"My boys went there all through school, and I never saw that white superintendent."

"They need to tear that old Pine Hammock School down. It's in such bad shape and nobody from up in Sheffield does a thing about it."

A few, however, questioned the concept of school integration.

"I don't want my kids going to school with white children."

"We're better off apart. They'll never treat our children as good as their own."

Buck alternated between the roles of moderator, judge, psychologist, and referee. Then, just before ten, a deep-voiced male identified himself.

"C. Clayton Cooper, Baltimore, Maryland."

Buck blinked. It was a name he knew.

"I understand you're friends with Desmond Henry," Cooper said. Buck acknowledged that he was, and that Desmond had covered integration activities in Twinton County.

"I've been listening to your program." Cooper's tone was measured and thoughtful. "It might be time for a rally in Twinton County. Would you help us get the word out?"

Buck was momentarily stumped. C. Clayton Cooper's reputation as an extreme left-wing civil rights leader was well-known. His Black Liberal Party had grown in leaps and bounds as a good number of younger Negroes, shocked by the violence coming out of the South, had grown weary of Dr. King's non-violent approach. There had so far been only sporadic reports of the Black Liberal Party inciting violence or damaging property, but from Buck's perspective, Cooper was looking to take it to the next level.

"Mr. Cooper, the black people of Twinton County appreciate your support, but peaceful integration has worked here so far. I think it's best that we let the local powers-that-be take what they've heard tonight and make decisions that will benefit all children.

"So that's what you think? Even after being fed that honky BS about three years. You know that cracker's plan ain't got a chance in hell of—"

Buck winced. The language wasn't appropriate for radio. "—Mr. Cooper, I'm going to have to let you go, but again, thank you for your concern." Hitting the disconnect button, Buck quickly closed out the show.

One thing he knew for certain; C. Clayton Cooper was a man best kept out of Twinton County.

THIRTY-EIGHT

"Did you get any sleep?" Dottie asked, pouring Buck a cup of coffee. She was off for another day of substitute teaching. He would be reading news from ten until two, then doing his usual shift.

"Not much," he replied. "Be honest with me, sweetheart, did it go too far?" Last night, he might have asked, 'Did *I* go too far?'; but after turning it over in his mind again and again when he should've been sleeping, he felt he'd only asked the questions that needed asking. All that remained was the issue of whether he should have pulled back sooner.

"It was difficult to listen to," Dottie admitted. "But he came across as so... *smug* in the beginning; like he knew there was a problem, but was going to take his own sweet time fixing it."

Buck took a sip of coffee.

"You're right, but... I don't know what came over me, honey. Maybe I hoped he would acquiesce. Decide the timeline needed to be moved ahead." Buck paused for a moment. "Maybe I finally saw him for who he is. Not the mythical figure that everyone holds him up to be, but just a man."

Dottie smiled sadly. "A man with his own shortcomings." She poured herself a cup of coffee and joined him at the table. "You know, Buck, I've had a few interactions with him. He's never disrespected me. Quite the contrary, he's always acted like he held me in high regard. I don't think he even realized there was anything wrong with the way things are, at least until recently. But last night was—"

From the living room, the telephone rang. Buck glanced at the clock as he went to answer it. Seven-twenty.

"Buck? That you?"

"It is. Good morning, Mr. Adams."

The station owner loudly cleared his throat, then apologized for the earliness of the hour.

"Last night's show has caused quite a ruckus. Can you come in early?"

Buck's breath caught. "How early, sir? I'm scheduled to be there at ten."

Silence for a few beats, then Mr. Adams answered. "Now."

***

Anticipating that it might be needed, Buck had recorded his previous evening's program in its entirety. The station secretary had been called in earlier that morning to type a transcript of the interview. Now, shoehorned in the tiny closet they referred to as an auxiliary studio, he and Mr. Adams replayed his interview with the superintendent. Hearing it from this side of the mic, Buck had to admit parts were difficult to listen to.

It was also great radio.

Mr. Adams had readily admitted that he hadn't tuned in the night before, something about a church meeting. Buck watched him closely as the tape played, seeing his face register concern, anger, and disappointment.

Everything you would want a listener to experience.

Then, when the interview concluded, they listened to two hours of listener calls, pausing only long enough for Mr. Adams to inform the morning deejay that he needed to stick around to do news.

The room was becoming claustrophobic, and Buck couldn't get a feel for what Mr. Adams was thinking as they listened to the calls. The anger and sadness in the voices raised emotions in Buck he hadn't felt the night before.

Then, they came to the call from C. Clayton Cooper. His voice had an edge; something about it unnerved Buck. He could see it did the same to Mr. Adams.

"Is he somebody important?"

Buck rubbed his beard. Unsure what to say for a moment. Mr. Adams motioned for him to speak.

"He's... somebody who is trying to become somebody bigger," Buck said cautiously. "Three years ago, when he was still Clay Cooper, he was part of Dr. King's movement; not an insider, really, but close enough to get his picture in a few national magazines."

"I suppose that's not bad," Mr. Adams said. "Dr. King has impressed me with what he's accomplished."

"But," Buck held up his index finger. "C. Clayton Cooper had a falling out with Dr. King over ideology. From what I understand, he grew tired of the non-violence and black people getting beat up. He left and started his own group. There hasn't been much written about them, but you hear things."

"Do you think he'll follow through?"

This was a tough question. Cooper and his ilk were unpredictable.

"I think... he'll go where the camera lenses are most likely to find him," Buck said slowly. "That definitely wouldn't be Twinton County. We're far enough from the big cities that any press coverage would be minimal."

"That makes me feel better." Mr. Adams moved to relax in his chair, then quickly straightened back up.

"Buck, you should have provided Superintendent Mister with the questions in advance."

They sat for a few moments, staring at one another. Buck felt something shift inside himself. This conversation could become anything he wanted it to be, but he reminded himself that Mr. Adams had come far in his support of Buck and civil rights in Sheffield. Now he was suggesting Buck should have throttled back, an assertion he wasn't sure he liked.

"Which questions should I not have asked?"

Mr. Adams perused the transcript, then went back and read it slower, finally placing his finger on a section. "How about here, where you asked him if he thought white students would enroll at Pine Hammock. Don't you feel that was antagonistic on your part, Buck?"

Buck glanced at his copy, refreshing his memory and formulating a response. "Parents being able to choose what school their children attend is the backbone of his plan, Mr. Adams. There's little question that black parents will want their children at Sheffield, particularly after you see what Pine Hammock School is like. But do you really think a white family will send their kids down there?"

Mr. Adams took a deep breath as he ran his fingers through his thinning hair. It was obvious that he was troubled. Five minutes passed without a word, as the station manager read and re-read the transcript. Finally, gathering what Buck supposed was resolve from some deeper source he didn't necessarily believe in, Mr. Adams laid aside the transcript and looked at him.

"When I bought this station, I was thirty-one years old," he said, his voice low. "Just about your age. I'd done news at a couple Philadelphia stations and wanted nothing more than to come out here and make a name for myself."

"I assure you, sir, this wasn't about making a name for my—" Mr. Adams motioned for Buck to be quiet.

"Please, let me finish. Anyway, I started with an investigative news story that doesn't mean much now, but in 1947, was huge – paving Main Street."

Mr. Adams smiled at the memory. "The city council hired Smokey Hartung to pave Main Street. I pointed out on the air that Smokey was the brother of Breezy Hartung, one of the city councilmen; a blatant violation of the city's nepotism policy."

Buck tried to envisage the usually taciturn Mr. Adams railing on the radio against the city fathers. He couldn't summon up the image.

"Well, I made my point. Shamed the city council into hiring a paving guy from Fruitland." He shook his head. "He wound up costing a third more than Breezy would have and did a piss-poor job to boot. Two years later, Breezy Hartung redid most of the job out of his own pocket. I lost a bunch of business over it. Some of it never came back."

Mr. Adams stood up and stretched. His shoulders were stooped and he looked older than he had the day before.

"The point I'm trying to make, Buck, is that in this business we sometimes have to tamp down on what we really want in favor of what's best for our livelihood. You and I have weathered storms before, and I've supported you, but this time the response is significant. Several advertisers – big ones – phoned me last night to say they'd be pulling their business if I didn't discipline you."

A feeling of fight or flight pulled at Buck, but he pushed it away.

"In four weeks you leave for Florida, and I believe you're going to do great things there. But for here, and now, it's about the survival of this station. I'll likely never fill your shoes, and most, if not all, the colored advertising you've brought in will dry up. Still, I have to hang on to what I've got."

When Buck stood, Mr. Adams' eyes grew wide. Fear? Perhaps, but Buck was the least fearsome-looking person in Twinton County. More like the uneasiness of having to do something that doesn't come naturally. This was hard for Mr. Adams, and Buck decided he would do what he could to make it easier.

"I'll clear out my things and be gone," he said, pushing open the door.

"Buck."

Buck turned. They were barely four feet apart, and he saw the concern his boss had for him.

"I was going to suggest you resign rather than forcing me to let you go," Mr. Adams said tentatively. "It might look better for you. Either way, I'm paying you through the end of the month."

Buck considered the option of resigning. With the paychecks continuing through December, it meant they would be free to head South whenever he and Dottie chose. They still had to find a place to live, and Christmas spent in the shade of a palm tree was alluring.

Then, other thoughts crowded in.

Mrs. Mitchell, her head bloodied, lying on the floor of the movie theater, smiling brightly despite the blow she'd taken, saying, "We done good, Buck! We done good!"

Dr. Watson at Miggetts lunch counter, eating a bowl of ice cream on the same stool where he'd been refused service years before.

Entire families from Pine Hammock trekking to the Twinton County Public Library to check out books.

Suddenly the palm tree wasn't so important.

"You'll have to fire me, Mr. Adams," Buck said steadily. "And keep the paychecks. I won't take them."

THIRTY-NINE

At ten-past-five there was a knock at the front door. Dottie went to answer while Buck stirred a pot of vegetable soup bubbling on the stove.

"Come in, Doctor."

Buck turned down the stove and stepped into the living room. Dr. Watson stood framed in the doorway, a heavy winter-weight trenchcoat hanging from his stooped frame.

"Why aren't you on the radio?"

"Well, I... the station—"

"Step inside out of the cold, Dr. Watson. Let me help you with your coat," Dottie said, taking note of Buck's discomfort.

"I know you got supper cooking and don't want to keep you. Buck, was it the interview with the superintendent?"

Buck rubbed the back of his neck. "Yes, sir."

A change came over the elderly doctor. His eyes contained a fire Buck hadn't seen, even that night at the lunch counter. He swore, loudly and profanely, using expletives Buck would have never thought he knew.

"You did your job," he said angrily. "You asked questions that needed answering, and as is usually the case, the white man couldn't answer for what he'd done."

Dr. Watson's harangue was interrupted by another rap on the door. Poop Chester, sober and awake, raged inside.

"He got you fired, din't he? Same bastard that set me up all them years ago got you too?" Poop's invectives made Dr. Watson's seem like nursery rhymes.

"Poop, settle down... Dr. Watson, there's more to the story than—"

Someone else was at the door. Dottie opened it and gasped. Buck scurried to her side. Jerome Gilliam and four other boys from Pine Hammock School were standing there. Behind them, Mrs. Mitchell was making her way up the oyster-shell-paved walkway. Other cars were pulling off the road. Within minutes, the living room was full. Sixteen people stood about, venting their anger in small groups amidst partially-packed moving boxes. The phone rang several times, but with the din it was pointless to answer. The temperature in the crowded room spiked, and Buck was perspiring through his sweater. Dottie scared him nearly to death when she climbed upon a folding chair to get everyone's attention.

"Buck and I appreciate your coming by. It's true he was let go by the radio station this morning. As you can see, we've decided to make our move to Florida a bit earlier than planned. We will miss you all and thank you for making us feel—"

"We need to do something!" Mrs. Mitchell's declaration met with resounding support, particularly from the high school boys.

"Let's go see that man at the radio station," one called out. "Who's with me?" His friends and a couple of adults raised their hands. In the background the phone continued to ring. Three more people arrived and, hearing the commotion, let themselves in.

"You need to say something," Dottie murmured, grabbing Buck by the sleeve as the gathering grew more boisterous. The feelings were real. They were angry that their voices had been stilled. Moving the folding chair

Dottie had been using to the center of the room, Buck raised himself unsteadily. Balance had always been a problem, and he thought he might fall until Jerome moved closer, offering his shoulder for support.

"It is true that—" When the phone rang again, Buck glanced at his wife, standing in the kitchen door, trying to keep the gathering confined to the living room. "Dottie, when it stops ringing will you take it off the hook, please?" Then, turning his attention to the gathering, he continued, "I'm no longer with WSCM. Regrettably, the station owner succumbed to the pressure exerted by a few advertisers and released me this morning."

"They's got some white guy on there playing Ray Charles and trying to sound colored." Though Mrs. Mitchell was yelling at a pitch much too loud for the tiny room, the others seemed to feed off it. Buck raised his hand for silence, then continued.

"Please remember the good we've accomplished over the past year. The businesses that have integrated, the institutions that have opened their doors to us." Buck's words were met with a couple amens and some light applause, but not so much that Dr. Watson wasn't easily heard over the din.

"It's not *enough*." As one, all heads turned to the gray-haired old man who'd tended to everyone in the room at one time or another. Usually congenial and soft-spoken, the doctor seemed bent on having his say.

"I've been the doctor in Pine Hammock for forty-one years. For twenty-five of those years, I wasn't given hospital privileges anyplace except the Negro hospital in Hermanville. It was a big thing when Sheffield integrated, but fifteen years later our people are still segregated in the colored ward down in the basement. More to the point, it's been my dream that a young person like one of these boys here," he pointed at Jerome and his classmates, "would take my position as town doctor. Despite the wonderful teachers we have, I don't think it can ever happen as things stand today. Our children don't have enough desks or books. Our teachers put up with classrooms with forty children. No school cafeteria. No sports teams..." his oration, as gripping as it was, was causing Dr. Watson to labor. He stopped for a minute, emitting a wracking cough. When he looked up, tears were trickling down his cheeks.

"Whitey says three more years, but as Buck and Dottie know, his plan is flawed. Most of our children will never see the inside of Sheffield School, and we certainly know that no white family's going to let theirs come to Pine Hammock. Why would they?"

He paused for another coughing fit. No one said a word.

"Something has to happen..." he continued, stepping back into the crowd that had grown by another half-dozen while he spoke "...I just don't know what."

Jerome used the opportunity to take center stage. Watching him now, Buck could hardly believe he was the same boy who'd taken a savage beating at the hands of Landon Biggerstaff fifteen months before. At sixteen, he looked and talked like a man, but usually displayed a gentle nature that disarmed most with whom he came into contact. Usually.

"That man who called in... C. Clayton Cooper, I've seen him on television. Maybe we need to take him up on his offer to come down. He could shake up those—"

"No!" Buck said loudly from his perch, squeezing Jerome's shoulder.

"You need to consider something like that very carefully," he said, looking at Jerome, but speaking to everyone. C. Clayton Cooper has some... different political views and could be a loose cannon."

"He worked with Dr. King," another boy said. "Since going on his own, he's helped Negroes in Kentucky and Ohio. I read about him, too."

"He really worked with Dr. King?" a man in his twenties, newly arrived with his wife and infant son in tow, asked.

216

"Used to," Jerome replied. "I think if we get him here, he'll spread the word. Mr. Jones got things started on the radio last night, but like Dr. Watson said, we need more."

The tide was turning, and there was little Buck could do to stem it. The allure of a nationally-known civil rights leader coming to Twinton County was turning the heads of even the older members of the community. As the discussion wound down, Buck cautioned Jerome and the others to consider C. Clayton Cooper's political leanings, but his warnings fell on deaf ears.

"We have to hope he's too busy to consider coming to someplace like this," Dottie said later, after the last of their visitors had left. "Because if he does show up, who knows what might happen."

FORTY

"It's from Professor Chivas," Dottie said, holding up the letter. "My schedule at Bethune-Cookman. I'm taking twelve hours and teaching nine. I'm going to be busy."

"We might not see each other until June," Buck said, carefully placing more of Dottie's books in a box. The packing was nearly done, and with some luck, they'd be in Florida within the week, staying for free in a duplex Vincent Payne owned until they found a place of their own. His offer was a godsend, as they were down to $341 in their passbook account at Maryland National Bank. It was December 8, twenty-two days before Buck started his new job. The day before, they'd divested themselves of Buck's dilapidated Dodge, adding eighty-four dollars to their cache. That would have to be enough.

There was a knock on the door.

"Try to keep them outside," Dottie whispered. Buck nodded as he made his way through stacks of boxes and pulled open the front door.

"Buck, Flora wanted me to bring you and Dottie this plate of food." It was Calvin Fuller, another Pine Hammock resident. It had been two days since Buck's firing and the subsequent gathering of outraged residents. Their fury had subsided, at least when they were around Buck and Dottie. Many, like Calvin, brought delicious meals and desserts; heaping plates of fried chicken, macaroni and cheese, and a cornucopia of pies.

"Thank you, Calvin," Buck said graciously as he accepted the covered platter. "I'd invite you in, but there are so many boxes stacked up there's not even room to move around."

"I understand," the large man said sadly. "I have to get to work, anyway. Flora and me is sorry about the way things turned out. You've done good for all of us and we won't forget it."

Calvin's was a familiar refrain, heard the past twenty-four hours from nearly everyone who showed up at the door. The first few times, Dottie had joined him in welcoming their guests, but the emotional toll was too much. These were good people who seemed at a loss to figure out what to do next. They'd followed with pride as Buck and Dottie blazed a local civil rights pathway. Now, with their departure, no one seemed able to step up and continue the fight, a fact that greatly saddened Buck and Dottie.

They'd met the day before with the older residents who'd integrated Miggett's lunch counter back in June. They were fervent supporters of the movement, but none seemed inclined to assume the mantle. Most of Pine Hammock's younger adult population put in long days on fishing boats or in fields and factories and were too exhausted to do little more each night than eat supper and fall into bed.

After Calvin said his farewells, Buck returned to packing. A few minutes before nine, Dottie pointed out that they were out of packing tape. Though cold, with temperatures in the low forties, it was sunny and beautiful, so Buck decided to walk to the store. School was out for Christmas break, and Buck passed a half-dozen children playing outside, many in jackets too thin for the winter chill. "Hey, Mr. Jones!" they yelled, oblivious to what had transpired over the past few days. "Tell Mrs.

Jones we said hey, too." Buck acknowledged them, most by name, as he continued down the road.

Happy's Market, a few blocks away, carried just about anything a person could need in Pine Hammock: food, cold beverages, and sundries in front, illegally-caught fish out back. The front door was warped and swollen, and Buck had to use his shoulder to push it open. The temperature inside was over eighty, thanks to a pot-bellied woodstove. Pleasant smells wafted from all directions. Bread, lunch meats, and peppermint candy among them. Happy's was a good name for the place, as coming here always made Buck feel that way.

"What can I get you, Buck?" Happy was on his usual perch, a high stool behind a huge cash register older than the man himself. With pinched features and a glass eye, some said he resembled a Negro Popeye.

Buck found a spool of packing tape and took it to the counter, grabbing a pack of malt crackers and some Juicy Fruit gum on the way. The conversation, as most recently, was centered on Buck and Dottie's forthcoming exodus from Twinton County. Buck was stuffing his purchases in his coat pocket when Biggerstaff came in.

For a moment, they froze, staring at one another. Nary a word had passed between them since Biggerstaff had fired him last summer. Buck had gone out of his way to avoid the principal and imagined Biggerstaff did the same.

"Happy, I need eggs and a pound of bologna," Biggerstaff said gruffly, looking past Buck.

Buck started toward the door, a path that would take him past Biggerstaff unless one of them moved down a side aisle. Biggerstaff watched his approach, his eyes flat and unblinking like a prize fighter staring down his opponent. Buck kept his gaze steady.

"Guess you got your ass handed to you," Biggerstaff growled.

Responses flashed through Buck's mind. Some aimed at getting under the man's skin, others more subtle. In the end, he chose to let it go.

"Take care, Happy," he said over his shoulder.

"You too, Buck. Hope we see you again."

He was pulling open the door when Biggerstaff said it.

"Chickenshit."

Buck stopped in his tracks. What was the man's problem? Turning slowly, he looked up at him.

"Was selling out to the white man a hard decision, Landon?"

Biggerstaff's breath caught. His fists clenched. Buck remained rooted in place, impassive. Ready to take whatever came. Biggerstaff rose slightly, so that he towered over Buck. His breathing grew shallow. He grabbed the front of Buck's shirt and pulled him closer, as he'd done in the hospital.

"Landon, get your damned hands off him." Happy was off his stool, clutching the splintered handle of a baseball bat. Biggerstaff could have easily taken it away from the old man, but the sight of Happy hobbling their way on painful arthritic legs gave him pause. He let go of Buck's shirt and took a step back. Buck wordlessly left the store.

***

"What's his beef with me?" Buck had made it home quickly, sparked by a rush of adrenaline.

"You've hit on it before," Dottie replied, stuffing a malt cracker into her mouth. "He's in one of the few prominent positions a black man can fill in a segregated community. Integration threatens him."

Buck paced around the room, flitting from box to box, but not accomplishing anything. "It's ironic, isn't it? Other than that cracker at the theater smacking Mrs. Mitchell with a jar, the only violence has been him against me; black man on black man."

The sound of the phone ringing brought their discussion to an end. Buck answered it while Dottie went to the kitchen.

"Buck, Desmond Henry."

"It's been awhile, Des. I should have called you, man. Dottie and I are leaving Twinton County."

"I've heard. Your interview is making the rounds here in the city. Somebody recorded it and started passing it around. We're going to print a transcript of it tomorrow."

Dottie entered the living room with a glass of water. She offered a drink to Buck, but he waved her off.

"Hi, Desmond," she called out as she returned to the kitchen.

"Buck, you need to know that C. Clayton Cooper is making some noise about a demonstration in Sheffield, maybe as soon as this weekend."

Biting his lip, Buck waved for Dottie to join him. He held the phone away from his ear, allowing her to listen. He briefly filled her in on what Desmond had said.

"Do you think he's dangerous?" she asked.

"Six months ago, I would have said no," Desmond replied. "In the last few weeks, though, his group has picked up support. They were in some backwater Kentucky town two weeks ago; fifty or so, staging a sit-in at a drugstore. It was going okay until Cooper got up on the counter and started making threats. Then somebody smacked a store clerk. They got out of town before anyone got arrested, but it was close."

Buck's first thought was screw 'em. He and Dottie would likely be packed up and out of town before anything happened.

"C. Clayton's been making noise about you getting fired. There are people here in the city who heard the interview and want to come down and demonstrate. The problem is, they don't need a guy like him leading them."

Buck rubbed at his beard. He saw the fear in Dottie's eyes.

"What do you suggest we do?"

He heard Desmond take a deep breath.

"For now, we wait. If I hear any more I'll let you know. Maybe it's just talk. Cooper certainly does enough of that. My concern is his using Twinton County as a stage to get himself known nationally. Whatever happens, I'll stay in touch. How much longer are you in town?"

"Today's Thursday. We planned on leaving Sunday morning."

"We should know more by then," Desmond said, clicking off. Dottie's face was twisted with worry as Buck hung up the phone.

"We can't leave if there's going to be trouble," she said.

"I disagree," Buck said. "If Mr. Adams hadn't let those white business owners influence him, I'd still be on the air. I could've headed it off before anything happened."

He could see Dottie was skeptical of a hasty departure, and felt a twinge of guilt himself. Still, what could they do now? Their platform had been snatched away.

"Let's finish packing, just in case."

FORTY-ONE

Buck was outside considering how to arrange boxes into the rental trailer they would pull to Florida behind Dottie's Studebaker. It was eleven-thirty and the winter sun had warmed the air into the mid-fifties, pleasant for Maryland in December. The boys he'd hired to help load would arrive at one. They'd made it to Saturday with no further word of trouble.

That was about to change.

Dottie opened the door and came outside, beautiful in a pair of black slacks and pink sweater.

"Desmond's on the phone."

He followed her inside.

"We're leaving tomorrow morning, so I don't want any bad news, Des."

"Do you know Jerome Gilliam?"

Buck acknowledged that he did.

"C. Clayton Cooper was on the Negro station in DC this morning saying he received a personal invitation from Mr. Gilliam to come to Twinton County. He and his group are leaving Baltimore at two today."

"Is he nuts? Jerome Gilliam is a high school boy."

"That matters none to C. Clayton. He'd been pining for an invite and he got it. This way, if things go wrong, he can say he was invited."

C. Clayton Cooper was a genius. Dangerous, but a genius.

"What do you think will happen, Des?"

For a moment, all Buck heard through the telephone line was the sound of typewriters clacking away in the background. Typical Desmond. At work on Saturday.

"A lot will depend upon how much encouragement C. Clayton gets. If the Negro population shows up in good numbers, or if the local law starts pushing back, he's likely to do anything. The best we can hope for is a quiet demonstration where the police stay in the background. Do you think you can make that happen? Do you even want to?"

Damn. One more day. If C. Clayton Cooper would have waited until Sunday, it wouldn't be Buck's problem.

But what to do now?

"Buck? You there?"

"I'm still here. I'll see what I can do to head off trouble. How many do you expect?"

"His brother owns a school bus company, so I'd imagine he'll bring a bus full from here; maybe thirty or forty."

"I guess I'd better get busy, then."

"Good luck." Desmond said. "I'm coming down to cover the story, so I'll see you later."

***

"Chief, I'm here as a courtesy to offer some advice."

The look on Sheffield Police Chief Russell Pannier's face as he looked across the desk said he didn't want advice. Still, he nodded for Buck to continue. Twinton County Sheriff Dave Masterson sat in the chair next to Buck. Unlike Chief Pannier, he was in civilian attire.

Buck gave them some background about C. Clayton Cooper, omitting his legal problems in Kentucky. Both listened thoughtfully. Sheriff Masterson jotted a few notes. Buck's experiences with Chief Pannier were minimal. He had kept his men at bay during the recent integration efforts, but there had been little potential for violence or destruction. How he and his men might react to C. Clayton was anybody's guess. Sheriff Masterson was a kind-hearted Methodist who treated Pine Hammock residents with respect. The few who voted had no issue casting their ballots for him.

"Buck," Sheriff Masterson spoke first, "I guess my first question is, why do you care? I went by your place this morning and saw the trailer in the yard. You've already got one foot in Florida."

Buck crossed his legs and turned slightly for better eye contact. "Sheriff Masterson, honestly my first response was to move up our departure and get out of here. Dottie, however, is a persuasive woman."

Sheriff Masterson offered an understanding smile. Chief Pannier showed no emotion.

"I'm going to make the rounds in Pine Hammock after I leave here," Buck said, checking his watch. "It's just after two. Mr. Cooper and the others will probably be here around six. I would imagine that word of his visit has already spread, but if I can urge restraint, I'll do it." Buck turned to Chief Pannier. "I would recommend not interfering with their demonstration, Chief. People in Pine Hammock are angry and this demonstration might serve as a catharsis for them."

"I don't know what the hell a catharsis is," Pannier said testily, "but I don't go in for demonstrations in our streets, especially when the people involved aren't from here. And by that, I mean this Cooper guy and the people from Pine Hammock."

"Do you have a city ordinance regulating demonstrations?" Buck knew the answer before he asked the question. He and Dottie had reviewed the Sheffield city laws before leading the integration of the Miggett's lunch counter. Still, it might help if Chief Pannier knew them too.

"I don't know about any ordinances, but if I want to stop 'em, I'll stop 'em."

"That's where you're wrong, Russ," Sheriff Masterson interjected. "It's the First Amendment. Violate that and next thing you know you'll have Eisenhower sending in the National Guard."

"Eisenhower ain't doing nothing of the sort, Dave. Now that pinko Kennedy… he'll have the niggers dancing in the street when he—" Chief Pannier glanced at Buck, his eyes wide with realization of what he'd just said. "Not you, Jones. I'm talking about them in the city." Buck said nothing. Sheriff Masterson shifted uncomfortably.

"I'll put a couple extra men on patrol tonight," the sheriff said. "We'll monitor the north and south roads into Sheffield. Russ, that leaves your boys to be available wherever the demonstration takes place. Let's not let anything happen here like what they had in Little Rock or down in Alabama, where law enforcement became the villains."

Chief Pannier ran a hand through his shock of jet-black hair, then leveled his gaze at Buck.

"Jones, tell your boy, Cooper that—"

"He's not *my boy*, Chief," Buck responded sharply. "I've never met the man."

"It was that disrespectful piece-of-shit interview you did on the radio that got him here, *boy*," Pannier responded, leaning forward in his seat, daring Buck to respond.

"Turn it down, Russ," Sheriff Masterson said, getting up from his chair. "Buck is here to help and you jabbing a stick at him isn't getting us anywhere." The sheriff offered his hand to Buck. "You head back to Pine Hammock and see what you can do. We'll take care of things on our end."

***

As best as Buck and Dottie could figure, seven-hundred people lived in a hundred and twenty-five or so

227

Pine Hammock homes. Many were extended families, with parents, children, grandparents, and aunts and uncles crammed together. Even dividing up the town between them, it quickly became apparent that time wouldn't allow Buck and Dottie to canvass the entire town. They decided to stay together and do what they could.

At some of their stops, there was no one home. At others, children came to the door, some as young as five or six, explaining that the adults were working. In cases where adults were home, Buck or Dottie made their appeal for restraint, but were often rebuffed. Interestingly, there was now as much anger toward the radio station as toward the schools.

"You told 'em how bad things are at the school and they took you off the radio," was a familiar refrain. "Somebody needs to let them people up at Sheffield know that we've had enough."

By the time they returned home, there was less than an hour until nightfall.

"What do you want to do?" Dottie asked, as she prepared a pot of canned soup.

"Get in the car, hitch up the trailer, and head South," Buck replied, partly in jest. She didn't smile. Outside, they heard cars driving by, several at a time, then a few moments of silence before more passed. It was rare for there to be more than a half-dozen cars pass by in an hour. That many had passed in the five minutes since Buck had arrived home.

"I guess we go to Sheffield," Buck said, declining Dottie's offer of some of her soup. His stomach was knotted, and only a peaceful conclusion to C. Clayton Cooper's visit would allay the discomfort.

***

A quick drive through Sheffield showed no evidence of Cooper's arrival. Many of the cars that had passed their house were now parked in a public lot near the movie theater. People were sitting in their cars, windows open as they waited. It was still in the low-fifties. Buck pulled in and waved to one of his former students.

"Tell me what you know, Hoy."

The boy, small, but with a baritone voice that made him sound older than his sixteen years, came to the car window.

"Jerome say that man, Mr. Cooper. He's gonna talk to people on the library steps when he gets here. That's all I know." Hoy, a dull boy in school, seemed excited by the prospect of meeting someone he perceived as famous.

"Do you hear that?" Dottie said after Hoy had returned to his gaggle of friends. Buck glanced around, trying to pinpoint what she was referring to.

"All I hear is a lot of talking," he replied.

"Not that. Listen carefully. In the background."

This time he heard it. Two-dozen cars parked with their motors running, had their radios tuned to the same station. Not the black station from Baltimore.

WSCM.

When he looked at Dottie, she nodded.

"It's worth a try," she said. "I'll wait here while you go."

***

As Buck expected, the front doors were locked. This was protocol for after-hours and weekends when the on-air jock was the only person at the station. He pushed a button that he knew sounded a bell in the studio, then waited, checking his watch every few seconds. It was after seven. Cooper and his retinue must be getting close.

There was a brief illumination of the dark lobby, a sign that someone had just opened the door to the studio. A moment later, Buster Key appeared. When he saw who had interrupted him, the jock flipped him the bird and started his retreat to the studio.

229

"Buster, open the door. It's important!" Buck rapped hard enough on the door to get Buster to look back. The jock considered his options, then moved to the door, unlocked it, and opened it just enough to speak.

"You don't work here anymore, asshole."

"Buster, look, get Mr. Adams on the phone. Tell him—"

"I'm not doing shit for you, gimp. Besides, the old man is visiting his daughter up North, so you're outta luck." Buster moved to pull the door shut but Buck wedged his arm in. This seemed to befuddle him for a second, but he recovered in good form.

"You wanna be a nigger with *no* arms?"

"Listen, Buster. There's about to be trouble downtown. A guy's coming to town and he's got people all fired up. I've tried to talk to everyone I could, but there wasn't time. If I could just go on the radio for a min—"

"Not a chance in hell," Buster spat. "You already cost me my weekday job. I'll be damned if you're gonna screw me over again." He tried again to close the door, but Buck didn't budge. For the better part of a minute they played a strange game of tug-of-war, before finally coming to the realization they neither had a chance of winning unless the other gave in. Breathing hard from the minimal exertion, Buster stepped back. Buck slung the door open and made a beeline for the studio. He was almost there when he heard an unmistakable click. When he wheeled around, Buster had a cheap pistol leveled at his chest.

"Don't think I won't use it," Buster said menacingly. "Probably give me as much pleasure as a good woman."

Buck froze. He didn't know if Buster Key was a violent man or not, but it wasn't the time to find out. Still, he had to give it one more try.

"Buster, please. Two minutes. I want to try to convince the people gathered downtown not to let this turn violent. You have to understand that." Then, another thought. "Mr. Adams would want you to."

Indecision mixed with anger on Buster's ugly face. Then, just as quick, it passed.

"I guess we'll never know," Buster said. "What I do know is that those coons wouldn't be tripping all over each other if you hadn't riled them up." He raised the pistol, lining it up with Buck's face.

"Get the hell out of here."

***

In the twenty minutes he was gone, the gathering had gotten larger and louder. Dottie waved him down at the edge of the parking lot.

"Buster Key pulled a gun on me."

She gasped, the reality of the situation dawning on her. Buck filled her in on the entire encounter.

"Things here are... strange," she said. People who we need here, like Dr. Watson and others from the sit-in at Miggetts didn't come. Mrs. Mitchell is here, but she's not acting like herself at all. Jerome and the high school boys seem to be in charge, and they don't have a clue."

"Maybe C. Clayton won't come after all." Buck checked his watch again. "They were due an hour ago."

From around the corner, a horn blasted loud and long. Jerome Gilliam came running to the parking lot. "They're here!" he yelled, waving for everyone to follow. The fifty or so people gathered in the municipal parking lot cheered as they rushed toward the corner closest to the movie theater. Chief Russell Pannier's men were nowhere in sight.

Three school buses with *Cooper School Transportation* emblazoned on their sides came to a stop on the street. Pine Hammock residents clustered around the door of the first bus and waited. After several minutes, the doors opened. Buck and Dottie watched from afar as twelve large men formed a human wall from the bus to the steps of the public library. Once the area was cleared, C. Clayton Cooper emerged.

The rowdy gathering cheered louder as Cooper made his way to the library steps, his body guards keeping pace. Even James Brown couldn't have gotten such an enthusiastic reception, Buck thought.

"They're acting like he's the second coming." Dottie's remark was meant to be cutting, but Buck noticed her eyes remained glued on the civil rights leader. They continued to trail behind the others. Then, turning onto Main Street, another surprise greeted them.

"I guess we know where Chief Pannier's interests lie," Buck said, eyeing the fifteen or so officers stationed along the walkway like streetlights, their backs to storefronts, protecting not the public but the enterprises behind them. Neither as much as moved when Cooper breezed past.

"I guess it doesn't matter if somebody gets hurt, as long as they don't try to vandalize one of those precious stores," Dottie said.

Reaching his spot on the library steps, Cooper turned toward the gathering and raised his hands for attention. It was a gesture for theatrical benefit only, as every face in the crowd was already focused on him. This was, Buck thought, as close to live theater as most people in attendance would ever experience. The protesters on the other buses, about a hundred in all, had silently disembarked and filled in the rear, pushing the gathering into the street and stopping traffic. Despite the possibility of someone – most likely a Negro – getting injured by a passing car, nary a police officer moved.

Out-of-towners were easily distinguishable from locals. Most were attired in a similar style. Tight black turtlenecks over black slacks and leather jackets. Men outnumbered women by two-to-one, but Buck noticed that they spaced out the women to make them appear more plentiful. None smiled. Their faces and countenances were grim. Unhappy. Angry.

"I expected you'd have a front row seat." Buck, initially startled by Desmond Henry uttering into his right ear, turned quickly.

"We're right where we want to be," Buck said, shaking the reporter's hand. Dottie gave him a peck on the cheek.

"I hear congratulations are in order," Desmond said. "You'll be great parents."

"We won't start celebrating until we're in Florida," Dottie said. Nodding in the direction of the library she added, "this was the last thing we wanted."

"I never expected this many," Desmond said, sizing up the gathering. "Buck, your interview with the school superintendent has resonated with a lot of people."

A full two-minutes passed before Cooper moved to the top of the steps. Jerome Gilliam and two of his Pine Hammock classmates approached to offer a welcome, but were quickly shooed away. Cooper wanted this stage to himself. He nodded at a man positioned as a sentry at the bottom of the steps who in turn addressed everyone present.

"Ladies and gentlemen, I present the Director of the Black Liberal Party, Mr. C. Clayton Cooper."

FORTY-TWO

Cooper again kept his audience waiting several beats before speaking. It was seven-twenty on a Saturday night, yet there wasn't a white face in the streets. The stores that lined Main Street typically remained open until nine, but not tonight. Inside, lurking in dim light near the rear as they attempted to remain inconspicuous, were gun-toting store owners.

Buck noticed that several of the police officers were gawking at the visitor. Cooper knew how to work a crowd, despite being slightly built and unremarkable in appearance. His most dominant characteristic was his eyes: dark brown and somewhat menacing.

"Change is coming to Twinton County."

His voice was clear. Some Negroes might say he 'spoke white,' without any trace of black dialect.

"Change is coming to Twinton County."

An amen echoed back at him. Then another. Then several.

"Now some of you might be thinking, 'but C. Clayton, change already came.' We can go into that library behind you and check out books. We couldn't do that before."

"Buck got us that!" The shout came from Mrs. Mitchell. Others echoed her sentiment.

"Thanks, Buck!"

"Bless you, Buck!"

It was obvious that Cooper didn't care for any show of support for someone other than himself. Bristling, he raised his hands for silence.

"Crumbs of bread. That's all they are. Checking out a library book from the white man's library. Eating ice cream at the white man's lunch counter. You might think that's pretty big, but, people, we are here tonight to help you go *the whole way*."

Cooper's declaration was met with cheers that started with the bus riders in the back and spread to the locals standing closest to the steps.

"Do you believe that?" Dottie looked as if she wanted to charge up the steps and strangle C. Clayton Cooper.

"Our buses made a side visit to Pine Hammock on the way here tonight," Cooper continued. "We saw where the white man has condemned you to live. I think it's safe to say that few of you are living as well as the people here in Sheffield. Am I right?"

The responses came from all corners, most from bus riders, but Buck heard a few familiar voices as well.

"You right!"

"Right on!"

"Got nothin' good as whitey got."

Cooper continued, "Now whitey will say you don't have nice things because you don't work hard enough. Or you don't take care of what you have. Am I right?"

More shouts of agreement.

"But you *do* work hard. How many of you work two jobs?"

Hands went up. Many.

"How many of you have been passed over for jobs because whitey thinks your blackness means you can't do good work?"

More hands.

"We cannot go around patting ourselves on the back for sitting next to whitey in the whitey-owned movie theater where whitey takes our money, or eating at whitey's lunch counter, because it's not enough. We need to go *the whole way*!

"The whole way! The whole way! The whole way!" Again, the chant started with the bus riders, but was quickly and fervently echoed by everyone. Desmond, having circulated around snapping photographs, circled back to Buck and Dottie.

"What do you think?"

"He's making some sense," Buck answered.

"I don't like him," Dottie said. "He has no right belittling the advances we've made."

"When we were in Pine Hammock, we saw your school… *the colored school*," Cooper declared, unbuttoning his leather coat. Despite temperatures in the low fifties, he was sweating heavily.

"Now I have a feeling that it's not as nice as the school that whitey has for his children. Am I right?"

Cheers mixed with laughter and jeering.

Cooper nodded his head knowingly. "Why don't we take a walk and a look at whitey's school. Anybody want to walk with me?"

"Yes!" The response was unanimous and loud. Buck noticed a couple police officers exchanging nervous glances.

The same burly men who'd cleared Cooper's walk from bus to library opened a path through the assembly into the street. Coming down the steps, Cooper made eye contact with Desmond, who nodded at Buck standing beside him.

"He wants you to walk with him," Desmond said quietly.

Buck glanced at Dottie, who made a cutting gesture across her neck.

"Buck Jones, will you join me for our little walk?" Cooper's question met with the most enthusiastic response of the evening. Unlike the earlier shows of support, this one started with the locals.

"Buck! Buck! Buck!"

Everything in him made Buck want to avoid the limelight, but that was becoming impossible unless he ran away. Reluctantly he shouldered his way through the crowd. When he glanced back, Dottie wasn't following. He moved to return to her, but was pushed forward by the surging mass.

Emerging from the crowd, he shook Cooper's outstretched hand. Smiling for the world to see, Cooper leaned close. "Follow my lead, but *never* get ahead of me." His emotionless voice belied his happy countenance. Together they started walking. The others fell in behind them.

"Where's the school?" Cooper asked.

"Three blocks, right on Grand. School's a block down."

"What the hell is with the cops? They're standing like they're in front of Buckingham fucking Palace."

"Guarding the stores."

"What happened to your arm?"

"None of your damn business."

Cooper let the rebuff bounce off him. His smile morphed into a look of determination when Desmond moved ahead of them and snapped some shots. Looking back over his shoulder, Buck saw the gathering silently moving as one. It was eerily beautiful, like some of the civil rights marches he'd seen on television.

"You still in contact with Dr. King?"

Cooper scoffed at the question. "Our philosophies are different."

"But you were pretty close? Once?"

He nodded. "Martin's approach depends too much on churches and white people. There are plenty of brothers and sisters out there who feel strongly about what we're doing, but have no interest in sleeping in church every Sunday. Besides," Cooper leaned in closer, lowering his voice. "I'm tired of getting knocked down by whitey's fire hoses and nightsticks. The next cracker that tries that might take one between the eyes."

Buck tried to hide his shock, but Cooper picked up on it. "There's only so far we can go... what's your name again?"

"Buck."

"There's only so far we can go, Buck, before violence has to become part of the plan. Be honest, man, haven't you ever wanted to bury a knife in some honky's heart?"

"Never."

Cooper laughed softly. "Then you haven't been on the frontline." He took a sidelong glance at Buck. "Besides, you're high yellow. That makes it easier. What are you half-white? Quarter?"

"None of your damn business."

Cooper laughed loudly. To observers, it probably looked like Buck had just shared a joke. Behind them a quiet serenade had started.

Ain't gonna let nobody turn me around
Turn me around. Turn me around.
Ain't gonna let nobody turn me around.
Keep on a-walking, keep on a-walking.
Marchin' into freedom land.

"Hear that?" Cooper asked.

Of course he heard it. How stupid did Cooper think he was?

"That's why we do this shit, man. That and the chance to be famous. Three years ago, I was waiting tables in New York City, barely scraping by. When I get a few more marches under my belt, my name will be better known than Martin's. I'll be in a league with Willie Mays and Jim Brown."

"What are your plans tonight?" Buck asked, noticing that several of Cooper's larger men were now moving toward the front of the march, mixing in with the locals.

"We're going to march up to the white school. I'm going to stand in front of these people and demand the superintendent show his face."

"He's won't be there."

"Don't you think I know that?" Cooper looked at Buck as if he were a child. "After that I'll let these people see how angry C. Clayton can get. I'll rail against the white man's apartheid. Maybe a bottle will get thrown through a window or somebody will break down a schoolhouse door. It'll be just enough to see if we can get a rise out of the fuzz."

"Fuzz?"

Cooper's laugh was almost taunting. "Pigs, Police. I'm hoping some of us get arrested tonight."

Buck grabbed Cooper's arm. "Wait a minute—"

"*Nigger, get your hand off me,*" he hissed. "Nobody touches C. Clayton."

Buck drew back as if he'd been slapped. The altercation, contained between the two men, went unnoticed as those following continued to sing.

Ain't gonna let nobody turn me around
Turn me around. Turn me around…

"These people aren't here to get arrested, Mr. Cooper. They came here because they want to build on the successes they've already had."

"Have you not heard a thing I've said? I didn't pay for three busloads of brothers and sisters to come out to the middle of nowhere to chat about what could be. We're here to *make* something happen."

"That's where you're wrong. We already are making things happen. The superintendent's interview on my radio show was just the first step. Things are improving here, and they're doing it without violence."

Shaking his head in disgust, Cooper replied, "Is that what this is about? Are your feelings hurt because we showed up and became the life of your little party?"

"It's not that at—"

"If you thought for a minute you were going to accomplish this on your own, you were seriously overestimating yourself, boy. Step back now and watch C. Clayton turn this place on its ear."

Ain't gonna let nobody turn me around

Turn me around. Turn me around…

"Boss." One of Cooper's men had stepped closer, just over his left shoulder. When they turned, he nodded down a side street. Another group of Negroes, forty or fifty, were marching toward them. Cooper stopped and watched their approach. When they were within fifty feet, a young woman stepped forward.

"Mr. Cooper, we are the Black Student Coalitions from Maryland State and Delaware State College. We request permission to join your march."

Cooper motioned her to come forward, as royalty might allow a servant to enter his space. The woman was attractive, and Cooper ogled her openly.

"What is your name, sister?"

"Helen Gooding, sir. Maryland State College."

"Well, Helen," he said, taking her hand and gently pulling her to his side. "We would very much like you to join us. In fact, I'd like you to march next to…" he looked at Buck, obviously forgetting his name again, "… this gentleman and me."

Wordlessly the other coeds fell into line as the march continued. Now two-hundred strong, the singing was louder.

Ain't gonna let nobody turn me around.
Keep on a-walking, keep on a-walking.
Marchin' into freedom land.

"What was the boy's name who came up on the steps?" Cooper asked Buck. "The school boy."

"Jerome Gilliam, but he's—"

"Jerome Gilliam, please join me up front." Cooper said loudly over his shoulder. Breathlessly, the boy came forward.

"Get a couple of your friends and have them come up behind us," Cooper said. Jerome quickly complied.

"Now you march on my right," Cooper said. "This… gentleman will step back to let you have his space." Then, to Buck, "Thank you for the role you've played, but we've got this from here on."

Jerome looked at Buck uncertainly before Buck nodded for him to take his place. Falling back, he searched for Dottie, but couldn't find her. He spotted Desmond on the sidewalk.

Dottie? he mouthed. Desmond shrugged.

***

He found her back at the car, sitting on the hood, waiting. As soon as she saw him coming, she lit into him.

"Are you stupid? This thing is going to get ugly, and you're right there in the front. He was using you, Buck. Are you too dense to see that?"

Nearby, a white policeman watched them carefully.

Buck crawled onto the hood beside her. "He couldn't even remember my name," he said quietly. "First chance he got, he had me step aside." He told her about being replaced by Jerome and the Maryland State coed.

"He read you like a book," she said, taking his hand. "He saw you weren't going to do his bidding, so he sent you packing."

They sat there, alone, considering the night sky. Eventually the policeman vacated his post for a spot closer to the action.

"Let's go home, hook up the trailer and head for Florida," Buck said, squeezing her hand.

"We can at least get as far as Mother and Dad's in Washington," Dottie said.

"I couldn't sleep if we did stop," Buck said, rubbing his beard. "I'm so hyped up by this..." he took a deep breath. "I might drive to Florida non-stop."

Dottie nodded and slid off the hood and into the front seat.

FORTY-THREE

The sun was rising as they entered Rocky Mount, North Carolina. Dottie stirred in her seat, yawned, and checked the surroundings.

"I'm hungry."

Buck had the *Negro Motorist Green Book* in his lap. "I figured you would be. Wright's Motel and Restaurant is seven miles ahead."

They hadn't spoken about what they'd witnessed in Sheffield. Nor had they speculated on how things turned out. Dottie turned on the radio and searched the dial before settling on a station out of Raleigh. They didn't have to wait long.

Three are dead and a schoolhouse is burned to the ground, following riots overnight in a small Maryland town. Mutual Broadcasting's Philip Chandler has the story from Sheffield.

Buck felt adrenaline begin to course through his body. Dottie looked at him gap-mouthed, her eyes wide.

It started with a radio interview last week on local station WSCM when the school superintendent was pointedly asked about segregation.

A clip of Buck's interview was played, along with the superintendent's evasive and uncertain answers.

Would you send your children to Pine Hammock, Doctor Mister?

When was the last time you were in Pine Hammock School?

When the superintendent's answers didn't meet expectations of the local Negro population, a demonstration was arranged in downtown Sheffield. Shortly after nightfall, a group of local people and student activists from two area colleges marched through the streets of Sheffield—

"What?" Dottie said sharply. "Not a word about Cooper!"

—ending at the Sheffield Public School where demonstrators called for the superintendent. When he didn't show, a smoke bomb was tossed through a schoolhouse window. Rocks and bottles followed, and within minutes many windows were broken. With Sheffield city police guarding local businesses against threats of vandalism, it fell to the Twinton County Sheriff's Office to step in and reestablish order. Sheriff Dave Masterson spoke with Mutual this morning.

When his voice came across the airwaves, Buck could tell Sheriff Masterson had been overwhelmed.

Soon after we moved into position, a protestor approached and struck one of our deputies with a blunt object, either a baseball bat or a cane. Another deputy was forced to draw his weapon in response. Unfortunately, the situation escalated quickly, and a deputy and two protestors were killed.

His heart hammering, Buck pulled to the side of the road. Dottie was weeping. The announcer picked up the story.

Dead are Sheriff's Deputy Wilbert Bramble, forty-seven, of Sheffield, and Lucius Murray and Jerome Gilliam, both sixteen, of Pine Hammock. According to police reports, Murray was wielding the bat.

Buck embraced his wife, willing the story to be a bad dream, but knowing better.

While deputies were securing the downtown area of Sheffield, a report came in that the Negro School in Pine Hammock was ablaze. Firefighters were dispatched, but were unable to contain the fire. The school was a total loss. Local authorities report that it was one in the morning before calm was finally restored. In the end, there were no arrests, but police are investigating and are said to have compiled a list of suspects who will be brought in for questioning. For Mutual, I'm Philip Chandler.

It was several minutes before they spoke. Dottie finally broke the silence.

"That bastard, Cooper. He started this." Her voice was drained.

"Not a mention of him," Buck said. "Two boys and a sheriff's deputy killed…"

"And Pine Hammock School?" Dottie exclaimed. "Why would they burn down the black school?" She started crying again. "Those poor babies. Jerome was in over his head from the start."

"He wanted to make a difference," Buck said sadly, "and look what happened."

"It was Lucius," Dottie said. "He always had a temper, but somebody put him up to it. I can't imagine that boy attacking a deputy sheriff."

They looked at one another. They knew. The instigator's identity was easy enough to determine.

"Should we go back?" Dottie asked. "They might need us. I'm sure C. Clayton Cooper isn't there this morning to take care of them."

"Let's get some breakfast, then try to call Desmond," Buck said, spotting the restaurant ahead.

***

"Newsroom. Desmond Henry."

"Desmond, it's—"

"Buck! Are you okay? Where the hell are you, man? Did they find you yet?"

"I'm okay. I just heard the news on the radio. It's terrible. Part of me thinks that if we'd stayed, we—"

"Stayed? What do you mean? You weren't there?"

"I was, but… remember when I—"

"You were there when it all went down, right?"

"I left right after I asked if you'd seen Dottie. She'd stayed behind, and when I went back to find her, we left. Cooper was scaring me."

"It was terrible, Buck. That boy, Jerome. He tried to help restore the peace after that other kid attacked the cop, and..." Desmond's voice tailed off. Buck could hear his labored breathing.

"What about Cooper?"

Desmond took a moment to compose himself. "Gone like the wind. When things turned bad, his people whisked him out of there. Those buses were on the road before the dust settled. The cops were running around like chickens with their heads cut off. They're trying to pin everything on the local people and the college students..."

When Desmond spoke again, his voice was barely audible.

"... and you."

"What? How am I being pulled into it?"

"They're saying you incited it. They're looking for you—where are you anyway?"

"We made it to—"

"Wait! Don't tell me. It's better if I don't know. Are you still in Maryland, because if you are..."

"I'm not."

"Oh man, Buck. Okay listen, I'm not a lawyer, but I think I'm giving you the best advice when I tell you to get in your car and get as far away from Twinton County as you can. Somebody's going to take the fall for this and given the airplay your interview's getting, that might be you."

Buck hung up and returned to Dottie. The waitress had bussed their table and her demeanor made it obvious that she wanted them to make room for more customers. She would have to wait a few more minutes.

"Should we go back?" Dottie asked.

"Desmond says don't," Buck replied, filling her in on their conversation.

"Buck, we can't just keep running. If they want you, they'll come find you."

"I'm innocent, Dottie, but do you think they can find a jury willing to believe a Negro? Do you remember what happened in Bristol County last year?"

Dottie's face creased with concern as she recalled the case of Reginald Ball, a Negro waterman who was awakened in the night by a sudden noise in his backyard. Creeping to a window, he saw a man removing the month-old outboard motor from his fishing boat. Grabbing his shotgun, Ball crept out of the house and got the draw on the intruder. When he announced his presence, the thief quickly reached in his pocket and pulled out what Ball thought to be a gun. It turned out to be a flashlight, and the suspect turned out to be a Bristol County Deputy Sheriff. None of this was known to Reginald Ball, who shot and killed the intruder. Even though the deputy was fully intending to steal Ball's motor, Ball was found guilty of manslaughter and sentenced to several years in prison.

"Let's head to Florida," she said.

FORTY-FOUR

BALTIMORE BLACK ADVOCATE
December 19, 1960

MARTIAL LAW IMPOSED ON RACE-TORN COUNTY

By: Desmond K. Henry

Following a second night of race-related violence, Maryland Governor J. Millard Tawes has imposed martial law in Twinton County. National Guard Troops were dispatched early this morning after local law enforcement officials stated they were unable to perform their duties.

The daylight hours of Sunday were quiet following what local leaders have termed a riot in Sheffield's main business district that left three people dead and the Negro school in neighboring Pine Hammock destroyed by arson. Soon after eight Sunday evening, police reported that local radio station WSCM also succumbed to arson. Employee Buster Key, 31, the only person in the studio at the time, escaped uninjured, but the station is a total loss. Local police indicate they have made no arrests in either case. C. Clayton Cooper, whose Black Liberal Party played a leading role in the Saturday night march through Sheffield has denied knowledge of the violence that took the lives of a Twinton County Deputy Sheriff and two Pine Hammock teens.

"We went to Twinton County at the request of local community leaders," Cooper told a reporter for the *New York Times*. "When I saw the evening's activities start to get out of hand, I immediately withdrew our people."

Cooper would not return calls to the *Baltimore Black Advocate*.

In mobilizing the Maryland National Guard, Governor Tawes has imposed a strict curfew of 9:00 PM and banned demonstrations by Negroes.

Sheffield Police Chief Russell Pannier felt the decision to bring in the National Guard was appropriate.

"They're (Negroes) trying to get what they want through any means necessary," Pannier said. "Saturday night was a situation where there were too many of them and not enough of us."

Regarding the loss of the local radio station, the chief was less circumspect. "While I feel for the owner, it was his radio station where everything started." Pannier was referring to a controversial interview conducted this past week of the local superintendent of schools, during which he tried to defend his laissez-faire approach to integration.

Twinton County Sheriff Dave Masterson was more restrained in his comments.

"While the loss of a deputy sheriff is a tragedy, our department will do everything we can to bring to justice those responsible for the deaths of all three individuals as well as those responsible for the loss of our local Negro school and radio station."

FORTY-FIVE

In the four days since they'd arrived, Buck and Dottie had remained secluded in the duplex Vincent Payne was loaning them. Though it was considered part of Butler Beach, it was on an out-of-the-way road a couple miles from the beach itself. Perfect for thinking through the future.

It was the day before Christmas Eve, but they'd decided to forego gifts, at least until Buck's paychecks commenced in January. Still, a nice meal seemed like a good idea.

"I'll call Vincent for a recommendation," Buck said, reaching for the recently-installed telephone. Following a series of transfers from one secretary to the next, he was put through.

"Buck, have you been reading about yourself?" Payne asked.

Buck's stomach clenched. "No, sir. We've not been doing much of anything."

"Get yourself a copy of yesterday's *Florida Times*. They're carrying a story written by your friend in Baltimore. Those people in Maryland want you to come back for questioning."

Buck's hand was shaking as he considered this. The day they'd arrived, when they picked up the keys to their duplex, they'd told Vincent about what had happened in

Sheffield. Some he'd heard, as the black newspapers around the country regularly shared stories, particularly when they involved civil rights. Buck had been initially reluctant to tell his new boss, but Vincent seemed unconcerned.

After securing a dinner recommendation he was certain his stomach wouldn't allow him to enjoy, Buck located Desmond's card and placed a long-distance call to Baltimore.

"Newsroom. Desmond Henry."

"I hear I'm making the news." Buck tried to sound casual, but knew Desmond could see through it.

"They're going to try to extradite you, brother. Inciting a riot. The police chief is saying if you hadn't conducted yourself the way you did during the interview with the superintendent, there wouldn't have been violence."

Buck took a deep breath. His hand still shook.

"I have no idea what to do with this information."

"Your hope is that Florida won't allow the extradition. That way, you'll be safe as long as you stay in state."

"Fat chance of that. One southern state asking another southern state to send back a black man accused of inciting a race riot. I might as well go to the local PD and turn myself in."

"Not so fast," Desmond said. "LeRoy Collins is Florida's governor for another week. He's been more outspoken against segregation the past year. If they ask for extradition in the next few days, there's a chance he'll deny it."

This was good news.

"What you need is somebody on your side. Maybe two somebodies. Hold on a minute." Buck heard Desmond lay the phone down with a loud clunk, then the sound of papers being shuffled. "Here we go. I'm going to have a lady get in touch with you. Her name is Cora Manning. White woman. She's a lobbyist who's been an advocate for affirmative action. She might be able to pull some strings with Governor Collins."

"I appreciate that, Desmond. More than you know."

"I know you do, brother. It's all for the good of the movement. I'll tell you what else I'm going to do. I'm getting on a plane tomorrow morning and flying down to interview you myself."

"Des, you don't want to leave your family on Christmas Eve."

"No problem. I'll fly into Jacksonville first thing, then head back in the afternoon. We'll have a feature story about you on the front page of fifty black newspapers on Christmas Day."

"Seriously, Des. I don't want you—"

"Pick me up at Jacksonville airport at nine-thirty. I'll be on the TWA flight from Friendship Airport."

FORTY-SIX

"Hey, you're that guy! Aren't you? The radio guy, from up North?"

It was the third time since they'd entered Jacksonville's Imeson Airport that someone had recognized Buck. Desmond's Christmas Day article had been picked up by the *Florida Times* and dozens of other black newspapers around the country. The first man to recognize him actually offered Buck ten dollars. He declined, but Dottie grabbed it, thanking the man profusely.

When they reached the gate for their Eastern Airlines flight to Washington, DC, they spotted several Negro passengers reading the *Times*. Since the current day's edition wouldn't hit newsstands until after lunch, yesterday's copy was still the latest. Buck's face was hard to miss, splashed as it was across the front page. While white passengers kept their distance, a Negro woman and her young son ventured over and took a seat next to them. Soon they were joined by two businessmen and a college student, all with newspapers in hand. They peppered Buck with questions.

"Are they going to extradite you back to Maryland?"

"Nothing's happened yet."

"Are you heading North to get away from the cracker legislators down here in Florida?"

"No, we have an appointment in Washington. We'll be coming back."

"Doesn't freedom of speech carry over to brothers and sisters?"

"I hope so."

The conversation ended with encouraging farewells as passengers drifted away to begin boarding.

"With all the excitement of the past couple days, it just dawned on me that I've never flown before," Buck said, pulling their tickets from his pocket.

"Me neither," Dottie said. "We went on exactly one family vacation growing up and that was two hours away, to Gettysburg."

"It was nice of Desmond to arrange everything," Buck said as they made their way through line.

"Did he ever say who paid?"

"He was cagey about that, but I think it might have been some people with Dr. King's group. He made sure they got an advance copy of the story."

The morning sun warmed their faces as they moved outside and walked toward the plane. At the top of the steps, the stewardess who was cheerfully greeting customers had an abrupt change in demeanor when she spied Dottie coming up the steps ahead of Buck.

"Second cabin," she said coldly, not bothering to check their tickets. They continued onto the plane and down the aisle.

"I think she has a case of the black person blues," Dottie whispered. A second stewardess, more cordial than the first, met them at the entrance to the second cabin.

"You missed your seats," she said sunnily. "You're in first-class." They moved out of the way for a couple other passengers to pass, then the stewardess led them back to the front.

"Rebecca, Mr. and Mrs. Jones are seated in Row Two," she said to the stewardess they'd first encountered, then turning to Buck and Dottie she smiled brightly and said, "Have a great flight."

It was obvious that Rebecca wasn't pleased with the arrangement. Starting in the row in front of them, she took drink orders, conveniently skipping Buck and Dottie as she made her way through the six rows that made up first-class. Dottie, seated next to the window, grabbed Buck's arm.

"She does *not* think she's getting away with this, does she?"

"Just let it slide," Buck said in a placating tone he immediately regretted. "I don't want anything to drink."

Dottie sat back in her seat, but Buck could tell from her posture that it wasn't over. They were a few moments from takeoff when Rebecca made another pass, this time with magazines. Again, the left side of Row Two was overlooked. Immediately after she passed, the pilot stepped from the cockpit and addressed the people in first class.

"Hi folks, I'm Captain Reed. We're about ready to takeoff and I wanted to personally thank you for flying Eastern. If there's anything I can do for you, just knock. Our door is always open to first-class passengers."

He had turned to reenter the cockpit when Dottie stood.

"Captain Reed, may I have a moment? Privately?"

The pilot glanced over his shoulder into the cockpit, checked his watch, then moved to Row Two.

"Yes ma'am, what can I do for you?"

Three minutes later, Rebecca was working coach. The happy stewardess from the second cabin was taking their drink orders and offering magazines.

"How did you know that?" Buck asked.

"It's federal law, sweetheart," she said. "They might try to put us in the back of bus, but if they try it on airplanes flying across state lines they can get massive fines."

Glancing toward the second cabin, Buck said, "It's a shame Rebecca didn't know that."

They laughed.

"She'll know next time," Dottie said, squeezing his hand.

***

The cab let them off at a non-descript office building three blocks from the Capitol.

"I must have passed here a hundred times growing up," Dottie said, glancing up the street.

"Which reminds me," Buck said. "Did you tell your parents we were going to be in town?"

"They're at Uncle Nemo's place in Hagerstown. I didn't want them to cut their time short for a two-hour visit. Uncle Nemo's getting older and not doing well."

In the vestibule, they consulted a directory. Buried amidst scores of lawyers, lobbyists, and consultants with long titles and elaborate firm names was *Cora Tasby Manning* and an office number on the second floor. No title. No firm name. They took the elevator to the second floor and passed a number of opulent frosted glass doors with names etched in gold or bronze. At the end of the hall, they found her office number in white paint on a plain brown door. They knocked, then pushed open the door. Inside was a small outer office with two mismatched chairs. No receptionist. No magazines. A door to the right was open. Inside, an immense woman was seated behind an oversized desk, animatedly talking on the telephone.

"You know the issues, Lyndon. You also know what's going to be expected."

Dottie raised her eyebrows. *Lyndon?* she mouthed. Uncomfortable with being in such close proximity to a private phone call, Buck wished there were magazines or something to divert his attention.

"Let's step outside," he whispered, reaching for the door knob.

Dottie pointed into the office. The lady was waving for them to stay, holding her fingers up to signal she'd just be a couple minutes.

"He and Bobby will minimize your involvement. Everyone knows that. How you handle it could determine where you wind up in sixty-eight... *Sixty-four?*... Don't even think about it. We need to do what we can to make sure he's there for eight years... don't be silly. You're fifty-two. Sixty's not too old... I know, but you need to be patient. Look, I have to run... No, that's the last thing you want to do. This isn't the Senate. You're not in charge anymore... okay, take care, Lyndon."

After hanging up the telephone, Cora Manning rose from her desk and moved into the outer office. She was tall. Probably over six-feet, with a short plain haircut, a matronly dress, and clunky old-woman shoes. Buck guessed her to be in her early fifties, but she could have been a decade older.

She grasped their hands warmly. "Buck and Dottie, it's a pleasure to meet you." She spoke with a tone that indicated she meant it. Her face broke into a grin that might be considered almost goofy if it weren't coming from a woman considered by many to be among the most powerful in Washington. "Come and sit down. I trust that your flight was pleasant?"

Buck peeked at Dottie, hoping she wouldn't bring up the incident with Rebecca the stewardess.

"Except for a racist stewardess, all was fine," Dottie said. Buck groaned inwardly, but said nothing. Cora Manning was a busy woman, according to Desmond. Taking her time to talk about a slight on an airplane was silly.

But, amazingly, she asked questions and listened attentively to Dottie's answers, even jotting down a few notes.

"You handled it perfectly," she said. "Eastern is looking to add flights to several southern cities. I'd say that word of your treatment will be passed up the ranks pretty quickly."

"We don't want to take more of your time than necessary," Buck said, attempting to move the conversation forward.

"Nonsense," Cora replied. "You came a long way. I've got as much time as we need. Desmond told me some of your story," she reached into her desk and pulled out a copy of Desmond's newspaper, the *Baltimore Black Advocate*. Like the *Florida Times*, Buck's picture was on the front page. "I read the rest in the paper when it arrived this morning." She smiled at Buck. "You've been quite busy, Mr. Jones."

"Yes, ma'am. That's why I'm here. Desmond thought you might be of help—"

"Mrs. Manning, who are the people in that picture?" Dottie was staring at a framed photograph on a bookshelf. Cora retrieved the frame, smiling lovingly at the two people in the shot.

"This is my son Earl and my daughter-in-law Vestal," she said proudly, offering the photo to Dottie for a closer look. "They live in Kansas City. I just got back last night from spending the week with them."

Buck peered over Dottie's shoulder. Cora Manning's son and daughter-in-law were a mixed-race marriage. They appeared to be over-the-moon for each other.

"How's it been for them?" Dottie asked.

"Mostly okay," Cora said, scrunching her face at the memories. "Earl works in maintenance at a home for unwed mothers. There've been problems with previous jobs, but this one is going well." She paused, took back the picture, and smiled. "He's looking at going out on his own. There are some businesses in Kansas City that like his work and want to hire him part-time."

She set the picture aside and made eye contact with both Joneses. "You're probably wondering why an old white woman from Missouri would have anything to do with your situation."

"Well, ma'am," Buck replied. "Desmond recommends you. That's good enough for me."

"It shouldn't be, and please call me Miss Cora. Not ma'am or Miss Manning; just Miss Cora. Even Lyndon, er, Vice-President-Elect Johnson still calls me Miss Cora. Now, let me take a couple minutes to explain why Desmond thinks enough to recommend me to you. It all begins with my marriage to a man named Levi Manning..."

For the next fifteen minutes, Cora Manning enthralled them with the twisted saga of a plain young woman with few marriage prospects who married a widowed farmer who became the leader of a white supremacy group. Despite Cora's plainspoken recounting of her past, Dottie was moved to tears, especially when she told of her love for a black man named Harry Davis, and how the white supremacists had killed him. More intense was the love she had for her son, a sensitive boy who had been mentally and physically abused by his father, but who'd grown up and married a Negro woman who had helped him find his way.

"The best day of my life was the day I left Levi Manning," she said. "The second-best has been every day since." She told how she'd secured a job working as a secretary for then-Senator Harry Truman, parlaying the experience into work as a consultant for politicians at the local, state, and national level.

"I could've been just as happy staying on that farm back in Missouri," she said. "Our best years were when Levi Manning was in prison and Earl and I were working with our neighbors." She retrieved a yellowed article from *Time* magazine, a feature story about a progressive group of black farmers called *The Grebey Island Negroes*. "They taught me more about farming in six months than all the years I'd spent with Levi combined."

"So just know," she said, clearing from her desk the photograph of her son and daughter-in-law along with the magazine article and the story about Buck, "I not only can help, I *want* to help. Now I suspect that your concern is fighting extradition from Florida to Maryland, correct?"

Buck nodded. "I'm worried about getting a fair trial after everything that happened."

"We weren't even there when the violence started," Dottie said. "We have a receipt from a gas station in Baltimore where we filled up that shows we were a hundred miles away."

"Still," Buck said, "I doubt there's any chance a southern governor would overturn an extradition request for a black man wanted for inciting a riot. Maybe the best we can hope for is that Maryland doesn't try to extradite me."

"They already have," Miss Cora said, holding up a sheet of paper. "Two days ago. It already made it to Tallahassee, lying on Governor Collins' desk until he gets back tomorrow. He took an extra day off after Christmas to be with his wife and daughters."

Buck looked at the floor, shaking his head. Dottie reached for his hand.

"I guess that's it then," he said quietly.

"Not necessarily," Miss Cora replied. "I understand that you've been away from Florida for several years, so I can't blame you for not knowing, but Leroy Collins has a reputation for being his own man, particularly when it comes to issues of race."

Buck looked up expectantly.

"He's Old South to the core, but they've taken to calling him Liberal Leroy for his stands on race. I think, if he knows the entire story, he'll consider not signing the extradition papers."

"Really?" Dottie asked, gripping Buck's hand tighter.

"Adrian, his Chief of Staff, knows of your situation and has promised to have Governor Collins call me first thing tomorrow. He's taken my advice before, and I would expect him to do so again."

Buck felt the weight of several days of worry slip from his shoulders.

"That sounds so... promising," he said, exhaling.

"Well, yes... and no. Leroy Collins I can work with. It's Farris Bryant that should be your concern. He'll be sworn in as Governor in eight days, and I can't see any way he'll deny the extradition for the reasons you mentioned – a black man accused of causing a riot."

Dottie sat forward. "Can the new governor overrule the old one?"

"I don't know the answer to that," Miss Cora said, picking up a fountain pen and tapping it lightly on the desk. "My gut feeling is that he could, but on a larger scale, I'm wondering if perhaps it wouldn't be better for you to return to Maryland on your own, before Bryant assumes office."

"Why would I do that?" Buck said, shaking his head.

"Think about it, Buck. You've received plenty of positive publicity in the Negro newspapers. I would anticipate some of the mainline papers picking up your story soon, particularly those up North. With all that in your corner it will be hard to convict you, I would think."

"Miss Cora, with all due respect, you don't know what these rural Maryland juries can be like." The words were barely out of Buck's mouth when he realized how ludicrous he sounded. Cora Manning had just finished telling them how a crooked judge threw her out of her home when her ex-husband had gotten out of jail years before. She knew better than anyone what could happen in a courtroom.

Miss Cora said nothing as she reached for the oversized Rolodex that dominated a corner of her desk. Finding the card she was looking for, she jotted down a number and handed it across the desk.

"Sam Lankford has defended some high-profile clients over the past few years. He's smart and he's good. More importantly, he's a Negro, and I think—"

"The last thing we need is to step into Twinton County with a Negro lawyer," Buck interjected.

"No," Miss Cora said, shaking her head, "I think it's the *first* thing you need."

FORTY-SEVEN

As expected, Buck's extradition to Maryland was denied by Governor Leroy Collins the next day. The evening newscast out of Jacksonville made note of it. The Governor's only comment was that there were extenuating circumstances that wouldn't allow him in good conscience to sign the request.

The newscast also included a picture of Buck that made his stomach drop to the floor.

"What's wrong, honey?" Dottie, sitting next to him on the sofa in their duplex, heard his breath catch.

What could he say? The picture of Buck Jones was also a pretty good picture of Pete Demopoulos. The beard and longer hair provided some level of disguise, as did the horn-rimmed glasses he'd started wearing in the fall. Still, what if some sharp-eyed Floridian noticed a resemblance between Buck Jones and that supermarket guy who'd died five years ago.

"Seeing my face on TV startled me."

Dottie laughed. "It's hard to believe you're that same ne'er-do-well that showed up in Pine Hammock eighteen months ago."

Buck grinned. "You mean that guy who didn't know it was bad manners to offer his hand to a lady?"

Their reverie was interrupted by a knock on the door. Buck went to answer while Dottie turned down the television set.

"Mr. Jones, my name is Sam Lankford. I believe Miss Cora told you about me."

Lankford wasn't much bigger than Buck. He was middle-aged, with short neat hair and a badly-wrinkled suit.

"Since this morning, I've flown from Philadelphia to St. Louis and down here to Florida," he offered as an explanation, having noted Buck's appraisal of his attire.

Buck extended his hand. "I'm sorry, Mr. Lankford. I wasn't expecting anyone and—"

"Quite frankly, I was concerned that you might not see me if you knew I was coming."

"I still might not, Mr. Lankford. My wife and I haven't decided how we plan to proceed."

Dottie appeared next to him at the door and introduced herself.

"I was just telling Mr. Lankford that we aren't sure what we're going to—"

"You're at the epicenter of an important civil rights issue, Mr. Jones. Handled correctly, it can make a big difference for our people. Not handled at all or, God forbid, handled badly, it could…" He didn't have to finish his sentence.

"Come in," Dottie said, pulling open the door.

Five minutes later, they were seated across from one another; Dottie and Buck on the worn sofa that came with the duplex, Sam Lankford seated in an easy chair with stuffing sticking out of one arm. There was a scarred coffee table between them.

"I'll get right to the point," Lankford said, pulling a stack of papers from a natty calfskin briefcase. "Your case presents some interesting issues for us as Negroes. Based upon what we're reading in the local papers up in Maryland, the prosecution in Twinton County is basing their case on your interview with the school superintendent. They claim that interview was the first domino to fall in what became an avalanche of violence."

"We're aware of that," Dottie said.

"My people beg to differ. We see this as a free speech issue. You asked questions that needed answers. Now, some might feel those questions shouldn't have been asked, but that doesn't take away your right to ask them."

"You used the word, 'we,' Mr. Lankford," Dottie said. "You said, '*we* see this as a free speech issue.' Who are your people?"

Dottie's question appeared to catch the attorney by surprise.

"Why… we're—Mrs. Jones, you don't know why I'm here?"

"We figured you wanted to represent us," Buck answered. "But the fact is, we don't have the money to afford you, even if we do decide to proceed."

For a few seconds, Sam Lankford stared questioningly at them. Then, slowly he gathered his papers, stuffed them into his briefcase, and stood up.

"I've made an egregious mistake," he said, his tone as conciliatory as the words he spoke. "Let's start again… Mr. and Mrs. Jones, my name is Sam Lankford. I'm the attorney that Cora Manning spoke to you about. I'm based out of Washington, but I travel all over defending clients in matters of race and civil rights. I'm in private practice, but am also of council to the NAACP…"

He paused for a second, then continued. "Dr. Martin Luther King and the NAACP Executive Committee sent me to offer my support and expertise at no expense to you."

Again, he offered his hand. Again, they shook. Again, he sat down.

"Folks," he said, again pulling out his paperwork, "we're going to win this case."

***

"And you're certain Buck will get out on bail?"

They'd moved to the kitchen table for more space. Lankford set aside his coffee cup and faced Dottie.

"Nothing is certain, Dottie. What I can say is there is a history of reasonable bail being set, provided the defendant has no prior felony record." He turned to Buck. "I'm assuming you don't. Would that be correct?"

Buck glanced away as thoughts of a morning six years earlier flashed through his mind.

"Buck, is there something we need to know?" Lankford's eyes bored into him.

"No, no," Buck replied, a bit too quickly. "Traffic tickets don't count, right?"

Manslaughter, Desertion, Bigamy...

Lankford smiled. "You paid them, right?"

Buck nodded. "Hucklebuck Theodore Roosevelt Jones has a record as clear as the driven snow."

"In that case, there's no reason for bail not to be granted. It's not like you're a fugitive. Extradition was denied and you're voluntarily surrendering anyway. What about your job at the radio station? Vincent Payne has a long record for supporting the cause. Have you talked about this with him?"

"He's aware of what happened in Maryland. As far as me going back, we've not spoken. I don't start work until January second."

"Get him on the phone," Lankford said. "He likes publicity, so I think he'll go along with the plan. If things go the way they're supposed to, you'll be back by New Year's Day."

Five minutes later, Lankford was back at the table with Payne's promise of full support and a letter for the judge assuring that Buck was gainfully employed.

"Okay, here's how we proceed. Today is Tuesday, the twenty-seventh of December. I'll contact the prosecuting attorney in Twinton County and let him know you'll voluntarily surrender on Friday, the thirtieth, at noon. Of course, he'll have to provide some assurances before we return – a peaceful surrender, the opportunity for bail, no time in a jail cell. If the prosecutor is a reasonable man, we should be in and out in a couple hours." Lankford jotted a few notes on a legal pad, then continued. "Between now and then, we're going to update your story for as many news outlets as we can. Desmond Henry can ensure that happens with the black papers, but we've got to get more from the traditional press outlets. We've got insiders at the big papers in New York and Chicago. If you'd be okay with it, we'll have them work through our public relations folks. They'll screen out the ones whose motives are less than savory. Are you up to more interviews?"

"How about television?" Buck asked, hopeful the answer would be no.

"The big networks won't give this much attention. They have thirty minutes to fill and more than enough news to fill it. A man walking into a small-town police station isn't as splashy as the Eagles-Packers game or France testing bombs." Lankford paused for a second, taking an appraising look at Buck and Dottie. "But just in case, Buck, trim the beard and get a haircut. You look a little frayed around the edges."

Lankford gathered his papers and got to his feet.

"The fight begins," he said. "My office will begin making arrangements. Stay close to the phone."

FORTY-EIGHT

The duplex became more like a circus tent as newspaper reporters traipsed through at regular intervals. By Wednesday afternoon, Buck had been interviewed eleven times for newspapers as close as Jacksonville and as far away as Dallas. The *New York Times* sent a tandem of reporters hoping to exploit the story from both legal and racial angles. Several reporters also took time to interview Dottie, who was turning into somewhat of a media darling. Buck had a feeling that some of them looked at her and looked at him and wondered how an undersized one-armed man who was unremarkable in pretty much every way had snagged a beautiful and dignified woman such as Dottie. Watching her handle the spotlight, he had to wonder himself.

Vincent Payne had stopped by late in the afternoon, ostensibly to offer support, but more likely to rub elbows with reporters and talk up his new radio station and its aim of promoting black causes. His efforts were not in vain, as Buck noticed two newspapers taking time to interview him in the front yard.

At eight-thirty, the last interviewers having left two hours before, Buck and Dottie had collapsed onto the couch after a quick dinner when the telephone rang. Dottie answered. Buck alternated between listening and dozing. Eventually dozing won out. When he awakened, it was after ten. Dottie had turned off the lights, covered him with a thin blanket, and gone to bed. He considered heading to the bedroom but decided to stay put. Thursday would be another full day of interviews, followed by an evening flight to Baltimore. From there, they would return to Twinton County on Friday morning.

***

Dottie awakened him with a cup of coffee and a plate of eggs and sausage. Buck glanced at his watch and sat up quickly when he saw it was eight-thirty.

"Don't rush. First interview isn't until ten," Dottie said, kissing his cheek. "Only four today, but we did get a last-minute request. A reporter from Yale University."

"Yale? Way down here?"

"She has family in Florida and is here through New Year's Day. You didn't even stir when she called. She sounded pretty excited, so I gave her the okay to come by at three."

Buck shrugged. "What's one more, I guess."

"If you don't mind, I'll excuse myself while she's here. We both need to take a change of clothes for the trip tonight, and your underwear has more holes than Swiss cheese. I'm going to run to Woolworth's in Daytona and get some."

"Honey, I can do that. I'll go after the Yale student leaves. You've done more than enough." He gently rubbed her still-flat stomach. "Besides, you need to take care of little Jones."

"Nonsense," Dottie said, smiling. "Besides, I might need a few things myself. Little Jones will be just fine."

Buck pulled her close and kissed her forehead. He liked how it felt, so he did it again.

"That lady reporter from Atlanta, you remember the one?"

Buck did.

"She pulled me aside after the interview, when I was walking her out."

"And...?"

"She knew."

"What? Knew what?"

"About the baby."

Buck stepped back, his mouth open in surprise. "How did she find out?"

"She has four children of her own," Dottie said, beaming at the memory. "She said she could see it in my face."

Buck looked into her eyes, then took in all of her. "I don't see it," he admitted. "I want to, but I don't."

Dottie laughed. "You'll see it soon enough, Mr. Hucklebuck."

***

The day was considerably less chaotic than the previous. Buck could anticipate most of the questions that would be asked and had his answers down pat.

"It's almost sad," he'd whispered to Dottie when excusing himself during one interview for a glass of water, "how few of them come up with original questions. They just keep asking the same things over and over."

At two-thirty, a *Miami Herald* reporter said his good-byes.

"I'll walk you out," Dottie said, grabbing her purse and giving Buck a peck on the cheek. "I'm going to pick up the things we need for the trip. I'll be back by five. We need to leave for the airport by six-fifteen, so get your bag packed."

"I'll get to work on it right now," he said, eyeing the couch and the chance for an hour of shut-eye.

"Don't forget the Yale student," she called over her shoulder, getting into the car. "Her name is G.A. Newsome."

"What kind of name is G.A. for a girl?"

Dottie shrugged. "Probably using initials to get ahead. Journalism is still a man's world."

***

The rap on the door brought Buck out of a deep slumber. Despite his best efforts, he'd succumbed to the allure of the sofa. He rubbed his eyes and shook his head to get rid of the cobwebs. Four on the nose. If nothing else, G.A. Newsome, female college reporter, was punctual.

He stood and stretched as she knocked again. Through small windows in the upper half of the door, he could see the top of her head. Blonde hair. Taller than average. He checked his reflection in a decorative plate on the tiny mantle, cursing at himself for not taking Mr. Lankford's recommendation for a haircut and beard trim, then reached for the door handle. When he pulled it open, she had her fist in the air, ready to knock yet again.

"Sorry, I was…"

The words stopped. Buck could summon up nothing more than silence as he stared at her. Lowering her hand from the door, she made eye contact, her confidence and stature both dwarfing his. She smiled. It was a smile Buck remembered though he hadn't seen it often. The most common facial expressions he remembered was unhappiness, anger, or a smug satisfaction from getting what she wanted.

Still, there was no denying it. It was her.

"Hello… Pete," she said brightly.

His first thought was to slam the door and run. But where? He was in the middle of no place and without a car.

Besides, the ruse was over anyway. Now, it appeared, inciting a riot was the least of his concerns.

He looked her over from head to toe. She was beautiful. Tall and pretty, intelligent blue eyes that pierced his soul. Might as well get it over with, he thought, pulling open the door and waving her in.

"Gwendolyn."

FORTY-NINE

She breezed in like she owned the place. For a split-second Buck considered knocking her over the head with a blunt object, then hauling her into the woody swamps beyond the duplex. It was a silly thought. The folks in the other side of the duplex were weekenders, but what if they'd come in overnight and he hadn't heard them? Better to ride this out.

"Have a seat." He motioned to the chair where numerous reporters had sat the past two days, but Gwendolyn opted instead for the couch, sitting down daintily and pulling a small notepad from her purse.

"I'm sure you've been peppered with the same ten questions over and over," she said, looking up at him still standing at the door. "I'll try to be original. So, tell me, how's life been since you left home six years ago?"

Buck shook his head, but said nothing.

"That question not original enough? How about this? What the hell is a one-armed man who's hiding from his previous life doing in the middle of one of the biggest civil rights cases in America?"

Again nothing.

"Are you thinking you can just stay hidden in plain sight, Pete? Or should I call you Buck? Or Hucklebuck? Speaking of whom, what happened to old Hucklebuck?"

"He… was killed."

This slowed Gwendolyn down. Buck saw a flash of suspicion in her eyes.

"Killed? My God, Pete, you didn't—"

"Don't be ridiculous, Gwendolyn, two guys tried to rob the warehouse. They…" Buck waved his arm in the air, not wanting to relive the sight of his friend's life being snuffed out.

Gwendolyn took a deep breath. When she spoke again, her voice was quieter. "The police picked up on the robbery, but not Hucklebuck. They found that car in a burned-out barn with your remains…" she snapped her fingers. "…those were Hucklebuck's remains."

Buck nodded.

She silently absorbed the about-face in facts she'd accepted for five years. After she didn't speak for several moments, Buck did.

"How's Elena?"

Gwendolyn smiled sadly. "Mother is… fine… I suppose. I haven't seen her since… hey, you're a grandfather, Pete. Step-grandfather, I guess. His name's Mark Thomas Newsome. He's three years old and pretty much rules my world."

"Congratulations, Gwendolyn, that's… great."

She shifted on the couch, smoothing the fabric of her navy-blue dress.

"Nobody calls me Gwendolyn any more. Either Gwen or G.A. And, yes, it is great. I'm happily married to a guy I met while at Montfried. His name is—"

"Wait a minute. You wound up staying at the private school? What about the money?"

Gwendolyn nodded gleefully. "Uncle Chris and Papú footed the bill, provided Mother sell the house in Gullford and move back to Sarasota." She leaned forward, conspiratorially, "You forgot life insurance, Pete. Mother searched high and low for a policy, but nothing. Shame on you."

Pete shrugged. "It was all kind of spur-of-the-moment."

Gwen's bracing laughter echoed off the walls of the duplex.

"Anyway, I met Byron at a mixer. He was a senior at Burkemper Military School. We started dating, got a little careless, and the next thing I knew, I was pregnant."

"You've done well, it would appear." The conversation was becoming surreal, and Buck was unsure where it was going, so he just jumped on and rode it. "Yale."

"Byron's family is rich, and his parents are wonderful to me. They're footing the bill for college and everything. Can you believe I'm pre-law, Pete?"

"You always could argue."

She shook her head sadly. "I know I was a brat back then, and I'm—"

"Brat?" Buck's show of fake shock brought more laughter. Then, just as abruptly, it stopped. Gwen leaned forward, motioning for Buck to join her on the sofa.

"Look, you don't have to worry about me giving up your secret. I was there, back then. I know how Mother treated you. I know how I treated you. My immaturity was such that I was willing to walk all over you to stay in Mother's good graces. Then, when you... left, her wrath turned on me. When I found out I was pregnant, she made a big show of disowning me. I could've crawled back into her good graces, but I just said screw it. Byron asked me to marry him, and that was that. Mother called a couple times, then moved on to whatever she's doing in Sarasota these days. She's never even seen Mark."

Buck relaxed slightly, liking what he was hearing but still not fully trusting Gwen.

"We have a girl in our journalism classes at Yale who is from a place called Galestown, not far from Twinton County. Last year, when you integrated the library, she brought an article to class from a local paper. They used your full name; Hucklebuck. That got my attention. Then, when you led the sit-in at the lunch counter the paper ran your photo." She paused, pointing at him. "The glasses and facial hair are good, but it's hard to hide that missing arm."

"You knew last summer?"

She nodded. "When it became obvious that it was you, I started doing some research. College graduate, radio deejay, teacher. Then the interview you did of the school superintendent became an underground sensation. You should win that case, by the way."

"Thanks. That's my hope. I—"

They looked up as the front door opened and Dottie came in carrying two Woolworth sacks. Stomach lurching, Buck stood; Gwen followed his lead.

"Hello," Dottie said, setting aside the bags and offering her hand to Gwen.

"Mrs. Jones," Gwen said. "A pleasure to meet you. I've been interviewing your husband, and it turns out we know a few of the same people."

"Really?" she asked, glancing at Buck. Before he could speak, Gwen did. "There's a student in my journalism classes from the Eastern Shore. She knew of you and Mr. Jones from the local papers. She shared the stories with me and I decided to do a feature for the *Yale Daily News*."

Buck tried to hide the deep breath he took.

"And you're from here?" Dottie asked.

"I grew up in a little town near the Gulf of Mexico called Gullford. My father was killed in the war and my stepfather was killed during a robbery."

"That's so tragic. I'm sorry for you…"

"Gwen. Gwen Newsome. Thank you, Mrs. Jones. I've done fine. I'm married and have a little boy. Life has turned out well, though we did lose my great-grandfather three years ago. We called him Papú, which is Greek for father."

Buck sat down heavily on the sofa. He hadn't considered the possibility that Papú might have passed away. Nor had he considered that anything might have happened to his parents.

Seeming to read his mind, Gwen said, "I still have my grandparents. They're missionaries in New Guinea. They were going for two years, but have been there for five. They seem to love what they do."

"How wonderful for them," Dottie said. Then, looking past Gwen, she spoke to Buck. "We need to get ready to go, sweetheart. The plane won't wait."

"Oh, I'm sorry to hold you up." Gwen turned from Dottie to Buck. "Mr. Jones, thank you so much for your time. It was certainly… interesting."

"Yes, it was," Buck said, getting to his feet.

"I'd like to stay in touch…" Gwen said, hastily adding, "to make sure your story is told."

"I'd like that too," Buck said.

FIFTY

"I trust your stay was comfortable?" Mr. Lankford said as Buck and Dottie stepped off the elevator into the cramped motel lobby. "Our budget for lodging isn't large, so we have to avoid extravagance."

"It was just fine," Buck said. "After the late flight last night, I could've slept anyplace."

Lankford led them to his car and navigated his way onto Route 50, the main artery connecting Washington to Maryland's Eastern Shore. Buck sat in front, Dottie in back.

"We're due at the courthouse at one this afternoon," Lankford said. "Provided we don't get stuck in traffic getting out of the city, we should be there with a few minutes to spare."

"Is anyone else from the NAACP going to be attending?" Buck asked.

"Just me. Our staff is spread pretty thin, so we divide and conquer," Lankford replied. "Mr. Wilkins, our Executive Secretary sends his regards. He's in Atlanta with Dr. King and some of his SCLC colleagues preparing for a series of lunch counter sit-ins like what you did in Sheffield."

From the backseat, Dottie flashed Buck a sympathetic smile. She knew he had hoped to meet Dr. King at some point.

"I wasn't able to accomplish much with Wheatley, the Twinton County Prosecutor," Lankford continued. "He stopped short of offering a bail agreement in return for your appearance. We'll have to hope that Judge Vickers is empathetic."

Buck perked up at this information. "What do you mean, *hope*, Mr. Lankford? I thought this was a sure thing?"

"Like I said at your kitchen table, Buck, nothing's a sure thing. Would you be willing to spend a few days in jail if necessary to advance the cause?"

"No," Dottie replied quickly. "I will not let him do that. We came back here voluntarily, Mr. Lankford. At the urging of you and the NAACP, I might add."

Silently, Lankford pulled the car to the side of the busy highway, turned in his seat, and faced them.

"Say the word, Buck, and I'll take you back to National Airport and put you on the first plane to Jacksonville. I can never guarantee that the judge won't try something out of the ordinary. We've done everything we can to make sure the case is receiving an avalanche of publicity. Judge Vickers would have to blind and deaf not to have taken notice. There will likely be a good number of press people in attendance today who will make sure that any injustices get out. Miss Cora has been working behind the scenes as well. Is it guaranteed that you'll walk out of court today? No. Is it likely? Yes."

The car became quiet. Buck stared ahead for several minutes, considering his options, then turned to face Dottie.

"Let's go to Sheffield. We didn't get involved to just turn tail when things became difficult."

For the better part of a minute, they faced each other, saying nothing, but communicating through their eyes as only a couple deeply in love can do. Dottie broke eye contact first, turning to Lankford.

"Take us to Sheffield, Mr. Lankford. And do your damned best to make sure my husband doesn't wind up in the white man's jail."

***

On the outskirts of Sheffield, they passed the former studio for WSCB. A side wall and craggy remnants of the front were all that was left. Buck grew sick at the sight of it and ordered Lankford to pull to the side of the road so he could vomit.

"You are not responsible," Dottie said. "Never forget that."

The entrance into Sheffield was like it always was, with no evidence of the lives that had been lost twelve days earlier. They passed the library and movie theater, then Miggett's. A month before, there would have been a myriad of black and white faces on the sidewalks. Today the faces were few and all white. Buck watched them raise their heads as Lankford's Cadillac passed, some offering a friendly wave that stopped in midair as they realized the driver was a Negro and that the man in the front seat was Buck Jones. Friendly faces clouded with contempt. A few flashed obscene gestures. When they pulled up in front of the courthouse, a gaggle of photographers and news reporters rushed toward their car. Behind them, between the car and the steps, two dozen protestors carried signs proclaiming *Jail for Jones* and *Keep Sheffield White*.

"How well do you know the area?" Lankford asked, warily taking in the protesters. "Is there a back way in?"

"Yes, sir, there is, but the protesters will be able to get around there as quickly as we can."

"Then let's take our chances and hope the cameras keep people on their best behavior." Lankford parked at the curb a half-block south of the courthouse. A hundred yards away, Buck spotted three black men approaching from the opposite direction. He recognized them as being from Pine Hammock.

"Stay in your car for a second, Buck," one of them said.

"What's going on?" Lankford asked.

"We're going to keep an eye on your car, Mr. Lawyer," another said. "We also got some people coming along who'll get you into the courthouse."

Sure enough, a light blue farm truck pulled around the corner and stopped behind them. A dozen men, again Pine Hammock residents, disembarked from the back. Lankford got out of the car and approached.

"Are you gentlemen armed? Because if you are, I can't let Buck be anywhere near you."

"No, sir," one said. "After everything that happened here a couple weeks ago, the white people are so scared of us, we don't need guns. Some of them may hate us with a passion, but they aren't going to mess with us, either."

Lankford nodded for Buck and Dottie to get out of the car. Hugs and smiles were shared among old friends. Dottie, who had been on edge for most of the three-hour ride, was visibly more relaxed.

Until a Sheffield police car pulled up behind them.

"This here's reserved parking," Chief Russell Pannier said brusquely, getting out of the squad car. "And you folks," he said to the men who were gathering around Buck, "are going to be arrested for unlawful assembly if you don't move along."

"What about them?" a man said, pointing to the protesters in front of the courthouse.

Pannier pulled a sheet of paper from his pocket, waiting a few extra beats while the reporters moved into closer proximity. "They got a permit," he said in a condescending gloat. "City Council passed an ordinance this past week." Then turning to Buck, he said, "So stick your nigger protest up your ass, Jones."

The Pine Hammock men seemed to shrink from the Chief's words, mumbling among themselves. A couple moved away. The reporters, on the other hand, clustered in closer as Lankford stepped forward.

"Chief, may I please see the minutes where this ordinance was passed?"

Chief Pannier chuckled. "I knew you'd ask." He retrieved another single sheet and held it out for the lawyer to see. "Approved, signed, and about to be enforced... with pleasure."

Lankford nodded, seemingly impressed with the Chief's anticipation. "May I ask one more thing, Chief Pannier?"

"Make it quick, boy; I've got work to do and niggers to arrest."

"May I see the minutes from the two previous meetings when this regulation was read?"

Pannier appeared confused, so Lankford continued.

"Because, Chief," he said, holding up a copy of the Sheffield City Constitution, any ordinance, law, or regulation must have two prior readings before being enacted."

"What about that, Chief?" a reporter asked. Another snapped his photograph, catching him with his mouth open and a befuddled look on his face. Quickly, the Chief stepped away, retreating to a triumvirate of men standing across the street. Two reporters who followed were shooed away, which did little more than attract the rest, leaving Buck, Dottie, and Lankford with their Pine Hammock bodyguards.

"How'd you know about that?" one asked.

"We see it quite a bit," Lankford said. "We try to be ready for every possibility."

They watched as the three men, whom Dottie identified as city councilmen, conferred with Chief Pannier. After a few minutes, they glared at the gathering and walked away.

"I guess we're clear to proceed," Lankford said. "Gentlemen, will you escort us to the courthouse."

"With pleasure, sir," one replied.

The day was clear and, despite bright sunshine, temperatures were in the upper thirties, about normal for

Twinton County in late December. Lankford took Dottie's right arm, and Buck took her left as they fell in behind three Pine Hammock men for the hundred-yard walk to the courthouse. Three more walked on each side of them, with three bringing up the rear. Cameramen scrambled ahead of them, turning often to snap pictures. White people lining the sidewalk stepped into the grass to clear their way. Their gazes were steely, but no one said anything until they were within a stone's throw of the courthouse steps. There, the only remaining obstacle was the protesters, and they treated the contingent as if they were invisible, marching in a tight circle that would require Buck and the others to step off into the grass to go around.

"Stop," Lankford said quietly to those surrounding them. The men on all sides complied, leaving them just twenty feet from the protesters. For a few moments, all was quiet, until Lankford broke the silence. Turning to the press he said, "Let the record show that Mr. Buck Jones has returned to Twinton County of his own volition to face the outlandish charges filed against him. Also, let the record show that as of this moment, he is being kept from the Twinton County Courthouse by a group of protesters. I will not risk the physical safety of my client by allowing him to proceed until the law in this town disperses or relocates this gathering."

This stopped the protesters in their tracks. Lowering their signs, they faced off against the Pine Hammock men, neither giving an inch. When one of the Pine Hammock men in front tensed his arms, Lankford touched his shoulder and the man relaxed, even smiled over his shoulder.

And there they stood. Each side waiting to see what would happen next. Then, a white man in a cheap suit opened the courthouse door and came out on the steps.

"Lankford?"

"*Mister* Lankford. Who are you?"

The man's face turned crimson, his haughtiness turning to irritation. "Victor Wheatley, Prosecuting Attorney. It's two minutes past one. You people are late. If you're not inside in three minutes, we'll start without you."

Before Lankford could respond, the press was on Prosecutor Wheatley with the force of a jet bomber.

"What are you going to do about the protesters?"

"Don't you agree that this situation is unsafe for Mr. Jones?"

"What about the Chief trying to disperse the Negro men?"

"What will you do if one of these protesters injures Mr. Jones?"

"Do you feel this is a safe environment, Mr. Wheatley?"

The Prosecutor, obviously not used to being besieged with questions, retreated to the courthouse, shutting the door behind him.

"Reminds me of when Dorothy went to see the Wizard of Oz," Dottie said, drawing a round of laughter from the others. The laugher stopped quickly, however, when a uniformed Sheffield cop stepped outside and removed the protesters.

It was time for court.

***

Buck hadn't expected to be as nervous as he felt when Judge Sterling Vickers stomped into the courtroom and sat down heavily at his station high above the proceedings. Judge Vickers probably did everything heavily. He was a massive man, six-five and three-hundred pounds, with a shock of premature gray hair, blue eyes, and an oddly shaped black birthmark over his left eyebrow that looked like a fly was perched there.

"One thing on the docket today so let's get started," he said gruffly. "Let the record show that Buck Jones is in the courtroom. Mr. Jones, you have returned to Twinton County to face the charge of inciting a riot. You understand this, right?"

"Yes, Your Honor."

The courtroom was packed, but silent. Whites in the main gallery, blacks upstairs. No intermingling. Buck had expected more of the confrontational vibe they'd experienced outside, but Judge Vickers had a reputation for a hair-trigger temper and no aversion to tossing people out of the courtroom.

As there was no seating reserved for the press, they clustered in the back and down the side aisles. The courtroom was stately, but not large, and the jockeying of reporters and photographers was creating a din that seized the judge's attention.

"The press will be silent or I'll clear you out of here," he thundered.

"We have a right to be here and you will do no such thing." The reporter, a young man from the *Philadelphia Inquirer*, was gone within a minute, barking threats as he was manhandled from the courtroom. Nothing else had to be said. Watching the exchange over his shoulder, Buck spotted Desmond Henry leaning against a side wall, camera around his neck. Their eyes acknowledged one another. Buck nudged Dottie and pointed at their mutual friend.

"This is a bail hearing for Buck Jones, a thirty-two-year-old Negro, formerly of Pine Hammock. The charge brought against Mr. Jones is inciting a riot. I will allow limited testimony before making a final decision." The judge looked at the prosecution table. "Mr. Wheatley, are you ready?"

Wheatley acknowledged that he was. The judge turned to Buck's side of the courtroom, his eyes boring into Mr. Lankford.

"And you are...?"

Lankford got to his feet, buttoned his jacket, and faced the judge. "Samuel Lacy Lankford, Your Honor. Attorney for the Defendant. Let the record show that my client, has returned by his own choice to face these charges. After reviewing the case against Mr. Jones, the Governor of Florida, the Honorable LeRoy Collins did not choose to honor Twinton County's request for extradition. We feel that his decision will be this court's as well, and respectfully ask that the defendant be released on his own recognizance."

Judge Vickers nodded. "Since we haven't even heard Mr. Wheatley's request for bail, let's save the argument, okay, Mr. Lankford?"

Lankford sat down.

"Mr. Wheatley, what are you seeking in this case?"

"Five-thousand dollars," Your Honor.

The judge nodded, his poker face giving nothing away. Lankford jotted a note on the pad in front of him and angled it so Buck and Dottie could read it.

I expected it to be higher.

When it became obvious that Wheatley was done, Lankford stood again.

"Your Honor, I have letters attesting to Mr. Jones' character and integrity from several notable individuals that I would like to submit for consideration. These include Mr. Jones' employer at a Florida radio station, the President of the college he attended, and the Reverend Martin Luther King."

Two distinct responses came from the gallery. Snorts of derision from those downstairs, gasps of amazement from the balcony. Hearing Dr. King's name mentioned in the Twinton County Courthouse meant something to both sides.

Judge Vickers accepted the letters, glanced at them, and laid them aside.

"Is there anyone in the gallery who would like to speak before I make a final determination?"

A hand went up. A female, mid-thirties, in a black dress. The judge waved her forward. She stood in front of him, and when she spoke her voice was so quiet Buck had to strain to hear.

"I'm Lucille Smoot. My husband, a sheriff's deputy, was killed by those terrible colored boys during the riot two weeks ago." She stopped and turned slightly, just enough to look at Buck. "That one there – the one-armed boy – his interview of Superintendent Mister got the others all riled up. We'd never had no trouble before then. They were getting their rights. The library. The lunch counters. There was no reason for what he did. It stirred 'em up to the point where they didn't know any better. Judge, the boys who attacked my husband got what was coming to them. The only person left who has to pay is that boy there. If you let him walk out of here I don't think he'll ever come back. I'm asking that you lock him up right now."

The lower gallery stood as one, applauding Lucille Smoot's bravery. Catcalls rained down from upstairs. Judge Vickers was having none of it.

"Clear the balcony!" he thundered. "Next time it'll be the entire courtroom!"

"Your Honor, you *cannot* do that." Lankford jumped to his feet and moved toward the bench. Buck noticed the bailiff make a move as well, his hand reflexively reaching for his sidearm.

"The balcony was the only seating area made available to Negroes," Lankford argued. "You've essentially taken away the opportunity for them to view these proceedings. That's a violation—"

The resulting camera flashes and surge of reporters trying to move closer raised a ruckus that drowned out the rest of Lankford's argument. Being heard wasn't a problem for Judge Vickers, however.

"We stand in recess," he boomed. "When we return, the balcony will be cleared, except for five colored people who are to be selected by their peers. They will be given seats in the rear of the lower gallery." He paused, glaring about the room, the objects of his anger obvious. "The press will be removed from the gallery and placed in the balcony. You are being unruly and getting in the way of Twinton County residents. Now, if there are no questions, we'll reconvene in fifteen minutes."

The press surged the defense table, firing questions at Buck, Dottie, and Lankford. Lankford signaled that he would address them. Two of the Pine Hammock men who had served as bodyguards entered the courtroom and tapped Buck on the shoulder.

"We've got a room for you off to the side. Would you like a cool drink while you wait?" Lankford nodded for them to go ahead.

"See you in a few minutes," he whispered. "And don't worry. Despite the theatrics, we're in good shape. The bail offer was acceptable as presented. The rest is all window-dressing."

***

The Pine Hammock men escorted Buck and Dottie to the small anteroom they'd secured, then left them alone.

"How do you feel?" Buck asked Dottie.

"Like we're in a car going five-hundred miles an hour with no roadmap."

He smiled and kissed her cheek.

"Seriously, Buck, it's unnerving not knowing what's going to happen. And all those white people seated behind us? I could feel their hatred burning right through me."

There was a quiet knock on the door. Desmond stuck his head in.

"Can I have a minute?"

Buck motioned him in.

"What can you tell me about Landon Biggerstaff?" Desmond asked.

They looked at one another. Buck nodded for Dottie to take the question.

"He was our principal at Pine Hammock. He seemed okay enough... at first. But later, I wasn't so sure."

"He offered no support for our efforts," Buck added. "When I lived in Mrs. Mitchell's place, he had a room across the hall. It started well enough, but I sensed he resented our efforts to integrate. I know he didn't care for me."

Desmond nodded thoughtfully. "Then it makes sense."

They looked at the attorney curiously.

"He's going to advocate for a higher bail."

***

"I'm Landon Biggerstaff. I was Principal at the Pine Hammock School. I have a teaching degree from Maryland State College. Currently I'm completing my master's degree at Harvard University."

Biggerstaff paused for dramatic effect.

"The night of December 17 was the worst of my life." Biggerstaff spoke succinctly, trying, Buck thought, to sound educated to the white people in court. "My entire adult life has been devoted to helping young Negro children find their place in the world. My opportunities to move beyond Pine Hammock have been plentiful, but I've always felt my best work could be done here."

"What the hell...?" Dottie whispered.

"Buck Jones arrived in Pine Hammock eighteen months ago, and I thought from the start that he had a chip on his shoulder. He drank to excess, stayed out until all hours of the night..." Biggerstaff paused again, staring into his lap. "... he played music on his radio show that I thought was too... flashy for people around here. Music with messages about sex and immorality... not right at all."

"Amen," a white voice said from the gallery, drawing a soul-shrinking stare from Judge Vickers.

"Moonie's – a speakeasy a few miles out of Pine Hammock – that became his second home. He hung with a rough crowd out there, and I found out later he was as rough as any of them."

Buck couldn't believe what he was hearing. Rough? Moonie's? He thought of Poop Chester fast asleep, his head resting on the table. It almost made him laugh.

Don't worry. Lankford wrote on his pad. *Theatrics. It'll be over soon.*

"Mr. Jones got off to a bad start at school. I had to go in the first day and restore order after he lost control."

Buck cringed at the memory of Jerome Gilliam being pummeled by the larger, stronger principal. If Biggerstaff had his way, students like Jerome would be chucked aside like garbage, rather than nurtured like he and Dottie had done. The same boy who'd been humiliated in front of his classmates had lost his life trying to break up a confrontation in the streets, and here was Biggerstaff using him to make a point. Damn him.

"As the year progressed, Mr. Jones became more and more insolent. He was starting to become well-known in Baltimore and Washington for the Hucklebuck skit he did on the radio."

Skit?

"The next thing we knew, he was bringing the wrong kind of people to town. I talked to him about it, but in the end, it became apparent he wasn't a good influence on our children, so our superintendent and I had to fire him."

Biggerstaff continued in a similar vein for several minutes, then finally got to his point.

"Mr. Jones might come across as a hero to the people in Pine Hammock, but in reality, he's a coward. He was extremely disrespectful to our superintendent on the radio and brought outside agitators to Twinton County. Then, when things got out of hand he ran away. In my opinion, if he posts bail, he'll disappear again."

The courtroom was quiet.

"Your Honor, I would like to question the testimony of Mr. Biggerstaff," Lankford said, rising to his feet.

"This isn't a trial, Mr. Lankford."

"If the court is accepting testimony willy-nilly, then it's becoming a trial, Your Honor. Much of what this man has said is hearsay and lies. If he's going to be allowed to say whatever comes to his mind, I'd like to call in several of the people you barred from this courtroom. They will definitely present a much different picture of Buck Jones than we're hearing from this..." Lankford pointed at Biggerstaff like one might an approaching skunk.

"I'll take your point under advisement," Judge Vickers replied tersely. "Just as I'll take into consideration the letter you gave me from Dr. Martin Luther King. By the way, Mr. Jones, are you and the Reverend good friends?"

Buck stared at the judge.

"The letter stands for itself," Lankford interjected. Satisfied that he'd made his point, Judge Vickers returned his attention to Biggerstaff.

"Anything else, Mr. Biggerstaff?"

"One thing, Your Honor. While a case is being built against Mr. Jones, I think somebody should check into his past."

"Stop him, Sam," Buck said quickly. "He has it out for me."

"Your Honor," Lankford was on his feet in an instant, his voice echoing off the walls. "Whatever this man is getting at, it has nothing to do with why we're here."

Ignoring the attorney, Biggerstaff forged ahead. "Somebody needs to check into the whereabouts of a man named Pete something-or-other. He lived in Florida and was found dead in the back of a car—"

"This is ridiculous!" Buck jumped up, standing beside his attorney.

"Your Honor, this man is a rambling idiot!" Lankford exclaimed.

"—It was 1955," Biggerstaff said loudly. "The man – Pete - owned a grocery store. I think Buck Jones might've killed him."

FIFTY-ONE

"Is there anyone else who wishes to speak? If so, step forward now."

Lankford had done his best to shoot holes in Biggerstaff's credibility, but it was hard with the accusations coming out of nowhere. He was able to extract a confession that Biggerstaff had been snooping in Buck's room at the boarding house, and that his claims were based upon some old newspaper clippings. As Biggerstaff stepped down, A couple reporters exited the courtroom, probably off to pursue the veracity of his claims.

"You want to speak on your behalf?" Lankford whispered. Buck shook his head.

"You need to say something, Buck," Dottie said, leaning close. "You can't just let his lies hang in the air like that."

"Your Honor, I'd like to speak."

Heads swiveled to the next-to-back row. Prosecutor Wheatley smiled when he saw who it was. Judge Vickers waved him to the front.

"State your name, where you live, and your occupation."

"I'm Paul Adams. I live in Sheffield, and I am the owner... former owner, I guess, of the local radio station."

"Proceed, Mr. Adams."

Adams tugged at the sleeves of the khaki barn jacket he'd worn to fend off the cold temperatures. Twice he glanced about the courtroom, the second time looking directly at Buck.

"As you know, my radio station was destroyed following a demonstration involving residents of Pine Hammock and some people from out of town." His diction was clear, precise, just as he spoke on the radio. Still, Buck sensed nervousness from his former boss.

"It was, everyone will agree, a terrible couple of days for Twinton County. Lives were lost, a school was burned down. My radio station..." his voice trailed off as his shoulders slumped.

"Say what you need to say, Paul," someone in the gallery encouraged. Mr. Adams nodded and pulled himself together.

"Your Honor, it's obvious now that there's going to be a trial... Buck Jones... for inciting a riot. People are saying his interview on my radio station set off the chain of events that resulted in two of the worst days we've experienced in these parts."

When several spectators uttered their agreement, Judge Vickers wielded his gavel. As Mr. Adams turned and gazed at the gathering, Buck saw a steely resolve in his eyes that hadn't been there before.

"He's going to let you have it," Lankford said. "Steel yourself."

When the room was quiet, Mr. Adams continued. "To those who assert that Buck is the reason for everything that happened, I have one thing to say."

Mr. Adams paused for a beat. Then another.

"Bullshit."

The gallery responded as if someone had just insulted a close family member.

"What are you saying, Paul?"

"You lost your radio station."

"Did somebody threaten you?"

Again, Judge Vickers banged his gavel for quiet. It took longer this time.

"Mr. Adams, do you know what you're saying?"

"Of course I do, Judge. Words are my livelihood and, in this case, I mean everything I say. Buck isn't the reason we've had problems." He gestured to the people seated in the courtroom. "We are."

The room grew rowdy again. Judge Vickers pointed out four people who were brusquely hauled out. Buck wasn't sure if they were the loudest, or if the Judge was making examples of them. Whichever it was, it worked.

"I fired Buck for that interview. That was wrong. I should have stood by him. When I offered to cover his salary for the next month, he turned me down. That's how strong his convictions are. I went home that night ashamed of myself for allowing a few advertisers to dictate the way I run my station."

"What about the coons who burned the place down, Paul?" A young man Buck had never seen before yelled from the rear.

"How do you know what color they are?" Mr. Adams snapped. "Chief Pannier's done nothing except pine to get Buck back here. Nobody's even bothered to find out who's responsible for the fire at my place or the one at Pine Hammock School."

The crowd quieted.

"Your Honor, not only do I plead with you to drop the charges against Buck, I pledge that, should the trial go forward, I'll be testifying on his behalf. Loudly and proudly."

"Nigger lover!" someone spat, causing yet another uproar. Ten minutes later Judge Vickers had the courtroom cleared of everyone except the press and those involved with the case. Once order was restored, he spoke.

"Mr. Jones, your bail is set at five-thousand dollars."

Buck took a sigh of relief. Dottie squeezed his hand while Lankford patted him on the back.

But Judge Vickers wasn't done.

"I also order you to remain in Twinton County until your trial, which is set for two weeks from this Monday, the sixteenth of January. Should you—"

"Your Honor," Lankford cried. "You're ripping away this man's right to make a living. He has a job in Florida where he's expected to be this coming Monday."

"That's my decision, Mr. Lankford. He's free to stay in the Twinton City Jail until then. At least he'll have a place to sleep and three meals a day."

Lankford sat down heavily.

"Besides," the Judge said, eyeing Buck, "I want to find out if there's anything to Mr. Biggerstaff's claim that this man might be involved in something larger."

***

Buck was roughly escorted to a holding cell in the courthouse basement with the understanding he would remain there until bail was arranged. Biggerstaff's assertions ripped through his mind again and again as he sat on a concrete pallet bolted to the wall. Those damned clippings from the Tampa newspaper. Why had he kept them in his room? He'd given up everything else related to Pete Demopoulos, why keep something as trivial as an obituary? Would Lankford and the NAACP spring for his release if the rumors grew? What would he tell Dottie?

It was two hours before he heard approaching footsteps, then the sound of the large metal door opening that separated the cell from the rest of the courthouse basement. A uniformed police officer led the way, followed by Lankford and Dottie. Buck expected the officer to open the cell door, but instead he left it closed as he stepped aside.

"We need to talk," Lankford said, stepping up to the bars. "Tell us everything."

Dottie hung back, eyeing him warily.

"First I need to talk to my wife... alone," Buck said. "Mr. Lankford, would you mind giving us a few minutes.

***

"I want the truth."

Lankford had stepped out, taking the police officer with him and closing the door behind them. Dottie wasted no time.

"I don't trust Landon Biggerstaff any further than I can throw him, but he didn't make all that up, either. What was he talking about, Buck? Tell me everything and tell me now. And I want to know what there is between you and that girl reporter from Yale. I saw the way you were looking at each other when I came home the other day. There's something there."

He considered lying; extending the ruse but knowing it wouldn't last much longer. It was a matter of time before the reporters put two and two together. The subterfuge was just about over. Now, it was just a question of how long.

"Gwen is my step-daughter."

Dottie gasped, but quickly composed herself.

"Start in the beginning and tell me everything."

So, he did.

FIFTY-TWO

Chief Russell Pannier was gleefully doing everything he could to ensure that Buck's stay in the Sheffield City Jail was miserable. If it wasn't the constant stench of a backed-up toilet in his cell or the tasteless pureed food, it was impromptu middle-of-the-night cell inspections. Despite the Chief's best efforts, however, nothing compared to the look on his beloved Dottie's face when he'd told her about his past.

That was five nights ago. Dottie could have handled the parts about him disposing of the assailants' bodies from the warehouse and even assuming Hucklebuck's identity. It was the part about his being married that had led her to wordlessly walk out of the jail. She hadn't been back. The next day, newspapers across the country told his secrets to the world, after a *Washington Post* reporter became the first to uncover his past.

"Jones, I figured you for a small-timer," Pannier chortled as he dropped off the latest editions of newspapers from Baltimore, Washington, and Philadelphia. "But you're a real pro. We've got you dead-to-right for inciting the riots, but now you're looking at abandonment, bigamy, and whatever the hell role you played in the deaths of those boys down in Florida."

Buck said nothing. Rather than being deterred by his silence Chief Pannier reveled in it.

"And claiming you're *a nigger*. Now that takes the cake. I've never known a white man stupid enough to want to be a coon. Were things that bad, Jones? Or should I call you Demo-poo or however the hell you Greeks say it?"

Buck stared at the wall, avoiding eye contact. Pannier grew quiet, but it was too good to last.

"Ain't seen nothing of the missus," he said with a grin. "She run off with that coon attorney? The only people who've asked to see you are the reporters. They keep calling and stopping by. You sure you don't want to talk to 'em? I know it gets lonely in here."

When he realized there wouldn't be any response, Pannier shoved the newspapers through the bars and left. Other than a drunk the first night, Buck had been the only resident of the Sheffield City Jail. The silence and uncertainty were starting to close in. Lankford and the NAACP had dropped him like a hot potato when his past was revealed. He didn't expect to hear from Lankford, but prayed every day that Dottie might come back. It was appearing more and more likely those prayers would remain unanswered.

The trial was another ten days away, after which he would likely be extradited back to Florida for questioning, with a probable stop in North Carolina to face miscegenation charges. There was little Buck could do to fight it. The NAACP support was gone, and he had no money for bail or a lawyer. Even if he did get bailed out, where would he go? The recent revelations that Buck Jones, the Negro civil rights champion was really Pete Demopoulos were causing a media storm. Whites and Negroes alike read with interest and shock about how his marriage to a Negro woman in a small town on the North Carolina border broke the miscegenation laws of that state along with the bigamy laws of every state from Maryland to Florida.

The most recent press clippings would do little to diffuse the uproar. One reported that Kirkmont College was considering the revocation of his degree. Another reported that Elena had been admitted to a hospital after learning that her late husband was alive. Conspicuously absent was any mention of Dottie.

With nothing else to do, Buck read through each of the newspapers, then read them again. The barred windows of the jail were ill-fitting, and a cold January wind kept the cell damp and chilly. The thin blanket he'd been provided did almost nothing to allay Buck's discomfort, and he'd realized the day before that he was now running a fever.

***

"Jones! Someone to see you!" The officer's bellow awakened Buck from a fitful sleep. It was daylight outside and still cold.

"If it's as cold in the cell as it is in this hallway, there's going to be hell to pay." Buck recognized her voice immediately.

The cellblock door opened and Gwen marched in. Her conservatively cut blue suit and briefcase made her look older. The guard stepped in with her and closed the door.

"We need privacy. And open the cell door."

"Can't do that little lady. We got rules, and—"

"I'm his attorney, and damn it you'll open this door." Chin jutting out, Gwen took a step in the cop's direction that caused him to retreat slightly. Wordlessly he unlocked the cell door and stepped out of the block.

"Call me 'little lady' again and I'll have your job," she yelled. "And if you even think of listening in, I'll go straight to Judge Vickers."

The cellblock grew quiet after the officer's footsteps faded into the distance. Gwen turned and offered her hand.

"I'm your attorney."

Buck shook her hand, waiting for the punchline. There wasn't one.

"I've already had twelve hours of Pre-Law and you've got nobody else. You need me and I still have a couple weeks before I have to be back at Yale."

"Is this wise?"

Gwen raised her hands. "Would you prefer to go it alone?"

She had a point.

"The first thing is bail. I've got a cashier's check for five-hundred dollars. That is the ten-percent required to release you. Next, we'll—"

"Where did you get the money? Did Dottie…"

"Pete, My husband's family is rich, remember?"

He nodded.

"Then we'll find you someplace to stay. There are a couple motels on the highway near Sheffield that—"

"Can't do that. They're white only."

"Pete, for God's sake," Gwen said, shaking her head. "You're *white*. The whole world knows it now. I'll get rooms for both of us, then I'll start working on your case." She paused again, knocking on the cellblock door to get the officer's attention.

"I'll be back to get you. We're going to win this case, Pete."

***

The Lone Pine Motel was bare-bones, but compared to the Sheffield City Jail, it was heaven on earth. The owner's initial refusal to provide a room for Buck was vociferously beaten back by Gwen's threat of a huge lawsuit that Buck was certain could never happen, but seemed believable enough to sway the owner. Gwen got him checked in then quickly jumped back into her blue Corvette.

"I've got a couple appointments," she said. "I'll bring you some dinner when I come back."

Buck turned the room's heat up to eighty, crawled under the blanket, and passed out. When he awoke it was daylight. The nightstand clock said eight-fifteen. A greasy bag of cold fried chicken sat on a small table in front of the window. In five minutes, he'd devoured it. He pulled back the curtain and glanced outside. Seeing no sign of Gwen's car, he crawled back into bed. The next time he awakened, the shade was open. Night was falling. Five-twenty. Gwen was seated in a chair by the table where he'd consumed his chicken hours before.

"Welcome back to the land of the living."

Buck eyed her warily. It was hard to believe it was the same Gwendolyn. The eyes, the blonde hair, all the same. The biggest difference was the smile. This Gwen smiled. A lot. She seemed happy. The brooding teen of years' past was long gone. Buck decided at that moment to trust her.

"I met your landlady," she said.

"Mrs. Mitchell?"

Gwen nodded, then reached into a sack at her feet, pulled out a pie, and sat it on the bed. "She sent this. Pecan. She wants you to know that not everybody has turned their back on you."

Buck lifted the pie and breathed in the sweet aroma.

"She also said that she knows who set the fire at Pine Hammock School. She and I paid a visit to Sheriff Masterson." She checked her watch. "In about ten minutes, Landon Biggerstaff is going to be charged with arson."

Buck dropped the pie.

"Biggerstaff? No way. If he was going to do something like that it would be the white school. He wouldn't burn down his own school. It cost him his job."

"Think again. The superintendent... the man you interviewed?"

"Doctor Mister."

"Yeah," Gwen snapped her fingers. "What a strange name. Anyway, he had told Biggerstaff that he would be an assistant principal at the white school when they integrate. Biggerstaff just took it upon himself to speed things up. He figured no one would ever suspect him of it.

Do you know the guy who runs..." she consulted her notes "...Happy's Market?"

Buck nodded. "His name's Happy."

"Yes. He was one of the few people who stayed in Pine Hammock the night everything happened. Almost all the others were in Sheffield. He lives above his store and says he saw Biggerstaff drive by three different times between eight and eleven. Only two other cars passed during that time, and he recognized both. One was a guy named Poop, and he was heading in the other direction."

"To Moonie's," Buck said.

"And the other was Sheriff Masterson. Plus... *plus*... Biggerstaff filled his car up with gas two days before the fire *and* the next Monday. Happy said he never fills up more than once every couple weeks."

"Could he be that stupid?" Buck knew the answer before he'd finished asking the question. Of course Landon Biggerstaff could be that stupid. He thought he was above reproach in Pine Hammock. Buck had seen it in the way he'd beaten Jerome and others who misbehaved. Despite his claims of attending Harvard graduate school, he was a bully who never left Pine Hammock because he knew there was no better deal anywhere else.

After a few more minutes, Gwen left for her room. Now wide awake, his heart pounding from the revelations, Buck laid back and stared at the ceiling. His thoughts drifted from Biggerstaff to Dottie. God, he missed her. He wondered if she thought of him, but decided they were probably finished. Were they even married, legally? He supposed not.

Eyeing the telephone on the nightstand, he debated calling her parents' house to see if she was there. Would she speak to him? There was only one way to find out. He picked up the receiver and got an outside line.

"Operator, I'd like to make a long-distance call to Capital-six-nine-two-five." He waited through a series of clicks as the call was connected. It rang twice before being picked up.

"Hello?" Dottie's mother.

"Gloria. It's Buck. May I speak to Dottie."

He heard muffled conversation in the background, then Dottie came on the line.

"Buck."

"Dottie, I'm out of jail. Biggerstaff is being charged with burning down the school. There's even a chance—"

"Buck Jones, I loved and trusted you."

His heart broke as she said those words. *Loved* and *trusted*.

Past tense.

"Please, Dottie. I know I've hurt you terribly, but it was so bad before..." He began sobbing. Getting control took several moments. "I... there was so much that..."

Then he realized the line was dead.

FIFTY-THREE

Once the press discovered he was out on bail, knocks at the door of Room 117 at the Lone Pine Motel became a relentless occurrence. Eventually Gwen prevailed upon the owner to put up a makeshift barricade of sawhorses and duct tape that created a ten-foot off-limits zone in front of the door. As with everyone she met, Gwen had won over Maury, the motel's crusty owner. She was also becoming somewhat of a media darling - G.A. Newsome, the stunningly beautiful and confident Yalie who was Buck Jones' legal representative. Naturally curious, the press started digging into her background. It didn't take long to find out how her past intersected with Buck's. When the questions started to arise, Gwen met them head-on in a press conference held, of all places, on the steps of the Twinton County Public Library.

"Pete Demopoulos was the closest thing to normalcy I had in my life back then," she stated. "I was young and out of control. My mother was more concerned with her social standing. Pete worked hard every day, even though he was treated badly on all sides."

Then came the questions, fired from all directions from grizzled veterans of the newspaper world.

"If he was such a great guy, why did he leave?"

"Life became impossible for Pete."

"Was he involved in the deaths of Jerry Mark Lester and Marvin Conrad?"

"Really?" Gwen stared down the reporter like he'd just asked her brassiere size. "Have you looked at the criminal records of those guys? They tried to rob the warehouse. Pete fought them off."

"Who was Hucklebuck Jones?"

"A friend to many. A poor deaf man who lived a simple life in the swamps until he was viciously stabbed by Lester and Conrad. Pete felt Hucklebuck's life should not be forgotten, so he sought to make his name mean something."

"How do you expect to win the case here in Twinton County, Mrs. Newsome? You're not even an attorney."

"The charges are ludicrous. The defense won't be able to find one person who testifies that Buck Jones's interview incited them to riot."

"What about the news that Landon Biggerstaff has been arrested for arson at the Pine Hammock School?"

"It further advances our claims that there was no incitement to riot. So far, the only person other than Mr. Jones who has been arrested was a man who openly stated that he didn't listen to the radio interview. The prosecution has no case against Buck."

From the rear, a black man raised his hand, waiting for Gwen to call on him. When she did, he wasted no time.

"Desmond Henry, *Baltimore Black Advocate*. Mrs. Newsome, given all that has happened, does Buck regret returning to Twinton County?"

"Buck… Pete regrets that his actions have caused hurt to others. He's grieved by the fact that his wife, Dottie, isn't here with him today. He's grieved that a good person like Mrs. Geraldine Mitchell, a widow and owner of the boarding house where he lived, was hurt defending civil rights. He's grieved that Jerome Gilliam, a student with a bright future, lost his life while trying to be a peacemaker." Gwen stopped and daubed at her eyes with a tissue. "None of that needed to happen, Mr. Henry." Gwen raised her hand, motioning to the library entrance at her back. "Buck and Dottie Jones integrated this library quietly, with respect and dignity." She pointed up the street. "They and several Pine Hammock residents integrated the lunch counter at Miggett's Department Store. Not a single Negro raised his fists in violence. These weren't violent people, Mr. Henry. They wanted only what others had: the ability to move freely around a community that they supported with their tax dollars. They wanted their children to go to good schools instead of rundown tinderboxes without the resources to prepare them for the world. Is that asking too much?"

There were a couple additional questions, but most reporters started packing up, realizing they'd just gotten their best quotes or soundbites. As they drifted away, Desmond Henry made his way to the base of the steps.

"Mrs. Newsome, I'm not sure if you're aware, but Buck and I—"

"I know all about you, Mr. Henry. I also know that you disappeared like the rest when Pete's past came to light."

Desmond hung his head. "You're right, and I feel terrible about that. When the NAACP backed away I thought it was best I did too." He paused, searching for the best way to make amends. "Buck's past doesn't negate the fact that this is still a free speech case. Is there a chance I can visit with him for a few minutes? I'd like to apologize and maybe do another one-on-one interview."

Gwen glanced around, making sure no one was listening. Satisfied, she came down the steps until she was standing face-to-face with Desmond.

"Sorry, Mr. Henry, but no interview." She pulled a slip of paper from her purse. "It wouldn't be right for a witness to interview the defendant, would it?" She pushed the paper into his hand.

"You've just been subpoenaed to appear in court, Mr. Henry. I'll be calling you as a witness." She winked. "Bring your best game. Buck needs you."

Unsure how she would be received in Sheffield, Gwen had parked her car a block away from the library. She was returning to it when a maroon Galaxie 500 pulled close. The front tire on the passenger side jumped the curb, startling Gwen enough to make her stumble back into a storefront. Regaining her composure, she glared through the Galaxie's passenger window. The driver was a large middle-aged woman whose face Gwen immediately recognized. When the woman invited her to get in, Gwen accepted.

***

Supper was other-worldly, yet their hostess had whipped it up in minutes. Her house, in a middle-class Washington neighborhood, was small but well-appointed. The furniture was plain, but obviously expensive. For Gwen, the experience of being in such close proximity to Cora Manning was like a dream.

"I'm glad you decided to stay here until the trial," Cora said, pouring Buck another glass of iced tea. "I tried to get ahold of you, but the owner of that motel refused to put my calls through."

"We've been getting inundated by reporters," Gwen said. "The owner's name is Maury, and he was a curmudgeon at first, but we won him over."

"*She* won him over," Buck said, nodding at Gwen.

"I can understand why," Cora said, smiling. "You're quite the celebrity, Gwen."

It was the first time Buck had seen his stepdaughter blush. She looked like a happier version of the child he'd known years before. It was obvious she was overwhelmed with being in the home of Cora Tasby Manning.

"Miss Cora," she said tentatively, "are you sure having us here is okay? Pete and I aren't very popular in most circles."

Cora waved her off. "Don't be silly. You were sitting ducks out there at that little country motel. The media has been respectful of your privacy so far, but there are still five days to go until the trial. Sooner or later they'll turn nasty."

"We really appreciate it, Miss Cora." Buck said.

"Well, Buck," Miss Cora's tone became more serious. "I don't know what happened all those years ago with the men who tried to rob you. And I certainly don't condone marrying someone when you're already married..."

Buck felt a tightness in his stomach. The last thing he wanted was for this wonderful woman to be disappointed in him.

"...but I also understand how circumstances can make people do things they'd rather not do. I've been there myself. At the least I can offer you a quiet place to prepare for what comes next."

"Again, thank you, ma'am," Buck said quietly. "I'm humbled by your courtesy."

"And, Gwen," Miss Cora's cheerfulness returned, "if you'd like, I know some pretty good legal minds that I can bring in to consult with you prior to trial."

Noting Gwen's quick change in posture, Miss Cora's tone changed. "Don't worry, dear. I didn't mean they'd take over. Quite frankly, I think at this point, changing Buck's representation would be detrimental. You've become the Jackie Kennedy of the legal set. But if you want some ideas that might help, I know people who can offer them."

Another blush. Buck considered it one of the most beautiful things he'd seen. Somehow Gwen had overcome her past, and she didn't even have to change her identity to do it.

"I'd like that, Miss Cora. I have some ideas, but there are some things I'm not sure about. But would these lawyers be willing to compromise their own standing?"

Miss Cora laughed. "The men I'm thinking of are brilliant, but they spend all their time in boardrooms and classrooms. Boring stuff, really. They'll consider this as renegade law; something they always thought they'd like to do before getting caught in the muck here in Washington."

Gwen appeared dazzled by the offer. "Well, if you think they would…"

"Consider it done," Miss Cora said. "For now, why don't I show you to your rooms. You'll be safe from the prying eyes of the press until the trial. Enjoy the solitude and use it to get ready."

Cora escorted them upstairs. After getting Gwen settled, she showed Buck to his room.

"I saw Dottie two days ago," she said when they were alone.

Buck turned quickly. "You did? How? How was she?"

"It wasn't hard tracking her down. I remembered her saying she grew up here. She's hurt, Buck. No woman is ready for the news she received."

Buck's eyes teared up. He turned away.

"Don't give up, Buck. I knew the minute I met you two that she loved you with a ferociousness that reminded me of my daughter-in-law Vessie. She and Earl have had to overcome so much, but they made it. You fight for Dottie with everything you have, but first, you fight for yourself."

FIFTY-FOUR

A mixture of snow and ice reduced traffic to a crawl. Fortunately, Miss Cora had anticipated the conditions and gotten them up early for the trip to Sheffield. The trial would start at one that afternoon, and a trip that normally took two hours stretched to five. About thirty miles out of Twinton County, the snow gave way to a cold slushy rain that made roads more passable. Miss Cora's friend, a prominent Washington attorney named Bennett Williamson, had offered to drive them in Miss Cora's car. Since they'd left Gwen's car in Sheffield, they gratefully accepted his request.

Buck wore a suit he'd picked up from a DC thrift store for four dollars. Gwen and Miss Cora had both offered to purchase him a new one, but he'd already taken enough of their time and money. Sitting next to him in the back seat, Gwen wore a winter white suit that made her green eyes stand out.

They parked and made their way to the courthouse without incident. The streets were empty, as the cold rain made even a few minutes outside unpleasant. Inside was a different story. Dozens of reporters and several television cameras crowded into the lobby awaiting their arrival. Questions were fired from all directions as Gwen led them to the courtroom. Buck noticed how the eyes of the reporters, especially the males, locked in on her. A few

308

recognized Miss Cora and Bennett Williamson and started asking questions about their involvement in the case. Responses were limited as they pushed their way into the courtroom. Inside, Gwen confidently directed Buck to the defense table, belying her inexperience in such environs.

"Are you nervous?" he asked as they got seated.

"Are you kidding? I'm about to represent you in front of all these reporters and cameras. Two weeks from today I'll be sitting in an archery class back at college. What the hell do you think?"

Buck laughed despite the tenseness of the moment. Bennett Williamson and Miss Cora were seated behind them, close enough to consult if needed. Three days earlier, Williamson and two of his colleagues had come to Miss Cora's house to help prepare Gwen, but she'd needed only a few pointers. When Williamson offered her a job with his firm after law school graduation, Gwen reminded him that she hadn't even started yet. It would be another year and a half before she finished her B.S.

The ludicrousness of his situation wasn't lost on Buck. He was a man exposed; accused of inciting a riot, the world now knew him as a white man posing as a Negro who had abandoned his wife and stepdaughter, only to be represented by the stepdaughter who wasn't even a real lawyer. A few newspapers were having a heyday with the more tawdry aspects of the story. Buck's two marriages, Gwen's estrangement from her mother, the real identity of Hucklebuck Theodore Roosevelt Jones. Gwen's mother Elena had, after initially refusing to talk to the press, started greasing the skids on her own behalf, speaking loudly and often about her husband's abandonment and her daughter's out-of-wedlock pregnancy. Elena's comments were actually starting to have a reverse impact, Buck thought. Two newspapers, one in North Carolina, the other in New York, had recently portrayed her as a crazy woman who'd driven off her husband and daughter.

"Oh, there's something else I need to talk to you about." Gwen sat aside her notes and placed her hand on Pete's. "The Prosecuting Attorney in Gull County, Florida is talking about making an example out of you. In his eyes, you're a white man who abandoned his family and took up with a black woman. Gull County is still very segregated, and a lot of residents will agree with his version of the facts. I'm worried about getting a fair trial down there." She nodded behind them, "Mr. Williamson is, too. Governor Collins is gone, and the new governor is a staunch segregationist. There's little chance of him stepping in on your behalf."

The nerves Pete was feeling amped up. "What should I do?"

"Get through this first," Gwen said. "Then, if it comes down to it, I have a strategy for Florida that I'll share with you. It's kind of offbeat, and I'm sure that Mr. Williamson or Miss Cora might not agree, but it might be preferable to facing a jury."

"Tell me."

"Actually, Desmond came up with it," she said. "But I think it's worth considering. It involves a sore spot for some down there; one I think we can exploit." Gwen leaned closer and lowered her voice. "You would have to—"

"All rise! Court is in session. The Honorable Judge Harland Jenkins presiding."

Pete and Gwen both jumped at the bailiff's announcement.

Judge who?

A murmur of confusion greeted the septuagenarian jurist who unsteadily climbed onto the bench, pounded his gavel, then waited for silence.

"Judge Vickers was involved in a car accident this morning on his way back from a law convention in Baltimore. His car slid coming off the Chesapeake Bay Bridge. He's in a hospital in Easton with serious, but not life-threatening injuries. He was adamant that the trial go on without him, so I'll be filling in."

More murmuring in the packed courtroom. Miss Cora leaned forward and whispered to Gwen and Buck.

"Retired judge from Prince George's County," she said, nodding at Judge Jenkins. "Taught at the University of Maryland Law School. Has a house down at Ocean City. Apparently, he was there when he got the call."

"Business first," the judge said. "Are either of the parties in this case adverse to my filling in?"

Gwen glanced over her shoulder at Williamson. He nodded that she should proceed.

"None, Your Honor," she said. Wheatley, the Prosecutor concurred.

"In that case, I do have one item," Judge Jenkins said, swiveling his chair toward the defense table. "Mr. Jones, you are charged with inciting a riot. You have representing you a young woman who is not a licensed attorney. Are you aware of this, sir?"

"I am, Your Honor."

"Please stand when addressing the court, Mr. Jones."

Buck stood. "I am, Your Honor."

"And you are satisfied that she adequately represents your interests in the case, Mr. Jones? The last thing we want is for you to come back later and claim you were underserved by counsel. If you feel uneasy about Miss Newsome's representation, we will adjourn until your fears are allayed."

"I wish for Miss Newsome to represent me, Your Honor."

"Fine, then, though I question your choice of representation, Mr. Jones, I do not question your right to choose her. Now, one more thing. Are you aware that charges have been brought against you in Florida, and that you will possibly be turned over to authorities there to stand trial?"

"I am, Your Honor."

"Then let's seat a jury and get started."

***

The jury was as white as the snow that had started falling outside. It hadn't proven hard for Prosecutor Wheatley to disqualify the four Negroes in the jury pool, as all stated that they had been friends with Buck and had no doubt he was innocent. In the end, the jury was six men and two women, ranging from twenty-three to seventy in age. Three farmers, two factory workers, a merchant, a housewife, and a retired schoolteacher. Their facial expressions ranged from excited to bored.

"Mr. Wheatley, please call your first witness."

"Chief Russell Pannier."

Chief Pannier was dressed in a formal uniform likely only worn to court and funerals. He strode to the front with the confident air of a man about to put away the bad guy.

Wheatley was also well-dressed for the occasion in a dark-brown suit and dress shoes that reflected the lights high up on the ceiling. He didn't bother to get up from his seat at the prosecution table as he walked Chief Pannier through the events of December 19. Referring to notes on a pocket-sized spiral pad, Pannier recalled the turmoil that led to the death of a sheriff's deputy and two Negro boys.

"For the better part of two hours, we lost control," he said tersely.

"Could that have been prevented?" Prosecutor Wheatley asked.

"If it weren't for the radio interview Jones did with Doctor Mister the week before, the people wouldn't have been all bent out of shape. Our coloreds have never caused trouble before." The chief pointed at Buck. "Not until that one came to town."

"Your witness," Wheatley said, nodding at Gwen.

Unlike her counterpart at the prosecution table, Gwen was quickly on her feet.

"Mr. Pannier, did—"

"Chief."

"Excuse me?" Gwen had been approaching the stand when Pannier corrected her. She stopped, momentarily confused.

"*Chief* Pannier," he said, gazing down his nose at her.

"Oh... okay. Sorry about that." Gwen took a breath. Buck could see her knees shaking.

"Chief Pannier, were your men actively patrolling the area of the march?"

He stared at her for a few beats, the replied, "What do you mean, *actively* patrolling?"

Gwen glanced at her notes, then back at the defense table. Buck wasn't sure what she was looking for, but he couldn't help her now.

"Uh... like were your men *actively* patrolling? Like being active?"

Prosecutor Wheatley stood for the first time. "Your Honor, the question is vague. Please advise Miss Newsome to be more specific."

"He's right, Miss Newsome. Your questions have to be clear. Please explain what you mean or withdraw the question."

Gwen looked at the floor like a chastened child. "I withdraw the question, Your Honor." She returned to the prosecution table and rummaged through a stack of papers, a process that took most of a minute. The courtroom remained quiet.

"Your Honor," Wheatley was standing again, "if Miss Newsome has no other questions, why don't we release Chief—"

"What did Mr. Jones say that incited the violence?" Gwen's words came in a staccato burst.

"I don't understand... what did he say? He said a lot." Chief Pannier's tone was irritatingly condescending.

"Your Honor," Prosecutor Wheatley interjected. "I know Miss Newsome isn't an attorney but do we have to do her job for her?"

Gwen's eyes darted between Wheatley, Chief Pannier, and Judge Jenkins. She appeared on the verge of losing control.

"I'll allow the question," Judge Jenkins said stoically. "The witness will answer."

"I've forgotten the question, Judge." Chief Pannier's response brought muted laughter from the gallery.

"What did Mr. Jones say that incited the violence?" Gwen regained her footing enough to restate the question.

Chief Pannier shook his head, his look one of pure irritation. "It was everything he said. The way he pounded away at Superintendent Mister. His questions were unfair. They—"

"Which questions were unfair, Chief Pannier?"

Pannier looked at the prosecution table, getting a slight nod from Wheatley.

"You just can't talk to the school superintendent like that."

"Like what?"

"Like… like one white man talking to another. Like they were… equals or something."

Gwen paused, allowing the chief's statement time to cook in its own juices. Buck eyed the jurors. Two were nodding in agreement with Chief Pannier's statement. One was asleep. A couple appeared to disapprove.

"Chief," Gwen continued, "I'd like to play the interview for you. We'll go question by question and you tell me at what point you feel Mr. Jones was inciting people to riot."

"Objection, Your Honor. I think Chief Pannier's trying to say that there wasn't one specific point when the interview turned, it was the overall theme that led to the rioting."

"Why are you telling us what he's trying to say?" Gwen retorted. "Isn't he capable of speaking for himself?"

"Objection overruled, Mr. Wheatley. Your witness has stated that the questions were asked in a way that could stir people to violence. Let's have him point out when this occurred. I assume you have a tape recording, Miss Newsome?"

Gwen reached below the table and picked up a large box. "Yes, Your Honor. I have it right here."

The gallery silently waited as Gwen set up the reel-to-reel tape recorder, running a long extension cord from the defense table to a plug on a side wall. She made sure everything worked, then looked at Chief Pannier.

"I'll stop the tape after each question, Chief. Please tell me if you feel the tone of that section of the interview was inciteful."

She hit a button and the reels started turning. Buck's voice filled the silence.

Most of our listeners, you might know sir, are Negroes. Many have been involved with the efforts to integrate local businesses and institutions, and they're wondering why it's taking so long to desegregate our schools. What can you say to them?

Gwen stopped the tape.

"Does that question raise any concerns, Chief Pannier?"

"Damn right, it concerns me. He's got no business asking a question like that."

"Why not?"

"Its disrespectful!"

"Disrespectful to Superintendent Mister?"

"Yeah. Nobody should talk to important people like that."

"I'll play it again, Chief. Please tell me which part is disrespectful."

The Chief's claim was ludicrous, and everyone knew it. Buck's question was delivered in his usual cool tone, without malice or disrespect. Looking around the courtroom while the question played again, Pannier reconsidered his stance.

"Maybe it's not *that question*, but there's plenty wrong with the interview. Play some more."

Gwen advanced the reel until she found the next question.

So, Dr. Mister, in September 1965, colored children will have the opportunity to enroll at the elementary and high schools in Sheffield?

"Is there something inflammatory about that question, Chief?"

A smattering of guffaws could be heard as Chief Pannier considered his response. Again, Buck was every bit the gentleman.

"Play some more," Pannier spat.

"I'll play Superintendent Mister's responses as well," Gwen said, pressing the button.

"That's right, we're excited about that, Buck. It's the right thing to do."

If it's the right thing to do, then why isn't it happening this fall?

"Right there!" Chief Pannier rose to his feet and pointed at the recorder. "He had no cause to put Dr. Mister in a corner like that."

Gwen looked at Judge Jenkins, who nodded at her to proceed. The next several interactions from the recorder were germane, with neither Buck nor the superintendent raising their voices. It wasn't until Buck's question about progress in Twinton County that the superintendent grew prickly.

Doctor, are you aware of the successes Twinton County has had over the past year in terms of integration? The library, stores and lunch counters, the movie theater?

Well, Buck, I don't live in a cocoon.

"What are your thoughts on that exchange, Chief Pannier? Was this the section that led to the riots in Sheffield?

"He's disrespecting the superintendent."

"Would you say a response like, 'I don't live in a cocoon,' was disrespectful as well?

Chief Pannier rubbed the back of his neck, his hand becoming slick with sweat. "He was getting tired of being hammered, so maybe he hammered back."

Gwen played more.

Then you are aware that, in almost every incidence, integration happened without violence or injury and that—

What about that colored lady? The one who got hit in the head? That's the kind of thing we're trying to avoid, Buck.

"Chief, was there something that Mr. Jones said that caused the superintendent to interrupt him like that?"

"He was being a disrespectful punk," Pannier said angrily.

"I'll continue to play the tape, Chief. If anything jumps out at you as being responsible for the riots in Sheffield, please tell me to stop."

Ten minutes later, the tape ended. Pannier didn't stop her once, even at a couple points where she might have expected he would. Buck came across as a professional, asking questions that deserved answers. He sounded much like the announcers on the big network stations. In the end, Superintendent Mister came across as a petulant child, growing silent and leaving when he didn't like the questions. Judging by what Buck saw in the jurors' eyes, they had expected a more volatile exchange.

"I have nothing else," Gwen said, returning to her seat. Miss Cora winked. Mr. Williamson nodded, a smile playing across his face.

"Call your next witness, Mr. Wheatley."

Wheatley rose. "Your Honor, we had planned to call Landon Biggerstaff, but in light of his recent arrest, we felt the word of Chief Pannier would be sufficient."

"You're saying you have no other witnesses, Mr. Wheatley? This is your entire case?"

The prosecutor turned and furtively glanced about the gallery, trying, it appeared, to find someone credible enough to testify.

"I'd like to take a recess, Your Honor," Wheatley said nervously. "I'll get ahold of Superintendent Mister and maybe a couple other people…"

While Wheatley pled his case to Judge Jenkins, Bennett Williamson reached forward and tapped Gwen on the shoulder. When she turned, he handed her a slip of paper.

Object to further witnesses. Ask for a directed verdict.

Gwen read it twice and looked again at Williamson. The attorney nodded. *Now*, he mouthed.

"Your Honor," she said, interrupting what had become a rambling monologue by Prosecutor Wheatley. "The defense objects to the calling of further witnesses. Mr. Wheatley had as much time as we did to prepare. We even drove here through a snowstorm so that Mr. Jones could have his day in court. One of our witnesses, Mr. Henry, did the same. Now Mr. Wheatley is trying to cover for his own lack of preparation."

"That's ridiculous," Wheatley said, angrily jabbing his finger in Gwen's direction. "We know what happened in Sheffield on December nineteenth. We know Buck Jones was responsible. Now the credibility of our police chief, an elected official of this city, is being called into question. Quite frankly, Your Honor, if Judge Vickers were here, he'd see through all this and give us the time we need—"

"Judge Vickers isn't here, Mr. Wheatley." Judge Jenkins voice remained calm, but his eyes blazed. By arguing that Chief Pannier's credibility was being questioned, the prosecutor had inadvertently questioned the judge's credibility, and that never played well. "And I tend to agree with Miss Newsome. You had plenty of time to line up your witnesses, but chose to hang your hat on Chief Pannier. Next time, perhaps you should consider doing your job."

"You have no right to—"

"I have all the right in the world, Mr. Wheatley, but if you'd like to debate that further, I'll give you the opportunity after this case is concluded."

The judge's demeanor invited no further rebuttal.

"Miss Newsome, please call your first witness."

"You Honor, I respectfully ask…" she glanced at the slip of paper in her hand. "…for a directed verdict."

A commotion ensued as spectators asked one another what this meant. Prosecutor Wheatley rose quickly for another round with the judge.

"There's no way in hell. In all the years I've practiced law in Twinton County, no judge ever considered a directed verdict."

"Maybe not, Mr. Wheatley, but perhaps no judge was every presented with such a shoddily prepared case. Now sit down."

As Wheatley sullenly took his seat, Judge Jenkins looked upon the gallery, raising his voice to be heard by all.

"Miss Newsome has requested a directed verdict. What she is asking me to do is make a ruling that her client, Mr. Jones, is innocent based on the evidence presented by the prosecution. It's a legal maneuver that isn't used often, because it effectively takes the decision out of the hands of the jury." The judge made eye contact with Bennett Williamson as he continued. "It's a request usually made by more experienced, savvy attorneys, but Miss Newsome has requested it and, quite frankly, I'm inclined to grant it."

Understanding what was happening, several reporters rushed for the door, causing a flurry of noise and commotion. Judge Jenkins calmly waited for the hubbub to subside before continuing.

"I've heard nothing from the prosecution that would lead a reasonable jury to believe that Mr. Jones caused the riot that occurred here last month. I find for the defendant and order him released."

***

The media din in the courthouse hallway was immediate and almost exclusively directed at Gwen Newsome. The flashes and clicking of cameras intermingled with questions about her performance and future plans. A star had been born, and Buck was happy to let her have the spotlight.

"We're heading back to Washington," Miss Cora said, coming up behind Buck with Bennett Williamson in tow. Buck gave her a big hug and shook Williamson's hand. "The directed verdict idea is greatly appreciated."

"Judge Jenkins has been around the block," Williamson said. "Your local judge might not have accepted it, but you got lucky today."

"What's next, Buck?" Miss Cora asked.

"I guess I head to Florida and face the music," he said.

They said their goodbyes and floated off. With Gwen still fielding questions from the quote-hungry media horde, Buck took a moment to look around. A few Pine Hammock friends waved as they made their way toward the exits. At the rear of the bustling flow he saw Chief Russell Pannier flip him the bird as he skirted the reporters and take his leave through an unmarked door. Desmond Henry made eye contact, pulled away from the throng of reporters, and approached. Buck opened his mouth to say hello when a familiar face appeared through the courthouse's glass doors.

Dottie.

"Hey, Buck, I just wanted to—"

Buck pushed past Desmond, his eyes never leaving her. When she spotted him, she came forward. They were steps apart when Buck was grabbed roughly from behind. Two men in street clothes flashed badges.

"We're from Gull County, Florida, Demopoulos. We're taking you back with us."

"Dottie!" Buck thrust his arm out, but was quickly pulled back.

"How do we cuff a one-armed man, Tony?" one of the Florida guys said.

"Put the other cuff on his belt," his partner said. Then, with his arm cuffed tightly behind him, they pulled him away. Dottie followed.

"Let me talk to him," she said, pushing past. One of the men strong-armed her, shoving her against a group of reporters still clustered around Gwen and sending Dottie sprawling to the floor. Seeing what was happening, the press turned its attention to the action developing behind them.

"Hold it!" Gwen yelled, getting in the face of the larger of the two men. "Show me your paperwork."

Dutifully, he produced an extradition form, flashed it, then jammed it back in his pocket. A reporter had helped Dottie to her feet and she limped to Gwen's side.

"Dottie, you came!" Buck seemed oblivious to the mayhem around him. His focus was on his wife. She raised a finger indicating she wanted a moment with him. The Florida lawmen relented but didn't release Buck from their grasp.

"Buck... or whoever you are... we're not married anymore. I went to North Carolina and got an annulment. I don't want to ever see you again." She shoved a piece of paper in his pocket, wheeled around, and left. Pandemonium ensued as reporters snapped pictures and shouted questions while others hurriedly followed Dottie out the door. For Buck, it was like time was standing still. He was seeing the throng of people closing in on him, hearing their questions, and feeling the tug of handcuffs from behind him. All of it seemed to play out at some strange heightened level he couldn't comprehend. Then, he felt his legs buckle. As he fell, the pressure of the men holding the handcuffs turned his arm at an impossible angle. The snap of breaking bone caused people milling around nearby to jump back, repulsed or horrified by what was happening.

Buck fell heavily to the tiled floor face-first, banging his head with a force that knocked out two teeth. Blood started to pour from his nose. The surroundings were turning gray, and given the news he'd just received and the pain he was feeling, Buck was determined to let the lights go out. Through the flash of cameras and din of reporters, the last thing he saw was Gwen's face as she kneeled and put her face close to his. Her stare was intense, her eyes locked on his. When she spoke, it was a whisper.

"I didn't get to finish telling you what to do about Florida... can you hear me, Pete?"

He nodded vacantly, his eyes rolled back in his head. Gwen grabbed his hand in hers, pulling on his arm enough to send waves of nausea throughout.

"If you can hear me, squeeze my hand."

He squeezed. It was slight, but enough for her to know he was hearing her.

"Pete, here's what you need to do..."

Gwen brought her face even closer, her hair brushing across his bloody cheek. He knew the lights were about to go out, but did his best to hang on to hear what she had to say.

"Make them think you're crazy."

PART FOUR

FLORIDA PANHANDLE
1961

FIFTY-FIVE

Mr. Jones, a man does not offer his hand to a lady. Were you raised in a barn?

We're having a baby!

Make them think you're crazy.

Buck opened his eyes, but Dottie wasn't there, so he closed them again. It was hard, sleeping during the day with the Florida humidity and bright sun streaming in from large windows. And the others – how they passed by and stared at him, some putting their faces within inches of his, their dank malnourished breath making him want to retch. The meds helped overcome some of the distractions. In the five weeks since being admitted, he'd mastered fake-swallowing them when dispensed by the bored night orderlies, then spitting them back out and hiding them under his pillow to take in the mornings when he wanted sleep. Daytime was for sleeping. Nighttime, when most of the staff was gone, was when Pete needed to be alert.

His arm still hurt. The doctor had done a shitty job of setting it. Five weeks later, the cast was off and the arm was slightly bent at an unnatural angle. No one had bothered to address his broken teeth, and breathing through his nose was still hard. The substandard care was typical of the medical staff at Panhandle State Asylum. He'd watched them when they were attending others,

324

carefully making sure they didn't notice he was awake. Dr. Feinbloom was in charge. He passed through once a week, barking commands at orderlies each step of the way. He'd viciously poked Pete in the ribs once, checking to see if he was eating enough, he claimed. That was as close as Pete had come to giving up his secret. For the most part, the others passed by with minimal communication.

His bracelet read, *Pete Demopoulos. Patient 1-61-19973. Agnosia.* The first few nights after he'd arrived, while the rest of C-Ward slept, Pete had studied the bracelet, trying to decipher what the numbers meant. The first three numbers were easy enough; the month and year he was admitted: January 1961. A guy two beds away had 11-52. He'd spent almost nine years of his life in this hellhole.

And the part about agnosia? That took a bit longer until he'd discovered it meant the inability to feel, usually brought on by brain damage.

Brain damage?

Make them think you're crazy.

Mission accomplished.

C-Ward was massive, two-hundred feet long by seventy-feet wide. Six rows of beds, forty beds to a row, lined up barracks-style from wall to wall, with a couple feet of passing space between each for staff to move about. It wasn't as if they did much moving. Other than twice-a-day feeding times, when spoonfuls of gruel were shoved into his mouth, it was rare to see the face of anyone who wasn't a patient. Pete had heard the orderlies refer to C-Ward as *Corpse Ward.* Looking around, it was easy to see why.

During the day, the patients who were ambulatory shuffled like zombies around the filthy ward. Pete observed them when he wasn't sleeping. Most were ghosts, emaciated shadows under perpetual shrouds of drugs and neglect. Some defecated on the floor as they walked, soiling the backs of their paper-thin hospital gowns. Others did things even more hideous. He'd watched patients force themselves on others, some victims crying out in pain, others unconscious or uncaring. One end of the room was for females, but over time, the beds had been moved about so that there was no longer a clear demarcation. One patient, a boy of maybe twenty, had lifted Pete's gown to gape at his private parts, before finding himself splayed on the floor as Pete kneed him in the face. After lying inert for a half-hour, he'd wordlessly gotten up and continued his slow march.

The only reprieve from the stench and filth had come three weeks before. He'd heard Dr. Feinbloom talking about it during his rounds. State Hospital Inspectors were coming, he'd warned the orderlies. The ward needed to be cleaned up. For two days, they'd grudgingly gone from patient to patient, manhandling them from their beds and dragging them to a room roughly the same size as C-Ward, except full of bathtubs instead of beds. Patients were dumped into the tubs where many remained for hours before orderlies vigorously scrubbed their bodies with brushes that sometimes drew blood. Pete had heard orderlies speaking of two patients drowning. It was abhorrent, and all for naught as the inspectors did little more than poke their heads into C-Ward before moving on. Pete wasn't disappointed, though. He had his own agenda.

At eight pm, evening meds were distributed. For most patients, this regimen consisted of a tiny but potent red pill that had them snoring within minutes. At nine the lights went out, casting the unit into a sea of snoring and moaning darkness. The night staff consisted of two orderlies, Pedro and Rocky, who were the devil incarnate. Their shift could be a reign of terror for patients who made the mistake of crying out or trying to get out of bed. Pete had watched them slap patients into unconsciousness. Fortunately, by midnight, both habitually disappeared into the Medical Director's office, where they watched television and shared a bottle of cheap booze. Their exit was Pete's signal to rise.

He had discovered another world beyond a metal door that could be jimmied with a nail file he'd taken from the unmanned orderlies' observation booth. A stocked kitchen provided ample nourishment to make up for meals missed during the day. Books, magazines, and the latest edition of the *Tampa Tribune* were available in an employee breakroom. And in a small unlocked room with a sign on the door identifying it as the *VISITING PHYSICIANS' OFFICE,* was a telephone. Pete closed the door of the dark office, picked up the phone, dialed an outside line, and made his call. It was the third he'd made since arriving. There would be more.

After the call was completed, Pete picked up the *Tribune* to see if there were any updates about his case. Given the proximity to Tampa of Pete's family business, the paper had provided extensive coverage. It was from the *Tribune* that Pete had learned that he'd been declared mentally incompetent to stand trial following the head trauma from his nasty fall at the Twinton County Courthouse. He thanked his lucky stars that he'd remembered Gwen's final admonition: *Make them think you're crazy.* It had been her way of providing him with an alternative to a trial and likely jail time.

In another edition of the *Tribune,* he'd found a picture of his parents leaving the hospital after their visit. That was two days after his arrival, the only time Pete had struggled to control his emotions, wanting very much to hug them and tell them he was going to be okay. Instead, he'd lain in a clean bed in a room he'd been jettisoned to so his parents wouldn't be exposed to the true conditions of C-Ward. He'd even pissed himself to make everything seem real. According to the *Tribune* article, Mr. and Mrs. Demopoulos were crushed that their son's life had come to this, but since there was little they could do, they planned to return to New Guinea.

There were several mental hospitals in Florida, and from what Pete could tell, he'd landed at the right place.

Now all he had to do was keep up the charade… and wait a little longer.

FIFTY-SIX

"How the hell is he *gaining weight*?"

Pete remained stone-still, despite Dr. Feinbloom's jostling him about like a rag doll. He'd screwed up and one of the day orderlies had noticed.

"What are you feeding him?" Feinbloom barked.

"Same as everybody else," the orderly replied meekly.

"But he's gained seven pounds. I've never seen anything like it."

"Maybe we should put him in isolation," the orderly suggested. "Perhaps another patient is giving him their food. Some pretty strange shit goes on here."

"His color's good," Feinbloom said, clutching Pete's jaw in a vicelike grip. "Who is he again?"

Pete heard papers being shuffled. "Demopoulos, the guy who left his wife and said he was a nigger. He led that riot up in Maryland."

Dr. Feinbloom snorted. "Well, if anyone needed confirmation of his insanity, that story should be enough."

The orderly laughed.

"Leave him here for now," the doctor said. "You're probably right about somebody shoving their food into his mouth. Maybe we'll get lucky and they'll choke the crazy bastard." As they moved on they continued laughing like fraternity brothers sharing a sick joke. Pete took a deep breath. Since he'd discovered the stash of ice cream in the kitchen freezer he'd been gorging on it several nights a week. It was supposed to be for patients but he'd never seen it on the trays around him.

Now that they'd identified him as something beyond a number, the clock would have to start again. Being unremarkable was critical to the plan.

***

"How many are there?" The voice came through the telephone line loud and clear, despite being a long-distance call.

"Three. Four if you count the woman," Pete said. "Two of the three men would probably pass. The third is missing an arm *and* a leg."

"Keep an eye on them. Decide which will be best. We'll talk again in two weeks. Maybe by then it will be time to move. And go easy on the ice cream."

Pete hung up, put on a lab coat hanging in the VISITING PHYSICIANS' OFFICE, grabbed a stethoscope, and eased open the door enough to peer into the hallway. Quiet as always. It was after one, and Pedro and Rocky had hunkered down to watch an old movie in the Medical Director's office, following a particularly brutal hour on C-Ward. A patient, a woman who was probably thirty but looked sixty, had refused the little red pill. Her argument was rational and well-stated, rare for C- Ward, but the orderlies didn't care. They'd teased her and slapped her, then Rocky pinned her in place while Pedro forced the pill down her throat. While they waited for her to drift off, they'd run their hands lasciviously across her body. A man in the next bed sat up suddenly and demanded they stop. They did, but only to turn against him. It grew bloody and horrible, but Pete forced himself to look. He wanted to remember. He wanted them to pay.

Pete snuck to the kitchen for a quick snack and his twice-a-week piss in the orderlies' coffee pot, then returned to C-Ward to make his rounds. There would be three stops.

Santos Marco Rodriguez. Patient 8-57-34210. Schizophrenia. Rodriguez was one of the three male patients missing an arm. Pete had observed him from afar. He'd had a few outbursts, but nothing more than many other patients.

"Mr. Rodriguez." Pete shook him gently, but he didn't move.

"Mr. Rodriguez, can you hear me." The man's eyes fluttered open. His mouth moved, but no words came out.

"Mr. Rodriguez, your family is here to see you." A lie, but one that was more likely than anything to get him to respond. His eyes opened again and stayed open. He tried to focus on Pete's face.

"Marisol?" His accent was heavy.

"Who is Marisol, Mr. Rodriguez?"

"Marisol? Marisol *esposa*... my wife."

"Would you like to see your wife, Mr. Rodriguez?" Rodriguez's eyes lit up.

"*Si... Mucho*. Marisol... but... Cuba... Castro." The man shook his head sadly.

"I'll see if Marisol can visit, Mr. Rodriguez." The man's eyes registered a flash of happiness before drifting back into the fugue from which they'd emerged. Rodriguez would be a bad choice. Too aware. Pete moved across the room to another bed.

Dewey LaPoint. Patient 12-60-64029. Chemical Lobotomy. LaPoint was the second candidate. He appeared to be late 20's and it appeared the chemical lobotomy either hadn't worked or had worked too well. Poor Dewey neither spoke nor registered any recognition of things happening around him. The only issue was his severed arm. He was missing his right arm. Pete had lost his left. Was it too obvious?

Pete shook LaPoint, but there was no response. He said his name several times, loud enough to cause the patient next to him to stir in his sleep before he resumed snoring, but Dewey still didn't move. Dewey LaPoint had potential. There appeared to be nothing remarkable about him. No defining scars, no sudden outbursts. From scouring the medical journals in the *VISITING PHYSICIANS' OFFICE*, Pete had learned that a chemical lobotomy was a regimen of medications that supposedly had the same effect as a real lobotomy. Yikes!

"Dewey," Pete whispered before moving on, "you might be getting out of here after all."

Elijah Butts, Patient 05/55/63775. Schizophrenic.

"Hello!"

Pete was so startled by Butts' greeting he stumbled backward, falling against another bed. The patient groaned as the bed lurched slightly.

"Be careful," Butts said cheerfully. "We're packed in as tight as ticks."

Butts was a short, compact man of maybe fifty, unkempt and smelly like most people in C-Ward. His eyes, however, were a different story. Bright and alert despite the late hour.

"Hello," Pete whispered. "How are you tonight, Mr. Butts?"

The man's eyes grew confused. "Butts? My name's Joyce Gilkey." He eyed Pete's coat. "Are you the new doctor? I've been waiting for you."

"Yes, I am. What can I do for you?"

Butts/Gilkey rubbed his forehead with a grimy hand. "It's still there. The other doctor said he got it out, but I can feel it. It hurts when I play tennis."

"I'm sorry, Mr.... Miss Gilkey, but I left my notes in the office. What's still there?"

"The pencil," Butts snapped, still rubbing his head. "It's been in my head since they admitted me. I keep telling them, but nobody is able to get it out."

Pete took a moment to ponder what he was hearing. Could it really be that easy to cure Elijah Butts/Joyce Gilkey? He considered going back to the *VISITING PHYSICIANS' OFFICE* for a pencil that he could lay on the bed. Then, when the patient woke up... poof! Healed! Would it help? Would it make things worse? While he weighed the pros and cons, the patient looked at him expectantly.

"I'll tell you what, Miss Gilkey. I'll make this a priority."

"Oh, thank you," Butts gushed. "The issue needs to be addressed. I've been unable to play tennis for two weeks, and I know my game is suffering."

Butts was still smiling when Pete left him. The man had been on the ward for over six years, but thought he'd recently played tennis. Butts had potential, but he was too full of life. The shorter the potential lifespan, the better it would be.

By unanimous decision, Dewey LaPoint had won the Pete Demopoulos Derby. The closest thing C-Ward had to the Miss America Contest. Dewey's prize? He would get to become Pete Demopoulos! Pete found himself humming the Miss America theme as he made one more pass by Dewey's bed...

There he is... Pete Demopoulos...

There he is... your ideal...

Maybe I'm starting to really go nuts, he thought, as he moved through the dark ward.

***

"Son of a bitch," Rocky grumbled, jostling Pete and waking him from real sleep. He was manhandled into a wheelchair, pushed into the bathtub room, and tossed into an empty tub, hitting his head heavily against the porcelain. Rocky turned on the hot faucet and the tub started to fill with scalding water. When it hit his foot, Pete reflexively pulled it away.

"Too hot for you, asshole?" Rocky grinned. "Then tell your family not to visit before nine o'clock. I've got enough to do without having to scrub shit from your crazy ass."

Rocky stomped off leaving the hot water running at full force. As soon as he was out of the room, Pete reached up and turned on the cold water in time to save himself from third-degree burns.

Family?

Visit?

The options were limited. Could it be Dottie? His heart started to race at the possibility. Could she afford the trip from Washington? If it were Dottie, the charade would end on the spot. He wanted her to know he wasn't *really* crazy, that it was all an act to avoid a long stretch in jail. More than anything, he would tell her he wanted to be with her and the baby growing in her womb. The desperate longing he felt for her hadn't dimmed. There were still nights when he thought of her endlessly, so much so that he'd considered aborting his plan in favor of an attempted escape over the walls that surrounded Panhandle State Asylum. It was a bad idea, he'd been warned during the regular phone conversations, but still... the chance to see Dottie again made the risk seem worthwhile.

But it wasn't going to happen. Dottie was finished with him, so the plan remained in place. But who could be visiting?

A clock on the far wall of the otherwise deserted bathtub room advanced quickly as the water cooled. It had been six-twenty when Rocky brought him in. It was now seven-forty. No one had come nor gone. Rocky would have probably gone home by now. They'd forgotten him. He considered getting out and sneaking back to the ward, but there was no towel nor gown. So, he waited. He'd gotten good at waiting, biding his time during the dozy parts of the day in anticipation of nightfall and the chance to roam.

Family?

Visit?

At five past eight, a siren went off, three short blasts. Pete had heard it before. It meant there was an incident on

C-Ward. Another fifteen minutes passed before a day orderly entered the bathtub room and spotted him, lying in the tub of cold water.

"Found him!" he shouted, then left, returning a few moments later with another orderly. They brought a towel and clean gown.

"Those damn night guys," the first orderly said, as they pulled Pete from the water and dried him off. "Look how wrinkled he is. They dumped him in here and left him."

"What are we supposed to do with him?" the second orderly asked as they placed Pete in the wheelchair Rocky had left behind.

"Put him in one of the private rooms," the first orderly said. "He has visitors. Mack's keeping them in the lobby until we have him staged.

***

Staged indeed. Before leaving, the orderlies took time to prop Pete up in bed and lightly slap his face a few times to give him some color. It was a room like the one he'd been placed in when Mom and Dad visited. Fresh linens, flowers, sunshine streaming through a large window. It reminded Pete of the visitations he'd attended at funeral homes where morticians went to great lengths to display the deceased to make people forget they were dead.

"His condition has been largely unchanged despite extensive efforts at rehabilitation."

Through the closed door, Pete heard the doctor's voice as he approached and knew he was talking about him. *Despite extensive efforts at rehabilitation? Is that what they called sleeping pills?*

"The fall in Maryland damaged something deep within his brain, and unfortunately, nothing seems to be helping."

Doc, if you only knew.

The door opened and Dr. Feinbloom entered.

"Come in and see him," he said, motioning for someone to enter.

It was his brother Chris and Chris's wife Becky. They gasped when they saw him. Pete made a point to stare at a spot on the ceiling, occasionally allowing his eyes to shut or roll back in his head. He knew his missing teeth, and unkempt hair and beard gave him a much-different appearance than the Pete of old. That's what he wanted.

"Can he hear us?" Chris asked, staring at his brother for the first time in more than six years.

"Probably. I mean, loud noises startle him," Dr. Feinbloom said, "but actually comprehend what we're saying? No. Most likely not."

"Will he ever regain his..." Becky paused. "...will he ever be *normal* again?"

The doctor shrugged. "Likely not, unless we become more aggressive in our treatment. That would depend upon you, Mr. Demopoulos. You're his next-of-kin. Would you consider alternative treatment methods?"

"Like what?"

"Electroshock therapy has been providing some promising results."

It was all Pete could do not to sit up and scream. He'd seen the results of electroshock on other patients. While it may be effective for some conditions and in some institutions, Pete suspected it was, like everything else at Panhandle State Asylum, administered willy-nilly without regard for patients' well-being.

"It sounds painful," Becky said.

"It can be, but the long-term benefits could be worth the discomfort."

Ask him about Morley Fanning! Pete's mind screamed as his mind flashed to a C-Ward neighbor. *He used to be able to feed himself. After two sessions of electroshock he was a vegetable.*

"We'll definitely think about it," Chris said. "Could we have a few moments alone with my brother?"

"Certainly," Dr. Feinbloom replied. "You can find me in my office." The doctor closed the door behind him. Chris moved to the side of the bed on Pete's left, Becky on his right. Both had aged twenty years in the six years since he'd last seen them. Chris's hair was mostly gone on top, and his eyes were shrouded in deep wrinkles. Becky was forty pounds heavier, her hair starting to gray around the edges.

"Dad said he looked bad," Chris said, "but other than the long hair and beard, he doesn't look *terrible*. At least they keep him clean."

Ha. Want to bet?

Becky leaned in, her face less than a foot from Pete's.

"Pete, it's me, Becky. Can you hear me?"

Sure, I can, Becky. You need to cut back on the potato chips and cookies. And maybe try a hair style that's more 1961.

"Nothing," Becky said, pulling back.

"Personally, I'm glad," Chris said. "It sounds terrible, but Dad was hoping he could recover enough to maybe do some menial work at the warehouse. I don't want to have to take care of him."

Peripherally, Pete saw Becky nod. "We already did our part. I'm not sure our marriage could have survived another year of Papú. Babysitting for Pete would put us right back where we were."

What?

"Don't worry about it, Becky," Chris said testily. "If Pete somehow were to snap out of it, he'd still have to stand trial for marrying the nigger woman. Then there's the issue of whatever happened at the warehouse..."

Chris grew quiet. Pete dared let his gaze drift enough to see his brother. His eyes showed something that wasn't there before.

Love?

No, that wasn't it.

It was fear, but of what? Fear of Pete coming back? He didn't think so. More like fear of losing something that he cared for very much.

"What?" Becky asked. "Something's on your mind. What is it?"

"It's just that... we've gone over this before, Beck. Things aren't as good as they could be. Pete, for all his faults, he knew the business inside and out. I think he could've helped us get by without selling the stores in Orchard City and Beardon."

Holy cow! They'd sold the stores he had remodeled. What the heck was Chris doing? Those should've been goldmines.

"I think you worry too much," Becky said soothingly. "We're making a nice living. Another fifteen years and we can sell out and retire to Naples or Islamorada."

Chris turned and looked out the window. From the back, he appeared stooped. The vibrant young man Pete remembered was gone.

"What you seem to be forgetting is that Demo-Fresh used to support three families and Papú," Chris said, gazing out the window. "You and I are doing okay, but the stores aren't doing anywhere near like they used to. Pete was right about us falling behind."

Of course Pete was right.

"Dad picked up on it when he was home. He could tell the company was struggling without even looking at the books." Chris's voice was filled with disdain. Whether it was for Dad or Becky, Pete couldn't say.

"Fifteen more years," Becky said again. "We can ride out anything for fifteen years."

Pete considered adding to the melancholy by soiling his gown, but the feel of clean cotton against his skin was too precious to give up.

"What are you going to tell that weirdo doctor?" Becky asked.

"About what?"

"About electroshock."

Oh crap. That again.

Chris turned and took a final look at his brother.

"Let's get out of here. He's starting to give me the willies, the way he just lies there and stares. I'll tell the doc to give him the juice. Maybe a few volts of Edison electric will bump him into the great beyond."

FIFTY-SEVEN

By necessity, Pete's countdown clock had been jump-started. True to his word, Chris had given Dr. Feinbloom the okay to begin electroshock therapy. The most recent notation in his chart notes, which Pete had been surreptitiously reviewing since starting his midnight rounds, was that treatments would commence the following week.

Strangely enough, as he considered everything that had to happen between now and then, the voice of the public-address announcer at Yankee Stadium played through his mind. Pete had heard him on the radio many times as a boy, listening to Sunday games with Dad.

Pinch-Hitting for Pete Demopoulos... Patient 12-60-64029... Dewey LaPoint.

Any guilt he might have for subjecting poor Dewey to electroshock was muted by the fact that the man seemed to feel no pain. Pete had pinched him, pin-pricked his feet, tickled him, everything. Dewey never flinched. Whatever had ailed poor Dewey before Dr. Feinbloom started the chemical lobotomy was gone now, along with everything else. He was a vegetable.

Which was sad. After he'd decided he was going to become Dewey LaPoint, Pete had started going through the man's file, which he'd easily pilfered from the unlocked records room. Dewey was thirty years old and had arrived at Panhandle State Asylum just a few months before Pete, following a previous commitment at another Florida mental hospital. Dewey had been committed by his father, a wealthy Tallahassee entrepreneur whose mayoral plans were railroaded when it came out that Dewey had impregnated the daughter of a family servant. Dewey was twenty-six at the time. The girl was fourteen. Notations by physicians at Sunshine State Mental Hospital, Dewey's first stop, painted a picture of a young man who was alert, but greatly depressed by the forced breakup of the relationship with his young girlfriend. When his condition deteriorated, Dewey's father faced the choice of taking him home or moving him to an institution better suited to handle his diminished capacity. That's how Dewey wound up in C-Ward.

Well, Dewey, Pete thought as he replaced the folder, *you're about to be free again. I promise to live your life to the fullest, just as I did for my buddy, Hucklebuck.*

***

Wednesday night would be busy, but nothing like Thursday night. Pete went on the prowl just after midnight, starting in the medical records room where he updated the form that required Chris's consent on treatment. A simple notation gave Dr. Feinbloom the authority to do whatever he thought was in Pete's best interest, no consent needed. Feinbloom would be like a kid at Christmas when he discovered he could do his tests without having to get in touch with family. Of course, the fact that he would be performing the tests on Dewey LaPoint was irrelevant.

After a quick snack, Pete moved to the medication room, using the keys Rocky always left behind when he and Pedro went off to watch the late-late movie on TV. Those two had gone on another rampage two nights before, all because an old man needed help getting back into his bed after falling out. They would be getting theirs,

Pete thought, smiling at the possibilities as he pocketed a selection of candy-colored pills.

The next hour was spent on the phone, initiating the plan that had been in place for weeks. Satisfied that everything was a go, Pete returned to the slumbering ward, crawled into bed, and slept like a baby.

***

An orderly named Ken was shoving a lunch of tasteless adult cereal into Pete's mouth when word came by way of one of the staff doctors.

"Secret inspection tomorrow. The Governor. They've had complaints."

The plan was underway.

"Shit. What are we supposed to do?"

"Head down to the back hallway. The boss is giving us our marching orders."

"Dammit! I was hoping to sneak out early." Ken shoved a few more spoonfuls into Pete's mouth, then left quickly. For the next twenty minutes, C-Ward was as quiet as night. Then, like a wave, they returned. Orderlies. At least a dozen, grabbing patients, shoving them into wheelchairs, and taking them out in such large numbers that they could only be going to one place. The bathtub room.

Pete watched and bided his time until his turn came. The clock marched toward four, and he knew by counting that he was among the last patients headed for baths. He was dumped into a cool tub of water that had already been used by several other patients, then hurriedly scrubbed. When the orderly deemed him clean, he pulled the stopper, allowing the water to drain while Pete remained in the tub. He was located near the center of the room and could pick up snippets of conversation among the orderlies. Apparently, a staffer from the Governor's Office with ties to the area had tipped off the asylum's administrator about a call the Governor had received from someone of high standing in the state who had seen firsthand the abhorrent conditions at Panhandle State Asylum. There was fear that the Governor might bring along members of the press. Pete did his best to hide his smirk.

The threats proved sufficient. While patients were bathing, the floors were being hurriedly polished to a high shine by the facility's custodial staff. By the time Pete was wheeled back and placed in his now-clean bed, the unit smelled of disinfectant, and the rows of patients were tucked under fresh white sheets resembling a series of snowdrifts.

Then, at seven the day shift took its leave, stooped and exhausted from their efforts. Panhandle State Asylum was shiny clean. Its patients, bathed, groomed, fed, and ready for the Governor's surprise inspection.

Pete watched the last of the day workers shuffle out, the doors closing behind them. A few moments later, the doors opened again. The night shift had arrived for duty.

Pedro and Rocky.

***

"Okay, you crazy buggers," Pedro called out from his perch in the observation room. "You've had your supper and your happy pills. It's lights-out time. We don't want to put up with any of your shit tonight, so *go to sleep*."

A few minutes later the lights of the observation room went out. By eleven, Pedro and Rocky were headed to the Medical Director's Office for movie time. Pete had heard them talking about it as they made rounds. Tonight's selection was a rerun of a John Wayne classic, *The Quiet Man*. How appropriate. While they were engrossed in their movie, another quiet man would be turning their lives upside down.

FIFTY-EIGHT

At midnight, Pete snuck into the VISITING PHYSICIANS' OFFICE for a final phone call. As he'd ascertained from the conversations he'd overheard through the day, the plan went as expected. The sanitarium administrator, the son of a political ally of the Governor, had only been on the job for a few weeks and was as gullible as the day was long. Rather than confirm the information he'd received about a visit from the Governor's office, he'd chosen to accept it at face value. This was what Pete had hoped for.

In a bottom drawer, behind empty file folders and old equipment, Pete located the medical bag he'd been filling for the past month. He didn't know how many of the items he would need, but he had plenty.

Donning a lab coat, he crept toward the Medical Director's office. John Wayne's voice came from the other side of the closed door, along with occasional snippets of conversation between Pedro and Rocky. Pete had expected them to be snoring by now. Had they retrieved their stash of moonshine from the usual hiding place? If not, the best laid plans could be for nothing. He decided to give them another hour.

Returning to the ward, he began removing identification bracelets from the wrists of sleeping patients. Many slid easily from arms thinned by malnutrition. For others, he used scissors. A couple patients who were awake despite their nightly overdose of sleeping meds asked what he was doing. Pete said something about updating information, an explanation that, along with the sight of his lab coat, seemed to appease them. When all patients were sans bracelets, he began the process in reverse. In cases where he'd had to cut away the bracelets, he pulled new ones from his bag. It had taken time to learn to use the machine that made them, but in the end, he'd gotten to where he could crank out a dozen a night.

By two-fifteen, the bracelets were exchanged. Not a single patient was the same person he'd been before. Just for laughs, he'd even mixed up a few men's and women's names. The last ID he placed was on his own wrist. It was one of the new ones.

Dewey LaPoint. Patient 12-60-64029. Chemical Lobotomy.

The original Dewey, gorked out several beds away, was now Pete Demopoulos, a man scheduled to receive electroshock treatments first thing in the morning. Given all that was about to happen, it was unlikely that those treatments would take place on time, but if they did, so be it.

Returning to the Medical Director's Office, Pete crept to the door and listened. Silence. Through a window covered by venetian blinds, he could see the dim light of the television, but there was no sign of movement. This would be the moment his plans would be made or broken. If he opened the door and Pedro and Rocky were awake, it was all over.

It was a risk he had to take.

But first, he decided to try something else.

He knocked on the door and scooted around the corner. If he heard it open, he would run for his life back to C-Ward. The last hundred feet would be the trickiest; a long hallway where the orderlies were likely to see him before he made it through the doors into the ward.

He knocked twice and ran.

Then waited.

And waited.

Nothing.

Tip-toeing back around the corner, he saw the office door was still closed. He opened it and peered in.

Rocky was passed out on a sofa.

But Pedro was staring directly at him.

FIFTY-NINE

Pete froze. His heart banged against his chest with the force of a hydrogen bomb. Pedro was glaring at him, pointing a long crooked finger.

"You..." Pedro started to speak, then gently fell forward, passing out onto the carpeted floor.

It was several moments before Pete took a breath. He realized he was shaking. Those meds were supposed to work quickly. Pedro must have the constitution of a bull. Thankfully, he was out now, and the drug cocktail Pete had mixed into their hooch would numb his brain to where he likely wouldn't remember their encounter.

With a few minutes to burn, he headed for the Records Room. Patient files were kept in two large metal cabinets, which he proceeded to open and start pulling files. Some he replaced in the same cabinets, albeit in different locations. Others he moved to other cabinets within the office. A few he removed and took to other areas of the hospital, where they were shoved in desks or dumped in the backs of closets. The file system was rendered a complete mess.

When that was done, it was three in the morning; still time for more mischief. Pete grabbed a pint of ice cream to steady his nerves, then went back to work. Pedro was the heaviest, probably two-hundred pounds. Getting him out of his clothes and manhandling him onto a gurney took a half-hour, bringing to mind epic battles landing large fish on Horace Atteberry's boat. Rocky was smaller, but not much easier to move. It was necessary, though, as Pedro and Rocky would serve as the centerpiece of his work. By the time he'd relocated their deep-sleeping forms to C-Ward it was four-thirty. Not much time left, but just enough to... oh what the heck. Why not?

A game of musical beds began. Even with sleeping patients in them, the wheeled gurneys were surprisingly easy to move about. An hour later, as the first signs of daylight crept through the windows, Pete stood at the end of C-Ward, admiring his work. The beds were still in perfect formation, six rows of forty beds each, but none where they'd been hours before. Between the ID switches, the misplaced files, and the rearrangement of the ward, it would likely take weeks to undo. Best of all, in a matter of days, he would be a free man.

Satisfied and bone-weary, Pete returned to the lone empty bed, pulled back the covers and lay down. For the second day in a row, sleep came easily.

SIXTY

"What the...?"

Pete was roused by the voices of four orderlies surrounding a bed two rows over. Pete buried his face in his mattress to keep from laughing out loud.

"I guess somebody should get the boss," one of them said. When no one moved, he did it himself.

"Should we try to wake them up?" another asked.

"I ain't touching 'em. Not like that."

"Me neither."

A few minutes later, the orderly returned with the harried-looking Medical Director in tow. When his eyes fell upon the scene on the bed, he looked as if he might become ill. The evening orderlies, Rocky and Pedro, naked and unconscious, were intertwined in a passionate embrace. Even a few of the early-rising patients started to giggle at the sight.

"Cover them up, and get them out of here now!" the Medical Director ordered. "The people from the Governor's Office will be here any minute."

"Boss, we got more problems," another orderly, working at the far end of the ward called out. "They ain't where they're supposed to be."

The Medical Director looked around, his face a mix of confusion and anger. "What do you mean?"

The orderly held up the arm of a comatose patient. "The bracelet says this nut-job is Mary Patterson, but when I lift up the gown, he ain't no Mary."

The scene quickly dissolved into something from a Marx Brothers' movie. Staff poured into C-Ward, checking bracelets against a master list of patients. While changing bracelets was smart, the game of musical beds was proving to be genius.

And it only got better. A few minutes into the mayhem, two representatives of the Governor's office arrived, escorted by a man Pete assumed ran Panhandle State Asylum. With them were two reporters. One, a female Pete heard introduced as being from the *Tallahassee Times*. The other, Desmond Henry, formerly of the *Baltimore Black Advocate*, now with the *Washington Star*.

Step Two of the plan was underway.

The Medical Director and orderlies were discreetly pushing the bed containing Rocky and Pedro out a side door when Desmond spotted them and made a beeline in their direction. The Medical Director tried to stop him, but to no avail. Before they could get the bed out the door, Desmond had snapped several pictures.

Things went downhill quickly from there. The Governor's staffers took copious notes that would be on his desk by the end of the day. While the Tallahassee reporter remained aloof, intimidated by the scene she was witnessing, Desmond worked with a vengeance. Within a half-hour, he had identified seven women and eleven men with identification bracelets for someone of the opposite sex. He tried to talk to several patients with minimal success. By the time he approached Pete, Panhandle's administrator was shadowing his every step.

"And your name is...?" Desmond picked up Pete's arm and looked at his bracelet. "Dewey LaPoint. Mr. LaPoint, I'm a reporter from a newspaper in Washington. Are they treating you well here?"

Pete said nothing.

"Well, sir, I wish you only the best and hope my investigative report will help make things better." Desmond surreptitiously stuck a slip of paper under Pete's pillow before moving away. When the crowd had moved past, Pete retrieved the scrap of paper.

Gwen says go as planned Monday at 1, but it won't be her picking you up. Worried about being recognized since pub from trial. College friend instead. Dottie is a no. Sorry the news isn't better on that front. Godspeed, Desmond.

The note changed everything. Pete had hoped Dottie would forgive him, but it appeared that wasn't happening. He turned slightly so that his face was partially obscured from the view of passers-by, then closed his eyes and started to weep silently. It was several minutes before he regained his composure and opened his eyes again. Still no one close, as the maelstrom had finally left C-Ward. Lying on his side, he gazed across the sea of blank misplaced, mislabeled faces, before noticing something most disturbing. One of the blank faces wasn't blank anymore.

Dewey LaPoint, the real Dewey LaPoint, was staring at him.

SIXTY-ONE

THE WASHINGTON STAR
April 30, 1961

CONDITIONS IN FLORIDA MENTAL HOSPITAL NOT SO SUNNY

By: Desmond K. Henry

From the outside, it looks like any of a myriad of state-operated institutions across America. An attractive 1890's era administration building fronting three brick and mortar structures on a pastoral campus of manicured lawns and neatly-trimmed shrubbery. Some might compare it to a seminary or convent.

Don't be deceived.

Inside Panhandle State Asylum is a world where patients are neglected and abused. A surprise tour led by representatives of the Florida Governor's office this past week revealed conditions termed as "abhorrent" by Governor C. Farris Bryant.

Despite institutional efforts to clean up the facility when word leaked of the visit, representatives found patients misidentified and misplaced, women and men sharing the same space, and evidence of widespread neglect. Particularly egregious were the violations in Panhandle State's "C-Ward" where the least ambulatory patients are housed.

Patient Elijah Butts was one of many whose identification bracelet was mislabeled. He has been housed on C-Ward since 1955. Butts, a gentle man who asked to be referred to as Joyce, described the work put into preparing for the visit.

"They never clean," Joyce said. "There's usually poop all over the place, but when they found out you were coming, they cleaned everything."

Joyce went on to describe how patients are regularly beaten for small indiscretions, such as crying out or refusing meds.

"The night orderlies, Pedro and Rocky, are the worst," Joyce said. "I've seen them hit people and take liberties with the ladies."

Evidence of the orderlies' lack of moral turpitude was on full display during the visit last week. Pedro Vizquel and Robert "Rocky" Dunham were discovered *in flagrante delicto* by Panhandle staff the morning of the visit. Both men were arrested for sodomy and fired from their jobs.

The investigation conducted by representatives of the Governor's Office found dozens of examples of patients being misidentified. Asylum Administrator George K. Rickerson stated that he did not believe this was typical of the facility. Rickerson submitted his letter of resignation the day following the inspection.

In a press release, Governor Bryant promised a quick and impactful response to the conditions at

Panhandle. The *Washington Star* will continue to follow this story.

SIXTY-TWO

C-Ward became a different place overnight, and while Pete had assumed there would be changes, he hadn't expected them to be so dramatic.

For one, his night adventures were eliminated. Rocky and Pedro were replaced by six orderlies who remained in the observation room all evening. Getting through the doors to the kitchen or using the phone in the *VISITING PHYSICIANS' OFFICE* were out of the question.

Then there were the meds. Whereas Rocky and Pedro would shove the little red pills into his mouth without concern of where they wound up, the new orderlies gently checked to make sure each pill was swallowed. Within a few minutes, Pete was dozy, despite his best efforts to fight it.

Fortunately, none of it mattered, as the plan was set to culminate on Monday.

Saturday and Sunday nights passed by in a hazy cloud of sleep, followed by long days in bed. Pete had become used to moving about during the night, and the confinement of the past two days was wearing. Fortunately, there were some positive aspects. The remaining staff, likely concerned about their jobs, became more attentive. Pete received a warm bath Sunday afternoon, followed by a few minutes under a heat lamp. The food was better, too, as the institutional gruel they'd received at every meal was replaced by a cereal that actually had some taste.

Another unsettling thing was Dewey LaPoint, who was now, of course, Pete Demopoulos. While he still never moved, Dewey's eyes always seemed to be open and staring at Pete while he laid in bed. It was beyond creepy, and Pete had taken to lying on his right side, facing away from his new namesake.

Just one more day, he told himself Sunday night, as he swallowed the little red pill and began to drift away. He considered what he might do first when he was finally outside. Trying to contact Dottie was his desire, but Desmond's note made him think otherwise, at least until some time had passed. Still, he wanted to know how she was doing. She was just a couple months shy of having their baby. Pete imagined her with a swelled stomach and decided she had to be the most beautiful mother-to-be any place. He had to see her, if only a quick glimpse from up the street. That, he decided, was a given. But first, he'd be flying to New York's Idlewild Airport. That was Gwen's idea. Her husband's family had a vacation place on Long Island where he could spend a few weeks preparing for his new life as Dewey LaPoint. Where would he go after that? He hadn't decided, but he dreamed of somehow convincing Dottie to join him. Desmond and Gwen had pledged their support toward making that happen.

Sleep came softly, coaxing Pete to follow. Knowing it was his last night in C-Ward, he acquiesced with pleasure. His resurrection, his third new life, began tomorrow.

SIXTY-THREE

Sunlight bathed C-Ward as Pete awakened. He'd slept longer than planned, and orderlies were noisily delivering breakfast bowls. As he had to be hand-fed, he knew he would be near the end. Turning from his right side to his left, he rubbed his eyes as they adjusted to the light. When he opened them he was staring at Dewey LaPoint.

And Dewey was staring back.

You crazy comatose bastard, Pete thought, not wanting to turn away from the new Pete Demopoulos. *Just like I did with Hucklebuck, I'll make your name one that people remember. And you...* Pete snickered, *...you'll be getting electroshock sometime this week. Enjoy that.*

With Dewey's gaze never leaving his face, Pete glanced at a wall clock across the ward. Eight-twenty. Another five hours and he'd be free. Happy with that thought, he looked again at Dewey. What he saw caused his stomach to lurch.

Dewey continued to stare at him, but in his clenched fist, he held a scrap of paper. When he saw Pete looking back at him, he smiled, winked, and placed the paper in his mouth, chewing and swallowing like it was a choice steak.

What the heck was that all about?

Then, a sick realization.

*It was the note Desmond had slipped under his pillow.
But how?*

While Pete continued to watch, Dewey moved his wrist toward his face and gazed longingly at his ID badge, breaking the spell only long enough to turn and smile again at Pete. Cautiously, so as not to bring unwanted attention from one of the orderlies, Pete lifted his own arm to look at his wristband.

Gone.

When he looked back at Dewey, the man was laughing silently. Realization washed over Pete like an ice-cold shower.

Dewey LaPoint had taken his ID badge... and his identity. Dewey wasn't Pete anymore. Dewey was Dewey. And Pete?

Pete was nobody.

There was no way in hell this was going to happen. Angrily, Pete threw back the covers of his bed and climbed down, intent on getting back the ID that Dewey had somehow pilfered in the night. As soon as he hit the cool floor, his legs gave way, a result of three days lying in bed. He staggered and fell to the floor, attracting the attention of two orderlies who ran to his side.

"Let's get you back in bed," one of them said, taking Pete's arm.

"Get your hands off me!" Pete yelled, nodding his head at Dewey LaPoint. "That man stole my bracelet!"

The orderly tightened his grip. "It's okay, buddy. Let's get you back in bed." Then, turning to his colleague, he said, "Marty, has this one ever talked before?"

"Hell if I can remember, Chuck. After Friday night, I don't know who's who anymore."

"My name is Pete Demo—"

Dammit!

Pete caught himself. "I mean Dewey LaPoint. That man is not me. He stole my ID bracelet and I want it back, *now*!"

"Easy, buddy," Chuck the orderly said soothingly. "That man isn't capable of getting out of bed. I think you just lost your ID someplace. We'll find it for you."

"Here it is," Marty said, bending and scooping up a bracelet from the floor under Pete's bed. "It probably fell off your stump…" he glanced at the bracelet, "You *are* Pete Demopoulos. You were right the first time." Then, turning to the other orderly, he said, "I think this one is schizoid. He thinks he's that guy over there."

"*I'm not Pete.* My name is Dewey LaPoint, and that son-of-a-bitch stole my ID!" Pete pulled away and threw himself at Dewey, landing square on the other man's back and scratching at his wrist to get the bracelet. Through it all, Dewey never moved. It took four orderlies to pull Pete off him.

"Let's take him to seclusion," one of them said. Exiting C-Ward, they passed Dr. Feinbloom.

"What happened?"

"He went nuts," Marty said. "More nuts, I guess I should say. He attacked a man; said he stole his ID bracelet. We're taking him to seclusion."

"Name?" Feinbloom asked.

"Pete Demopoulos," Marty said. "Here's his bracelet."

"*I'm Dewey LaPoint!*" Pete screamed as he tried to break free from the guards. "The guy Pete is a fake. He took my ID bracelet in the middle of the night, Doc. You've got to believe me."

Dr. Feinbloom looked him over carefully, then nodded.

"He's Demopoulos. I remember the missing arm. His brother was here and gave us permission to start electroshock." Feinbloom consulted his files, then held up a signed form that Pete had placed there himself. "It looks like the brother has given up all rights."

"The other guy is missing an arm, too!" Pete wailed. "And my brother didn't give up anything! I forged that and put it in there myself."

This brought Dr. Feinbloom up short. Pete could see his mind working on the new information. After a few moments, he placed his hand on Pete's shoulder, turned and spoke to the orderlies.

"Put him in Isolation Room Three. I'll begin electroshock this afternoon at quarter-past one."

***

At quarter-past one an orderly came into C-Ward, consulted a clipboard, and moved down the rows until he reached his destination.

"Are you Dewey LaPoint?" he asked. Dewey stared into space. The orderly, unsure what to do, checked his identification bracelet. The visit by the Governor's Office had been Friday, three days earlier. Since then, some of the mismatched identification bracelets had been straightened out, but there was still much uncertainty. Satisfied that he had the right patient, he gently picked up Dewey and placed him in a wheelchair.

"Your sister is here to get you," the orderly said, pushing him out of C-Ward for the last time.

After a stop for a set of ill-fitting street clothes from a supply room, they made their way to the Administration Building. When they reached the Asylum Administrator's office, a petite redhead of maybe twenty-five rushed to Dewey.

"I'm so sorry, Dewey! Mama and Daddy are sick about everything. They sent me to get you out of here right away." The redhead hugged him tightly, then turned to the harried interim administrator who had assumed his position just five hours before.

"You should be ashamed!" she cried. "My brother came here to get better, and now…" she couldn't finish, the tears came hard and fast. The administrator stared blankly like a deer caught in a car's headlights. She was the fourth person today who had come to claim a family member.

360

"I wasn't here when..." the administrator paused. "... when all the things happened, but I can promise you there will be changes."

"Maybe so," the redhead spat, "but you've had your chance with my brother and you blew it."

"Still, Miss... LaPoint, before we can release your brother, we need to review his case. Unfortunately, we've not been able to locate his file yet. Please understand that it's—"

"It's *bullshit*! That's what it is," the redhead shouted. "And if you try to stop me from taking him, my family will be suing you and this godforsaken place by the end of the day!"

Any fight the interim administrator might've had left was gone. He waved his hand feebly for them to leave. Ten minutes later Dewey LaPoint and his surrogate sister were pulling away from the grounds of Panhandle State Asylum.

***

"Time for your treatment."

Two of the orderlies who'd tossed him in earlier entered the isolation room and assumed positions on each side of Pete, expecting more of the same resistance as before. This time, Pete was calm, getting to his feet and smoothing his gown. He'd spent the past two hours considering how he would handle things. Acting impulsively and striking out obviously weren't the answers, so he would wait until he was face-to-face with Dr. Feinbloom. Then, he hoped they could have a rational dialogue.

***

"Everything you need is in there," the redhead said, motioning to a knapsack on the seat between them. "Gwen tossed in some of your old papers, too." Dewey picked up the knapsack and looked inside. An Eastern Airlines ticket from Mobile, Alabama to New York, two changes of clothes, a worn wallet filled with personal effects, and three-hundred dollars.

"Gwen and I went to school together at Montfried. I'm a drama major at Florida State," the redhead said proudly. "I hope I did a good job of playacting your sister."

Getting no response, she continued. "It's a four-hour drive to Mobile, but Gwen thought it was a good idea to get out of Florida as quickly as possible. I'll drop you at the airport and she'll meet your plane in New York, then help you get situated. What do you think of that?"

Dewey nodded and smiled, then put his head back and dozed contentedly.

***

"Mr. Demopoulos, it's good to see you've calmed down," Dr. Feinbloom said as he entered the examination room. Pete had been waiting for more than a half-hour, and the sight of the electroshock equipment on the shelves at the foot of the exam table was starting to make him queasy.

"Want us to stay, sir?" one of the orderlies asked.

"Just until he's sedated," Feinbloom replied. "I don't want another situation like we had with him earlier."

"You won't have one, Dr. Feinbloom," Pete said, trying to sound as rational as he could. "But may I speak with you for a few minutes first? I have some things to say that I think you'll want to hear."

"Certainly. Give me a second to get your sedative prepared, then I'll sit down and we can talk. It's encouraging to see that you've emerged from the agnosia."

"That's what I want to talk to you about. I never had—"

Raising his finger for Pete to stop, Feinbloom said, "Like I said, give me a moment to go prepare the sedative."

With that, he left the room. When he returned, he was holding a small syringe. The sight of it caused Pete's pulse to quicken.

"This will pinch, then you'll feel nothing," he said, as he approached.

"Wait. You said we could talk, remember?"

"Oh, yes." Feinbloom took a seat on a stool beside the exam table, but held onto the syringe. The orderlies moved to a spot behind him, close to the door.

"What do you want to tell me that is so important?"

"Doctor, this is going to sound bizarre, but I've been faking my condition the entire time I've been here."

Feinbloom raised an eyebrow but said nothing.

"I knew if I didn't do something drastic, I'd be tried for bigamy, desertion, and maybe even manslaughter or murder, so I faked everything. I realize now it was a mistake and want to make things right."

"Impossible."

Pete shook his head. "No, sir, it's not. I've been acting the entire time. The night orderlies didn't check to see if I was taking the meds, so I didn't. After lights out, they would go to the Medical Director's office and watch TV. When they were gone, I roamed the hospital. It was me who moved the files and changed patient IDs. I orchestrated the whole thing."

Feinbloom motioned for Pete to proceed.

"My plan was to assume the identity of another patient. Dewey LaPoint. Three nights ago, I exchanged bracelets with him and had someone from the outside coming to get me. Then, somehow, the real Dewey woke up and figured things out." Pete shook his head. "Sir, I think he was faking just like I was."

For a few moments, the room was quiet. Then, behind Feinbloom, the orderlies started giggling. He angrily turned and shushed them.

"Why would you need to trade identities, Mr. Demopoulos? It doesn't make sense."

"Sure, it does. I'm here because the courts deemed me mentally incompetent to stand trial. If I tried to leave as Pete Demopoulos, I would've had to go back and face those charges. But as Dewey LaPoint…" Pete waved his hand, allowing Dr. Feinbloom to reach his own conclusions.

The doctor nodded sagely. "It's starting to make sense, Mr. Demopoulos… except for one thing."

"What's that?"

"None of what you've described ever happened. You're having delusions."

Again, more silence as the import of what he was hearing began to seep in. Pete sprang from the table. In an instant, the orderlies had him pinned on the floor.

"Delusions?" he screamed. "I'm not having delusions, you quack! You know as well as I do that this place is a badly-run shithole! Now if you don't cut this charade and let the authorities know that I'm mentally okay, you'll find yourself on the front page of every newspaper in America."

"I think not, Mr. Demopoulos," Feinbloom said coolly. "We have an outstanding facility, despite what the papers say. Allowing you to tarnish that image further is unacceptable."

"Wait until Desmond Henry finds out that you let the wrong person out!" Pete yelled. "He'll finish taking you down!"

"That's not going to happen, Mr. Demopoulos." Feinbloom pulled a sheet of paper from Pete's file, waving it in front of him. "Because, as you see here, I have a release from your brother, allowing Panhandle State Asylum to assume control of all medical decisions. With this—"

"I put that there myself!"

"Oh, sir, I think not. It is an official form; definitely real."

"You're never going to survive this, Feinbloom. Your reputation is going down the toilet by the time I'm done..."

Pete stopped in midsentence when Feinbloom nodded to the orderlies. Their grips on his arm and shoulder tightened, making it impossible to move. The doctor raised the syringe as he moved in closer.

"I'll give you this sedative, Mr. Demopoulos, then we'll begin the treatments. There will be some pain, but in the end, I think you'll like the way you feel. Now a word of caution... because of your condition, we might have to administer higher doses of electricity than is otherwise recommended." The doctor smiled. "I'm sure you understand. And if this doesn't work, perhaps we'll consider a lobotomy like we intended for your friend, Mr. LaPoint."

***

The rest of the drive was silent. At five-thirty they pulled into the Mobile airport.

"Well, good luck!" the redhead said brightly. Dewey smiled and exited the car, making his way to a pay phone just inside the terminal.

"I'd like to make a collect call to Betty at the Happy Hatter Café in Tallahassee." He recited the number from memory, then waited.

"What's your name, sir?"

"Dewey."

"Thank you. I'll place that call."

A male answered, then retrieved Betty.

"Dewey? Is it really you?"

"It is, sweetheart. I'm sorry I've not been able to call sooner, but—"

"It's okay! I can't believe I'm talking to you now. They said you were like a vegetable or something. Did you get cured?"

"It's a long story that can wait. The main thing is, are you still willing to be with me?"

He could hear her choking back tears.

"More than anything, Dewey. I've not even looked at another man. And little Dougie needs his daddy. He's getting so big, Dewey. You'll be proud."

It was Dewey's turn to become emotional.

"Okay, here's what you do, Betty. Is your cousin in Missouri still willing to give us a place to stay for a few weeks?"

"Anytime, darling. Freddie and Glenda live in a little town called Tipton. They'll take us in."

"Then you need to go to the Western Union office tomorrow. I'll wire money for a plane ticket. Get on the first plane to Missouri you can. We'll get married as soon as you get there."

Betty started to cry again.

"I'll do it," she said between sobs. "I'm so happy."

"Oh, there is one more thing."

"Anything!"

"For this to work, I've had to change my name. Sooner or later the people at the hospital will figure out that Dewey LaPoint shouldn't have been released."

"What's your new name?"

He pulled a tattered driver's license from the knapsack the redhead had given him and recited the name. They giggled when they heard it.

"I'll see you in Missouri!" Betty said joyously. "Dougie and I love you!"

"And I love you, too."

***

When he startled awake, he couldn't feel his legs. And his jaw hurt, bad. Like someone had slugged him. Had Feinbloom administered the electroshock, or had he let the orderlies take him outside and kick his ass?

The room was dark. It was C-Ward, he thought. But then again, maybe not.

He looked at his bracelet in the dim light of the large room.

Pete Demopoulos. Patient 1-61-19973. Agnosia

That wasn't his name? Was it? Wasn't he someone else?

Maybe so, but did it really matter now?

***

"Hello, sir, can I help you?" the attendant asked brightly.

"I was wondering," Dewey replied, handing her his ticket, "if I could exchange this. I was supposed to go to New York, but there's been a family emergency and I need to get to a place called Tipton, Missouri."

The attendant checked the ticket against a master schedule. "The closest we can get you is Kansas City," she said. "You can leave here in ninety minutes, have a layover in Dallas, and be in Kansas City at midnight."

"Close enough," Dewey said, offering a smile. "Thank you for your help."

"There is one thing," the attendant said, as she began filling out a new ticket. "There's no name on the original ticket. Can I see your driver's license?"

"No current driver's license, I'm afraid," Dewey said sheepishly, pulling out his wallet. "I've been ill for quite some time and my license lapsed. I do have this old one from Florida, but it's badly dated."

The attendant looked it over for several moments. "A 1949 driver's license? And no picture?"

"Like I said, I've been in the hospital for a long time. The picture got lopped off in an accident. I plan to get another as soon as I get to Missouri."

"Sir, this says you're a deaf mute."

"I used to be," Dewey blushed. "That's why I was in the hospital so long. It was miraculous, what they were able to do for me."

A tear came to the attendant's eye as she looked at the tattered license.

"I'm so happy for you, sir. It's a miracle indeed," she said, handing him the license with his new ticket. "This is one-way ticket, sir. Are you moving to Missouri permanently?"

Dewey nodded. "My girlfriend and I are getting married and living there with some of her cousins. She's a lot younger than me, and our families weren't happy that we were together, so we're getting a fresh start. We've been apart while I've been in the hospital, so you can imagine how excited I am."

"Oh, how wonderful! I wish you only the best, and I must say, you have a most unique name."

Dewey glanced at the old driver's license and smiled. "It is, isn't it? I'm not sure what my parents were thinking, but I'll bet I'm the only Hucklebuck Jones you'll ever meet."

SIXTY-FOUR

The next time he woke up, it was daylight. His jaw still hurt, but not as much, and he could feel his legs. He was in C-Ward. Definitely C-Ward. When he looked at the clock, he saw two. Two clocks, not two o'clock.

A couple orderlies noticed him stirring and came to his bedside.

"Doc shocked the shit out of this one." The guy who spoke was one who had tossed him into the seclusion room. Marty was his name. The other one was new, but judging by the way he laughed at Marty's humor, he was no less vile.

"More today?" the new guy asked.

"Oh yeah," Marty laughed. "I wish I was going to be here to see it. He called the doc a quack and said he was somebody else. I saw the chart. Feinbloom's going to shock him into the next decade, then slice his brain like a slab of salami." Marty playfully punched the new guy in the shoulder. "And you get to watch!"

They laughed and joked as they reapplied the arm and leg restraints. Pete silently cursed himself for not making a run for it while he had the opportunity, but knew he probably wouldn't have gotten far. Even in a prone position, the room seemed to bend and dip around him.

"You guys..." he said, struggling to find what he needed to say, "I'm Buck... Pete Jones... no, I'm—"

"You're Sally Shit-Out-Of-Luck," Marty said, glancing around before slapping Pete a good one on the cheek. "The next time I see you, you'll be crapping your drawers and calling me mama."

***

When the two clocks finally started to converge into one, Pete saw it was half-past-noon. Despite his best efforts, he'd fallen asleep again. His head had cleared enough to comprehend that he was facing another round of Feinbloom's experiments. That thought made him frantic. Looking to his left, he spotted another patient seated on the edge of his bed; a man of at least seventy, glancing anxiously toward the exit door. Next to the door, the observation area that had been fully staffed by orderlies the last few days was empty.

"Hey, what's your name?" Pete called out.

The old man either didn't hear or didn't comprehend. He fidgeted as he watched the door, his gown shifting open in back to display the telltale signs of starvation.

"Hey, sir," Pete said louder. "Look back here. Can you help me?"

The man looked over his shoulder at Pete.

"Can you loosen these straps? They're starting to hurt."

"Can't help. Waiting for 'em to come get me for my bath." His voice was strong for such a weak body. The accent was all New York.

Pete looked around for other patients who might be able to help, but most beds were empty. Since the visit by Desmond and the people from the Governor's Office, the patients who were at least marginally ambulatory were being loaded into wheelchairs and pushed into hallways and outside areas. Other than the old New Yorker, the few remaining patients were sleeping or comatose.

370

"Sir, please… what's your name?"

"Miklos," he replied, still not turning to look at Pete.

"Miklos? Are you Greek?"

The man nodded. "Santorini."

"My name is Demopoulos. I'm Greek, too."

Miklos looked over his shoulder tentatively.

"You look like a coon."

"I have my grandmother's color.

"She a coon?"

"No, but her family comes from an area of Greece where people are darker."

Miklos considered this for a moment.

"What was your name again?"

"Demopoulos. How about helping me with the straps, Miklos?"

"I knew a cabbie in Brooklyn named Sandor Demopoulos. Any relation?"

"No… I mean, wait a minute… Yeah, he's my uncle!" A little fib couldn't hurt, especially if it convinced Miklos to help with the restraints.

"Sorry to hear that. Your uncle was a crook and a womanizer."

Uh-oh.

"Yeah…" Pete scrambled for a response. "We ran him off after we found out. A real deadbeat, Uncle Sandor."

"Good decision," Miklos said, returning his gaze to the door. "They should be here by now to take me to my bath."

"While you're waiting, Miklos, won't you please help me with these straps. Like I said, they're too tight. The orderly said he'd be in to take them off, but you know how busy they get around here."

"You can't count on those bastards for nothin'," Miklos said angrily.

"Exactly! Now why don't you come over and help a fellow Greek."

With Miklos staring at him, Pete tried to look as pitiable as he could. It must have worked, because the old man slid off his bed and shuffled toward him.

"All right, but if they show up to get me for my bath, I'm gonna go."

"I understand. All you have to do is unclip that thing down there." Pete pointed with his head at the strap that stretched across his arm at his waist. "Once you get that one, I'll get the rest."

It seemed to take Miklos an hour to make the twenty-foot walk from his bed to Pete's, but it couldn't have been more than a few seconds. Watching the man's shuffling approach, Pete planned his strategy. There was a fire exit at the far end of the ward, with an alarm that never worked. If he could make it that far, it was a hundred and fifty-yard run to the wooded area that bordered the asylum's north side. Another twenty yards beyond that was the ten-foot brick fence that separated the property from a melon farm on the other side. The fence would be hard to scale, especially given how shaky he was. Adrenaline could accomplish a lot, though.

"Make sure you don't tell 'em it was me who took these off," Miklos said as he finally arrived at Pete's bed.

"I promise, Miklos. We Greeks need to stick together."

Miklos studied the restraint as if it were an abstract painting, tipping his head from side to side.

"Just push the button," Pete coaxed. "It will fall right off."

Miklos turned to look toward the door. "I don't know why they haven't come to get me yet," he complained. "I always get my bath at twelve-thirty."

"They'll be here soon, Miklos. Now, push the button and let me get up."

"You're a real pain in the ass, you know?" Miklos groused as he pushed the button and released the restraints. Pete shook his hand to bring feeling back to it, then went to work on the leg restraint. It was lower on the side of the bed, on the opposite side from his arm, and the effort caused the room to begin spinning around him. Damn electroshock. When he got out of here he swore he would sue that bastard Feinbloom and the nut house that employed him.

And finally, with a reluctant snap, it released. He was free. He jumped from the bed and made a beeline for the fire exit. He arrived just as the door was opened from outside.

It was the new orderly, the one from earlier, who had laughed when Marty slapped him.

"What are you…?"

Pete feinted right, then made a move to dive under the orderly's outstretched arms. He scrambled past, but tripped in the process. Before he could get to his feet, the orderly sat down heavily upon him, pinning his arm and legs to the concrete.

"I was just coming to get you, buddy," he grinned. "The doctor says it's time for your next round."

SIXTY-FIVE

"Put him in Four," Dr. Feinbloom said brusquely as they passed by. "I've got two more before him. It'll be an hour."

"You're going to regret this," Pete said angrily from the gurney where he was securely restrained. Then, mad at himself, he wondered why a line from dozens of B-movies was the best he could do with his life on the line.

"I doubt that, Mr. Demopoulos," Feinbloom smiled, patting his arm as he continued down the hall. "I sleep like a baby every night, knowing I'm keeping the world safe from nut-jobs like you."

The orderly silently pushed the gurney down the hall and into a sickly green-colored holding area. Once there, he closed the door, sat down heavily on a folding chair, pulled out a pack of Lucky Strikes, and lit up.

"Smoke?" he asked Pete.

When no response came, the orderly reclined in the chair, lit up, and slowly enjoyed his cigarette. Pete looked the room over from floor to ceiling. Two doors: the one through which he'd been wheeled in, and another that he was unsure about, possibly a utility closet. No windows, no telephone. Nothing. Just the orderly, puffing his Lucky in a contented bliss.

Was this the way it was going to end?

"Have you seen what they are doing to me? To us?"

The orderly opened his eyes, took another puff, and looked at Pete.

"It's a hellhole," he said simply.

"So why do you work here?" Pete asked testily. "Why aren't you out there doing something about it?"

"The visit last week from the Governor's Office is going to take care of that," the orderly said. "That and the column your friend at the *Washington Star* wrote."

What? He knows about Desmond?

The orderly continued, "He'll win an award for that story. A year from now this place is gonna be much different. And Feinbloom? He'll be in a Tallahassee jail cell."

"Did you say my *'friend'*?

The orderly nodded. "Desmond Henry. Your friend. Do you think you're that much smarter than everyone else? That screwjob LaPoint wasn't the only one who had you figured out. They all know now. The new administrator, the orderlies. Even Feinbloom. Why do you think he's moving so quick on your electroshock? He knows it's a matter of time before they storm the place. The last thing he needs is to have you testifying against him."

"If that's the case, then why—" Pete pulled hard against the restraints, but was unable to move. "—how much longer do I have?"

The orderly shrugged apologetically. "Feinbloom plans to give you enough juice today to make you a vegetable. If he has enough time, he'll lobotomize you into oblivion. I'd say by this time next week, you'll be alive in name only and he'll be scrambling to find an island that doesn't extradite."

"And this doesn't bother you?" Pete yelled.

"Shhh," the orderly leaned forward, his hands in the air, the butt of the cigarette smoldering between his fingers. You want him to hear you?"

Sweat began to flow from every pore of Pete's body as he came to grips with the reality. He was going to die. He'd never see Dottie again; never get to hold their baby.

Nothing else mattered, he realized, other than them. The prospect of dying before his child was born was enough to bring a flood of sad, desperate, and angry tears. He thrashed against the restraints, causing the gurney to shake violently.

"Easy, buddy," the orderly said. "Don't do that." His casualness provoked Pete to try harder. The bed squeaked and lifted slightly off its left-side wheels.

"Stop already." The orderly stood up, tossed the spent cigarette on the floor, and came closer. Pete thought he was going to be struck, but the orderly moved to the end of the gurney and unsnapped the harness holding down his legs. Pete flailed his legs trying to get enough momentum to kick out, but stopped when the orderly calmly raised his hands.

"Not necessary," he said, as he loosened the restraint around Pete's waist. Despite the emotions he was feeling, Pete eyed him warily. Fifteen seconds later, the last straps were removed and he was untethered. Still, Pete didn't move. What if it was a trap? What if the orderly wanted him to try to make a break for it, just so he could chase him down and inflict further pain. Pete had seen it before, and this time he wouldn't have to wait long to find out.

Checking his watch, the orderly glanced at the door leading to the hallway. Pete saw nervousness in his eyes.

"In about four minutes a black Lincoln Continental will be parked outside. You're to go through that door." he pointed to the room's second door, the one Pete thought might be a closet. "It's a utility room. In there you'll see another door that leads outside. Go out and to the left, toward the woods. You'll see the car. Get in the back seat and crouch down. Don't lift your head or ask any questions until you're told the coast is clear. Understand?"

Pete blinked away the remaining tears and shook his head.

"Why? What's going to happen to me? It's a trick, right? I don't trust you."

"Would you rather trust *him*?" The orderly didn't say who, but the slight nod of his head toward the hallway told Pete he was referring to Feinbloom. Considering this, Pete sat up and put his legs over the side of the gurney. His gown yawned opened at the knees.

"I almost forgot," the orderly said, grabbing a medical bag he'd brought into the room. "Put these on."

Pete opened the bag and pulled out a pair of khaki pants and a blue shirt. "Maintenance" was monogrammed on the shirt pocket.

"There's shoes and socks, too. I forgot a belt."

Pete quickly changed into the clothes, never taking his eyes off the orderly.

"Who are you?"

"Doesn't matter."

"Well, at least tell me your name. You obviously have some tie to the outside."

"That doesn't matter, either. Let's just say you have some pretty good friends and leave it at that."

Pete sat on the floor and started to tie the shoes, always a difficult chore with one hand. The orderly watched him for a moment, then reached down and did it for him.

"It's time."

Pete got to his feet. The clothes were roomy and he'd have to hold the pants up by the belt loops or they'd fall down. Still, the hopefulness he felt made that irrelevant.

"What will you do when he comes back?" Pete asked.

"I won't be here," the orderly said simply. "My work is done. Now..." he motioned for Pete to make his exit. Pushing open the door, Pete halfway expected there to be a cadre of orderlies waiting for him in the next room, but there was only a large washing machine, bottles of bleach, and a pile of filthy gowns. He stepped past, turned the handle on the door and was met by blinding sunlight. Barely able to see, he turned left and took off on a dead run, slipping and almost falling several times on the grass while he prayed no one was watching his staggering escape. Then, without warning he crashed into something large and fell backward. Shielding his eyes, he looked up and saw it. A black Lincoln.

"Hey, wait a minute!" The shout came from behind him, but he didn't turn to see who it was as he got to his feet, pulled open the car's back door, and dove toward the floorboard. Even before the door was closed, the car moved away. A dark blanket was tossed on top of him from the front seat. He covered himself and got as low to the floor as he could. That was when he tasted blood. When he'd banged into the car he'd split his lip. He raised his hand to feel the extent of the damage and realized that he was shaking violently.

More than anything he wanted to know who was driving the car and where they were going. Certainly, by now Gwen and Desmond knew he hadn't shown up in New York, but could they have made the trip south so quickly?

His thoughts were put on hold as the car slowed. He heard the sound of the front window being lowered, then a voice from outside the car.

"Blessings to you, Father," someone said. "Thanks for taking time to come out. These folks might be nuts, but they still need God."

There was no response from the driver as the car pulled away and picked up speed. It was another ten minutes before Pete detected they were pulling off the road onto a gravel surface. The driver stopped and turned off the car, then Pete felt the blanket being removed. When he dared to glance up, his gaze was met by the familiar twinkling eyes of his old friend, Horace Atteberry.

"Welcome back, Pete! I've missed my favorite fishing buddy!"

EPILOGUE

SOUTH FLORIDA
1961

SIXTY-SIX

The place was called Bean Point, an isolated beach on the northern tip of a sleepy Florida island called Anna Maria. It's crystal-clear turquoise waters marked the point where the bays of Tampa and Sarasota became one with the Gulf of Mexico. The sand was like sugar, and breezes from the west massaged the skin of the few sun-worshippers who took the time to trek to its shores.

It was the perfect place for a wedding.

The eleven guests began arriving at six, an hour before the ceremony. As different from one another as any group could be, they ranged from the wealthy and powerful to workaday folk. They were young and old, black and white, rich and poor. The conversations were stilted at first, as they tried to find common ground. Cora Manning saw the disconnect and immediately went to work; bringing people together.

Dr. Elijah Watson had spent his life tending to sick and ailing Pine Hammock Negroes. Hal Demopoulos was spending the second half of his life ministering to New Guinea's spiritually sick and ailing.

Paul Adams was fascinated with politics, and reported on it regularly to his listeners at WSCM. Desmond Henry reported the politics of race and civic injustice for the *Washington Star*.

Gwen Newsome's husband Byron had learned the art of wine-collecting from his father. Moonie Cephas made hooch.

But no one could resist the sight of a cooing baby, and Gwen and Byron Newsome's son Edward brought everyone together. Corrine Demopoulos and Geraldine Mitchell, the Pine Hammock boardinghouse operator, took possession of the two-year-old, happily granting the others the chance to hold and play with him. Slowly but surely the group gelled.

And then it was time.

At six-fifty, Horace Atteberry brought his black Lincoln to a stop two-hundred yards away at the head of the only road leading to the secluded area. Horace and Pete got out. Horace wore a conservative navy suit and maroon tie. Pete was in a light gray tuxedo, the empty sleeve folded back and held in place by a cufflink. He was clean-shaven and his hair was cut close. The teeth knocked out at the Twinton County Courthouse had been repaired, thanks to a Caribbean dentist. The ghostly pallor of six weeks before was replaced by a sunbaked bronze. He appeared healthy... and nervous.

***

Seeing them all for the first time in so long had brought an uncertainty to Pete as he and Horace walked across the sugary sand toward the small gathering. While gratified by who was there, he also noticed who wasn't. There were four. Two who hadn't been invited, two others who had been but declined.

They smiled at him as he came closer. Mrs. Mitchell and his mother were side-by-side, chatting happily while tickling little Edward who appeared to want to be anywhere but there. Dr. Watson, dignified in a decades-old suit, nodded his approval while Pete's Dad beamed. Even Moonie winked and gave him the thumbs-up sign, which was probably as much as anyone would hear out of him.

Desmond Henry closed the gap between them, brushing past Pete's outstretched hand to pull him into an embrace.

"You ready for best-man duty?" Pete asked.

"Of course, but would you mind if I take some pictures for the paper first?" Desmond's response brought a laugh. The only people who knew Pete's location were right here. By the time word got out that he was in the United States, he would be long gone. It had to be that way, at least for now. Miss Cora and Horace were working with influential people in Washington and Tallahassee to make things right for his permanent return, but there was still much to do. The fact that their union was still against Florida law was the least of their worries, especially since Miss Cora had secured for them a District of Columbia marriage license.

"Right over here," Horace said, steering Pete to a spot where a white canopy had been set up. On cue the others took seats in white wicker chairs placed in two rows. It was time to begin.

There would be no music, other than the sound of waves washing against the shore a few yards behind them. Horace took his place in front of Pete. It would be his second official act since sending twenty dollars to the mail-order diploma mill and receiving the certificate proclaiming him a Pastor in the United Spiritual Church of West Florida. His first act had been saving a life at the Panhandle State Asylum.

Horace motioned for the guests to sit. Pete's mother and father sat on the left side front row. There were two empty seats where Chris and Becky, his brother and sister-in-law, would have been seated if they were invited. Since they weren't, Dr. Watson took a front-row seat, leaving an open spot between himself and Pete's parents.

Across the aisle, Miss Cora and Mrs. Mitchell sat proudly, filling the seats that normally would be reserved for the parents of the bride. Unlike Becky and Chris, they had been invited, but declined to attend after all that had transpired. Pete still held out hope that they would come around.

When they noticed Horace looking expectantly over their heads, the guests turned as one, looking toward the lone house that stood within sight, a two-story home constructed eight feet off the sand to protect it from the inevitable flood or hurricane. Horace had built it three years before, during what he called the first phase of his transition into retirement. A door opened and Gwen stepped out; her pink silk dress reflecting the sun's rays. She waved shyly at the guests, then turned and waited.

Pete's breath caught when her shimmering white dress came into view, then he began to cry. It had been months since he'd seen Dottie, and she was more beautiful than ever. The sight of her large round belly made him want to laugh, but he was already crying, so that would be difficult. Instead, he just gazed at her, happy for another chance to spend his life with the woman he worshipped.

As Dottie and Gwen moved across the sand, Pete saw they were barefoot. Following their lead, he kicked off his loafers and peeled off his socks, a move nobody noticed, as their eyes were glued on the bride as she glided toward them.

"She's beautiful," Mrs. Mitchell exclaimed.

"Mmmm-Mmmm!" Moonie said, bringing a round of good-natured laughter from the others.

When Dottie was twenty yards away, Pete could see her eyes. They were clear… and happy. Months ago, in the Twinton County Courthouse, he thought he'd never see those happy eyes again. It had taken much time and intervention from Miss Cora, Horace, and Gwen to help her see that she loved Pete enough to forgive him. Fortunately, as he knew all so well, Dottie was a determined woman. Once she'd agreed to marry him again, she'd stipulated that they not be together until the wedding. As much as he wanted to be a part of final weeks of their baby's growth in Dottie's tummy, he'd happily complied.

Both understood what the next few months would bring. They would be taking Horace's new boat, actually a small yacht, and relocating to Jamaica. Gwen's in-laws had a place there. The baby was due in four weeks. After that they would stay and live until it was okay to return to the U.S. The more Pete considered it, however, the more certain he was that they just might stay. He remembered from their trip to Florida's Atlantic Coast how much Dottie had loved the beach life.

And then, she was there, beside him. Their eyes met for the first time in months, and Pete felt new love wash over him. It was going to be okay, he knew with a certainty like he'd never known before.

With that thought, he reached out and took her hand, happy to find that she was reaching for his.

ACKNOWLEDGEMENTS

To everyone who read my first two books, *Harvest of Thorns* and *Shunned*, thank you!

To the folks of Dorchester County, Maryland and especially my hometown of Galestown, though this story is fiction, you'll find names and occurrences that might seem familiar.

Thanks to my sharp-eyed editor Judy Falin Dellinger and her husband John.

I appreciate my friend, Suellen Wheatley Wilkins for sharing remembrances of the real Hucklebuck.

My wonderful team of beta-readers provided valuable feedback. Thanks to you all.

And thank you, Lord, for giving me the time, interest, and ability to write these words. Without you, I'm nothing.

ABOUT THE AUTHOR

Paul E. Wootten is a writer, educator, blogger, and former usher with the Kansas City Royals. He and his wife Robin live in Bradenton, Florida and Kansas City. You can get in touch with Paul at his website, http://www.paulwoottenbooks.com or by e-mail at paul@paulwoottenbooks.com. His previous novels, *Harvest of Thorns* and *Shunned,* are available in traditional or e-book versions.

Made in the
USA
Monee, IL

15821989R00226